P.E.N.
New Fiction II

P.E.N.
New Fiction II

Edited by Allan Massie

Quartet Books
London New York

First published by Quartet Books Limited 1987
A member of the Namara Group
27/29 Goodge Street, London W1P 1FD

Copyright © 1987 by Allan Massie

British Library Cataloguing in Publication Data

P.E.N. new fiction: thirty-two short stories
   1. Short stories, English   2.English
fiction—20th century
I. Massie. Allan
823'.01'08FS   PR1309.S5

ISBN 0–7043–2622–1

Typeset by MC Typeset, Chatham, Kent
Printed and bound in Great Britain at
The Camelot Press Ltd, Southampton

Published with the financial assistance of the Arts
Council of Great Britain

62374

Contents

Introduction

These stories represent some choice fruit from an abundant tree. It is more difficult to have short stories published than it used to be; nevertheless a form so flexible, various and challenging is bound to continue to appeal to writers as long as some outlets exist. The range of writers represented here is evidence of that.

Selecting stories for such an anthology is a tricky business, ultimately an expression of personal taste refined, one hopes, by experience. Almost five hundred stories were submitted; it would have been possible to compile an alternative collection of almost equally high quality. Inevitably I have omitted – often reluctantly – many stories which other editors would have rejoiced to include. It would be arrogant to claim that this collection represents anything more than my own choice of the stories among those submitted which gave me most pleasure.

Fiction is partly a means of exploring and evaluating experience, partly an imaginative extension of experience, and partly, like other arts, a matter of making an aesthetically satisfying object. Few stories are completely successful in effecting a true marriage of these elements. Yet it is for something that tends towards such a perfect fusion that one looks, while listening intently at the same time for a clear personal voice, a distinct rhythm, and savouring also the choice of words and images. In his introduction to the first of these anthologies, Peter Ackroyd found 'one common feature among those selected . . . the presence of a sustained and convincing personal voice'. I have listened for that too, and think it is to be found here.

A number of the writers appeared in last year's collection, which gives a pleasing sense of continuity. Some are established writers whose work would be welcomed by any magazine publishing fiction. Some are new, and it is for these that publication of this sort is especially valuable. All have, as I say, given me pleasure – the first purpose of literature; I hope they will please readers also.

Allan Massie

GILES GORDON

People who live near the Heath

She telephoned to ask if we'd come to lunch, me and my wife, no name given to her, although they'd met on various occasions, been introduced, talked and laughed; as if she were an appendage, chattel; on the fifteenth, the Sunday; not this Sunday, it was the eighth, would be the eighth, the one after, the fifteenth; we wouldn't get the date wrong, come on the wrong Sunday? Lunch, at lunchtime, yes; about twelve-thirty, or a little after if you're running late.

She gave her name, announced herself at the beginning of the conversation, when she asked if it was me, after she had decided to ring me, to include us in the list of invitees for her lunch party, one more no doubt to tick off on the list drawn up on the back of a manila envelope. The telephone had rung. I'd got up from the chair in which I'd been sitting, rereading the brief I'd been trying to master, and answered the phone.

The name she proffered in return for the acknowledgement of mine was not one I knew, not one I recognized, thinking back, grasping for, a name in a context, trying not to drown, searching for the familiar. It wasn't, the surname, a name I could recall. It struck no resonance, no association in conjunction with the first name given, Eleanor, a name I like and recognized. I could vaguely remember an Eleanor or two but I didn't expect them to telephone me, to make contact in that way, reach me at home, intrude on my private life. They didn't have that knowledge about me.

Eleanor I recognized as a name but I couldn't relate the voice to an Eleanor I knew, identified. I could not marry voice and name, Eleanor, to a persona, the image of a remembered individual; identify it like an encircling, trapped butterfly and think: That is Eleanor Archibald. Or another Eleanor. Instead, she said, squawkily, as if from a lifetime of too much nicotine:

—This is Eleanor Dalziel.

And I realized who it was, as she gave the name; but it was the wrong name, not hers; not the name of the voice. It was Eleanor Donaldson. Why then did she say: This is Eleanor Dalziel, pronouncing it not as presumably spelt? Why should she assume that anyone she telephoned would recognize the voice, and know; and not be fooled by the false name, the name unknown, not related to the voice? Had she forgotten her own name, got it wrong, was searching for something else? Had rung my number, the number of someone she thought she didn't know, trying to find an identity in the void? I am no psychiatrist, no doctor, not one made or trained to ease the anxieties of others, unless a lawyer may be so construed.

Then, matter-of-factly, without my having responded, queried anything, she changed her name.

—Eleanor Donaldson, she said, as if it had been my fault that she'd presented the wrong name, mistaken the code or password.

—I can hear you're in the middle of a dinner party.

—No, I said shaking my head, expressing surprise; not that she could see. The gesture, the protest was wasted on her. She wasn't to know that we had eaten hours ago, that I was in the sitting room not the dining room. I apologized, surprised, for the noise, not that I could hear it, was aware of it other than as the sound of children, a household. There was, I suppose, the buzz and excitement of children in the count-down towards Christmas; talk of presents wanted, and to be given: more, gratifyingly, of the latter than of the former; Algy, the white boxer, gnawing on his new marrow bone, pink and glistening: the first in weeks and also a remembered, past pleasure; the television gabbling, blinking away in a corner, images and soundtrack, a foolish programme about John Lennon, the one-time Liverpool militant. What, were he undead and around today, would he do for Liverpool? I wanted to tell Eleanor Donaldson that since Mrs Thatcher had come to power one job in five in Liverpool had vanished, like sand surreptitiously stolen from the shore; but she would regard that as irrelevant.

—Eleanor Donaldson, she said. —A lot of your friends, and your wife's, are coming you know. As if we had different friends which, up to a point and in certain ways, we did but how could she know that, how could she know them as friends of ours, Jill's and mine?

—I only ask people who live near the Heath. Adjacent. Too far from it, and I'm not talking about South London, and you never know what's going to happen; what's going to happen to *them*, I mean. I don't mean – did you think I did? – what they're going to do to the party. That would not have occurred to me. But people who live around the Heath, don't you agree? You know what you're getting, the kind of person. It's not *too* complicated. If they come from the other side, you just don't know. Between twelve-thirty and one then. You're not going away for Christmas, not that that would make any difference on the fifteenth?

I knew she was not inviting the children, that she was excluding them. She was the kind who would, one of the relatively few. I did not know her in such a way that I could guess the reason. The children, simply, were not invited.

—Not this Sunday. You've written the date down?

It was a Friday when she rang, just after ten o'clock. I was working, reading a brief tied with the inevitable, ironic red ribbon. I had wrestled the ribbon away first from the cat, one of the cats, whose paws had played with it, flicked it about; and then from the dog who had chewed the end of it as if he had, well, unravelled the thing, the papers the ribbon secured. The brief, sans ribbon, was in my hand as I spoke to Eleanor Donaldson.

—I'm afraid, I began, having got a word in, staunched the flow by dint of letting her rattle on to an illogical end.

—What? she boomed, like a giant wave crashing against a blinking lighthouse.

—It's jolly nice of you to invite us . . .

—Yes, I was thinking that.

—But the children . . .?

A pause. I'd stopped deliberately; didn't know how to continue; hoped that she'd pick up the cue, whatever line might follow. I'd thought, perhaps I had thought, hoped against hope in a manner of saying, matter of speaking, that they'd have been welcome, at least tolerated. Not that *they'd* want to come, they'd moan for days – Do we have to? Why did you say we'd come? – but that, as she knew we had them, that they existed, had lives, she'd assume that they'd come in tow with us; which is not for a moment to suggest that the dog, the cats, the goldfish, the hamsters, the gerbils, or the orang-utans, had we had any, would be invited as well.

—Oh, lock them up in the shed. That's what I always did.

It was only later, the next day, bruised by the encounter on the telephone, the unexpected aggression, even violence of the conversation, that I realized something I hadn't previously known: Eleanor Donaldson had had children. I realized how little I knew about her. She had never told me she had children, a family. Indeed, as far as I knew there was no Mr Donaldson, if Donaldson (as opposed to Dalziel) was her married name. We had never, previously, had this kind of conversation, this level of communication. We did not know each other, insofar as we did, in this way. We hadn't, before, thought of one another, responded to each other, as parents, as fellow perpetrators of the next generation, one as father, the other as mother, though not of course of the same children. In no sense were we a couple. Together, we were usually little other than two voices communicating shallowly but not, I trust, unpleasantly with one another.

—Lock them up in the shed.

How could she know we have a shed? Is everyone expected to possess a shed? She had not visited our house, at least not with our knowledge or awareness. Even if, improbable though it was, she had walked up and down our street, the back garden, in which the shed was, was not visible from any vantage point.

We had invited her, last year or the year before, I cannot remember which but I know it was only once after seeing her a few days previously, to our Christmas party. It was a wine and cheese evening between Christmas and Hogmanay, the dead days before the end of a year, the dead days before the beginning of the succeeding one. If you bring a bottle it will not be rejected, it will most probably be consumed that evening, but truly you will not be expected to come armed, not necessarily thanked for bringing one if you do as usually wine so brought is of inferior vintages, drab years, with especially ugly, that is to say aesthetically unpleasing, labels from such emporia as Peter Dominic or Peter Somebody at bargain prices. In short: Is it better to come empty handed to a cheese and wine party than to bear an indifferent, even undrinkable bottle? Less a rhetorical than a philosophical question.

The shed? There is not space, what with the lawnmower and the green coiling hose and the tools – fork, spade, shears and so on – and flower pots and canes and stakes and a trug and rubber gloves and paint pots and father's ancient bicycle and an axe and a saw and other carpentry tools and nails and accoutrements of the kind that reside in a garden shed, in garden sheds generally and in ours specifically. Were there space, lock the children in and they'd be asphyxiated by the stench of creosote.

It was like a war cry, a new idea: *liberté, égalité, fraternité.* Lock them in the shed. Why had no one thought of it before? More convenient than the guillotine, cheaper than a prison. She pronounced the new idea, The New Idea, as if for months it had been the only thing to do. Murmurs and mutters, a groundswell of individual and communal, private and public, opinion had irrevocably been leading to it. There was, simply, no other way of coping with children. Let them not eat cake, especially Christmas cake.

Later, in the dining room where my wife was plunging and thrusting at the sewing machine, mending the gash in a child's cordurory trousers, I told her about the absurd telephone conversation, Eleanor's invitation. She said —If *you* wanted to go you'd have gone. You've already turned somebody else down for the fifteenth.

Her attitude was tough, unfair and yet, in a sense, true. Our children had been invited to the Dalton's, who'd asked us for the fifteenth but we hadn't, any of us, wanted to go; nor did we feel an obligation. She insisted, did Jill, that I would go to any party to which I was invited. The fact that we'd rejected the Dalton's invitation belied this. I like to think that I am discriminating about the invitations I accept. The truth, of course, lies somewhere between but this kind of truth is of little interest to third parties.

At the table alongside her mother Marjorie did her French homework, telling us wallies to shut up as otherwise how could she get her French right? Is *pain* pain? No, it's bread.

—*You*'ve already turned somebody down for the fifteenth, she said, as if she hadn't been consulted, as if it weren't a mutual decision; as if it hadn't been an act of complicity, of trying to find some privacy, stillness, peace in the weeks leading up to Christmas, the children's time. Was wine more likely to be drunk at a party than water at home at this time of year? Water was unlikely to be drunk in our house, except at the height of a hot, sticky summer. Except, that is, by Algy, slurping and sucking with his tongue, and the cats, Fido and Lodo, perpetually thrusting their red-letter-day tongues into the creamy tops of milk bottles, even the tops of milk bottles without cream, assuming dairy cows still yielded cream.

All this was in the future. Eleanor, as was her swingeing wont, changed tack, to a degree: —I do so hate those evening things at the end of the year, as if people haven't time for you during the day and don't even give you a decent meal; as if everyone's trying to mop up their obligations before the witching hour.

—Oh, I said. We're going to rather a lot. Well, a few.

—In the evening? With the children? she expostulated. Whether it was more reprehensible that the children had been invited or that we were planning to have them accompany us was not clear.

—Yes, I said, my voice defensively shrill, with a touch of

vibrato to emphasize my belief in the appropriateness of the decision. I immediately regretted the emphasis as I thought, forgetting the others already invited: my God, she'll change the time of her party, she'll make it another day or even, in spite of what she said, an evening.

—Oh, you lock them in the shed in the *evenings*, she spat, a purr of satisfaction laundering her voice, as if my attitude had at once become clear, acceptable.

Should I explain that there was no electricity in the shed, that it is a hazard getting to it with our unweeded and untended garden, more like the Somme than the Somme for the last couple of years, representing more an attitude of mind than an inability (though that too) to organize flowerbeds and keep the lawn trim? The ground was covered with pits and ruts and craters, from Guy Fawkes' night fireworks, and dog mess and even the possibility, just the possibility, of terrifying Raymond, the doe-eyed rabbit from the house at the end of ours, the adjoining garden, who has found a way through, from garden to garden, a tunnelling rabbit who, I have grown to think, enjoys giving our dog potential heart attacks, so madly does Algy cavort when Raymond appears.

No; instead —Our system of baby sitters . . .

Whether she interrupted the feeble sentence before I concluded it I do not recall; that is, I do not feel morally bound to tell. Besides, the motivation, as so often, is immaterial; the attitude of mind, the resentment or the opposite behind the words and their force are what count; and the level of her aggressive passion. We *do* have a baby sitter or two still but we rarely use them and that is a different story, an altogether separate one. One once became pregnant but babysitters do, sometimes; less often though than they might. Are you honest? Are you fair?

—So you can't – *won't* – manage the fifteenth?

There was nothing I could say, in response to that. Would her call go on for ever?

Then —I *never* see you now.

Our relationship, hers and mine, was casual; non-existent

7

really, as relationships go; we'd not had more than a drink together, during an interval at the theatre, and rarely on our own. But what do we know of the lives, the relationships of others; the depths or the shallows? Skating on fragile ice, or falling through. If we met, it was never more than three, four times a year; and not prearranged; by chance. I liked her well enough, in the way of casual encounters. We did have, as we suggested on the telephone, friends in common, even a secondary occupation. Our interests, in a general way. But to invite one another – which we'd both done – to our respective houses was a suggestion of either courtesy or despair. I'd done it first, last year or the year before. Therefore I was courteous before her, or in despair first. And yet . . .

It would be hard to define precisely, rigorously what there was 'between us'. Yes, we had friends in common, absolutely; people we both knew; but neither of us (certainly not me) would think of inviting them to our house. Our friendships were in public rather than private places. Public friendships turned private by one party can cause embarrassment, the end of the friendship. If such people were invited home, they would wonder why, puzzle as to the motive, the objective: was there no one he (or she) knew better to invite? It would destroy the ease, the equilibrium of meeting, unexpectedly and thus not without a modicum of mutual surprise and pleasure, in public places.

As to inviting certain people to parties, they might think: how extraordinary that he invites me to his party, as one of say fifty, or a hundred. He cannot have many *proper* friends. Appearances to the contrary – he always seems *friendly* – in truth he cannot have many good relationships. He must be, at heart, solitary, a bit lonely even. How unexpected, and sad. Yes, he must be lonely, which is probably why he grins all the time. Then a further, logical thought: His wife, what's her name, I never remember it, doesn't grin. She doesn't go around grinning, even when you catch her eye. Which perhaps is why *she's* lonely. Maybe he grins as much as he does to compensate for her straight face.

The truth is: you do not know. I do not know. Circumstances and opinions are the best we can do.

On another occasion, some years before, another friend or acquaintance, if you wish to make that somewhat arbitrary and, linguistically, ill-defined distinction, invited us to lunch. We had first met at the house of mutual friends, two couples meeting at the Golders Green home of a third couple. They lived, the mutual friends, in a large basement flat in Bloomsbury, a literary square. They had no progeny, though had they done so the children would surely have left home given the ages of their parents, unless the children had been born later than is usually the case. Whether the couple had had no children by inclination or mischance I do not know. You cannot discover such things without asking and normally you do not enquire; either you don't know people well enough or you know them, as it were too well; the moment, the opportunity for asking having passed, faded away, disappeared.

It was a Sunday, too, that invitation; for lunch. A buffet, standing up. Which wasn't to say, the host commented to Jill on the telephone when inviting us, that there wouldn't be things worth eating. There would. It was just that they didn't have that many chairs. If people wished to sit on the floor that was their business but if it was wet, and it probably would be, their clothes would be damp.

—You know we have children, said my wife.

—No, came the sharp, urgent reply; as if, had they known, they wouldn't have dreamt of asking us. He stormed on: —It wouldn't be possible. We don't have a garden to put them in.

On that occasion a shed was not mentioned. What is a garden without a shed but without a garden there is no need for a shed.

Then a further, practical thought came to him: —Besides, at this time of year it might snow.

Which, I'm sorry to say, wrapped up the matter, including the next generation. It didn't snow, in fact it was warm for the time of year. We had lunch at home that day with our children. Eeny-meeny-miney-mo.

Eleanor said —You mustn't let your work get you down. She

was, I felt, but maybe only because I wasn't relishing the conversation, twisting a corkscrew into a corked bottle. Turn, turn.

—No, I shouldn't I said, clutching the far from brief brief which remained in the hand which I wasn't using to grapple with the telephone receiver that was conveying her tirade.

She scented victory, I thought, the life being drained from me. Like an hour glass, I felt the sand running away steadily, irrevocably.

—Work, children and dogs, she said. —I don't know.

No one had mentioned dogs. We had never spoken of pets, animals, specific beasts or otherwise. Why should she think animals were a major item in my life? Algy hadn't barked in the background, provided unmusical accompaniment. Her mention of dogs, unless of dog eating dog and on that she had feasted sufficiently, was gratuitous, more mad than offensive.

—You shouldn't let them dominate you. *I* never did. I think the worse of you for this.

So she had dogs, too. These disclosures were bewildering. Why was she telling me all this? Then I realized that she wasn't referring to dogs but, still or again, to children. Why did she continue to think the worse of me when we'd not before had a cross word between us? I didn't want her, anyone, to think the worse of me but without reason . . . why then there was no opportunity of defence.

—In twenty years' time they'll still be with you, if you don't fight it now.

Fight what?

—Their controlling your life, telling you what to do.

How many children did she think we had, and what ages. Were some of our children, and we in our middle-forties, still in the womb, not even there yet? Was I regarded by her as the proprietor of some timeless, permanent children's home?

—If they're dominating your life now, getting you down, what'll have happened in twenty years' time? You ought to think it over before it's too late.

The irony was that Jill, when the children were younger, felt that they hadn't dominated my life anything like enough; that is, more exactly, that I hadn't allowed myself to become involved sufficiently with their upbringing. In that accusation, for I saw it as such, there was truth. Eleanor Donaldson, naturally, could be objective; cut through the length and dross of individual lives. She understood relationships, people. Dogs too, no doubt.

In twenty years' time I would, I trust, have retired; the youngest of our three children would be thirty-one. If the apron strings hadn't by then been cut . . . But they weren't apron strings now.

I'm not so sure about myself but mankind tries instinctively to be rational, to seek for and provide explanations. I was back in the present, anxious to be practical, determined that the conversation shouldn't end like this, her continuing to rail, me to listen limply, acknowledge some remarks, deny others.

—Our middle child is away from home.

—Then there's no problem as far as he's concerned. It is a he, I suppose?

Why she supposed that I do not know but yes, Lady Bracknell, it is a he.

—No, he's at boarding school; and he's home for the holidays that weekend.

—The fifteenth? she said darkly. —You're not thinking of the eighth?

—No, the fifteenth. He's been away for weeks. We wouldn't want to be away for a couple of hours the weekend he's back.

But I'd got it wrong, he wasn't back that day. I'd deliberately, knowingly got it wrong. She was forcing me to lie, stupidly.

She had stopped talking. Her voice, the voice of the telephone conversation, echoed in my ear, made circles, waves.

More quietly she said —We're only across the Heath. The tone of her speech was transformed, a different person; two voices in the one mouth. Who the 'we' was I did not know. She and her house, perhaps, or an animal secreted there, a cat, or a guard dog maybe.

She was passed retiring age, Eleanor was. She'd been kept

on, at her own request, because she was good at her job. She was at least twenty years older than me, a generation. Her husband, if there had been one, might have gone away or died. It was assumed that there wasn't one about the place – she was never seen in public with a man who might have been her husband – but he could have existed, belonged only to her private life, their private life.

It was believed that she had had an exceptionally brave, essential war but she spoke of it neither voluntarily nor when pressed. Whether this was because the thought of all those decades ago appalled her or because she was not permitted to, the official secrets act having been signed in her youth, was not known. Both views circulated. Either way, her young life was too painful for her to want to discuss, she was insulated against it. She had no desire to rake over the embers of a life that had been lived, more selflessly than most; a life she didn't mean to live, expect to happen. The bravery, such as it was, had not been intended, expected. She was, in truth, terrified to contemplate what she had done more than forty years ago and it was those years she could never come to terms with.

I was a mewling, if not puking, infant when she was gaining glory.

—We're only across the Heath.

There was begging in her voice.

—Please come. You don't have to stay long.

Her voice broke. I could think of nothing to say to comfort the lonely woman, or how to support her. There was a terrible fear in the air, a hollow on the line between us.

I said —We'll come if we possibly can.

—Even if your wife can't come, and the children, come on your own.

—I will try, I said; believing I would. She knew that I wouldn't.

We both acknowledged now that there was no party. That is, no one would turn up for lunch with Eleanor Donaldson on the fifteenth—unless I did.

G.E. ARMITAGE

The End of the War in Vietnam

'Get out! Go.' Sixteen years of marriage folding in on itself,
sharpened, distilled, reduced to this.

'You want me to go?'

'Ha ha ha. Out.' She held out her arm and jabbed with her
finger towards the door like a villainous landlord in a silent film.
She was pale with anger and her finger shook. I'd known it was
coming, but had never imagined it would be so simple or so
clean. I told her I'd go. She said, 'Good.' I waited for her to
lower her arm, but she kept it rigid, a test of us both. There
were tears in her eyes, but whatever they were, they weren't
tears of regret. I found myself asking her where I was supposed
to go. Everything else between us was irreparable, but the
precise act of our physical separation – of me leaving the house
and finding a bed for the night, a meal, hot water, clean clothes
– that was what truly defeated me. She told me to go wherever I
liked, that she didn't care. I almost apologized for having asked
her. I left the house, manoeuvred my car from beside hers out
of the garage, and drove away.

I spent the night at a motel close to a motorway feeder. I'd
stayed there before – before we'd moved to the district; and
since then, when there had been entertaining to be done. The
manager recognized me and asked if I was alone. When I told
him I was, he said, 'Ah, yes,' and, 'Perfect.' He was the kind of
man who still liked to click his fingers and think that someone
would jump to obey him. I told him I had no luggage and he
said, 'Ah, yes,' again.

I drove home the following morning and found the house

empty. I sat by the phone and attempted to rearrange my day's schedule. I cancelled appointments using the excuse that my wife was ill. No one questioned me or became suspicious. I rang her parents and listened to what her mother had to say to me before hanging up on her. I sat in the garden for the rest of the morning, drinking, and unable to get out of my mind the thought that she was being unreasonable – not because of what she wanted, but because she finally wanted it now, at such an inconvenient time. The firm was preparing for its Autumn Sales Drive and Christmas markets. I had a sales team to organize and encourage.

It was then the height of summer, and I thought about the holiday we had looked forward to, but which we would never now have.

By early afternoon I'd fallen asleep. She returned at three and woke me by banging doors and drawers. She came out to me and saw the half-empty bottle by my chair. I tried to laugh and sound reasonable. There was a second when I thought she might cry, or confess to having been stupid, or ask me to forgive her. I saw us upstairs on the bed together, naked in the strong sunlight, and thinking it, almost willing it to happen, I knew what had forced us apart. When we were first married she used to worry if I had a hair out of place, or it my tie was a quarter of an inch askew.

'You,' she said.

I wanted to say, 'Me.' Instead I nodded and smiled a neutral smile. I have a whole range of smiles. I've been trained in sincerity, understanding and spontaneity.

'What about work?'

It cannot have been what I truly believed, but I said that I thought what was happening to us was more important.

She laughed. 'Only now.'

I wanted to explain to her about the pressures I'd recently been under, but there was no way of making them sound like anything but the lame excuses they had always been, the release from which had been the motel and other nights. She lifted the bottle by its neck and poured herself a drink in my glass.

Everything she did made a point about her contempt for me. She told me she'd seen a solicitor. I nodded. She knew where I'd spent the night without asking. She looked from me to the lawn and said it needed cutting. She asked me about my day's appointments and hid her surprise when I told her.

'This is it,' she said, as though trying to fix for herself an absolute point of separation. If I'd said anything about getting everything settled amicably and cleanly she would have laughed in my face. I said nothing. She looked calculatingly at the house.

The sun shone on my back and head, and together with the drink gave me a headache. I told her I didn't want to argue with her. She made a final contemptuous noise and said it was no longer a question of what I wanted. She apologized immediately afterwards and said she'd hoped I wouldn't have been there.

All this happened a long time ago – 1973 or 1974. I could be more specific – to the date and hour – but because of how I still think of it, it would serve no purpose.

I resumed drinking to finish the bottle and she went back into the house and her presence became no more than further banged doors and drawers and long periods of unbroken silence. I assumed she was there to collect whatever she needed for the next few days and would then return to her parents. Over the phone her mother had said that she thanked God that there had been no children. By hanging up on her I had resisted an even greater cruelty.

When I went into the house she said that she was ready to leave. She would return the following morning and from then on intended staying. I asked her how sudden her decision to throw me out had been. She looked guilty and then accused me of being drunk. I tried to deny it. She said she'd appreciate it if I took what I wanted and was gone by the time she returned. We began to sound like actors in a bad television play. She said we needed time apart before the larger issues were settled. I asked her what she meant, but if she answered I never heard. She went and I have never since heard a slamming door that didn't in its own small, unexpected way remind me of her.

Six months later we had become part of the machinery of our separation. Her solicitor shook my hand as often as she had used to kiss me. I began to see her more frequently, and because the machinery protected us both we became more friendly towards each other. We discussed what was happening to us as though it was happening to someone else, someone we knew only vaguely.

'Whatever else happened, it would always have come to this,' she said, wanting me to believe it, convinced herself that it was the only absolute truth of our marriage.

'I suppose so.'

'Suppose so?'

'OK. Yes, I know.' It was the nearest we were to come to an argument in our new state. I saw in her again the qualities which had first attracted me to her and wanted to ask her if she felt the same. But if she'd admitted it we would only have laughed. She began to speak of things we'd done together only a year ago as though a decade now lay between them and us. I pretended not to remember the incidents as well as her. It gave her a strength I never found.

'You still have your work,' she said.

'I still have my work.'

'You can't deny that it's what –' There was a half question in her insistence.

'It wouldn't serve much point now to deny it.'

'No.'

The silences became more important than the words and we were still being careful about what we said to each other. She said that I'd started taking her for granted, and I let her know that it was what I would have expected her to say. I told her she was right and she smiled. When I looked directly at her she looked solemn.

The house had been up for sale for a month. I made a joke about being a prize-winning salesman and having to lower the asking price for a quick sale. She said she didn't care.

'About the money?' I said.

She half shook, half nodded her head. We were laying the

foundations of another familiar argument, but because it no longer mattered neither of us pursued it. She felt safe within the machinery; I only felt exposed by it. I wondered if there was any suffering to come, or whether the real suffering was only a creation of other people's imagination, looking on from outside.

I left her and returned to the office. The Office. A newly appointed Marketing Director had arrived and I was staying with him in his new home prior to the arrival of his wife and children. Everyone had extended their sympathy and under-standing to the limit. All that mattered now was that my work for them did not suffer. They understood everything they needed to understand without any explanations from me. I'd seen others lose an edge by indulging in unnecessary self pity, or by pretending that they were somehow suddenly liberated, new and keener men. I learned how to comouflage my own small mistakes with those of others. I drank more and ate more and exchanged one routine for another.

On that first night, sitting in the motel room overlooking the lights of the motorway and moving traffic, I watched a man and woman in the car park below as they carried two small sleeping children from their car to the reception. I finished the bottle I'd started at home and started on another. Seeing the man and woman and the children wrapped in blankets, a vivid seven-year-old memory returned. I held it until its every detail was fixed, and was then unable to shake it from my mind.

I was at a Sales Conference in London. The firm for which I'd been working was in the process of being taken over by a much larger and more prestigious one. I and several others had been invited down to observe, be impressed and report back favourably. The conference was held in a large, impressively furnished room at the top of an equally impressive hotel. The view of the sky through almost 360 degrees dominated everything that was said. It was an easy room in which to disguise one's boredom. Attractive secretaries belonging to the other company came and went with coffee and messages. When the doors closed we said things about them and laughed among ourselves as men together do. My capabilities and potential were still topics for speculation, and I was still learning by example.

At lunchtime, when we were relaxing with drinks, one of the secretaries, an older woman, came into the room and announced that there had been a disaster in Wales – something about a colliery tip and a schoolful of small children. Someone shouted at her to leave and not disturb us. There were red marks around her eyes where she'd rubbed them dry before coming in. She looked disbelievingly at the man who had shouted and then repeated what she'd said. He said he'd heard her the first time and told her again to leave and not return. They stared at each other. The rest of us hung in silence. After a few seconds the woman left and the door closed silently behind her, its gentle click the signal for us to resume our conversations. The man who had shouted apologized to us for the woman's behaviour. Several of his colleagues poured wine and spirits into our glasses. We forced the silence from the room and laughed loudly at the first joke to keep it out. The phone rang, and the man who had shouted answered it and left us for a minute. The rest of us continued to fill the room with reassuring noise. The man's short absence exposed either the shame or the fraud in us all. There was a flutter of nervous laughter to which we all contributed. Some discussed what might have happened to make the woman cry. Whatever it had been, we all decided that it was less important than what we were all there to achieve. Someone said sufficiently loudly that the man who had shouted was the influential chairman of several other important companies. He returned a moment later and answered questions with dismissive movements of his hand. A glass was touched with a pen, and in the ensuing silence he apologized again to us all – mostly, he said, for his own behaviour. He asked for our forgiveness. We gave it. He explained that there had been a radio news report of something having happened, as yet unconfirmed, and that we all needed to wait. Everyone felt relieved – 'not yet confirmed' – our concern had been uncalled for, our apparent callousness now forgive-able. We all assumed that he'd left the room to apologize to the woman. It was enough to assume it; no one asked. The man then came to each of us individually. I was introduced to him and he shook my hand and said that he was sure I'd go far as a result of the merger.

It has often been remarked that everyone now over the age, say, of thirty, has some idea of where they were, or what they were doing, or whom they were with on the day President Kennedy was assassinated. And if they didn't know, the question has become important enough for them to find out. Not to know is to be excluded from something on a worldwide scale. But for me, it was never the motorcade and the blurred, frozen frame of film – a head and a smudge – but the announcement of the disaster at Aberfan and the images of it afterwards: the small covered bodies in a small hall awaiting identification; politicians walking from house to house along a terrace, shaking the grainy hands of bereaved parents trying to smile, stepping into cramped, gloomy interiors and looking around them as though they had wandered into a closet by mistake.

The important man who had shouted at the woman and shaken my hand had been right – I went far; I became successful. Everything I wanted to happen happened. It got me where I am today.

The divorce and division of the property proceeded smoothly. We even came to think and talk of it in the same easy and convenient phrases used by our solicitors. It was what she wanted and what I came to accept. We became for each other a forgettable excuse for everything that had ever been wrong with our lives. I moved out of the Marketing Director's into a new flat. I tried, at forty-five, to become the bachelor I had never been. People stopped sharing the glances which signalled their uncertainties. Life continued. The framed certificates of salesmanship and achievement continued to fill the walls.

My wife remarried five years after our divorce became final. I saw her once, and her new husband was as unlike me physically as it was possible to be. They were walking together along a city street, holdings hands whenever the crowd allowed, making a game of releasing grips and reconnecting as people came between them. I haven't seen her since.

The day after she'd told me to get out, when I'd gone back to the house and sat in the garden and become drunk, and when she'd returned and banged the doors and told me of her intentions, I'd spent my last night in the house. It had been warm during the day, but by eight or nine in the evening had become cold inside. I went into each room and refamiliarized myself with its every perfection and fault. I even searched the cupboards and shelves to see what they might still contain of us. The light died on everything I looked at.

At ten I sat and watched the television news. The war in Vietnam was drawing to its real end and long-term American prisoners were being returned home. A massive silver plane taxied to a halt, steps were wheeled up to it and a band began playing a patriotic tune. A newsreader read out the entirely superfluous details of what we were seeing. The door at the top of the steps opened and a stewardess stepped out. Behind her appeared a man in uniform, half saluting, half shielding his eyes from the bright light and searching the waiting crowd beneath him. Here was Air Force Captain Ronald Bliss being greeted in San Antonia by his wife Charlene after having been shot down over North Vietnam in 1966 and held captive in Hanoi for seven years. He is carrying a bouquet of white flowers over his arm. Another camera watches the crowd part and follows the woman who begins to run across the open space towards the aeroplane and her husband. He sees her and runs down the steps and across the runway towards her. On either side of the running man and woman are uniformed soldiers saluting with white gloves. The woman has long thick black hair, and it and her white skirt move up and down as she runs. The film slows, savouring the unrepeatable seconds towards its climax. The man and woman raise their arms towards each other at precisely the same moment, drawn into the same powerful vacuum. Neither of them slows their momentum and they collide into each other and each holds the reality of the other and the woman is lifted off the ground and spun in a circle, accentuated by her hair and white skirt, which rise again and exaggerate her movements. A microphone catches their few words and the sound of their mouths. The camera holds them as they convulse and merge. And then it freezes them, and around the world the war has ended. Watching them, seeing them held against the background of a sky and crowd in a single figure and expression, it is easy to believe that no two people will ever kiss or cry or run towards each other in precisely the same way ever again.

IAN J. RANKIN

The Wall

Something there is that doesn't love a wall,
That wants it down.

(Robert Frost, 'Mending Wall')

In 1967, a small boy disappeared in the Highlands of Scotland. Six years later, he walked back into civilization and the headlines. He could growl and hack and chirrup, but he could not form a simple English sentence. Six years it had taken for the wilds to throw their immense and incalculable net over him, and it took me six intensive months to help him regain human speech. During that time, I would gaze into his eyes, but never once was I allowed into his mind, into the memories of that alien world.

Now, however, I was being rowed across a sound off the north-west coast of Scotland, towards what promised to be a stranger experience than even that of my six months with the wild boy.

I had been working in the University of Glasgow for eight years, wrestling with the problems of helping the dumb to communicate. At most, I could look forward to a minor professorship as acknowledgement of the valuable work done long ago; my eight years at Glasgow had done me little good. My research had taken me up a darkening lane, at the end of which stood a wall.

I had gazed at this wall for some time, then had gone to the most anonymous bar that I knew of in that city of anonymous bars. I had supped beer for a while, seeing again before me that wall, representing some mystery beyond and the impenetrability of that mystery. Then I had walked home.

As I unlocked the door, I felt the push of some mail on the carpeted hallway. I scooped up the bundle of letters and took them through to the living-room, turning on the television out of nothing more than the instinct of years. Amongst the mail was a crumpled envelope from the Outer Hebrides.

It was a long, rambling letter from, of all people, a professor of philosophy. His handwriting was atrocious, and he took nearly three pages to get to the point. He offered me a challenge, a challenge which I would find stimulating, and which, had I any sense of the metaphysical, I might even find to contain an element of black humour.

Never the most metaphysical of characters, I sat down to watch Star Trek before telephoning him with my agreement to travel north on the very next day.

And now a wind-lashed fisherman was rowing me across the sound towards the tiny island of Cullsay. Between vicious sprays of sea-water, I explained to the fisherman that the word 'sound' derived from the Old English word for swimming. He nodded towards me, but not at me. He was a Gaelic-speaker, with only a smattering of English.

He understood my fear of the water around (and occasionally above) us, however, and chuckled to himself, nodding past me as if in collusion with the waves.

At the landing-point, I wiped my mouth while the fisherman tied up his craft. We made towards a small, turreted castle, built so that it faced the island's only peak. It was as if a prior age had decided that some working monument would be needed to remind the future of what the past had almost been. All I cared about at that moment, however, was the damp state of my clothes.

'Dr Rankin, I'm so pleased to meet you. I'm Professor Edwin Dulwich.'

Though there was a good breeze still blowing outside, inside the castle the temperature was near-tropical. My jacket steamed visibly as it lay across one of my bags, both of which were themselves damp with spray. A wild-haired man in a baggy, off-white suit shook my hand with surprising firmness.

'Come in, please.'

I was shown to my room by the Professor, who insisted both that he be allowed to carry one of my bags and that I call him Edwin. While I washed, I asked if he could be more specific about the disease from which Frederick Copeland was suffering. He shrugged his shoulders. It was quite mysterious, he said. Not quite a stroke, but not arthritis. Copeland had not been feeling well for over eight years, but the first real physical signs of what the Professor called 'ossification' had been simple cramps, diagnosed at first as rheumatoid arthritis. Quickly, however, it had begun to creep through Copeland's whole body, stilling his limbs.

'Could it be multiple sclerosis?'

The Professor shrugged again: 'Apparently not.'

At the worst possible moment, Copeland being in the midst of his three-volume *Mankind and the Images of God*, the disease had begun to affect his speech. Soon, while his mind raced, it became clear that only a few people could understand what the philosopher was saying. Moreover, Copeland could no longer write, and, like Milton and others before him, the genius depended upon amanuenses to draft his ideas on to paper. Edwin Dulwich was a necessary adjunct to this operation, since he could understand Copeland's often abstruse trains of thought, and so could see where the copyists had perhaps made mistakes in their transcriptions.

All very workmanlike, in the manner of a monastery of old, except that now *no one* could understand a word Copeland said, just as his thesis was nearing completion.

'You can see the irony, can't you?' said the Professor as I followed him downstairs, almost fully recovered from my ordeal by water. 'Inside his head may be the answers to some of my profession's oldest questions, but nobody can make out what it is he's trying to tell us. One thing though,' his eyes becoming as strong as his hands had been, 'he says it with real passion, whatever it is. Passion, virulence almost. Oh, Freddy's found something all right, something *big*.'

With that, he opened the door to a large room filled with the remnants of the day. I saw the chair immediately. A young woman was seated on the floor beside it, notebook blank at her side. She had been holding one of Copeland's hands, but dropped it guiltily when we entered.

The chair itself faced a french window, which led to the castle's garden and the magnificent view beyond. The mountain swept upwards in the distance, and the sun seemed to have settled directly behind it, so that a single tree atop the peak threw an unnaturally long shadow down the hillside and across the garden.

'Magnificent view, isn't it?' said the Professor. 'We had to knock down the garden wall to give Freddy a better look at it.'

And, in his chair, Frederick Copeland began to chuckle, his trembling hands lying across his crotch. He studied the view with hooded eyes, his head twitching in time with the great hands.

The Professor crouched before him and spoke gently, his eyes intent on the philosopher's as though meaning could be conveyed by thought alone.

'I've brought Dr Rankin to see you, Freddy. All the way from Glasgow. I thought you'd like to meet him as soon as possible.'

The Professor motioned for the girl to leave, which she did, glancing towards me and leaving the notebook on the floor. I approached the huge wicker chair.

I had been told that Copeland was fifty-three. He looked nearer seventy, as patients often will. Long, white, recently-combed hair ran down either side of his head from an imprecise centre parting. He was wearing a loose smock and baggy trousers. He had been shaved erratically, and bristles sprung up in little clumps around his throat. But his eyes were clear, and he raised his head a little in order to fix me with his stare. Then he began to speak.

The disease had done much damage to his jaw, but worse still had left his tongue almost completely immobile. It stuck to the base of his mouth like a wounded animal, panting and struggling to rise. Finally, he rested, breathing hard through his nostrils, his eyes heavy. The Professor was smiling at him, so I smiled too: I had not understood a word of the utterance.

'You can see Freddy's problem now, Dr Rankin, can't you?'

I could, but what could I do about it?'

'Is Mr Copeland taking any drugs at all?' I asked, trying to sound professional.

'A sedative now and again, but nothing much. I can show you.'

The Professor took me away from the tired old body, towards a small three-legged table upon which were arrayed bottles and phials of garish-coloured medicines.

'I need some time to think about this,' I whispered.

'Certainly,' replied the Professor, more loudly than was necessary.

'Did you understand what he was saying?' I asked, again in an undertone.

Edwin Dulwich laughed and shook his head: clearly it was now *my* problem.

Outside in the hall, having said goodnight to the two men, I met the girl again. We smiled at one another, and I asked for her name.

'Moira,' she said, still smiling, and then, her eyes on mine, went quite willingly back into the room of lengthening shadows.

Three nights later, I lay on my bed, wishing that I smoked and thinking about Moira. I had already told the Professor that the problem looked, to me, insurmountable, but he had shrugged his shoulders. I was all that they had. No one was doing any better than me, so I might as well stay.

I had tried working Copeland's jaw myself while he attempted a few words and phrases of my own devising, to see how much my manipulation could make his sounds resemble the words. At one point, with my fingers under his throat and inside his mouth, he had begun to chuckle uncontrollably, his eyes filling, and I joined in, an amateur ventriloquist with his dummy.

Thank God, I thought, that the man could still smile at his horror.

I had also started reading the notes thus far dictated, and some of Copeland's earlier writings besides. He was as full of madness as the best philosophers are, and as full of eternity. His philosophy whirled around a central, simple image of man as a positive entity, and the irony of Copeland's present predicament was made all the more vivid by my reading of him. When I came to study the recent notes on religion, I found that he was indeed working towards some kind of revelation. Did mankind use religion, or was it more a case of religion using mankind? How could a religious sensibility tolerate pogroms, witch-hunts, Belsen, Dachau? What the philosopher made of these initial questions was beyond me, but towards the end of his thesis he began to hang things together in a new order, as though the house had been given a spring-clean and he had seen that certain elements looked better when grouped in a new way. He rearranged ethics and metaphysics, and came to his conclusions.

Or rather did not, for the work stopped just short of that.

After a week, I had found a method of communication with Copeland. It was, to say the least, crude. I held his shaking head lightly and asked him questions. He was able to twitch in a certain manner for 'yes', and in another way for 'no'. So it was that I was able to extract from him a few important answers. Yes, he told me, he was at the end of his thesis. He had worked things out to his own satisfaction.

As I asked him more questions, he began to shake more violently, and his breathing became strained. I crouched before him and looked into his eyes. He fixed them on me, and there was rage within him, and fear.

It seemed my questions had touched a nerve. He refused to

27

answer any more of them, and just sat there, staring from his window, his great parchment hands slapping together slowly in his lap, admiring the view.

Moira served a simple lunch in the dining-room. I was alone with her, the Professor having gone across to Barra to collect the mail. I asked Moira to sit with me. She did so. I asked her to tell me about herself. She laughed and lapsed into Gaelic, knowing that I would not understand. We both laughed then, and I guiltily thought of the philosopher in his room, watching from his chair as the sun crept round the castle.

'Were you born on Barra, Moira?'

'I was, yes.' Her voice rose and fell like the churning sound itself, as though she were part of the spray and the salt. Her hair was dark and curled like the waves, too, and her face was round and open.

'How long ago was that?'

'Some years ago now.'

'What do you think of the work Mr Copeland's doing?'

'He's a fool, that's what I think, if you'll forgive me for saying so.'

We were silent for a moment, until Moira, looking out of the window, said, 'An dorchadas a' fàs.'

'What does that mean?' I asked.

'The darkness is growing,' she said.

Over the next two weeks, I began to relax into my task, replacing Glasgow in my mind with my new environment, and with Moira.

The garden-room, as we came to call it, was the scene of daily struggle towards communication, but there was always slight progress to record at the end of the day. Outside that room, struggle was the last thing in evidence, apart from my struggle to communicate with Malcolm the fisherman, who turned out to be not a fisherman but the castle's handyman.

Moira and I would walk round the castle and the garden, while Malcolm tinkered with an old motorbike which was kept in the makeshift garage at the side of the castle.

I called Frederick Copeland 'Freddy' now, and sat with him for hours at a time. Sometimes Moira would sit with us, mending things or scrubbing vegetables, always smiling, while Professor Dulwich sat against one wall, telling me about his life in Cambridge and his long relationship with Freddy, scouring his pipe with a small knife, sucking on it casually without ever filling it with tobacco.

On a day like any other, Freddy chuckled and spoke, and I was able to understand what he said. I crouched before him.

'Freddy, did you just say that you remember the day Edwin stopped smoking?'

His eyes gleamed. His head twitched: yes.

'He says yes.'

The Professor was stunned. He rushed over to give me a stinging slap on my shoulder. I explained again to him that I had been working with Freddy on the enunciation of certain words, and from repetition and concentration I could now tell when he uttered certain words, just by the tones and the sounds he used.

'My dear man, you're a genius! Isn't he, Freddy?'

Moira smiled on me, too, but there was still a long way to go.

Soon, Freddy had a working vocabulary of thirty-five utterances, and we enjoyed slight conversations together. He was very keen to find out about my past. I told him about my failed marriage, my adventures with the wild boy, and my recent feelings about my work, culminating in my personal wall. He twitched, sympathetically.

'At least you have your work to look forward to,' he said.

I asked him what he meant.

'My work is complete, finished. I've nothing to look forward to now but this blasted view from my window.'

'Better to look through a window than have to stare at a wall.'

'Oh no, not always, Ian.'

'I don't understand.'

'Don't try to.'

His face had lost much of its illumination, and he saw my bafflement.

'Don't worry,' he said. 'I like talking with you. Tell me, do you believe in God, Ian? I mean, in any kind of God at all?'

'Maybe.' I paused. 'I don't know.'

By now, Freddy's speech seemed lucid to me, though the others still heard only the pitched, gargling sounds of a drowning man. Edwin felt especially frustrated at not being able to comprehend Freddy's utterances. This made Freddy chuckle.

'But can't you get him to finish his work now?' asked the Professor.

I shook my head, as Freddy's breathing became louder.

'We need a larger vocabulary still,' I said, 'but we'll get there.'

'OVER MY DEAD BODY!' roared Freddy from his chair.

'What did he say?' asked Edwin, but I, horror-struck, wouldn't tell him.

The vocabulary tested itself out over the course of another three weeks, as did my relationship with Moira, and I thought myself very clever on both counts. It became apparent that Freddy could finish the work any time he felt like it. I coaxed him towards completion. After all, I told him, I would have to return to Glasgow soon, or they would have my blood.

'You won't leave, Ian. You like it here. You like Moira, too. Besides, you'd feel frustrated if you left without having helped me to finish my work. It would be another of your walls.'

'Is that why you won't finish it, Freddy? Are you afraid of losing me?'

It had struck me only then: were I to leave, Frederick Copeland would be returned to his solitary confinement. But it did not seem to be that which was troubling him.

'No,' he said, 'I won't keep you here. It would hardly be fair. I don't mind sitting here and thinking to myself, looking at my mountain. But I can't finish the work either.'

'Why not?'

But his eyes were distant again, dreaming over the mountain-top, roaming free over the Hebrides, over Britain, over humanity. I could not bear to have those eyes ignore me when the truth was so near.

'Damn you,' I said, 'I'm not your prisoner!'

I rushed to the window and began to pull the curtains together, dragging the heavy velvet material until only a thin rent remained, then tugging to close that single crimson gash.

'How do you like *that* view, Freddy?' I hissed.

Freddy stared on in the near-darkness, but there were tears in his eyes now, tears for the first time in weeks.

'What's wrong with you? Why won't you finish the book?'

He stared at the curtains, ready to defy me even in this, until I began to believe that he *could* see through them, and then, like a frustrated child, I left him to his darkness and his memory of a view.

I went in search of Moira. I couldn't say what it was I was hoping for, but she had been filling my mind for weeks. Her smile was as warm as the best words are, and we had sat together often in the insect sounds of her knitting. It was for her as much as for Copeland that I had stayed on at the castle way past my leave period, and way past the University's reminders that I must return at once.

I had even tried to learn Gaelic, but found it too difficult. I was a schoolboy still in every respect.

Moira was not in the kitchen. I walked into the garden, ignoring the curtained garden-room. Coming around the side of the castle, I saw the old motorbike standing outside the garage, surrounded by a clutter of tools and nuts and bolts. There was a sound from within the garage. Peering through a crack in the badly-warped wood, I saw Moira and Malcolm against the back wall. Malcolm: the fisherman, the handyman, Moira's lover.

I crept away from the scene, and returned to the garden room, kicking open the heavy door.

He had his eyes closed, tears drying on his cheeks, his nose moist. I cleaned him up in silence, then opened the curtains. The sun had fallen behind the mountain, and the shadow of the tree was again gigantic, striding like a legend towards the castle.

'I'm sorry, Freddy,' I said, crouching before him.

'It's my fault,' he said.

'Hardly.'

He looked at me.

'Hear me out,' he said. 'It's what you've been wanting, isn't it? You're right, of course. I could finish my book right now. The argument would take, at most, three hours of dictation. But I can't.'

'Because then I would leave?'

'No, no, no.' He was emotional now, as if reassuring a child that dragons did not exist.

'Then why?'

'Because of the end of all that reasoning, all that conjecture. An argument with no holes in it, the perfectly argued theory on Man and Religion. The conclusion I've reached . . . well, I don't want anyone to know what it is. It's as simple as that.

'You see, Ian, I'm *glad* that I'm like this, glad that I can't speak, or at least couldn't be understood until you came along. I was relieved, you see, because I interpret it as a supreme sign . . . *the* supreme signification. Instead of an old man's speculations, here we are with a concrete, irreducible fact. And because I believe that this disease *is* a sign, I'm not about to make public any of my reducible, mundane theories. It wouldn't be right. It wouldn't be good. That's all there is to it.'

'That's all? You mean that's what you've been trying to tell them all along?'

He chuckled.

'Yes,' he said, 'that I had no intention of finishing the book. But you, you worked so hard and came so close. *You* solved the speech difficulty, and I felt that I owed it to you not to clam up.'

I thought back to the wild boy. I had forced human speech into him as though he were a tin-can, against his will. And here I was, engaged in the same exercise. Suddenly, speech seemed tainted, guileful.

'What will you tell Edwin?'

I shrugged my shoulders.

'I suppose I'll tell him that it's not going to work after all. That I have to get back to Glasgow. That's all.'

We looked at one another, and by now we really could communicate without words. I hugged him then, and felt his face rubbing against my shoulder. Then I telephoned to Glasgow, telling them to expect me back, if they still wanted me, in two days' time. While I was on the telephone, Moira came into the hall. She smiled at me, and I, speaking into the mouthpiece, smiled back.

And I sit at my desk here, my research packed into two filing-cabinets at my back, facing a wall that I regard now as a curiously comforting thing, perhaps even a barricade of my own unconscious design, still to be surmounted, and all the better for that.

There are some walls you'd rather not have knocked down. Frederick Copeland, his hands clapping, his view fixed, knows that, whatever he knows.

KATHRINE TALBOT

Bedfellows

Frau Meyer was writing to her husband. She tried to contain her naturally large and flowing script, squeezing it up on the narrow, slippery camp paper. One was only allowed two one-page letters a week, and her wrist felt cramped with the effort of writing small. Otto, only a few miles up this Isle of Man coast in Douglas, had no such problems, for his writing was small and neat, his business-trained mind tidier than her undisciplined outpourings. There was never, at the end of his letters, the sudden need to write along the sides of the sheet because the most important point had been forgotten.

'I shall never get used,' she wrote, 'to the intimacies of the bedroom.' She looked across the room at Frau Finkelstein with whom she shared a bed, and who now sat reading. Could the older woman guess what she was writing? Only ten years her senior, Frau Finkelstein, at fifty-nine, looked an old woman. Presumably she had had a hard life, perhaps an unfortunate background, Frau Meyer guessed, though the older woman's status as the wife of an Oxford professor was cultured and *comme-il-faut*. Frau Meyer's expansive good nature may indeed have struck the other woman as vulgar.

'She is clean, thank God,' Frau Meyer had written when they had first arrived, 'I suppose I should be grateful.' She thought with horror of some other bedfellows she might have had. There had been women on the boat who were no better than common prostitutes, and to share with a young girl would have been embarrassing and noisy.

The two girls sat near the window to catch the best light for their knitting. They were certainly industrious, always preparing lessons or knitting for other internees to make money. Their two dark heads were together and they were giggling again. Neither of them was as yet twenty, and at that age they were still able to bounce back after any blow, though one of them had said in a moment of self-pity, 'I shall spend the best years of my life here.'

After the lights were turned off at ten, Frau Meyer and Frau Finkelstein could hear them singing canons and rounds in their double bed next door.

Bed. That was the worst of it. How she hated, even after six months, to feel the old woman's body next to hers. '*Sie hat Blähungen*,' she now wrote of the other woman's wind which, after all, she couldn't help, poor thing, and then wanted to cross it out but feared that the censor would be suspicious of a blotted letter. How ugly it looked, and how unkind. But her husband would laugh, and the thought made her smile. He would like her vulgarity, and it cheered Frau Meyer to think of Otto amused, of Otto so sure of himself, his money and his influence. 'I'll soon have us out of here,' he'd written more than once. She moved her broad shoulders, settled her magnificent bosom and wrote more fluently and more gaily, allowing her writing to grow larger as she covered the page. Then, contemplating her well-manicured nails, she wondered what little treat she could buy for her three fellow-inmates tomorrow to make up for her unkind thoughts.

She had plenty of money. She boasted that she was spoilt, had always had a second-best fur coat. This pampered life, and her happy, childless marriage, seemed to have kept her young and resilient. A few months of internment would not break her spirit or her good humour. But the small discomforts came hard – the double bed, the awful food.

Mrs Hill, the landlady, came in with the supper tray, and Frau Meyer removed her letter and writing materials. There was no need to look at the tray to know that it was brawn again, for it was Tuesday and the day for it. It kept her awake all night with heartburn, a dreadful sensation in her chest, and was no doubt one of the causes of Frau Finkelstein's trouble. Pinkish and fat, the gelatinous parts never quite transparent and tough to the fork, the four slices lay on the dish, and on a plate next to them four hunks of spongy white bread and a square of margarine. There were four small tomatoes but not, this evening, four portions of processed cheese. She heard one of the girls sigh. They were always hungry, buying buns and milk with some of the money they earned with their knitting and the English lessons they gave, an hour for a penny. But it took a lot of lessons and knitting to buy buns on top of the necessary toothpaste and shoe soles.

'No cheese tonight, Mrs Hill?' one of them said.

'No cheese tonight. Can't run to it.' The landlady's expression and tone of voice belied her comforable figure and round face. She was small and sturdy and should have been good-natured, but her mouth was set in a hard line of greed. They had invented the legend that she counted the grains of sugar in the sugar-bowl. Probably ungenerous by nature, her years as a seaside landlady in a small backstreet house of this tiny resort had taught her to keep her guests only just content. With the internees there was no such necessity. The Government paid, and she no doubt felt it to be her patriotic duty as well as her pleasure to keep her four lodgers as short as possible. They sometimes heard her high, shrill laughter from the kitchen where she ate with her husband, entertained her neighbours, and no doubt mocked the 'funny' accents and incomprehensible manners of her 'Germans'.

Frau Finkelstein put her bookmark into her book and gathered up her dictionary. As well as taking lessons, she was trying to improve her English by reading, but it was hard work. She had never thought of herself as quick, now age and fear had slowed her wits learning was as hard as stonebreaking. What an incomprehensible language this English was, with its queer pronunciation and its impossible words. She worked hard for her lessons, learning 'plough', 'cough' and 'enough', but it made very little sense, and nothing stuck in her mind. It was all right for the voluble Frau Meyer who made up in quantity what she lacked in correctness. Frau Finkelstein who loved Mozart could hear quite well how wrong her bedfellow's English sounded, but that lady was so gay with it, so uninhibited, she chattered away without a care. As for the girls, their young minds and nimble tongues had adapted quickly, straight from school, and they now tried to instruct the elderly to earn money, feeling pity for their pupils not unmixed with contempt. They wouldn't understand until they were old, Frau Finkelstein knew, the agony of mind she suffered in these surroundings; their separation from their fiancés filled them with melancholy and an almost voluptuous sadness and could not teach them the agonizing lack she felt who had never been parted from her husband before.

To her who had brought up two children, had lived in many places and learned to mix with many people, had left her own country and language, emigrated to hated Oxford and made a sort of home again, the professor was husband, father and god, an infallible presence who gave her fearful soul support and her hopes substance, who cherished her and, by leaning on her, gave her strength. Without him, here, she felt she was nothing, insubstantial as her reflection in the mirror, so thin, pale and bent, not worthy of consideration by her bedfellow who bared her handsome bosom without thought that it might offend, or the two girls who teased her to jolly her along and reminded her of her daughter.

They sat down to their supper. Frau Meyer poured the tea. She, if anyone, was 'mother'. They talked in German and discussed once again how they could rid themselves of the hated brawn. Once, in the summer, they had sent it back, whereupon it had appeared twice weekly for a time. There was no way out. Frau Meyer had on this occasion bought a pot of French mustard which made it more palatable. They all dug in gratefully, the good lady from Berlin was kind. It was what the brawn did to them later that could not be avoided, for even the girls with their young digestions were not immune from its after-effects.

A walk after supper might have helped, but now it was

curfew and they were trapped in this room, in each other's company. It made them think of the coming winter, curfew time getting earlier and earlier, the girls wondered how they would fit in their classes, whether they could find more knitting. They would need money for gloves and wool to knit themselves sweaters, they would need stockings, and they could not risk being penniless if, in the far-off future, they received the order of release.

Frau Meyer and Frau Finkelstein thought of the contracting days, and though they did not much like walking, and only Frau Meyer did much visiting, the prospect of the many hours in this ill-assorted company made them wish uneasily to be at least free to walk about within the circumscribed confines of the little seaside town.

It did not seem to them a pretty little town, hardly more than a village, quieter sister of its twin which, facing the Irish sea, had a long uphill promenade culminating in a pavilion restaurant of comparative gaiety, now boarded up, and a row of more or less affluent small hotels neatly painted in recent peacetime.

In the smaller resort there were mostly fishermen's houses, grey stone or pebbledash, huddled towards the 'point' which stuck out into the sea and held a Methodist church as stark and forbidding as a prison. The centre of the town had a few shops, butcher and baker and Co-op, woolshop for the knitters, and chemist and barber-shop attached. At right angles to the central street with its parish church surrounded by a shady cemetery, short streets of two-storey terraced houses with little front gardens behind fuchsia hedges ran uphill for a short stretch, stopping short of the low trees and scrub which bordered the open moor where the barbed-wire fence ran and the view widened towards the west and the Irish sea. And, as in peacetime, the families in the small houses made do with the little back rooms and let the front in summer, so now each house had made room for its quota of internees.

Below, as one turned the corner from the shops, the seaside centre of the town emerged, a tiny promenade above a yellow

38

beach, and, facing the sea, a row of more official boarding houses leading to the Grand Hotel, a cream-coloured, plain structure with only rocks and dunes beyond. The boarding houses were all alike, all attached to each other, thin, gaunt houses like a row of elderly chorus girls, with curtained first-floor windows behind which the treasured front rooms lurked, a tall flight of stairs leading to a high-up, pedimented front door.

The 'big' hotel itself was not so very large. They had discussed, separately, whether to ask for a transfer there. The food was said to be better, and there was an advantage in the anonymity of being one of a crowd of two hundred, with no landlady on the premises. On the other hand it was noisy, the 'modern' double rooms were tiny, and there were days, if not weeks, when there was no hot water. Also they all felt that the devil they knew was preferable, their grey backstreet house down towards the point, and that any change might well be for the worse.

How strange it was, Frau Finkelstein thought over her last cup of tea, that she should find herself in this company, that they should have been blown together by the whim of the British Government's internment policy and the way they had come to sit, by chance, in the little train that had brought them from Douglas where their boat from Liverpool had docked. Pure chance had brought her into the compartment where the girls had already settled, and where Frau Meyer, having found the next compartment full, parted for this reason from the companions she had been with on the boat, thrust herself at the last moment.

She had come, she had said, from Barrow-in-Furness, a name which was meaningless to Frau Finkelstein, and when the voluble lady had told her of this northern industrial town and her husband's business, Frau Finkelstein has been subtly repelled. She imagined tall chimneys belching smoke, dirty houses, and a man as ebullient and cocksure as his wife. Frau Finkelstein herself had come from Oxford in many difficult stages. Like one of the girls she had spent several nights encamped at a racecourse in the Midlands. The ghost smell of a thousand horses still seemed to cling to her clothes.

She had been taken from her Oxford home that Monday morning (already long ago in the history of that long week by the time they arrived in the Isle of Man on Saturday) on the point of going shopping, an ordeal she tried to get over before the other housewives, who did their washing then went to the shops. The shock of what was virtually an arrest, though half expected for some time, had made her tremble, but she had not cried. Her husband, ready to go out to give his first lecture of the week, had been taken in another car and she had not seen him again.

This had been May 1940, and Holland and Belgium had fallen, France too for all they knew might have been conquered by the time they reached the island. Their week's journey had cut them off from the larger realities. They had been brought from all the corners of the kingdom, assembling and reassembling as ever more trainloads of women converged and travelled towards Liverpool.

The girls, though they had been brought together from two widely separated parts of England, had both left their employers' washtubs. Though the moment when the police called had been dreadful for both of them, the thought of the unwashed clothes still aswirl in the sink gave them, in retrospect, a small feeling of gratification. Fond though they were of their respective 'ladies', they were pleased to think of them doing their washing, for once, themselves. They had both ended up in housework, the only employment permitted, though one planned to become a teacher and the other a librarian. They were both therefore somewhat inclined to show off their intellectual superiority.

Arrived at their destination, they had been taken off the train and divided among the hotels and boarding houses, and now the four of them sat over their empty cups and, as she lit her evening cigarette, Frau Meyer said as so often, 'How Hitler would laugh to see all us Jews in this place.'

The irony of their situation was, of course, an often discussed wonder. That they should have come so far, fleeing from Hitler because they were Jews, to be imprisoned here on this small island. Frau Finkelstein could not bear to hear them discuss their situation once more, going over the same ground again. They were all three optimists, the girls because of their age, Frau Meyer by nature. Frau Meyer was critical of the English who were glad enough, she said, to make use of the refugee Jews, and she generously included the professor as well as her industrialist husband, but had herded them into internment at the first opportunity, unable to differentiate between the Nazis, all so patently safely outside, and this huddle of Jews and innocents. She quoted her husband's opinion that there wasn't a chance of England winning the war, and that it was just as well they (the Meyers and so many others) were on their way to the USA.

The girls wouldn't agree. Though they too were supposed to be on their way to 'America' when their quota numbers came up, one had become engaged to an Englishman and hoped to stay and marry him, the other had been bitten by the bug of English patriotism and could allow no talk of defeat. They defended their internment as if they had some stake in the Government whose 'guests' they were. The muddle that had thrown them all together in a heterogeneous heap of female humanity was, they said, a muddle without malice. The very innocence which led the authorities to leave the Nazi spies outside showed how benign the regime was, inexperienced in such matters. England would certainly win the war since its cause was just and its motives pure. Frau Meyer smiled knowingly, but the girls called her cynical and spoilt.

Frau Finkelstein liked the girls' idealism but couldn't believe in their conclusions, nor could she bring herself to agree with her bedfellow whom she thought insincere, her warmth artificial. She had once, in an early letter to her husband, called her '*die fette Berlinerin*' and it was one of her fears, lying awake in the middle of the night in the enforced familiarity of that double bed, thinking of her husband and imagining the comfort of his hand in hers, that she might grasp one of Frau Meyer's fat

41

little hands with their cushioned wrists.

Frau Mayer had just looked at the tiny jewelled watch on her wrist when Mrs Hill came in to take the tray. She glanced at it, stacked by the girls, empty of crumb or drop of tea. 'They'd eat you out of house and home,' she thought, continuing in her mind the conversation she'd been having with a neighbour. Then, drawing the blackout curtains, she saw the vicar pass outside. He was no more than a foot from her the other side of the window pane, dark-clad, small and rather stout in his clerical outfit and hat. Whatever was he doing here at this time of night, she thought, on a Tuesday? She didn't care for him, of course, despised that church's ritual, the organ and the stained-glass windows, the vestments and the visits from the bishop. When the knock at her front door came, she clicked her tongue in vexation. With these heathens in the house, no wonder that, on top of everything, she should be exposed to a visit from the church.

'Who was that?' one of the girls asked.

'The vicar,' she snapped, and the girls looked at each other under the light above the table where they were arranging their work for the evening. Frau Meyer, contemplating her letter to her husband, wondered whether she had forgotten anything.

Mrs Hill and the vicar were heard in conversation in the hall, Mrs Hill's voice excitedly objecting to what the vicar was saying.

'Whatever is he doing here!' Frau Meyer exclaimed. Mrs Hill's dislike of the Church of England had been made abundantly clear.

'I don't like the sound of it,' one of the girls said, for she remembered how in the summer, at the time of the *Arandora Star* disaster, the vicar had gone from house to house to tell those women who'd been newly widowed that their husbands had been drowned.

'All right then,' Mrs Hill was heard to say. She came in.

'The vicar's come to see you, Mrs Finkel. You'd better take him upstairs to your room. There's nowhere else. My husband is having his tea in the kitchen.' She sounded offended.

Frau Finkelstein rose and left the room.

At this Mrs Hill blushed scarlet and her scowl became a pout.

'Her husband's died,' she said as the two sets of steps were heard to ascend the stairs. 'The professor.' Then she left them to sit in stunned silence.

Upstairs Frau Finkelstein adjusted the blackout and turned on the light, gestured the vicar to the only chair. The last of her English had deserted her. She sat on the edge of the double bed and had difficulty with her breathing. The vicar, stout and ill at ease, had also found the stairs a strain. He looked at the toilet stand, and his confused mind took in the bottles and pots of Frau Meyer's creams and lotions, and he thought to himself: you wouldn't think she'd use that sort of stuff, giving, in his confusion, the old lady a searching glance. Then he saw that she was old and broken, that he was about to give her the final blow, and his heart revolted against his task and against the fate that had cast him in this role, obliged to give bad news without consolation, for he could at least offer hope and the love of their redeemer to his parishioners, but whatever they believed in, these Jews, it was not Jesus Christ.

Frau Finkelstein looked at him. The silence had lengthened. She knew what he had come to say and instinctively wanted to help him break the awful news but could not find the words.

'My husband,' she finally babbled.

The vicar nodded. These women! He thought of his wife, comfortably at home, waiting with his supper. What could he say.

'I'm sorry.' He remembered the speech he had used again and again that brilliantly fine day when he had plunged, so it had seemed to him, half the women interned in this small town into widowhood. He'd had help from the Chapels, of course, but he had felt, perhaps because he was not a native here, a special responsibility. 'I'm sorry to have to bring you bad news. Your husband died this afternoon. I expect you knew he had a weak heart? That it might happen at any time?'

What had they wanted with an old man like that? Why hadn't they left him at home in Oxford or Cambridge or wherever?

43

'Weak heart, ja,' the old lady repeated. She sat slumped forward on the edge of the bed as if she herself had a pain in her heart or her stomach. The vicar got up.

'Would you like a glass of water?' he asked. What a cold and uncomfortable place this was, he thought. The small shabby mat had slid from beside the bed, and the old woman's feet seemed to scrabble on the old, shiny linoleum. She was getting up. She looked about her as if caught in a trap.

'Mein Mann,' she said. The vicar had learned what that meant. It had been an education, this internment, he'd said to his wife. Now he nodded. He hoped she would cry. He disliked tears less than the dry-eyed grief of some women. He could leave her in tears, call one of the others. But he could not leave her like this. She looked at him like one demented. He wondered whether she would attack him with her knobbly old lady's hands. Her head nodded on her thin neck.

'Let us pray,' he said firmly, not caring whether she understood.

'I am not religious,' Frau Finkelstein said in a rigid, teaparty voice.

But it was his only defence, and, giving the floor a look of dislike, he knelt by the chair he had abandoned, and putting his head into his hands began to pray. 'Almighty and merciful Father . . .'

Downstairs they were very quiet. One of the girls had had an impulse to run upstairs to be with the old woman to help her understand, or to interpret for the vicar, or to stop her understanding and send the vicar away. But the thought of death and Frau Finkelstein's natural grief had stopped her. It seemed too heavy a task.

'Should someone go up to her?' the other girl asked. She too was repelled by the idea of grief, by the way the widow would now be set apart, unapproachable in her bereavement, inhuman in her hour of absolute abandonment.

'I'm not much good at this,' Frau Meyer said. She had turned pale under her make-up. 'I'll go up presently.'

The enormity of the night ahead struck her. She felt cold

panic, for it seemed to her that she would have to share her bed with Frau Finkelstein and her dead husband.

MARGARET BROWNE

The Country Bus

He waited for her in the sun and in the rain.

With infinite slowness the country bus trundled along the winding road, a green beetle pulling to a stop – doors folding back, magic yet slightly menacing. His mother would move down the steps carefully then sweep him up in her stout freckled arms.

Walking weighed on her.

Sometimes they would dawdle up the hill hand in hand – other afternoons he ran ahead, jumping over potholes, taking joy as he grew older in the longer leaps.

At the top of the rise the stern brown barn commanded the hill, silent now because the apple women had finished for the day. What was left of the afternoon belonged to them until his father returned to the farm.

Night trespassed on his windowsill. Blackie, the cat, slipped silently through the window and rested on the quilt when all was quiet. The rhythm of the animal singing was a great sea of sound drifting in and out – outside in the green galleries of the orchard leaves and branches whispered. His ear was satisfied, his brain content. Unknown to him the moon blanched the trees silver while the vixen from Walker's Copse romped with her cubs in the yard.

Six days a week his mother went to work in a café. Father supervised the apple women or hired himself to the farmer who owned the many acres beyond the orchard. The fields were smooth beige, then white where chalk seams broke through. On the days when he was alone he joined the apple women in the oleaginous barn for lunch.

'You got bread and jam again today, Benny?' It was Ruby Skillet, a thin intense woman, her hair so dark it looked black-painted.

'I like bread and jam.'

'That's right, Benny.' It was plump Mrs Oliver speaking. 'You stick up for yourself. I'll give you one of my ham sandwiches.'

'Did you hear Beech Lodge is going over to lettuce? Signing on packers next month?' Mrs Crabtree remarked.

The little flock of women arrived each morning dressed in ancient mackintoshes, wellingtons, felt hats which had come out of the Oxfam shop. Voluble with the latest meteorological information and gossip they fanned out to do the various tasks in the orchard. The Grace sisters, tall and gentle as giraffes, smiled at him if he followed. The women were concerned with apples, the pruning of trees, grafting, staking. They carried the scent of apples in their clothes and hair so it seemed part of the orchard seeped into their veins. In summer faces glowed. Only thin Ruby Skillet with her tight mouth never bloomed or blossomed. He marvelled how Mrs Oliver, round as a robin, could ascend long ladders, pick Beauty of Bath with deft fingers, making sure never to bruise though her hands were as hard as his father's last. When the light was on his face and he smiled the women wondered at his beauty. Once when he was alone with Mrs Oliver she had spoken to him seriously.

'Benny, has your mother ever mentioned school?'

'No,' he answered.

'Anyone called round to ask? Any letters?'

'I don't think so, Mrs Oliver.'

'I work it out you should have gone last September . . .'

People had knocked on the farm door but he did not open it. At least not after Ruby Skillet had told the story of the wolf dipping his paws in flour. For a week he had glimpsed wolves hiding in the orchard – black wolves with questing noses, big furry heads. Spring brought the gypsies with willow pegs and snowdrops still callow. Watching them from a side window he saw them sorting clothes into two pyramids, odd garments begged from neighbouring farms and bungalows. The unwanted pyramid was left behind, scattered by wind and trapped on the black spikes of hawthorn for days.

The postman came bringing letters but more often than not they ended up behind the big clock on the mantlepiece. His mother smoothed the pages carefully with her hand and wore her glasses to read them until the side-piece broke – after that she never bothered.

Once a year the rat catcher came, an elderly man with naïve dignity. Two white terriers trembling with enthusiasm and energy would tear through the barn and outhouses putting the hens off lay for a week. Ruby Skillet would burst into deprecatory laughter for the rats were never there when the dogs called. Ruby did not laugh often.

'I looked through your kitchen window this morning.'

'You shouldn't ave! You had no right!' He was quite shocked at her behaviour and not a little afraid.

'Them windows is so dirty I could see precious little. Your Ma should get the farm cleaned up and the kitchen in particular. There's people talkin'. About the farm being run down and the way it is. All the others are planting lettuce – something to fall back on. Something to keep the wolf from the door.'

One day in late spring when the blossom was pink and white on the bough he waited for the bus as usual.

When the doors drew back only two young boys with a dog appeared.

He watched the bus disappear along the winding road which he believed went on forever and felt the quickening beat of his heart.

Waiting for the next bus he stomped his feet like Mrs Crabtree in her green wellingtons but a chill seemed to settle around his shoulders. An hour later the next bus passed without stopping, the bright lights mocking. At dusk it was his father who came down the hill and took him home. There had been no message from his mother. Anger was in his father's face and in his quick movements but they could only wait.

In the morning the apple women arrived earlier than usual. Ruby Skillet went into the orchard and swore fierce hot words which seemed to hang on the very trees.

'That won't achieve anything,' muttered Mrs Crabtree.

Mrs Oliver shook her head then tutted.

The Grace sisters moved off quickly to the lower end of the land.

It was a hard frost.

At break they were oddly silent but he told them his news. Ruby Skillet's mouth opened and the cigarette dropped out of the corner and fell on her skirt. Mrs Oliver, opening the corn bin, swund round, her arm spread wing-like.

'Your mother wasn't on the bus?' The Grace sisters put their flasks down. 'She didn't come home?'

'She didn't let you know?' Ruby Skillet's eyes narrowed. 'He knows where she works surely?'

'A café usually has a telephone,' ventured Mrs Oliver.

'The phone box out here isn't working,' said Mrs Crabtree. 'My husband says it's a disgrace. Glass all broken too . . .'

'And there was no note? No message?' Ruby Skillet persisted.

He could only shake his head.

They left more slowly than usual, straggling along the bridle path. First, Mrs Crabtree taking long strides, then the Grace sisters picking their way carefully over the mud. Ruby Skillet and Mrs Oliver brought up the rear. At the end of the path they all paused as if wondering if they should leave. Ruby Skillet glanced back at the farm and then vanished.

'We can manage on our own,' said his father, 'until your mother comes back.'

When he was alone he found her old straw summer hat with the cloth flowers, slightly almond perfumed, and put it away safely in a drawer with her broken glasses. The big mantlepiece clock stopped. A badger set discovered by the Grace sisters did not awaken his interest. He wandered down the hallways and corridors of the orchard, on his own.

The apple women gave him news.

'In the newspaper on Saturday,' said Ruby Skillet.

'That she is "missing from home",' said Mrs Oliver angrily. 'How can anyone just go missing in this day and age?'

'They gave her description,' said the Grace sisters. 'It may help them to find her. It gave the address of the farm.'

'My husband said, "Surely that's not where you work,"' said Mrs Crabtree, '"all over the front page of the local rag."'

'In the corner,' corrected Mrs Oliver. 'Two small paragraphs.'

'What does it mean?' he asked.

'God knows,' said Ruby Skillet in disgust.

'He moves in mysterious ways,' confirmed the Grace sisters.

'That isn't what I meant,' said Ruby Skillet, one eye on the bullfinches.

The children from the bungalows had never been friendly but now they stared at him strangely. The women in the sweet shop had been abrupt when he took the lemonade bottles back and had been reluctant to give him the money back. Dwarfed by the counter he avoided her inquisitive eyes and left as soon as he could.

'Benny, have you no relatives?' asked Ruby Skillet.

'Grandparents, uncles,' said Mrs Crabtree.

'Never heard of any . . .' he answered.

A cold wind seemed to touch the apple women. They bunched together in the barn, bulky in working mackintoshes.

'Is there no news of your mother?' The Grace sisters spoke timidly as though afraid of the answer.

'No . . . No . . . No . . .' he shouted and ran away.

Weeks turned into months. Now he kept away from the barn and went for long walks, knowing the time by the feel of the day, making impromptu meals on his own, avoiding his father. The roadside banks were flooded with scarlet poppies, short-lived libertines brightening the day but withering quickly once he held them in his hot hand.

His father had not been clever with the farm – now he was not clever with explanations.

'It's only for the time being', he said. 'As soon as things are better I'll send for you.'

When they took him 'in care' he didn't seem to mind. He was startled by the throng of people standing along the side of the bridle path. Ruby Skillet was there, hissing and spitting like a kettle and wearing a green dress which he knew to be the 'Kelly Green' she had bought in a chain store and kept for best. The Grace sisters stood on their long indefatigable legs, craning their necks to watch the car pass. He saw the woman from the shop and other people who lived in the bungalows on the lower roads. Mrs Crabtree was standing by the side of a red-faced man who was wiping beads of sweat from his forehead.

The car slowed to take the corner of the bridle path then passed on down the rise, jolting over potholes. A gash had appeared, deep-throated in the biggest bird-cherry tree by the barn – he wondered if it would bleed left unattended. Looking through the back window he saw Mrs Oliver standing at the top of the hill, her face crumpled as if she were laughing or crying. The swallows who nested in the eaves of the barn circled and dipped behind her in wide curves. Summer was at its zenith. She was lost in the dazzle of sun.

When they reached the main road the country bus was slowing down to stop. He did not turn his head to watch.

PETER PARKER

No Snow in Genesis

Winter came quite suddenly that year. One night of unexpected snow was enough to muffle the world. Children, turning in their sleep, would awake to a new silence and gaze in chilled wonder out of upstairs windows on to the altered streets. Several couples, who had not done so for months, moved together beneath sheets as white as the ground outside their houses. Some partners mistook this need for warmth for a more complex desire and slept easier, while others elbowed husbands and wives back across the cold expanse which divided them. A few old people began to die.

As curtains swished back in unison – six forty-five in Etruria Avenue, SW12 – the new world was revealed, as timeless as a Christmas card. People who thought about such things were newly awed by the elements, while others wondered whether the buses would be running.

'I always wonder why there was no snow in Genesis,' she said. 'I mean in the bit about creation.'

'You don't get snow in those parts,' he reasoned.

'Which parts?'

'You know. The Middle East. All those Arab places.'

'What has that to do with it?' she asked, more vexed than truly puzzled.

'Well, that Garden of Eden. I mean it must have been in that neck of the woods,' he said. 'I mean Adam and Eve would have needed more than a few leaves if they'd woken up to Arctic conditions.'

'What I mean,' she persisted, despite long years of disappointed and fruitless wrangling, 'is that when I see everything covered in snow, it all seems clean and new, as if the world had been born once again; and so that is why I feel that there ought to be snow in Genesis.' She took her comfortable dressing-gown off the hook on the back of the door. A small pimple of material stood out between her shoulder-blades as she wrapped the tie around her waist. Some days – *most* days – she wondered why she bothered.

'But the Garden of Eden was a jungle, wasn't it? Full of snakes, and pineapples and mangoes and things.' He was trying to remember the contents of a drink they had for breakfast called Tropical Cocktail, which came in a garish carton and tasted like petrol. 'You don't get snow in jungles, do you?'

'You don't get jungles in Israel, either,' she said quietly.

'You might have done before Adam and Eve were kicked out,' he said.

'I don't think you're supposed to take it all literally,' she said. 'It's a poetic expression of the beginning of the world. All I'm saying is that when you see the snow, before anyone has gone out in it and left tracks all over it and begun trampling it to slush, when you see that you get some idea, if you're of a sensitive and imaginative disposition, of what the new world must have been like when first glimpsed by mankind.'

'Well I'd have had a few words for my Maker if I woke up to this sort of weather. Especially if I was in the Holy Land.'

'Branflakes or Swiss-style?' she asked, pulling open the bedroom door. But she did not wait for an answer. As she closed the door upon him she thought she heard him mutter something. Possibly 'porridge'.

The strip of garden had been made neat by the uniform white which blanketed it. Its ungiving soil had been buried, its few shrubs reduced to mere bumps. She preferred it that way. He had never been one to stick at anything – apart from his job, thank God – and when the first neglected seeds failed to sprout he had abandoned the narrow borders. Someone at the pub had sold him some spiky bushes which he had grudgingly thrust into the black stony earth. They had never discovered what these bushes were. Unpruned they straggled into dark, shapeless clumps which bore neither flowers in the summer nor berries in the winter. She could never decide whether they improved the look of the garden or whether the beds would have been better left as raw gashes on either side of the lawn. Perhaps he could be persuaded to take an interest in the garden when he retired. She dreaded the thought of him closeted with the television from Breakfast Time to Close Down, passive but unreceptive through old films, quiz shows, Blue Peter and programmes in Hindi. Really you might as well have him put down.

But oh how lovely it was outside, as yet unspoilt by human intrusion. From the warmth of the kitchen she gazed out across the neutral landscape. One could almost be in the country, she thought with a pang like a sharp little jab of hunger. She would go to the Common, she decided, excited as a child. Then, with adult disillusion, she imagined the Common after the commuters had shuffled tracks across it. It was as spoiled as a wedding cake.

The cistern flushed upstairs and then she heard the faint wasp buzz of his electric razor as it began mowing paths across his chin. He would be running his hand before it, straightening out the corrugations of flesh, smoothing its angry passage. His eyes would scarcely register in the mirror: the image was too familiar even to prompt the interest of vanity. Suddenly she couldn't bear the thought of the Common ruined before she had seen it. She poured boiling water into the teapot and jammed a cosy over it.

'I'm going out,' she shouted up the stairs as she rummaged about for long-neglected wellington boots. The razor hummed on. 'I said I'm going out,' she shouted again. The insect alighted with an indistinct click.

'What?'

'Your breakfast's on the table. I'm going out for a walk.' She pulled a woollen hat over her dark hair, pushing the loose strands up beneath it with gloved fingers.

'You're what?' came the voice, louder now, with the creak of an opening door. He had heard, of course. She was not going to repeat herself endlessly. 'Where?' he said. She fumbled clumsily with a buckle.

'To the Common.'

'You're mad,' he said. 'The woman's off her head.' The woman smiled. No imagination, she thought. It would be beyond explanation. Guavas in Palestine, the old fool.

The door has a glass panel in it. A ship was in full sail across it, tilting on green billows, its shape boldly outlined in lead as if by a conscientious child. The pure white light, reflected off the snow, brightened the panel to a breezy summer morning. One could almost hear gulls. No post. It was only to be expected that it would be late on such a day. She imagined the bright red vans emerging stripily from their covering of snow. Jangling keys in her coat pocket, she turned the handle and the door swung in upon her. Light and silence washed into the hall as if the snow has drifted in upon her boots. Never had the avenue seemed so quiet and new. It was waiting for her.

He stumped back into the bathroom and switched on the razor once more. Even as a child he had disliked snow: he was the sort of person people aimed snowballs at. He shuddered at the memory of the painful thud against his bare neck followed by the chill and trickle inside his collar. His wife, he supposed, had been the sort of child who would have been doing the throwing. Utterly irresponsible. And now she was rushing off to the Common without so much as a by your leave; without, he suspected, getting him his breakfast. It was the same in summer, flinging back the bedclothes, pulling back the curtains in Etruria Avenue and exlaiming over the sun. As if one should not expect sun in June and snow in December. Once he must have found these girlish enthusiasms attractive; naïvety sat well upon a young woman and it was quite probable, although he could neither remember nor imagine it, that his heart had responded. Catch at the heart, the skipped beat, the racing pulse – such long-forgotten symptoms of emotion had clinical explanations no doubt. At any rate, had he experienced them today his first thought would have been: coronary. He blamed the colour supplements. Too much knowledge, it made a man worry. She lapped it all up of course, and now there was lumpy brown bread with stuff like axle-grease, apparently produced from budgie seed, to spread upon it. Mrs Braithwaite changed her husband, the jovial Irish voice mocked from the television. Out of the corner of his eye he had seen her glance at him. The razor worried at an awkward little patch at the corner of his jaw.

He was a man whose natural gait was a shuffle. The backs of his slippers had long since been concertinaed flat and they slapped at his bare soles as he made his way back to the bedroom. Her nightie lay across the bed like a wraith, pale and suggestive. He undid his dressing-gown and dropped his pyjama trousers to the ground, stepping out of them clumsily. He pulled on a pair of underpants, steadying himself against the bed, his mind a blank. It was possible to dress without thinking, like walking along a familiar road or breathing. He did not even pause to consider which tie he should wear; his hand stretched out negligently to take one from the wardrobe door at random. As he tied his shoelaces he came to once again. Appleyard had galoshes so as to preserve his shoes from the snow. He remembered this from last year with a twinge of distaste. Appleyard would, of course. While everyone else's shoes turned patchy during the day in the warm office, Appleyard twinkled about smugly, shod in dry shiny leather. But how ludicrous he appeared as he buttoned on the galoshes; like someone with a deformity. Goodnight, Mr Appleyard, the elderly secretary had said in a voice warm with maternal approval. Appleyard, needless to say, was unmarried.

Finding himself fully dressed, he scooped his discarded pyjamas from the floor and tossed them on to the bed where they fell into relaxed proximity with her nightie. He shut the door upon their intimacy and went downstairs. In the hall stood his umbrella, furled and secretive, and his leather briefcase, locked inside which was last night's evening paper. The kitchen was still and empty, the only life a thin shimmer of steam rising from the spout of the teapot. He glanced, as he always did, at the electric clock above the cooker, then at his watch. Turning on the radio which she kept tuned in to the same station – he was not sure which – he reached out for the packet of Branflakes. *And if you've just joined us, a very good morning to you* . . .

The snow made a curious noise when you trod on it, something between crunching and squeaking, and it retained the imprint of your sole in starling detail. She turned to look back at the even pattern she had made. Cars were mere hummocks, as if abandoned for decades; here and there the chromium grin of a bumper or the bleary eye of a headlamp shone through the blanket. They did not have a car, for there was nowhere – apart from work – for them to go. Everything they needed was at hand or a short ride away by London Transport, just as the estate agent had said. She enjoyed walking, gaining from the most casual excursion a feeling of achievement and autonomy. He, on the other hand, had never walked further than the nearest bus-stop. He was not overweight and did not look unhealthy but there was something about him that precluded excercise. She imagined the tracks he would shortly be making through the snow – the heavy footprints joined by long scars where the toe dragged, inappropriately suggestive of exclamation marks.

The street were deserted, for people were still at breakfast, warming their hands around cups of tea, speculating about the disruption the weather would cause at their places of work. Supervisors from Kent would arrive terse and late. *British Rail apologizes for the cancellations* . . . They could afford to linger. And there it was, revealed as suddenly as the sea, calm and expansive. Just as when the first glassy blue had been glimpsed from the car window and her small hands had clutched excitedly at the red spade's handle, she felt that this belonged to her. Her brother, married now and in Canada, had shared her excitement, a bright ball tossed between them. Now it was hers alone and she hugged it to her, a talisman against the disappointments of the world. Beyond the avenue of trees the Common spread out as smooth as icing. Already cars, buses and lorries were moving cautiously along its sides, marking it out. She crossed the road and stood at one corner feeling that all she had to do was to reach forward and scoop it up like a tablecloth and it would be hers forever. Idiot, idiot, she said, laughing out loud. She stepped out and began walking, the line of her progress as straight and neat as that of a sewing-maching across linen. When she reached the centre, she knelt down, then keeled over sideways to lie as if asleep, curled upon a vast, cold counterpane.

He had to stand the whole way, jostled by damp, muffled people, holding himself rigid with distaste. The dense, warm air inside the bus shimmered with steam rising from drying clothes. He could not read his newspaper, so it lay neatly folded within his locked briefcase. It amused him to think of his wife's curiosity about the briefcase. He had seen her cast covert glances at it as she passed it in the hall. He had never said anything and she had never asked, but he knew that she spent much time speculating about the contents of the case. It was in the nature of his business – taxation – that he should be handling confidential documents and it was only natural to assume that the details of the income and expenditure of individuals should be kept under lock and key. As indeed they were at the office. Such secrets, of little consequence one would have thought to anyone but the officer and his client, remained in their files. But she was not to know that. It pleased him to dwell upon that insatiable tic of hers. It pleased him further to think that the briefcase held no secrets, ever, only a newspaper whose information was available to anyone who cared to spend a few pence. He concentrated upon this while standing in the bus and the journey, which should have been almost intolerable, passed swiftly and pleasantly for him.

'Are you all right?' The voice was warm with concern but it

broke upon her like the beam of a torch upon sleep. 'Are you unwell?' It was a voice which had been educated to a classless, professional politeness, the voice of a doctor or the better sort of waiter. She supposed that she would have to open her eyes. 'Here, let me help you up. You'll do yourself no good at all lying there you know.' The light dazzled her and then, against the white, she saw the edge of a mackintosh and the heel of a shoe. The man was squatting beside her and she felt his fingers close upon her arm just above the elbow. 'Upsadaisy!' The world tilted, like the horizon when a ship wallows. Sitting up, she blinked, taking in the landscape, now scored with dark lines where people had walked.

'Thank you,' she said, without conviction.

'Did you lose your footing?'

'No . . . no,' she said as if trying to remember, to produce a rational explanation of the circumstances in which this kind stranger had discovered her, a middle-aged woman sprawled contentedly in the snow in the middle of the Common.

'A dizzy spell?' the man suggested helpfully as she rose unsteadily to her feet. 'Perhaps you ought to sit down? On a bench I mean,' he added hastily, evidently prepared for the woman to sink back into the snow.

'Spoilt, spoilt. All spoilt,' she said.

'No, I think it will brush off,' said the man, assuming that she was referring to her coat which was caked in damp, compacted snow.

'But I saw it,' she continued. 'I came here and I saw it and it was mine.'

'No harm done,' the man was saying. Her mind registered this confusion but put it to one side. She turned to look down at the ground, at the shape she had made there. As clear as a fossil in stone the curled imprint of a human was outlined in the snow.

The house, although empty, was alive and warm. Soft light glowed at a downstairs window and the radiators clicked and hummed as they obeyed the thermostat. Like the burglars he had attempted to fool when he installed the timing device, he imagined the house occupied. He stood beside the gate savouring the moment. It was past eleven.

Seeing him standing there gave her an unpleasant jolt of surprise. He had not heard her footsteps, muffled by the remaining snow, and did not turn as she approached but stood there gazing at the house. Perhaps he had been to the police, she thought, the old fool; and the concern she projected on to him made him seem to her vulnerable and touching. This concern, of her own creation yet more real than any concern he would have felt, convinced, moved and deceived her. She stepped back off the pavement behind a shrub that protruded conveniently over the wall of Number Fourteen, and from this vantage point contemplated her husband.

He had in fact been in a pub all evening, warming himself in the convivial atmosphere and in the scenes of distress he had conjured up for his wife. The creations of his own defective imagination, these scenes were as garish, flat and unconvincing as those flickering across the television screen suspended above the bar. What was important, however, was that they were real to him and it does not matter what you or I or anyone else in the bar, or even his wife (who, being elsewhere at the time when she should have been distraught in the kitchen, was in a better position than any of us to dispute their authenticity) might have thought of them. They had warmed him, as live as coals, and he had sat on, drinking moderately, a contented man.

She had in fact been in a train rattling back through the glinting suburbs to Victoria. She had travelled out to the countryside to see the unbroken white of fields. She wanted to hold on to the day a little longer after the bemused man on the Common had left her alone, perched in her coat upon a bench, like a large bedraggled bird. She couldn't bear the thought of her husband sitting across the table from her, inert and unreceptive to her joy. Some tedious meteorological dissertation, gleaned from the television, would be trundled out, and the day would crumble and melt away, as insubstantial as the snow which had transformed it. In the railway carriage she had sat back as warm and as content as if she had pulled the landscape around her like a cloak.

'Hello,' she said, emerging from the snow-bowed laurels. He gave a start, as if caught in some mildly criminal act.

'I got held up,' he said defensively. Then: 'Where have *you* been?'

'Oh, I just popped out,' she said, smiling at the absurdity of it all. 'Have you eaten?'

'Yes,' he said. A curly sandwich and two packets of crisps, but it would be unfair to ask her to start cooking at this time of night. They walked up the path together.

'Good day?' she asked.

'Yes. And you?'

'Mmm,' she said and opened the door.

He checked the lock on his briefcase, then propped it, with the furled umbrella, against the stairs.

'Cocoa or Horlicks?' she called from the kitchen. She stood at the table, not listening to his reply although she heard him say something. Possibly 'Ovaltine'. She looked out on to the garden, illuminated blue by the light from the kitchen window. Already the thaw had begun and sharp black thorns pushed through the melting snow.

A Business Meeting

1

Stare Crow arrived at 2.30 pm. Early office afternoon. Greeted upon entry by the receptionist he was led to the room of partner Marcus Clay. Mr Clay sounded a conventional welcome. They shook hands. Mr Clay lifted his telephone receiver and told the telephonist he was in a meeting and was not to be disturbed. Mr Crow seated himself and glanced around the room.

Crow noticed four identical, large, black-framed photographs, each hung in the middle of each of the otherwise empty four walls. In the previous years of his annual visits he had been confronted with a more complete visual silence. Crow commented on and asked some polite question about the picture.

'Yes indeed. An interesting photo. It was taken last September. It's of a hopping race. The junior staff of the firm organized and participated. They asked me to take my camera along. This is the result. It was taken from just behind the finishing line which the contestants are approaching head-on. Curious how they're all at a slope is it not? That's because when hopping on one leg the axis of balance of the body alters and to compensate for this the hopper must lean to the side.'

While talking Marcus was looking at the copy on the wall to the right of his visitor. While listening Stare was looking at the one behind and above the head of his host. Stare Crow expressed interest in and comprehension of the information he had been given. He continued to look at the picture. A typical City of London background of straight line, glass and concrete surface, and tones of grey colour. The race had been 'run' over square paving stones. The twelve male figures were in an uneven, horizontal line, most clearly distinguishable from neighbouring ones. All twelve were at an angle away from the vertical and sloping from top left to bottom right of the picture. The right feet were at or near the ground and the left feet were held higher away from the ground. Faces wore intent expressions, happily grimacing towards a spot on the ground a pace or so in front of the right feet. Bodies were clothed in jacketless dark suits, shirts and ties. Some wore braces. Some were nearer the camera than others.

After taking this scene in, the visitor turned his thoughts to the business matter he had come to discuss. Conversation resumed. Crow reported that he and Lord Herdstalker had been through all four sets of the Perthshire Castle's annual accounts. Lord Herdstalker wished to discuss the tax and investment planning questions arising from the accounts. But at a later date. Today Crow was to talk about a more mundane matter. The figure for debtors in the Castle Inn accounts.

The partner had at hand a set of the relevant accounts. 'Page five. Yes. The figure is £45,585. What about it?'

The castle official indicated he was unable to work out how such an amount came about. His knowledge of the business and the records at the inn suggested a much lower figure.

'I see. You require a reconciliation. Mark Andersen was in charge of this job. Excuse me,' continued Clay. And into his telephone, 'Hello. Yes, Clay here. Will you put out a call for Mark Andersen and tell him to come along to my room? Thank you.' And to Crow, 'He'll be along in a minute.'

Stare Crow was recalling Mark Andersen from the latter's visit to the castle to prepare the accounts. Very tall with long blond hair he had been accompanied incongruously by a small, bald assistant. At a lunch Crow had learnt little about his character. Mark had spoken his few words softly and from an air of deep melancholy which three lunchtime pints had done nothing to dispel.

Crow looked for Andersen in the photograph. He was easy to pick out because of his height and hair. He was behind at least some of the others. Crow asked Clay how Andersen had performed in the hop.

'Not very well. Last by a long way. He really is abnormally tall and I suppose such a build is unsuitable for the thing. It was sporting of him to join in at all. He'll be along in a minute.'

Darwin-Taylor toilets. Gentlemen. Enter Mark Andersen, followed soon after by fellow employee Robert Nisbett.

'Nice lunch Mark?'

'Can't complain.'

'Drinking with Marcus? A client? Friends?'

'Not with bloody Marcus.'

'Why not?'

'He won't drink at lunchtime.'

'You do.'

'Yes I do, why shouldn't I?'

'I don't know.'

'Well, there you are then.'

'I don't know but I thought there might be some rule or other about getting back to the office at a certain time and in a condition for work. But maybe I'm . . .'

'Actually I was on my own.'

'Why was that?'

'To increase the chances of drinking lightly.'

'Well that is a good thing I'm sure. And now I suppose you're going back to the work room?'

'No, not yet. I'm waiting 'till I feel more like working.'

'MARK ANDERSEN, TELEPHONE PLEASE.'

'Oh that is really too bad, but you could always ignore it.'

'Ignore what is almost certainly the weekly report from the steam engine club? I do not think so!'

'See you later then.'

Exit Mark Andersen.

Mark walked along the corridor and stopped outside the door of Mr Clay's room. The telephonist had told him he was expected. He knocked and entered.

'Hello Mark. Please sit down.'

'Good afternoon Mr Clay, Mr Crow.'

'Mr Crow is asking about the figure for debtors in this year's Castle Inn accounts. Can you tell us how the figure has been arrived at?'

'Oh in the usual sort of way.' Mark had been drinking heavily over lunch and his customary air of melancholy was well and truly dispelled. His mind was relaxed and he could still think in a general sort of way.

'Yes but . . .'

'But for a more detailed justification we need to refer to the working papers. And to Robert Nisbett. He worked with me on the job and debtors I left to him.

'Thank you Mark. If you collect the working papers file I will try to get Robert.'

Marcus Clay again spoke into his phone. 'Hullo. Yes. Tannoy Robert Nisbett and send him along. Thanks.'

Stare turned his attention once more towards the photograph of the race. He spotted at once Robert Nisbett who was without hair and the smallest of the line of contestants. Robert hopped on a foot wearing a white plimsoll. His non-hopping foot was shod in a black shoe. He seemed to be doing well. Mr Crow asked a question. Mr Clay answered. 'Yes very well as a matter of fact. He was a clear third and closing rapidly on the second place man.'

Clay paused for thought but then added only that Robert would be along shortly.

Darwin-Taylor toilets. Ladies. Re-enter Robert Nisbett quasi-accountant. Thinking.

I was right. It is blue tissue in the partners' and in the gents' toilets. I've got to get rid of all this pink stuff in here before anyone notices. I just hope no one already has.

Now. I can leave the pink in this cupboard until I need it. Which won't be next week, it's to be white toilet rolls then. But maybe the week after. To be honest I've forgotten the rota. Blue, white, green, lavender, pink? Or is lavender the same as one of the others? And what about yellow? When I get a moment I'll work it all out again and I'll write it out this time. Right now I must give this mirror a good polish.

'BOBBY NISBETT, TELEPHONE PLEASE.'

I don't have time to answer some stupid call.

Finished. Now I wonder if the partners' is as clean and tidy as I left it before lunch. Cleaning the toilets in this place is no fun. You clean one, say the gents, and you go on and do the ladies and the partners'. Then you go back and have a look in the gents and as often as not it's as if you'd never been there in the first place. Still. A job's a job.

Bobby Nisbett left the ladies' toilet.

When the call went out for Robert Nisbett, the partner was reviewing the situation in his mind. He was not worried. Lord Herdstalker and himself got on very well. The occasional problem arose but was always sorted out. Herdstalker knew that misunderstandings and mistakes were bound to arise every now and then. He kept his reactions to them in perspective and seemed satisfied with the firm's normal level of competence. Clay's former dealings with Crow had also been satisfactory. True, it was difficult to be sure of Crow's motivating values. Loyalty to Lord Herdstalker? Satisfaction from a job carried out responsibly? Fun with figures? Clay thought not. But in any case, he sensed that Crow would not make trouble for Darwin-Taylor or its staff unless he was left with no option.

Nevertheless Clay was now fully alert. Robert Nisbett was about to be brought into the affair and this was disquieting, for Clay knew something of the man. The eyes of the partner moved to the photo on the wall behind Crow and focused on the figure of Robert Nisbett. Sufficiently co-ordinated to put his fitness to good effect in the hopping race he had done well. On no other occasion had he been known to perform well while in the employ of Darwin-Taylor. He had difficulty with numbers. multiplying, dividing, subtracting, adding, even copying them. After several disasters in his first few months of training he was adjudged unfit to continue work of an accounting nature. He was a popular figure in the office and it transpired that he was offered an alternative job with the firm. Robert accepted a slight reduction in salary and was appointed 'lavatory attendant'. Robert cleaned the toilets and Marcus assumed that this was what he was involved with at that moment.

Mark returned with a file tucked under his arm. Marcus spoke to the woman on the switchboard. 'Have you got Robert Nisbett yet? Well try again.'

'BOBBY NISBETT, TELEPHONE PLEASE.'

When this second call went out for Robert he was asleep in the ladies toilet. The mention of his name woke him up.

'The tannoy for me once more,' he said aloud. 'I suppose it might be important.'

Robert made his way to a telephone.

'Hullo . . . Hullo, Bobby Nisbett speaking. Oh certainly. I'll go along straight away.' Marcus Clay wanted to speak to him. He hoped that it didn't mean trouble.

Nisbett made his way along the corridor, knocked on the appropriate door and entered diffidently. At the forefront of his thoughts were memories of unhappy-stop-unlucky interviews with partners in the past.

'Thank you for sparing us your time Robert. You know Mr Crow from the castle. It is the Castle Inn accounts we are concerned with. The figure for debtors. Mark tells us there are no papers in the debtors section of the file.'

'That's right, I remember throwing them away. Now why did I do that? Let me pause for more memory. Blairalyth Castle Inn. Debtors. Yes, that was the people who owed money to the pub. I remember I had a lot of trouble with them because there were so many sales and cheques just before and just after the year-end. I didn't know how to sort them all out. I asked you Mark but it was the morning after we'd spent the night in the inn and neither of us was in a mood for talking. Anyway, I really wanted to know so I phoned the office to ask my old manager Wanker Gillity what he thought. He wasn't in his room and although Maureen tannoyed and tannoyed I never did get to discuss the debtors with him. It was then that I threw away my workings because I thought it was easiest to use the same figure as the year before. Later I added an amount which was the cost of some improvements to the Lounge Bar. Later I added the balance of a bank account we'd forgotten about . . . So I suppose it became a sort of dump account. If I may make a suggestion we should change the account to read 'odds and sods' instead of debtors.'

How was this insolent rubbish going down with Crow? Badly of course. But disastrously? Clay thought that it needn't be so. He composed his expression and his thoughts and started to speak the moment Nisbett had finished talking.

'Thank you Robert. Thank you Mark. You can both go now.'

The door opened, stayed open long enough for the two to exit, and shut again.

'I am sorry Mr Crow. It is obvious to us both that the question you have has not been and cannot be answered properly. My apologies to yourself and Lord Herdstalker. The accounts will have to be revised. I will review all material figures and give special attention to the areas Nisbett has had anything to do with. May I add that for some time Nisbett has not had any accounting duties and is now employed in a purely administrative capacity. Treat the several copies of each set of accounts that the castle has received as draft sets. Revised accounts will be with you within the fortnight.'

Stare Crow nodded easy aquiescence. They stood up. The discussion was at an end. Leaving the office they walked towards reception. As they shook hands Crow surprised the accountant by again mentioning his room's framed pictures. Crow went so far as to ask if it would be possible for a copy to be sent to the castle, where, he felt sure, it would be received gratefully by Lord Herdstalker. Clay felt he had no choice but to agree. He knew Herdstalker was perversely interested in a wide variety of creations. 'Yes I am certain that it can be arranged.'

After Crow had gone, Clay walked quietly back to his room, one or two things troubling him. How on earth, he asked himself, had those photographs managed to get on to the walls of his room? If only he had got back from his business lunch a little earlier he might have had time to remove them. The afternoon would have been a lot less disturbing. Why on earth, he asked himself, had he agreed to take part in the hop? Thank goodness that the picture on display saw his own obscured by other figures.

Clay sat down and tried to relax. His natural width, rounded by good food and a quiet life, was made imposing by the cut of a suit jacket. Relax he couldn't. Had other pictures been taken? Was Nisbett sane? Would Herdstalker take exception to all this?

2

Crow emerged from the building, stepped on to the city street and into the cold January air. He was in a high good humour. Such a comedy of manners as he had witnessed brought a smile to his mouth and a pace to his pulse.

Crow was a man of above average height and of slim build. His face was often devoid of expression and this accounted for its unlined aspect at forty years of age. The features were regular, standardly proportioned and symmetrical, save for the lack of an ear on the left-hand side of the head. The right ear was discreetly positioned fitting close to the skull and this seemed to prevent the unusual feature detracting from the impression of the man's appearance. Most liked the look of him. Stare was of the opinion that his appearance was acceptable. Occasionally he derived an amount of succour from it.

He thought back through the afternoon. He had enjoyed the photo. He thought it through. Work imposed rules of behaviour on people. The effort to abide by the rules could result in psychological conflict. In this case creativity had been engendered, a form of beauty and madness made manifest. Crow's eyes brightened and his pace quickened.

There had been a time when Crow had looked for a more

vigorous interaction with the world. Adventures in strange places, affairs with intriguing women. But for some long time now self-analysis, self-control and self-development had become his life. For such he required little. A little isolation, the odd meeting, and the occasional word exchanged in trust or humour or friendship.

Crow smiled again as he recalled the delivery of a Robert Nisbett sentence. While smiling he was walking. Walking quickly to the station from where a train would bear him away to the lands he'd been raised in.

It was snowing. The snow had been falling thickly and the pavements had quickly become white. Most surfaces presenting a near-perpendicular angle to the falling snow had become white. The air was cool and clear. Sights appeared sharp and noises sounded crisp. Across the way two children were playing in the snow. Their red, plastic anoraks and happy laughs jingled in the air. Stare turned in their direction and spoke aloud a few, true, simple words about the weather.

FRANCES FYFIELD

Not Another Wedding

To be fair, I wasn't in a good frame of mind when our Eileen told me she was getting married. Oh, I know he's a nice lad and all that, and I tried to enthuse a bit, so that she wouldn't start asking me what was wrong with him, or carrying on about not being too young to get wed. These days I feel so tired when one of the kids rounds on me, it makes me feel worn out. Anyway, who was I to tell her to wait a bit when I married myself before I was twenty? Thirty-eight years and four little monsters ago. So I was nice to our Eileen, pretended I was pleased, but inside, I wanted to scream, what's the point, you don't know what the hell you're letting yourself in for. As it was, I didn't of course. I just pretended I was in a bit of a hurry, and sat on the bus from her little flat to town, grinding my teeth, I was so upset I could have cried.

I suppose I was being a bit selfish, I'd been so proud of her, fighting her Dad, cutting loose, getting her own flat – somewhere it'd be nice for me to pop and see her on my own. I didn't interfere, didn't give a damn that it was dark and a bit dirty. The less my youngest knew about housework and the more she spent on clothes, the better, I thought. As far as I was concerned, my last daughter should be decked out in furs, nose in the air at all the blokes and never touching a dishcloth. Why not? Secretly, because it flew in the face of everything I'd done, and because Mary, my eldest, who talks as if she was Queen Victoria, would have been scandalized to hear me. I'd been pushing my own version of woman's lib at our Eileen since she was a baby. Kept telling her, see the world, always make the men pay – and wait; get away with as much as you can as long as you can, don't let them tie you down. No reason for it when you're as good-looking as Eileen. That might not be what other people think this femi-whatsit stuff is all about, but I don't mean that I wanted her making herself ugly and getting all serious. I wanted her to be clever and brave, a sort of Charlie's Angel, really glamorous, coming down our street with everyone oohing and aahing at her clothes. How she got them was her concern, as long as she didn't get her hands dirty. But had our Eileen taken it in? Not a bit of it. There she was, the sexiest girl in our road, desperate to get stuck with an ordinary bloke, not even a rich one, over the moon for nappies and babies. Oh, I was sick about it.

As I sat in a café in town, brooding, lady that I am, I could have spat, lonelier than I'd ever been. Chatting to our Eileen in my head, 'Look, love, this marriage business goes on for a long while. You'll do everything for him to begin with; then you'll have a baby, which'll be the last time in your life anyone will spoil you. And another one or two, to break the routine. Then you'll be twenty years on, and realize, when they're fighting with you, that all you've done for years is shovelled rubbish, fed the helpless animals, washed up. Your life in their sandwiches. And that good-natured lad of yours will have worn out three armchairs, and if he's fool enough to ask you, after a drink or two, if you love him, you'll think he's got indigestion or something, it'll have been so long since you thought about it. 'Don't be so stupid', you'll tell him.

It went over in my head, I got that worked up, I nearly went back to tell her there and then. No, I thought, you wouldn't have listened at her age. But my mother had been telling me different; she told me that men looked after you, you had to have one like a good coat. Don't know where she kept her brains. I did nothing, kept my mouth shut, and went to go home. Catching sight of myself in a shop window was the final straw. I saw a little, middle-aged bundle, nicely turned out, bargain coat, our Mary's second-hand shoes, nice bag, but still a woman who had written all over her, as clear as a convict's uniform, 'housewife and mother, has never done anything else'.

I got indoors, still bad tempered, and told George the news. 'Oh yes', he said. 'That's nice.' He didn't take his eyes off the football results when he added. 'I thought she'd do that. It'll be good for her.' 'Good for *him*,' I snapped back, before going into the kitchen, to clatter round making his food, feeling like poisoning it.

The meal was a bit silent. He's like that, George, doesn't ask for explanations, if he knows there's any chance he'll get them. Not that there were any this time, there was just too much to explain. Best left. Perhaps because I was so cheerful, he shuffled up about half-past nine, off in search of drink, nice enough to ask me if I'd like to go too, in that toneless way that only asked for one answer. 'No thanks,' I said. Not that he's a bad man, George; he was a nice lad like our Eileen's when I married him, and he's a nice man now. But I carried on where his mother left off and, like most men, he's still a child. I didn't know any better, nor does he now. Still, I supposed, I'd been luckier than most. He's always been in a job, he's careful, doesn't drink much, though he likes to overdo it from time to time. And I've looked after him, scrimped and saved for all those years, and raised four babies. Sorry, five; I didn't include George. If that's luck, it wasn't the sort I'd wanted for our Eileen.

'You know what,' said George, when he swayed in from the pub, having spread the good tidings, 'there's something else to celebrate – it's our wedding anniversary tomorrow.'

'Oh yes,' I said, 'and who's celebrating?' George gave up his attempt to be sociable, went into his shell and stayed there for weeks. It was as well I had our Eileen's wedding to think of, because I wasn't right in my mind at all. In fact I was as miserable as sin. Dreamed of getting away, getting a career, as they say in the magazines. But what? It wasn't as if I had nothing to do, what with George, who could no more feed himself than fly, to say nothing of the dog, the cat, the neighbours' strays, including Jones's grandmother, half the kids in the street whose parents go to work, plus my grandchildren,

Old People's club, all the costumes for plays at the local school – it goes on and on. Time wasn't hanging heavy, just all my life dragging on me like a sack of potatoes. Nothing done, nothing done at all, and what was to come, more of the same. I wanted to change, burn the house down, learn something new, stop being taken for granted, do something clever. As it was, I muttered and grumbled my way towards Eileen's party. Thank God she didn't want a big fuss, I couldn't have stood it. But Dad had to find the cash for a hall and a buffet again. I'm glad our middle kids were boys, and someone else paid the bill for them getting married.

What a business. It should have been simple, but it wasn't. Eileen in tears about her dress, our Mary sulking because her Jacky, who's just twelve, wasn't required as bridesmaid, and God knows what else, with me, everyone's favourite target in the middle. But the day arrived. Still heavy at heart, I put my grin on with my hat, fixed it with a pin to keep it in the right place, and went to the Registry Office. Fretted all the way through wondering if George would polish off all the food before anyone else could have a go. But all was well.

I suppose it was a good do, I'm told it was at any rate. But it was a strange and smashing do for me. Somehow my whole down-in-the-dumps mood changed for some reason, because of lots of little things really, nothing dramatic, no blinding light. First of all, I found myself looking at our Eileen (she looked really lovely) pawing over her husband, she couldn't take her hands off him, and I thought to myself, Well, I'm glad I'm over most of that sort of thing. Not that George doesn't like a bit of a cuddle from time to time, but he's not as regular with it as he used to be, by any standards, which is just as well, because neither am I. And when I thought that, I found myself laughing, I don't know why. I suppose I was just realizing what a lot of things there were in my mind that would never upset me again, and that set me off thinking that perhaps I was better off than I thought. Then there were the speeches. I was slightly giggly by this time, but our Eileen's new husband really touched me. He said in his speech that he was proud to have got our Eileen.

74

'Hear, hear,' I shouted (George shushed me), and he went on to say if Eileen turned out like her mum, he'd be proved right in thinking she was the best girl in the world. And he thanked me for all our hospitality – he's not got much of a family himself – and said how much it had meant to him. Eileen must have sensed my mood and told her old man to flatter me a bit, and it worked. I was sitting there with the kids and their kids, and I looked at them with my eyes peeled all of a sudden. They were beaming at me, a bit drunk, but not bad, and I thought how nice they were. That's what I've done, I thought, raised four nice kids. All of them good-looking, kind, and none of them idiots. And what's more, they like me. I suppose I'd not noticed before that they were really quite proud of me, even when they were joking about me. It may be because they all kid themselves they still need me, while I know they'd manage without, but that doesn't matter. I was well cheered up one way and another, not by any means because I was full up with wine, although that helped. Perhaps, I thought, I've got a few things done after all. There they were, in front of me, looking marvellous, all my grey hairs, my great achievements. God, I was proud of them.

Our Mary's Jacky was sat next to me. She's my favourite, talks to her Gran a lot, looks like an angel, nobody's fool, top of her class. It's our secret of course, that we're one another's favourites. It wouldn't do for the others to know. And I thought, as the speeching went on, it's a bit late for me to change, it's just about too late for Eileen, but what about Jacky? I must have a word with Mary – make sure Jacky does her homework, and doesn't ever learn Domestic Science. I was sitting there, imagining telling one of the neighbours about Jacky in a few years – 'My granddaughter. She's a scientist' (it could be a doctor, or a lady detective, I'm not fussy). 'She's not wed, doesn't need to be. Blokes queuing at the doors. She can buy her own fur coats, and she's got a smashing car . . .'

That's how it'll be if I have anything to do with it. I'd better start work. She's brighter than our Eileen and I'm more determined. With all that in mind, I was even pleased to have a dance with my clumsy great sons. Our Raymond told me I was looking great (he meant for my age) and for once he wasn't joking. Then I danced with George, who was a bit uneven. He said to me (I can't remember the exact words, he isn't very direct at the best of times, which this wasn't) that I'd probably be wanting a few changes now that all the kids were settled; perhaps I'd be wanting the house altered; perhaps I'd want to go out more, go away more often; perhaps, he hinted, I'd even be wanting to move. I said yes, to everything. Poor George. He was terrified. Without trying, I'd got him worried sick that I was going to turn his world upside down. He wasn't the only one I'd worried either. Let him sweat for a bit, I thought; it was nice to know I could still get under his skin.

That night, after we'd all sat up late, laughing over the party, and gossiping, I went to sleep sort of peaceful and resigned, happier than I'd been for months. George was still twitching, much to my satisfaction; I wasn't going to put him out of his misery. I knew by then, of course, that there weren't going to be any changes, well, not many. I wasn't going to alter, it was too late for that. I am what I am, and it isn't bad at all, or at least not so bad that I wouldn't be doing fine if I just carried on. There's still so much to do with them all.

Nothing wrong with spreading a bit of unrest though. If being what I've been and being what I am can make me a spoiled old lady, I'll work on that one too.

DAVID WELSH

A Mugging

I'd seen those two boys before. Since I'd been a child I'd gone on long walks when it grew dark and I hadn't abandoned the practice when I came to live in Clapham. On one of these walks, about a week before they mugged me, I saw those boys. They were white, around sixteen, one dark and one fair, slightly built but tough-looking. They were walking ahead of me, talking animatedly, gesticulating with their hands. It didn't occur to me then, but perhaps they were talking about me, as a likely customer for their attentions, that night or another.

What I noticed about them that first night was their jackets. Teenagers often wear that style, a leather jacket, brown or red, with a curved pleat at the back below the shoulders suggesting a cape, two straps with silver buckles on the shoulders, and two more straps with buckles around the waist forming a sort of cut-off decorative belt. There were rows of them at Arding and Hobbs, the local department store, and earlier that day I'd noticed a black boy wearing one as he puffed out smoke at a bus-stop in the Wandsworth Road. Those jackets interested me, flashy bits of junk, the current uniform of the little urban toughie. A week later, the two were to be wearing the same jackets, but circumstances would not permit detached interest.

The day I was mugged was a Saturday. I'd spent almost the whole of it in my flat, working on a book I was writing for schools, on law and order. Around nine in the evening I'd rejected the idea of going to the Salisbury, the gay pub I frequented: I didn't think the handsome Greek I fancied would be there, and anyway I wanted to go on with my work. Inside the flat, as I typed on, it was warm and quiet. The only sounds were the clock ticking on the wall, buses passing on the road and trains on the line. I was writing a chapter on prisons and the alternative methods of dealing with crime, and had just finished the section on the new scheme whereby the criminal is confronted with his victim, when I began to feel the need of some fresh air. It was shortly before eleven at night. I gave my steamed-up glasses a quick clean, double-locked the door behind me, and emerged into the night.

It seemed deliciously fresh and cool. There was a slight wind swaying the trees, few stars, no moon. I walked fast, and was soon lost in the dark, leafy tangle of streets to the north of Clapham Common. Thousands of people lived in those streets, in tall Victorian houses and modern blocks of flats shaded by trees and overgrown yards. But apart from a few late-night parties in upstairs rooms and the distant shouts of homegoing revellers, I wasn't conscious of people around me. I wandered along as usual, absorbed in my thoughts, talking and singing a little to myself, enjoying my solitude.

I had just rounded a corner when I saw the two boys following me around it. They gave little starts as they saw me, as if to say: now we've got you. I took two hurried paces more, but by then they were matter-of-factly pushing me against the wall in the dark garden of a block of flats.

'Give us yer money,' said the dark one, as the fair one pinned my arm against the wall.

'I haven't got any money. God, I'm sorry,' I said, my voice rising in panic.

The dark one smacked me hard across the face. 'Give us yer fucking money,' he said.

'I haven't got any, I told you,' I said desperately. This was true. I never carried money on these walks, since I never needed to buy anything. He hit me twice more in the face. 'Give us yer money, you fucker.'

I was holding my door-keys in my pocket with my free arm. I mustn't lose them, or not being able to get back into the flat would complete my misery. The dark boy hit me several more times in the face. I wasn't capable of fighting back so concentrated on remaining on my feet, a human punch-bag.

I was calm. I didn't feel much pain. In between the dark one's blows, I caught a sudden glimpse of the blond boy, jerking my arm against the wall and looking at me almost wonderingly. There was something wary, foxlike about his eyes.

Suddenly it was over. They turned smartly on their heels the way they had come. They did not look back. They strutted their shoulders, arms slightly akimbo. The jackets completed the sudden effect of cocky teenage masculinity. Their gangsterish little mannerisms seemed mildly comic. I watched them go, rather ruefully, blood streaming down my face.

I stood there a moment. My attackers had vanished and the dark street was empty. I put my tongue cautiously around my lips and then used my hands gingerly to feel inside my mouth. I still had all my teeth: that was a relief. I knew I'd better start off home. My flat wasn't far, I still had the keys, and when I got back I would phone the police. As I began walking, the meaninglessness of what had happened suddenly struck me. I had been on a walk; now I was resuming it. How pointless, how irrelevant to my real life, the intervening minute had been.

I walked along slowly. Every so often I passed people walking the other way along the street, in ones and twos. I hurried past them in the darkness. I did not want them to see me. There was something horrible and unnatural about my state: I felt almost ashamed to be seen like that, as if I were responsible for what had happened. As I walked on I began to be surprised at the number of people about. It was really almost a busy street, but very dark, so you couldn't see the people's faces as they emerged from the shadow of bushes. For all the good these people had been to me, I might have been on a country road.

I was almost back at the path leading down behind my block of flats when I realized I hadn't got my glasses. They must have been knocked off during the encounter. I stood irresolute a moment. My flat was so near, shouldn't I walk on? But no, those were expensive glasses, and if you wanted to find

79

something you had lost in a strange part of London, you must return immediately. The next day I would never find them. I turned back, walking faster than before. As I neared the place again, I had a moment of panic. Suppose they were hanging round the scene of their crime and saw me returning? But no, that was nonsense. It would be too risky and pointless to hang around. Indeed the place was deserted; the crowds of passers-by seemed to have vanished.

I looked down at the bushes. I couldn't see my glasses, or anything much. Really, had I any hope of finding them? Was this even the exact place? But I'd come back to find them, and look for them I must. I began feeling around in the under-growth, and was soon rewarded by feeling them in my hands. Apart from a little blood on one lens, which I wiped off, they seemed undamaged. I put them on and hurried off again immediately. This time I passed no one and within five minutes had regained the flat.

How lovely it was to lock the door behind me and walk into the warmth of my own well-ordered interior. Only half an hour had passed since I had left this security. If only I had never gone! I went into the sitting-room first, but then almost immediately into the bathroom to inspect the damage. The lower half of my face was covered in blood, my nose had been knocked sideways, and there were bloodstains on my coat and shirt. I began to clean up, then stopped. Perhaps I'd better show the full damage to the police, on the analogy of touching nothing after a burglary. I went into the sitting-room and phoned the local station. A woman answered. I said I'd been mugged and gave my name and address.

'No, I'm afraid I didn't really see where they went,' I said, 'towards the Wandsworth Road, I think. Yes, white youths, around sixteen, one fair and one dark.'

'Right, I'll send some officers round to see you immediately,' she said.

'Thank you . . . oh, and tell them not to be too shocked when they see me. I'm afraid my face is a bit of a mess.'

'Oh, don't worry about that, sir,' she said warmly. 'They're used to dealing with that kind of thing.'

I put the phone down and then noticed that there was blood on the receiver. It was a smart green phone, and the blood looked incongruous on it. I wiped it off hurriedly, and went into the bedroom to change my shirt before the officers came.

They arrived after only a few minutes, two young male officers. The slightly older one, obviously the senior, was a large, fair man with a pleasant but rather craggy face marred by spots; his junior, also blond, had the newly hatched well-washed-behind-the-ears look that very young recruits often have. They came into the sitting-room, radios chattering, looking rather large and clumsy in my small metropolitan flat.

'Hello, sir,' said the senior one, 'you've obviously suffered a nasty attack. Would you like to tell us what happened? If you feel able, that is. You look badly beaten up, if I may say so.'

'Oh, it's not that bad,' I said. 'I can certainly tell you what happened, anyway.'

'Good, then I think you'll probably have to go to hospital. Your nose looks as if it's broken.'

'Oh, I don't have to go to hospital, do I?' I said this, rather self-consciously adopting the British stiff-upper-lip role, but really I half-wanted to go to hospital.

'Well, I think you'd better go,' said the policeman, 'but tell us what happened, and then see how you feel. Now, you said on the phone, I think, that two youths attacked you. Where exactly did this happen?'

I had a map of London on the wall, and used it to point out exactly where the mugging had happened. As I did so, I wondered whether I was seeming absurdly fussy by pinpointing the incident, as it were, on a map. But I also felt rather proud of my own calmness and fortitude. At least I could endure blows, even if I hadn't been capable of fighting back.

'Can you describe the youths, sir? You say they were white. Would you recognize them again?'

I hesitated. I felt certain I had seen those youths before, and during the encounter had been trying to take note of their faces. But most teenage boys do not look very individual. 'Well, they were both around sixteen, one fair and one dark. They were wearing brown leather jackets, the type with a pleat at the back and shoulder-straps with buckles on them.'

'Would you recognize them again?'

'Well, I think I would if I saw them again tonight, or tomorrow. Especially the dark one. But I'm not sure I'd recognize either of them again if I saw them in a week, say.'

They looked at each other. I could see they were giving up the case as hopeless.

'Excuse me, sir,' said the senior one, who was doing all the talking, 'but do you have any idea why these youths attacked you? As you'll appreciate, we get a fair few attacks in this area. But in our experience it's usually women who get attacked. It's quite rare for young men to be picked on.'

I hesitated again. I did have the uncomfortable feeling that these boys had recognized me and had perhaps picked on me for a mugging. Perhaps they saw me as an obvious eccentric, wandering around the streets as I did. Perhaps this had even been a queer-bashing. But I didn't want to raise these questions with the officers. Their attitude seemed respectful enough, but if I told them I was gay, or if I seemed peculiar in any way, perhaps it would change. 'No, I'm afraid I don't know why they attacked me,' I said.

The younger policeman, who had not spoken at all, now asked to use the toilet. After asking if he could sit down, his senior sank into an armchair, looking suddenly more relaxed and informal as he did so. He looked at me, still standing: 'You're coping with this very well, sir,' he said, 'but why don't you sit down?'

I looked at him, noticing him as a human being for the first time. I did have various preconceptions about him. My attitudes, generally, were conservative, and I made it a point not to share the fashionable hostility towards the police of many gay people, at least until experience proved me wrong. My feelings were complicated by the fact that I often found policemen sexually attractive: their clean looks, their short hair, their uniforms at once mildly threatening and rather comically reassuring, the sense policemen gave of being ordinary, unsophisticated and virile which is so attractive to the intellectual.

But this man was not handsome in any such ideal sense: a featureless, rather over-earnest face. But I now began to think there was something rather pleasant-feeling about him. His attitude was respectful, but it was also concerned in a way I could not have expected. He represented a different model of masculinity than had my attackers: controlled strength, simple manhood but admitting sensitivity.

'No, it's all right, I'll stand,' I said, 'but thank you for you help. You're doing a good job. I really think it's mindless the way people criticize the police so much these days. When you've been attacked, you're glad to have a policeman around.'

I felt rather pompous as I said this and, of course, despite my expressions of confidence, there was little hope they would solve the crime. But these were my real opinions, and I wanted the officer to know that I appreciated his efforts.

'Well, I think most of the public *do* want us around,' he said, immediately adopting the avuncular community policeman tone which is obligatory for the force nowadays. 'Most of the public want to help us. We have got our critics of course, who hasn't? Some people like to criticize, I suppose. But that's why we do try hard to explain our role to the public.'

I remembered my book on law and order, in which I had discussed such questions, and wondered whether I ought to mention it, perhaps even use him for an interview. But I decided against it. It would introduce a note of irrelevance, levity even, into the proceedings.

I thought about what I'd written earlier, the scheme whereby the attacker is confronted with his victim. This seemed rather ironical in the light of current circumstances. Would I ever be confronted with the two boys? Could such an awkward, even absurd situation be made to seem serious, useful? Come to think of it, those boys were probably still at school, grumpily finishing their course at Vauxhall Manor or Stockwell Park before going on the dole. They might even use my book! It might give them a few insights, help them go to the top of the class. I smiled a little at the absurdity of my thinking this. The policeman must have been surprised to see me smiling, but I knew I couldn't share the joke. He would think I was mad.

The return of the younger policeman from the toilet recalled my mind to serious business and my bloody face. The first one said, 'Right, I'll call an ambulance now. I think I'd better come with you to the hospital. You're quite badly hurt.'

I nodded. I was getting to like him more and more. I hoped he would come in the ambulance.

Unfortunately the police station, when phoned, vetoed the idea. There were too many crimes in Clapham that night, apparently. He called the ambulance, I collected money and a coat, and the policemen saw me off when the ambulance arrived. An upstairs neighbour was watching the scene with barely concealed curiosity. I talked a little to the ambulance attendant during the journey, but it seemed a very long ride.

The hospital was a bright, cold, depressing place. I filled in a form for a receptionist, then saw a black nurse, who handed me over to a doctor. All these people treated me pleasantly enough, but with brusque indifference. They made it plain that they saw hundreds of cases like mine: you're nothing special was their depressing message.

The Asian doctor was the most cheerful of the three, almost jovial in fact: 'My, my, you've had a nasty attack there. Dear, dear, you're going to have a couple of big, bad black eyes tomorrow. Real juicy ones. My, my, it's terrible the attacks now. My, my, yes. Now just hold still, and I'm going to wash you nose out. Lean back.'

He manoeuvred me back into the chair, tied a bib around me, and began to sponge my face expertly. I felt the blood flowing in streams. That was the worst moment, worse than the attack itself. I felt so powerless, my blood draining away. If I had broken down at all, it would have been then.

After I had been treated, I went out into a hall where various young hoods, friends of that Saturday night's woundings, were waiting. The receptionist called me a taxi. I didn't speak on the drive, while the black taxi-driver just grunted softly to himself. I didn't recognize the streets we passed through, and it was difficult to see much through the window. Sometimes a traffic light threw up a sudden bowl of brightness like a punctuation mark in the endless sentences of streets. This London, how dark it seemed.

Once home, I briefly phoned my mother; as it happened, she was coming to see me the next morning. I had to wake her from sleep, and she was terribly surprised and distressed to hear about me. I didn't talk long, saying I would explain more in the morning. Then there was nothing for it but to go to bed. The world's business with me that day was over.

I couldn't go to sleep immediately. I went back to thinking about my attackers. Were they too lying in bed at that moment somewhere quite close, I wondered. Would they feel at all sorry for what they had done? Probably not. My mind speculating idly, I suddenly saw them as they might be in a few years' time, hanging around in the rougher gay bars, hoping to earn an easy twenty pounds or steal more. They would stand there alone, looking as hard and indifferent as they could, but also isolated, even vulnerable under the appraising eyes.

A gay man would approach one of them, mainly wanting him for his tough-looking body of course, but also ready to take a benevolent interest in a personable working-class youth, perhaps help him on a bit. But the boy would not respond to his friendliness, would answer in few and curt words, making sure he knew that money was wanted.

Back in bed, the boy would lie there like a lump, giving nothing, but the next day he'd expect to be given a meal and, if it were Saturday, allowed to stay to watch the football on television. Eventually, the gay man would throw him out and he'd attempt to blackmail a few more pounds as he left. One day one of them would roll a guy over for money and be sent to prison, but it would never occur to them that there might have been better ways of turning such situations to their advantage.

There was something sad about all this, sad for them. Their skills seemed so outdated for the demands life would make. The male's simple urge towards violence had been comprehensively devalued by the modern world; force it still admired, but allied to cunning, sophistication, smooth talking. Just as Norman knights in their chain-mail would have looked more awkward than awe-inspiring clanking through the counting-houses of the Venetians, so these boys were ultimately weak, fists in a world of brains.

But they'd been able to triumph over me, hadn't they? The strong inflicting themselves on the weak, that male world of violence and domination, was still there, would indeed go on for ever, although driven into the dark alleys of cities for simple youths to practise on the unprotected and the natural victims. Partly I lived in a different world – the dinners with women friends, the discovery of common interests in books and music, the restaurants and concerts. But a more fundamental part of me had gone to meet what it would find in those dark streets, just as the boys had perhaps come hunting for me. For them the world provided no more glorious assertion of their power than to smack their fists into someone's face. But didn't an intellectual like myself deserve to be hurt and punished eternally by such careless, splendid young thugs? I began to have sexual fantasies about them, imagining their lithe, white boys' bodies in which the prentice muscles were beginning to burgeon. I thought how much I could love a man who hurt me and then loved me afterwards. But what if they'd had a knife? I twisted in the bed in terror at the thought. My masochism was a fantasy which could only exist because I hadn't really been hurt, not terribly anyway. I became conscious of myself lying alone in the bed, alone in the flat, London all around me: the concrete mazes of underpasses, the dark railway arches of disused lines, the sheerly rising walls of monster flats, friends saying goodbye and immediately becoming lost in the indifferent crowds. But strangers could rise from the darkness as suddenly as friends vanished, with knives and other fearful implements in their swiftly curving hands.

As long as I lived here, these streets would fill me with fear, real fear, not something half-pleasant which you could toy with.

For hours I lay awake, miserable, my thoughts confused. Finally the dawn, blessed light of day with its chorus of birds, enabled me to sleep.

Now I am left with a pervasive sense that something, anything, might happen, a permanent looking over the shoulder which has not left me in the two years since the attack. Things can happen suddenly to sharpen this unease. The other day, for instance, I passed a boy in the street who I thought might be the blond youth who attacked me. He was with a friend and, as I passed, I could hear him saying something about someone having been beaten up near Clapham Common. Paranoia? He also had that wary, wondering look in the eyes that I remember. And he was wearing the same brown leather jacket. Coincidence?

But of course I never will be sure if it was the same boy. The whole incident was so fleeting, after all. A minute's confrontation, and then my attackers vanished. Despite my fears and fantasies, I'm never again likely to be confronted with them.

CAROL BARKER

The Petition

One day, quite late, Mr Nugent climbed into the tree at the bottom of the garden and refused to come down.

'Will you be staying there long, do you know?' his wife, a middle-aged woman of indeterminable shape, asked.

'I'm an ape!' Mr Nugent gibbered matter-of-factly back at her and he got into a squatting position to prove it, curling his fingers round until his hands were all knuckle at the end of loose-hanging arms. He pulled off a few leaves and stuffed them into his mouth.

'You won't be wanting your dinner then,' Mrs Nugent said, steadfastly controlling her voice in the face of this new manifestation of her husband's thoughtlessness.

Mr Nugent continued, greenly, to munch his leaves, as he sat there, on his haunches, in the tree,

'Right,' she said, 'just as long as I know,' and she stamped back up to the house, leaving impressions of her expensive leather shoes at regular intervals up the lawn.

Mr Nugent uncurled his fingers and lowered his bottom on to the branch, letting his legs dangle in the air. 'Mrs Nugent has never really understood me,' he thought, as he dug the fibrous bits of leaf from his teeth with his thumb-nail. With his other arm he encircled the trunk of the tree, and he sat there, some twenty feet up in the air, swinging his legs backwards and forwards.

The trouble with Mrs Nugent was that she made no allowances for individuality. Mr Nugent had these urges, at times, to escape – from work, from routine, from her – and get away from it all in a tree. She would pursue him, clucking up and down like a broody hen, and 'Get back where you belong, Mr Nugent. We all have our place to fill after all,' she would say, only too pleased to explain to him exactly where his place was and in what manner he would do well to occupy it.

Mr Nugent chuckled to himself when, by a multiple association of ideas, his thoughts made their way back to his wedding-day, nigh on twenty years before. 'Mr Nugent,' the reverend gentleman had asked, 'do you take Miss Naseby' – as Mrs Nugent had been then – 'to be your lawful wedded wife?' Mr Nugent had looked down at the floor, up at the reverend gentleman, across at the then Miss Naseby and replied, 'Can I think about that one for a moment?'

(Which only went to show that he had suspected even then.)

'Hee hee hee,' Mr Nugent laughed, as he sat on the branch, making the leaves quiver. He clutched the trunk with both arms and shook, rocking rhythmically like a metronome, until he nearly fell backwards out of the tree.

'Ah dear,' he sighed to himself, ribs all on fire from their breathless heaving. He let go of the trunk with one arm and fumbled in his pocket for a handkerchief, for laughing always made his nose run, but he found he hadn't taken one off the pile that morning. So he pulled off a leaf, blew his nose into it and let it drop, speculating, only very idly, on the probable efficacy of nasal mucus as a fertilizer.

Mr Nugent began to whistle one of the music-hall songs his father used to sing. After whistling for a bit, he broke into voice. 'Rolling round the world, looking for the sunshine, that never seems to come my way,' he sang in his cracked tenor.

As he sang, he thought it was surprising how much you could see sitting twenty feet up in a tree. Just went to show what you missed scurrying around at ground level all the time and Mrs Nugent not giving you a moment to yourself because she could always find a job for you to be doing and, if she couldn't find one, invented one rather than let you sit quietly in your armchair and think. The postman had just emptied the letter-box down the road – final collection of the day – and was climbing into his red van to drive off. Mrs Davidson, next-door-but-two's horrible infant son was scrawling on the pavement with a lump of chalk, no doubt purloined from some off-limits source since, at seven or eight, he was already showing marked criminal tendencies. And there was Mrs Davidson herself coming out of the house in her furry slippers and floral apron, disenchalking her son, clipping him round the earhole and dragging him off in. The Newbolds' cat – a smelly brute of a thing that gave even the more disreputable members of the feline species a bad name by permanently gate-crashing the house and trying to mate with the furniture – was scrabbling under the rose bushes in Mr Wyman, next-door-but-three's garden.

It was restful, though, peaceful, sitting on his branch with just the birds for company and the occasional creepy-crawly thing that came up the trunk or dropped on to his shoulder from above.

When a large, ugly earwig landed on his knee, Mr Nugent remembered how hungry he was. Even one of Mrs Nugent's improbably named dinners would have gone down with a little more ease than usual. Mr Nugent glanced about him and composed a menu, which, based on available supplies, came out something like: Chilled leaf. Roast rack of leaf with braised leaf and leaf au gratin. Leaf gateau with freshly-whipped leaf. His hunger sharpened. He pulled one of the leaves off and chewed it purposefully, but it was far too bitter. Nutritious, perhaps, but neither sustaining nor pleasant. He wondered, as the street-lamps along the road flickered into orange life, how many leaves he would need to eat as per his body-weight in order to survive. Perhaps he'd have to eat constantly like cows and grass. In which case, how many days' supply would his tree yield? And what did apes eat anyway? Not that he was one, which made the question academic, if still interesting from an environmental point of view.

It was dark now. House-windows were lighting up and curtains being drawn. Mr Nugent hummed to himself and, in order to forget his hunger, he tried to compose a poem about sitting in a tree in the dark. He stabbed the darkness with his finger, wrinkling his forehead into folds of verbal concentration. 'De-dum-de-dum-de-dum-de-DUM, de-dum-de-dum-de-dum-de . . .' No, no, that was no good; didn't scan. How about . . .? He began stabbing again, but couldn't think of a rhyme for 'earwig' in any case. 'Fear big'? No; he couldn't use that. It ought to be 'big fear' and even poetic license didn't extend to a reversal of such magnitude. 'Queer twig' then? he thought, but wasn't happy with that idea either.

Mr Nugent stayed in the tree all night. It was the end of summer, but the nights, even at the deepest hour, were tolerably warm still. He managed to sleep by putting one leg either side of the branch and leaning his back against the trunk. Not very comfortable, but manageable. He daren't risk stretching his legs out along the branch in case he dropped off – first to sleep, then out of the tree.

In the morning, he woke early with the rising sun, the birds' dawn chorus and a sore rump. Branches, he discovered, could be cruel to the tenderer parts of the human anatomy. He twisted round so that both legs dangled over the same side of the branch and shifted his weight from one buttock to the other – like you do in the theatre when the play's boring, the seats are hard and you wonder how many more scenes there can possibly be until the interval.

Mr Nugent felt replenished by his night in the tree. Doing something a touch out of the ordinary always gave him a fresh perspective on the normal routines of life. He thought, perhaps, given the time, he might even get used to it.

As dawn was still quite early in these days of late summer, it wasn't until two or three hours later Mrs Nugent, as Mr Nugent had known she would, came down the garden towards him. She had even got dressed for the occasion. Mr Nugent had not seen his wife external to her dressing-gown at this time in the morning since they were first married.

She planted herself squarely beneath the branch and looked up at him very crossly. 'Mr Nugent, what do you mean by still being up there?' she demanded, sacrificing grammar to the call of righteous anger.

Mr Nugent let go of the trunk, crooked his elbows with a hand resting either side of his breast-bone, flapped his arms up and down and said, 'Tweet, tweet.'

Mrs Nugent went very red in the face and shook her fist at him. 'We'll see about this,' was her parting shot before she stormed back up the garden to the house.

Mr Nugent sat on his branch and waited to see what would happen. Several possibilities occurred and a long ladder was common to all of them. Except the one where Mrs Nugent returned wielding an axe with her powerful shoulders and lumberjacked him out of the tree.

The fire-brigade, he reckoned, must come high on the list, though he didn't much like the idea of being rescued from the tree like a cat. At least, if it came to it, he could go down miaowing.

He watched the house and saw Mrs Nugent's face looking out at him from an upstairs window. She shook her fist again in an I'm-going-to-get-you-just-see-if-I-don't manner, so Mr Nugent stretched out a hand, broke off a sprig of leaves and stuck it in his ear, at which point Mrs Nugent's face disappeared.

The sun was quite warm now and Mr Nugent rolled up his shirt-sleeves to catch the heat on his arms. He removed the sprig of leaves from his ear where it was beginning to scratch and settled himself more comfortably against the tree-trunk.

When, some twenty minutes later, he saw Mrs Nugent coming down the garden again, accompanied, this time, by Mr Wringer his boss at Whitebone, Fleesam and Fleesam, the firm of accountants for whom he worked when not otherwise engaged in expressing himself freely in trees, he began to whistle 'Underneath the Spreading Chestnut Tree' – quite lyrically, he thought.

This appeared to disconcert Mr Wringer who hesitated at some point in the middle of the garden – or perhaps it was simply the fact of seeing, for the first time, his employee, with whom he was not used to dealing outside the office environment, looking down at him from twenty feet up in a tree – until recalled to his task by the steely hand of Mrs Nugent beneath his elbow.

'Now look here, Nugent,' Mr Wringer began as he approached the tree, 'this won't do at all. Mrs Nugent – your wife' (he added, though Mr Nugent did not think the clarification at all necessary, but that's what years in the accountancy profession did for you), 'has told me all about it. And really,' he finished weakly, 'it won't do at all.'

Mr Nugent pulled off a few leaves and began to float them down on to the head of his boss, so that Mr Wringer retreated a few steps and darted his eyes about, as though afraid there might be witnesses.

'I want you to get down at once, Nugent,' he said stiffly.

'I'm an ape,' Mr Nugent called and began to bounce up and down on the branch in ape-like agitation.

'He's not you know,' his wife put in. 'Don't listen to him.'

'My dear Mrs Nugent,' Mr Wringer said, 'I know what I'm doing.' He took two steps forward and, speaking quietly, said, 'All right, Nugent we both know you're not an ape. So I want you to come down from the tree and then we'll talk things over nice and sensibly.' He stopped and flashed a smile at Mrs Nugent.

Mr Nugent had gone very quiet.

'There,' said Mr Wringer, triumphantly.

Then, 'All right,' said Mr Nugent from above, 'in that case I'm an orang-utan.'

Mr Wringer's smile slid from his face, slowly, like a holed ship slipping beneath the waves. He struggled with his professional training for a bit, then raised an accusing, pointing finger.

'Damn it, Nugent, stop arsing around and come down from that bloody tree.' He stepped forward, grasped the trunk in a bear-hug and began labouring away. 'Damn you, I'll bloody well shake you out,' he gasped hoarsely.

And he always seemed so calm and unflappable at work, Mr Nugent thought, chuckling to himself.

Then word got round.

Mrs Nugent made numberless trips down the garden, bringing with her a friend or neighbour to have a look at Mr Nugent making a spectacle of himself in a tree, and her such a respectable woman too, it was a sin; giving the neighbourhood a bad name like that. Still, that was men for you – no sense of marital obligation. 'That's right, Mrs Nugent.' 'Who'd be a married woman?' 'All work and no thanks. Mine's just the same.'

Mr Nugent entertained them by eating a leaf now and then or he raised himself to a standing position and lifted one leg in the air, toes pointed ballet-fashion, so that they gasped and clutched at each other in alarm. He stuck leaves in all the acceptable bodily orifices until he was bored with the smell and taste of them.

The family doctor came, but, in the absence of any twenty-foot-long instruments, could not make an examination, so mumbled, instead, something about Mr Nugent looking a little off-colour. And went away again, leaving a bottle of vitamin pills and no instructions on how to administer them.

That nice man Mr Wyman next-door-but-three, came and had a look. He stood beneath the tree, hands in pockets, rocking on his heels, and looked up sadly from beneath repressed eyelids.

'Really, you shouldn't, you know,' he said, but his glance was full of hungry admiration.

'It's a disgrace, Mr Nugent,' Mrs Wyman shrilled, pulling her husband away as though afraid he might be contaminated. 'Mrs Nugent in tears too.'

Mr Wyman shook his head slightly and trailed his wife back up the garden, turning for a fond backward look now and then until Mrs Wyman caught him at it and dropped a pace behind to make sure he couldn't do it again. It made Mr Nugent feel quite melancholy to see him.

The Press arrived after that.

'Why are you sitting in a tree, Mr Nugent?' they called; fresh-faced youngsters – doubtless unwed – assigned to the fill-up stories and glad of a change from 'The bride wore ivory silk trimmed with lace.'

Mr Nugent turned round on his branch and gave them his back. They lifted their equipment – cameras and microphones – and rushed round to the other side of the tree.

'What are you protesting against?'

Mr Nugent yanked up the neck of his pullover until his face was hidden in acrylic. He leant against the trunk of the tree and sat there, headless, among the leaves.

'Up to the house,' the reporters yelled and stampeded away to get the relevant details from Mrs Nugent.

Even the Newbolds' cat paused in passing, sparing a few moments from a busy schedule to sit beneath the tree and blink up, unimpressed, at Mr Nugent with its yellow, dead-pan eyes. Then, before moving on to continue its never-ceasing quest for amenable females, it didn't omit to have a quick squirt against the trunk since it wasn't fastidious.

It was afternoon now and the activity, the comings and goings of earlier, had quietened down. Mr Nugent came out of his pullover, sucked on a few leaves, staving off the pangs of hunger, and was glad of a bit of peace. It was, after all, what he'd climbed the tree for in the first place.

He began humming softly to himself – 'A Room with a View'.

And, while engaged in actually surveying the view, Mr Nugent was surprised to see Mr Wyman coming back down the garden, anxiously glancing over his shoulder at every two or three steps and treading carefully, rather like a fugitive afraid that a cracking twig will give his whereabouts away to the enemy.

'Oh Mr Nugent,' he began as though meeting him unexpectedly in the street. 'I've brought you some bananas.' He threw them up. 'I thought you might be hungry.' Mr Nugent caught them and nodded his thanks, too busy peeling back the skin of the first one and cramming it into his mouth for verbal gratitude. 'And I thought I'd better warn you. They're going door-to-door. A petition. You know, just a friendly warning. I'd better go. There'll be hell to pay if she misses me.' Mr Nugent stuffed in a second banana as his neighbour first started back up the garden, then stopped. 'It was a brave attempt,' he said. 'I . . . I . . . admire you for it. Only wish I . . . um . . . had the courage myself.' He came back to the tree and pressed his hand flat against the trunk. 'What's it like?' he whispered hoarsely up to Mr Nugent. 'You know, to get away from them for a bit?' He looked nervously over his shoulder and, without waiting for an answer, which, bunged up in his third banana as he was, Mr Nugent couldn't have given anyway, added, 'Good luck,' and went away, back up the garden.

Mr Nugent couldn't make much sense out of the 'warning'. A petition? What petition? (He peeled a fourth banana.) He felt a great deal of sympathy with his hard-pressed neighbour; poor man, had more than his fair share of it what with being married to Mrs Wyman, and out of deference to his, no doubt, well-intentioned message, Mr Nugent kept a close eye on things.

At first all was peace and calm. Mr Nugent hummed to himself and scattered banana skins round the bottom of the tree. He idly chased earwigs up the trunk with a leaf, mentally chastising them for not rhyming with anything. He watched the birds that alighted on the branches of his tree and speculated on their business, as they no doubt did on his. He enjoyed the new-found experience of tranquillity.

Then they came: eight or ten of them, in a pack, Mrs Frangle of the Residents' Association at their head. They looked purposeful and resolved, and aligned themselves precisely beneath the tree, each fixing Mr Nugent with an accusing gaze.

Mrs Nugent was there, leaning heavily on the arm of a neighbour. So was Mrs Wyman who turned red at the sight of the banana skins and started to count them, having a few minutes earlier discovered the theft of a bunch of seven from the fruit bowl on the sideboard at home.

There were no men.

Mrs Frangle took a step forward, removed her gaze from Mr Nugent, swept it over the assembled sisterhood and returned it to the occupant of the tree.

'Mr Nugent,' she said in an unpleasant, fog-horn voice,

evolved from a lifetime of shouting other people down, 'we have brought to this – unhallowed' (shuddering) 'place, a petition that we want you to hear.' The women set their jaws in readiness. 'I have been asked to read it to you. It runs: "We the undersigned, being the women of this neighbourhood, friends and neighbours of Mrs Nugent, whom we know and esteem, do wish to register, most strongly, our protest at the unacceptable action of the said Mrs Nugent's husband, Mr Nugent. We unanimously declare that we deem this action anarchic, inconsiderate, untenable and ridiculous in the extreme. We demand that the said Mr Nugent, husband of the said Mrs Nugent, to whom he is bound by the firmest rules of matrimony, do forthwith descend from the tree and return to his wife's side, where it is his duty to be and to remain."' Mrs Frangle paused and lowered the paper from which she had been reading. 'I should, in fairness, point out that we,' running her eyes over the group who smiled one by one as the spotlight of her glance fell upon them, 'are only a small representative body of the signatories herein gathered,' raisng the paper. 'Do you wish to hear the names?' The women behind her nodded vigorously. 'Very well.' She took breath. 'Mrs Nugent, of course, Mrs Frangle – myself, that is – Mrs Newbold, Mrs Wyman, Mrs Peasman, Mrs Dunwithy, Mrs Hastings, Ms Richards – Ms? How did that get in? – Mrs Shorthorn, Mrs Flipper . . .

Mr Nugent clutched at the tree trunk as the names bludgeoned his ears.

'. . . Mrs Cocky, Mrs Wedgewood, Mrs Maltings . . .'

He felt the eyes in the upturned faces of the women beneath him awaiting his every move.

'. . . Mrs Jemmy, Mrs Harding, Mrs Bloodstone . . .'

He had always known he would have to come down in the end, but had imagined it would be in circumstances more favourable to himself. The taste of escape was sweet; victory would have been sweeter still. Looking down, though, he saw Mrs Nugent smile weakly, but bravely, at the neighbour supporting her, free herself from the helping hand and step forward to receive her husband, her arms ready and waiting to fold him to her bosom. Mr Nugent swallowed.

'. . . Mrs Broadbeam, Mrs Chipper, Mrs Beasting . . .'

Mr Nugent rolled down the sleeves of his shirt, buttoned them at the wrist, and pulled down the arms of his pullover over them. He looked up into the canopy of leaves and patted his branch. Then he sighed deeply – once.

'. . . Mrs Nojoy, Mrs Bracewell, Mrs . . .'

Mr Nugent . . .

. . . stopped dead.

Before he had made so much as a preliminary move, a loud cry suddenly cut across the air. The roll-call of names abruptly ceased. Mrs Wyman went rigid and her eyes and mouth opened in harness as though she had swallowed a fly and could feel its passage down her throat. The band of women swung slowly round on its axis and looked up and over whence the voice had come.

'Cooee,' called Mr Wyman from where he was sitting on the roof of his house. He had one arm round the chimney-pot and waved vigorously at them with the other. When he saw he had their undivided attention, he raised his arm, fist clenched, and in a voice surprisingly firm and baritonal for a man of his size, weight and apparent stature (though Mrs Wyman, for one, was convinced she would never believe in anything after this), he began to sing 'Fight the good fight with all your might'.

Everything else had gone still. Nobody moved. Nobody breathed. There was just that noble voice ringing out over the rooftops and the gentle quivering of the leaves on the trees.

ELSA CORBLUTH

The Grapevine Tea

It was a breezy evening, ruffling my cassock as I went in, early, as usual. At this time, only a handful of people occupied the chairs, one here and one there, widely spaced, except for that lady in a beige coat and – I took him to be – her son, pale, in a blazer. A stout gentleman had his plump hands resting in front of him and the old lady knelt, shaking very slightly. The first few, as with the ones who stay there after the service, interest me rather. Mrs Larkin, in her old-fashioned fur collar (she does remind me of my Aunt Cicely), passed by me to take her usual place near the front. We exchanged slight smiles of recognition, tempered by our mutual reverence for the place of our meeting.

By the time I was in the pulpit the nave was full. The choir was in very good voice. We have a number of young girls in our choir. Their voices are very pleasing. It is, indeed, pleasant and reassuring to see and to hear such young people singing to the glory of God.

I was confident about my sermon. There was a time when I used to have my doubts – no, never about my faith – but regarding my ability to bring the Word to my congregation. I would wonder if I had composed the sermon to the best effect, and even whether my voice would project sufficiently to the people at the back. But this was when I was fresh out of college – and that was a great many years ago, a time about which I seldom have occasion to think nowadays.

On the Sunday evening of which I am speaking, I heard, with some degree of gratification (but not, I trust, self-aggrandisement), my own voice soaring strongly out and up,

99

into that great edifice, as, indeed, the youthful voices had, with their well-practised hymns. In a cathedral, sound, when it is suitable sound, which it almost invariably is, always soars.

Evensong is a very beautiful service, and, I think, my favourite, if it does not appear slightly lacking in respect to think in such terms of the services.

My sermon was well prepared, early in the week. In fact, I usually write my next Sunday's sermon on Monday, or, at latest, Tuesday, while my recent Sunday's sermon is still fresh in my mind.

On that particular evening, my sermon was on Matthew. I have no need to repeat it in full, as it may be found on my file for last September – the second Sunday of September, to be precise. 'When the Lord called Matthew,' I told the congregation, 'he abandoned everything in his life up to that time and obeyed the Call. When God calls us, we must do likewise. When God calls you, you must leave everything in your present life and answer the Call of the Lord.' I descended, satisfied but, I sincerely hope, appropriately humble. I am indeed privileged, and this must never be forgotten. It is, one might say, a unique privilege, and one of which I am doubtless unworthy in this life, to be Canon of this, one of God's most beautiful houses.

The sidesmen were going round with the collection bags during the final hymn, and then I gave my blessing, and the congregation quietly rose – that is, after the Dean had made his little announcement about the Canon – myself – being pleased to take tea with any who cared to accompany him to his fine house in our historic close with which many of us are already familiar.'

It was the duty of Sister Clare to address members of the congregation as they began to disperse. She is a very fine Sister, extremely beautiful, in a totally unworldly way, naturally. She is – like a medieval painting, I have observed to myself, more than once.

I made my way to my home. I am very fond of our close, its ancient cobblestones, its splendid archway. Autumn was going to be early. A few leaves already blew about.

Sister Clare and her helpers had had the cups ready before the serivce. Now it was merely a question of reboiling the kettle and brewing the tea. Some of my cups are of very fine china, with a charming motif, one might call it, of a purple-fruited grapevine which is, inevitably, repeated upon the tea plates. The tendrils have always given me a sense of appreciation. The saucers, however, are plain white, but with slightly scalloped gilt edges. I generally use two tea services, knowing that I have, easily accessible, additional cups and saucers, should these be required owing to a greater than usual influx of visitors. After Evensong, I expect mainly adults to arrive, hence I deem it safe to put into service the grapevine set. Also, Sister Clare has a very steady hand.

We always have assorted biscuits for these occasions. I find these very popular.

Sister Clare had already ushered in the first-comers, and was efficiently managing the finishing touches – milk jugs, the tea itself, in two teapots, the rather elegant grapevine one and another, serviceable, if less distinguished. We have one of those large tins of biscuits – Huntley and Palmers, I believe it was that week. They keep rather well in those, if we do have a residue. Sister Clare's slender white fingers arranged the biscuits upon the two plates, mixing the varieties pleasingly. More people were trickling across the courtyard. 'Don't stand on ceremony,' I reassured them. 'Do come inside.'

Among those already in the room were the lady in beige with her, perhaps fifth-form, son, the elderly lady (ah yes, Miss Phillips), Mrs Larkin and her friend, whose name I can never remember, and a lady, perhaps in her late forties, fifty or so (I am not very good at judging ladies' ages), tidily-dressed, if just a little unusually for a lady of her years attending Evensong, in fairly well-pressed – jeans, as these are now more generally called, although I still tend to think in terms of slacks (which *were* a rarer phenomenon, at least in church), a lightweight pullover – I forget the colour – and with long, lightish, greying hair held back by a patterned scarf. She was evidently on holiday. I am not suggesting that such attire is remarkable

101

nowadays, in such circustances. I had never seen her before, and had observed her arrive after the service had commenced and slip quietly into a place right at the back (without kneeling on entering, as is customary), near, as it happened, to Sister Clare – which is, no doubt, why she found her way to my house that evening. Sister Clare is always particularly eager to bring holiday visitors to our little tea-gatherings.

Far more remarkable, it would seem, was one of the later-comers to the house. The stout gentleman I had half-expected. 'Mr Morris? – do come in. Norris – thank you.' But at Mr Morris's – Norris's – heels, ducking through the open doorway, and dropping a small, very dirty, knapsack on the floor beside the chair for which he made, and on which he at once sat, was a fairly young man. His clothing was decidedly shabby, crumpled – and, I am afraid, not at all clean. His boots were muddy. His hair was long, tangled and greasy, with a band of some description around his head and across his forehead, Red-Indian fashion. He was bearded, untidily. He even exuded a faint, but disagreeable, odour. He helped himself to a biscuit. 'Yes, do,' I said, involuntarily, I am afraid, looking askance at the condition of his hands.

I helped Sister Clare fill the cups and pass one to each, offering the sugar bowl and tongs. I always make quite sure I speak to each person individually at least once. They have come to my house for fellowship and it is my duty to give each one a little of my attention, or, as it may be, concern, to this end. Do not misunderstand, me. It is a pleasant enough duty, in general. Those members who come, at Sister Clare's persuasion, or of their own volition, and myself, we are all, in the main, desirably relaxed, even, I must say, mildly jovial. Uplifted, it is hoped, by the service, and, certainly, refreshed by Sister Clare's tea, it has become, for those among our flock who regularly join me after Evensong, and for myself, one of a busy week's most pleasant hours.

Mrs Larkin and her friend always stay to help Sister Clare with the washing-up afterwards, thereby earning an extra blessing – if I may be permitted to say this without impropriety.

On that occasion, I heard Mrs Larkin remark to her friend, as she did every Sunday evening at precisely the same time, 'Nobody knows what I did for that man,' and Mrs Larkin's friend answered her, as indeed she always did, 'No, I know, dear,' adding, as ever, 'except God, of course.' 'Of course,' said Mrs Larkin, applying a discreet handkerchief, and Sister Clare would refill her cup and the friend would pass her a biscuit.

The stout man tends to take one of those biscuits with a small round disc of extremely stiff red jam on top of them. I dare not touch these, owing to my dentures. I can manage a shortcake however, or even, on occasion, a custard creme.

I was speaking with the elderly lady, and we were discussing the sale of cathedral postcards, when I heard, with one ear, so to speak, the lady in the headscarf address the – person – in the headband, asking him, politely, how far he had come. 'Next street,' he answered. I heard her attempting not to react with surprise. I turned to the lady in beige, and, directing my words, *sotto voce*, at the level of her son's well-combed head, said, 'I wish they'd *wash!*' like an almost naughty, but admissible, secret joke. The beige lady received my secret message with a swift hidden smile and the son took his cue from his mother, and did likewise. After all, this individual had chosen to present himself to God in such disarray, so did I in fact owe him total, unquestioning respect, as a child of Christ, even out of his hearing? If so, then this, surely, very small sin of mine might only serve to display my erring humanity, from which no man, even a man of God, is free? I do not, after all, presume to rival God Himself in my forbearance.

By this time, the scarf lady was facing in our direction, and aiming a tiny wry grin of assent at me. I began to speak to her. Yes, she was here on holiday – that was, she was staying in the town for just two nights before going on to a centre a few miles away, where she was to attend a course in literature. Yes, she had enjoyed her stay very much, had joined a guided tour, seen the city wall, Roman remains, the Tudor houses (the genuine, as well as the copies), the canoeing in the river and, finally, the cathedral. 'The cathedral is very beautiful,' she said.

'We are very proud of our cathedral,' I answered.

'The stained glass,' she added, 'especially the blue – and those wonderful monsters carved underneath the old choir seats.'

'Misericords, yes,' I agreed, 'they are remarkable.' Then, 'A literature course, you said? What is your particular interest in literature?'

She seemed to hesitate. 'Well, I like a lot of things.'

'Have you read P.G. Wodehouse?'

'Well, no, to be honest –'

'Oh, you *must*!' I became quite animated. 'He's delightful – *very* humorous. There is a *mar*vellous passage. It begins, "The genteel moon – "'.

She laughed, and the atmosphere was very genial. We were both laughing. Then she said, 'My real interest is poetry.'

'Which poets?' I said.

'Oh, a lot – but one I like is R.S. Thomas – he is a clergyman, actually – yes –'

'I don't know him.'

'Well, you could try him – *he* has something to say about the moon. Read his poem "The Minister". It's in his collection *Song at the Year's Turning*.'

I did not know, then, whether or not I would remember the name of this poet, or his poem. In any case, this seemed like the end of our conversation for the present. I glanced round, making a mental note of the people I had yet to single out, and converse with. There seemed a tacit understanding that this particular conversation was at an end. Then, and there was something in her voice as well as the content of her question which alerted me to attend to her, 'Look, I wonder if I might ask you something more serious?'

'Yes, of course,' I answered, at once just slightly apprehensive because caught off my guard, so to speak, and, at the same time, confident that I would know what to reply, suggest, conclude, when she had asked, stated, opened, whatever it was on her mind.

With a gesture almost of impatience I pointed one of the old ladies who seemed to have been waiting for me, and no other, to fill her empty cup, towards the table where a teapot stood. 'Yes?' I said to the literary lady. There was a brief, but I sensed, rather tense, pause, during which I was aware of tea being poured, and biscuits being crunched, around me.

'The sermon –' she said, with a hint of breathlessness, 'I would like to ask you about the sermon.'

'Of course – do,' I encouraged.

'It was Matthew. Matthew's call to God. God calling Matthew.'

'Yes? God did call Matthew.'

'My daughter thought she had a call to God.' I was going to speak, but she went straight on: 'She thought she had a message from God to go and work in a hostel for homeless women. She was there twelve hours and one of the homeless women burned the place down. Ten people died. My daughter was one of them.'

I do not remember exactly what I said. But I remember what she said: 'You are probably always hearing of terrible things happening – I know that – but God was supposed to have told her to go – she believed that. She had become a Christian – got baptized in the Baptist Church – then went to a Catholic hostel. She used to say "I am Christian", meaning not of any one sect. If she'd gone to a council hostel, not a religious, voluntary, hostel, it would have had fire precautions, and she wouldn't be dead.'

'Didn't this one have fire precautions?'

'No, it had nothing, nothing at all.'

'I thought they had to have.'

'Not by law. And they chose to rely on their faith. She was our only daughter, healthy, "pretty" the papers said. She wanted to go to India to help Mother Teresa. She got no answer to her letter to India. Then she wrote to the Mother Teresa hostel in London. We were relieved she was not going to India. When they said "Come" she left everything – home, family, boyfriend – and went. She prayed to God, and God, she thought, said "Go". The nuns were up at 5 a.m., praying, the next morning, and that is when the fire was started. God didn't tell them. When they found it, it was too late. They did all the wrong things – panicked, left doors open, hadn't a clue. No one had warned them. They believed God would take care of them. My question is, if God really did call my daughter to do his work, why did he not allow her to do his work? They put her on the top floor –'

I must have given the type of reply one normally gives in such testing circumstances, those explanations designed to give comfort and to lessen some anger felt towards the Almighty, because she said, 'Those are things other people have told me, about God's will, about his 'mysterious ways', I am asking for new answers. You have studied these things. Mother Teresa herself wrote to us. She made it sound all too simple –'

'The best answers are often the simplest ones.'

'Hers are simplistic. I have gone into tiny country churches and into great cathedrals. There are no answers, are there, if you are honest?'

I said, 'I know this is terrible for you,' or something like that, 'but –' and I searched my mind, my educated, my trained, cultivated, specialist mind, for something she might not have heard before. I spoke slowly: 'There is one way you could look at it – she died with her *ideal intact*.' I will not forget her look. She did not weep. I think I could have done something about that. I *do* see people from time to time in all kinds of terrible predicaments. Some of them burst into tears, or even angry rages. They are in the desperation that is beyond reason, and out of reach of reasoning. I can put my hand on their heads, and bless them. But this woman? My voice had to remain kind to her because of her situation.

She said, 'If I were to believe that it *was* God's will to burn a girl of eighteen to death, and her ideals with her – to nail a man of thirty to a cross and leave him to die, slowly – and never to tell anyone what has happened to them apart from the burning and nailing –'

'The Bible – the Resurrection –'

'Never to tell *me*, never to tell *you* – if I did believe that, I would believe the world in the hands of a power so malicious that –' I thought I saw an actual cloud go over her face – or was it across mine?

'My daughter died at Easter,' she said.

I had read many Christian thinkers. The fabric of my life, and all life, as I understood it, depended on the doctrine that suffering has a Purpose, that death is the way into Life. I am not saying that what this woman said, or was, made me hesitate in my faith. I am not saying that. But, like taking a comma out of one of my sermons, like deleting one letter, like breathing in or out for an infinitesimal time longer than is customary to the breather – no, there is no way I can tell it.

There is one thing with which I am burdened, and that also is difficult to tell, even to tell myself.

'I prefer,' she concluded, 'to have no God.' Then, 'There is something else you could read – a play by Lorca – a Spanish poet and playwright – *The House of Bernarda Alba* – Bernarda's last speeches –'

She and I both saw that the conversation was truly at an end. I extended my hand. We shook hands. I said, 'Thank you for telling me.'

'Thank you for the tea.'

As she went out, the light coldly green, just after sunset, and I heard her go away over my cobbles, under my archway, I found myself momentarily almost envying her – what? Her freedom? A freedom from the burden of belief? But what freedom could there be without God?

I do not know if anyone had overheard our conversation. We had spoken quietly, and the others were speaking among themselves. But, if they did, they all, naturally, left it to me whether or not I would refer to it. I said nothing, and when Mrs Larkin's friend reminded me that it was her turn to do the flowers next, with Miss Spiller, I assented, eagerly. I quite forget what topics I touched upon, with whom, but trust I left no one out. Gradually they went away, and only Mrs Larkin and her friend and Sister Clare remained. It was incumbent upon me to hover, until the washing-up was completed.

Finally, I had the house to myself. A faint hint of light remained in the sky as I went upstairs to my study. I did not switch on the light. I sat at my desk, very tired. I have not been young for a long time, and now I am no longer middle-aged. I took off my cassock, only standing for a moment to raise it to my waist, and let it fall on the back of my chair. I loosened, then removed, my clerical collar. I must have dozed.

My dream began with a street, which I took to be in Northern Ireland. A young English soldier hung, star-shaped, on barbed wire. He had a beard and round his head was an Indian-style band. A child, whose name was Catholic, because its mother kept crying out the name into the night, lay in its blood on the road. Then a great cloud of smoke went up into the sky, a volcano beginning, not from a mountain, but out of the curve of the earth, a cloud that spread out and shaped itself into a giant tea-table. There was a clanging of bells, which became more slow and regular, and the word 'fire' was muttered by old ladies eating biscuits. Then Sister Clare floated across in front of me. It was out-of-doors. Her habit was blowing about. She came closer, and I could see it was not her habit, but her skin, hanging, black. I looked for her long pale fingers, but there were only jagged, snapped-off branches, also black, where her arms should have been. I looked for her face.

Then something hit my face.

That may have been when my head fell on my desk.

I opened my eyes. I could not tell whether I was still dreaming or now awake.

Outside the window was a tree with horns.

A voice – very like my own, as it sounds in my own head when I preach in the cathedral – came out of the horned tree: 'Be still and know that I am God.'

I looked at my clock. It was 4 a.m. I had not undressed, washed, prayed.

I rose up slowly. Feeling very remote, I went into my bathroom. I performed a shortened version of my bedtime preparations – toilet, a brief wash and change into my loose, comfortable pyjamas – all in the dark, or almost dark – a glimmer only from street lights beyond the arch. I did not wish to hear the sound of bath or shower running. I was alone, and would disturb no one, but I did not wish myself to be disturbed. I had left my clothes in the bathroom, but the housekeeper would do whatever needed to be done with them when she came in the morning.

In bed, I could not remember whether I had prayed or not. I had forgotten to open the window. Feeling in need of air, I arose again and opened the window, moderately. A leaf floated in, and lay on my dressing table beside my silver-backed hairbrush (which I have no cause to use nowadays). The leaf was dry and brown, and its veins made a drawing of a miniature tree.

I awoke at nine, much later than normal.

Mrs Priest was already bustling about, lighting the fire, vacuum-cleaning, preparing my breakfast.

Later in the morning, when she was about to go to the shops, I asked her if she would go to the public library and obtain two books for me, if these were in stock. I explained to her that I had remembered authors and titles to the best of my ability, but she might require some assistance in locating them.

She did bring them both. I looked at 'The Minister' first, combing through for references to the moon. I found:

> . . . You who never venture from under your roof
> Once the night's come; the blinds all down
> For fear of the moon's bum rubbing the window.

Well, that is a good Shakespearian word, I suppose. There is also somewhat stronger language elsewhere in this poem. Yet the author is a rector. This is confirmed in the foreword to the book by John Betjeman (whom I have read).

Near the end of 'The Minister' I found this:

Protestantism – the adroit castrator
Of art: the bitter negation
Of song and dance and the heart's innocent joy –

You have botched our flesh and left us only the soul's
Terrible impotence in a warm world.

I found myself hoping that Mrs Priest had not looked inside
the book. It was, however, rather unlikely that she had, I
decided. My own reaction I would, so to speak, shelve, for the
moment.

Apart from ecclesiastical works, I have read mainly for
recreation, Wodehouse for example. Life must not be exclus-
ively solemn, I have always maintained.

Lorca, I learnt from the introduction to his 'Three
Tragedies', when in his thirties, was 'murdered at Granada by
Nationalist partisans, just after the outbreak of the Spanish
Civil War'. What would his Bernarda Alba have to say to me? I
asked myself: I turned to the end, as had been suggested to me:

> . . . Cut her down! My daughter died a virgin. Take her to
> another room and dress her as though she were a virgin. No
> one will say anything about this! She died a virgin. Tell them,
> so that, at dawn, the bells will ring twice.
>
> . . .
>
> And I want no weeping. Death must be looked at face to
> face. Silence!
>
> Be still, I said!
>
> Tears when you are alone! We'll drown ourselves in a sea
> of mourning. She, the youngest daughter of Bernarda Alba,
> died a virgin. Did you hear me? Silence, silence, I said.
> Silence!

'I have no other daughters,' she had told me.
'With her ideals intact,' I had told her.

When I next saw Sister Clare, I had a matter of some little
delicacy to mention to her:

'Sister Clare, allow me to compliment you on the zeal with
which you gather members of the congregation at Evensong
and bring them into my house for tea and conversaton . . .'

Sister Clare's face lit faintly with subdued expectancy. 'I do not, however, really wish to – overcrowd – my room, so that only a few may be seated, and I can hardly get round to speak with everyone, if you follow my train of thought?'

Sister Clare nodded, the merest traces of confusion crossing her fine features.

'I feel it would be more desirable, on the whole, to extend a *particularly* warm welcome to our – regular – visitors – those who assist with the flowers, the postcards, the – washing-up, and so forth. That is not to say that a strange face is *never* welcome – such as those on holiday who come to our cathedral in place of their usual place of worship for example . . .'

I am not quite sure whether I made myself totally clear, but I suspect that Sister Clare was able to follow my musings.

Sister Clare has a very fine countenance. I would not wish to see it – dare one say, coarsened – however slightly, by a taste for the evangelical – that irresistible smile which was beginning to shepherd all and sundry into my house in the close on Sunday evenings. Her desire for converts should not lead her to lose her sense of proportion or even a modicum of her dignity, or forget her obligation to the more familiar among our congregation.

Our little interview gives me reason to believe, nevertheless, that Sister Clare and I now understand one another to quite an extent.

MARY HADINGHAM

Theo's Divorce

The news was all over Philadelphia in a matter of hours. Theo
Simmer was divorcing his wife after forty years! His old partner,
Gus Henniker, drew the whole thing up for him and took the
papers around to Horterr Street. No warning. Didn't even
discuss it with Emily – and you know what a lovely person she is
– perfect wife and mother. Couldn't believe her ears. Just back
from a church social; still wearing her hat and removing her
gloves, her maid said.

He's seventy years old. Let's see, she must be nearing seventy
herself. What grounds? Mutual imcompatibility, that thing
that's so difficult to prove, and generally means that there's no
real reason. Of course, the Simmers are a nest of lawyers. Four
generations of them. Believe me, if they say so, it can be done.

Emily was so stunned that she waited for a week, confined to
her bed, attended by Rachel, her maid, who kept the world
informed about what was going on via the telephone and the
back door. Then, she summoned Carl, her eldest son, from
New York. Her other children are out of reach, one of them is
in Brussels, another in Montreal. Benji, the youngest, died in
Vietnam. Her daughter Kate is on the West Coast. Carl arrived
with his wife Babs.

'Make him see what he's doing to us, Carl. Tell him I can't
bear it.'

His mother tore at a lace handkerchief, which fluttered like a
flag between her restless hands. As soon as Carl managed to
calm her slightly, her spasmodic energies drove her wild again.

'I will. I promise,' he soothed. 'But you've got to calm down.'

It has been the shock of his life to see his rock-ribbed upright mother reduced to this trembling ghost.

'Tell me about it, Mutte.' He reverted to their childhood name for her.

She rocked to and fro irritably. 'I've no idea where he's been for the past six months . . . New Mexico, I think. You know how it's been. He goes his way, and I keep things going here. He's resigned all his commissions. Left everybody in the lurch . . . doesn't seem to mind a bit. All I ask is that he turns up sometimes for the family's sake.' She turned her pale gaze on him. He nodded in sympathy.

'When he does come, he might just as well not have bothered. He just sits there with his black glooms. Not speaking to anybody. But, lately he hasn't even made an appearance. He missed Lou's graduation, and Lou is supposed to be his favourite. He's grown that awful beard . . . you know it's always a sign of something when a man grows a beard. He's either giving up, or trying to be something special. Have you noticed that?'

Carl let his mother talk on. Just when he was lulled into thinking that his elderly parents were safely entering some peaceful harbour at last, they broke out with this last kick of life. He felt his dyspepsia coming on, and surreptitiously swallowed one of his anti-acid tablets.

He said, 'I'm seeing Henniker later today. Maybe I could get him to change it to some kind of formal separation, a new will, that kind of thing. Would you go for that, Mother?'

There was a nervous tremor of her head, but her eyes lit with relief. 'Oh yes, Carl,' she sighed with a long trembling breath. 'All I want is for him to let things be. Stay as we are. And try to be dignified about it. Not spread ourselves all over the newspapers, and turn me into a fool. And I won't have people saying he's crazy.' She started up convulsively again. 'Doctor Cooper says he isn't anyway.'

Two large tears slowly formed and spilled over her reddened lids.

'Make him stop, Carl.'

He took her handkerchief and tried to wipe her tears away with awkward hands. The family so seldom touched or embraced one another. 'I'll try,' he promised. 'I'm seeing Father now. I asked him to come here.'

Carl descended the stairs to the landing below where his wife, Babs, waited for him. Her frown was a little squiggle of lines in the centre of her large fair brow. 'Well?' she demanded.

'She's pretty upset. Looks terrible. Seems he wants to be rid of all of us. Believes he's got a right to be free at his age.' He knew that he was betraying his role as a mediator who shouldn't take sides, but it was a relief to let go.

'Why doen't he shoot himself! That's what a real man would do!'

He seized her by the shoulders. 'Shut up, Babs. He's my father, for God's sake.' He drew strength from her and then let her go. 'Don't go saying things like that to Mother.'

Theo sat in the large guest room that overlooked the Japanese garden that he had created with such enthusiasm on his retirement. With eyes closed he could trace the design of grey boulders, sanded paths, fish pools, conifers and dwarf trees. But, it was only a toy, and belonged to that flare-up in his sensual life when he had made a lot of trouble for himself by chasing women, trying to up-date his clothes, and joining athletic clubs to recover his body. That episode was as remote to him now as the long passage of his career and married life, and he was closing the door on all of them.

He sat in perfect stillness, upright but relaxed, arms balanced along the rests of the chair, with his hands drooping down, fingers softly curled.

'Hullo Father. How are you?' Carl entered the room briskly, meaning to set a tone to the encounter.

Mother was right, he thought, after one look. That was a meaningful beard. It was like a black spade at the chin, but the areas around the nose and cheeks were thickly covered with coarse and grizzled hairs. That was how Carl had remembered him, but now, a new and secondary growth had sprouted below his mouth in a snowy white and soft-looking goatee. His head was covered with hair of the same silken texture. It was hard to tell how he looked under this camouflage; perhaps a little bloated as if he had been given steroids.

'Mother's upset,' Carl ventured.

His father made a slight fluttering gesture with his hands.

'Don't you care?'

'It's not important.' Theo's voice was husky, and cracked over the word 'important'.

'Goddamit, don't you know that everybody is talking about us!' Carl was enraged, and took a turn about the room.

'It'll pass. They'll forget.' Carl had to stoop to hear his words.

He took a grip on himself. 'Look, Father, Simmer's name is going to be mud around here if you go through with this thing. It's so unnecessary. You owe the family something. Why can't you come to some kind of private arrangement. Henniker will be glad to draw it up. I'm sure he hates being associated with your idea of a divorce . . .' He stopped as Theo raised a hand as if brushing away a bothersome fly.

The truth is that ever since he re-entered the house in Horterr Street with its disturbing associations, Theo's trouble has become more acute. For some time now, the world doesn't speak to him, and he doesn't speak to the world. He has developed these gestures (so infuriating to the onlooker) to take the place of speech. He has shut off contacts the better to listen to his inner monologue which is far more significant that anything in the object world around him, persons included.

In fact, lately he has sometimes seen himself divide. There is a train going out of the station, and he is left on the platform, only the platform is rolling backwards, too. He struggles to resolve this conflict, but first he must renounce his marriage, his sons, grandchildren, and the house in Horterr Street. He should have done so years ago. Now there is little time.

Although he looks so oddly calm outside, all his energies are on the boil within. The peace that he longs for is the aspect of indifference that he has seen on the faces of Buddhist monks or mystics. In New Mexico where his bones felt light and dry, and his breathing clear, he thought that he was coming close to his desire. He had spent some months in a commune there, but it proved even more of an effort to get involved with strangers. They had wanted him to apply himself to some litigation over land for them. It had taught him that he was putting on more chains. He would never live in a community again.

He made an effort to return from the spinning void. Carl's words took form again. His son reminded him of somebody. Who can it be? He rarely re-enters the past now, but he recalls that his Uncle Joseph had just that rigid way of holding himself with clasped hands. Uncle Joseph had turned the family upside down in his day, too, by entering a Trappist order.

Theo looked resignedly at his son. 'Do what you like. I want to leave in a day or two.'

Carl shook his father's hand warmly, feeling his triumph. 'I'm glad, Father. We'll fix it up for you . . .', although it's a pity that it ever happened, he was going to say, but stopped, checked by his father's passive hand and lack of response. 'What are you planning to do? Where can we reach you?'

Reach him, indeed. No one can reach him, but he answered quietly, 'Jim Hartnett's letting me have his fishing shack on Squamm Lake. I'll be there for a while.'

A few days later, Theo is seated by the water's edge on a small island which lies at the eastern end of Lake Squamm. It is early morning. Little muddied wavelets lap against the side of the dinghy which swings out from its moorings. His feet are bare, and he is wearing a singlet and trousers. A spider has spun a diaphanous web between two twigs, almost at his feet; the dew sparkles on it, and reflects the cold clear sunlight.

Theo's car is parked over at Ed Baines' general store at the north end of the lake. He hired his boat there and crossed to the island at dusk. Squamm Lake was formed after the glaciers receded. It is fathomless at the centre. When he reached this spot, Theo took the car keys from his pocket and dropped them over the side.

The bag of groceries which split open when he put it down inside the shack yesterday, is still untouched on the wooden table. He brought a bottle of brandy and a tin of coffee, too, but he has drunk only water, and eaten some rye bread for breakfast. He has slept and not slept all night, wrapped in a blanket on the bunk bed, and listened in the wakeful hours to the lament of a pair of loons passing and re-passing over the lake.

He saw the steely flash of their wings when he went outside this morning. The bag of groceries, the swaying boat, the curtain of trees that enclose the deserted lake, the pile of wood that must be brought in for the fire if he is to eat and be warm – even the spider's trembling web, all these nearby things are at the rim of his consciousness. They register, but he does not really respond to them. Just so he has seen the holy men of India planted among the refuse and the rotting carcases, or in the midst of a scene crowded with animals and men, oblivious to all.

He waits for something to happen. He is not sure what form it will take. Perhaps a terrible rapture or a blinding light. That is what the mystics describe, but it is all hearsay. He has not met anyone in his travels yet who has actually experienced it . . . He waits for the 'peace that passes all understanding' or something like it. It will empty his brain of all his intolerable thoughts, and fill his bosom. As he sits there he puts his hand on his chest, and feels the muffled beat of his heart.

What if he has left it too late? Gone the wrong way about it? He should have stayed in Burma, and joined the men walking bare-footed up the mountains a dozen years ago when his first promptings began.

He started to rock to and fro. What if he had surrendered his humanity for nothing? Where had he read those awesome lines 'the waste sad time stretching before and after'? He considers eating something, but the impulse passes. He has encountered an entirely new timescale, for the sun, which he saw rise a moment ago, is already setting over the Squamm Mountains behind him. It seems to have happened in the blink of an eye.

He experienced this in the desert once before.

It is late at night when Theo stumbles to his feet in the darkness.

A week later, a county officer from Holderness, a young man called Jim Anderson, made his way across the lake to Squamm Island. Three days of heavy rain had filled Theo's boat which lay wallowing near the shore. Jim called out from the landing. The door to the shack was open. He placed a hand on either side of the door frame and peered inside. Groceries were spilled out on the table. Some marauder, a chipmunk, perhaps, had been at the flour bag, and padded his prints across the surface. Jim picked up the bottle of brandy which was still sealed. He looked across the room to the shelves stacked with fishing equipment done up in plastic covers, and saw the ample tins of food and provisions there.

He cleared his throat, and called doubtingly again. 'Mr Simmer?'

He turned and laid a hand on the stone fireplace. It was cold and unused, although there was plenty of wood piled nearby. A red blanket lay on the floor beside the chair which was drawn up to the table, like a human clue planted in a mystery. Jim started at a sound. Squamm Lake and the island are spooky places, especially off-season. He knows all the legends about the depths of the lake, and the ghosts of the Indians who trapped beaver here in the past.

The sound is the vibration of the wooden walls, which makes the dust fall, nothing more.

Jim left everything undisturbed in the shack and closed it up. He spent an hour or so searching the island, and the woods close by on the mainland. Finally, he looked with binoculars along the spine of rocks which link the island to the shore, under water, but just visible, festooned with long sulphur-coloured weeds that swayed in the currents.

When he returned to headquarters, a combined search of the countryside was organized. Carl was summoned once again, and present when the waters around the island were dragged.

There are so many deep vaults in Lake Squamm. Over the years there have been many drownings, and few bodies are recovered.

'So, he may be down there, all right,' Jim Anderson said clumsily to Carl.

But then, there are the mountains, and he might have got across the lake somehow. Carl accompanied the helicopter pilot who scoured the hills. In the end it was decided to leave the case open for awhile.

'He seemed a real nice gentleman,' said Ed Baines. 'When he said he was a friend of Jim Hartnett's that was good enough for me. He was quite spry. He managed the boat as if he knew what he was doing. Said he'd come back over in a day or two and get more of his things from the car . . . in case he planned to stay, that is. There ain't hardly any fishing this time of year, but he said he knew that. And it's lonesome over there at the end of the lake . . . but he said he didn't mind being lonely. What's that? No, I wouldn't have said he was upset at all.

'Well, when he didn't come over, we thought it was just the rain kept him away, but we thought we'd just better check him out. I'm hoping he may turn up . . . maybe he just wandered off someplace, but there's the boat, and it don't seem too likely. I'm real sorry about your father.'

It seemed to Carl that Ed Baines' summary of his father's last days, and the impression he left were the best possible memorial. Baines, a stranger, had seen Theo as capable, self-sufficient, a possible survivor. Carl was exhausted by the search, and depressed by the inconclusive verdict he would carry back to Emily waiting in Horterr Street. He wished with all his heart that it was he who had seen his father with this humanity.

D.J. TAYLOR

After Bathing at Baxter's

For quite a long time – longer in fact than either of them could remember – Susy and Mom had canvassed the possibility of an extended summer vacation. Later at night in the apartment, Mom listlessly fanning the dead air, Sunday mornings coming back from church along the side of the freeway, over long, slatternly turn-of-the-year breakfasts their conversation turned inevitably on the single topic. Sometimes, Susy thought, Saturday afternoons mostly when she lay on her bed smoking and contemplating the rigours of the past week, it was only this activity that gave their lives any purpose, that without the brightly coloured travel brouchures, the timetables advising coach journeys to Des Moines and Kansas, life here in Tara City was bereft of meaning. Mom incubated similar ideas, seldom expressed. 'Nothing keepin' us here,' she had once remarked, with uncharacteristic acumen, and then more pointedly, 'Ain't as if ya had a career or anything'. It wasn't. Susy had rather resented the stricture about careers (there had followed an argument on who the fuck did Mom think paid the rent?) but she appreciated the distrust of milieu. Lulu Sinde, who had married a local dentist, reckoned she had put down roots in Tara. 'Yeah. Like in fuckin' concrete,' Susy had retorted, half jokingly. 'Like I was born here,' Lulu had said, dimly aware that her husband's decision to run for mayor demanded a certain patriotism. Susy had not said anything. Driving back down the freeway, past the first strew of advertising hoardings and the neon sign that read WELCOME TO TARA CITY, she has said a great deal.

Mom and Susy were not people who did things in a hurry. Last time the apartment needed painting it had taken a year for them to decide on the appropriate shade. The installation of a central heating system (two radiators and an immersion – shit, this was Tara) trailed thirty months of low-spirited bickering. It was not to be expected that such a momentous step as removal would be entered into without a period of procrastination. Three years back when they had been on the point of vacationing in Florida Mom had recollected that coach journeys disagreed with her and in any case what was the point in going two thousand miles just so that you could lie in the sun? The picturesque leaflets of Tampa Bay and the virid swamps were consigned to the dustbin. Eighteen months back Mom had floated the idea of staying with Aunt Berkmann in Tucson, had sought and obtained Aunt Berkmann's approval, had even, with unusual foresight, made arrangements for letting the apartment. Two days after that the fast-food chain owner to whom Aunt Berkmann acted as personal assistant decided to go to Europe. It was, Aunt Berkmann's letter explained, 'too good an opportunity to miss'. The episode had annoyed Mom considerably. 'And she fifteen years older'n him,' she had remarked, both appalled and envious. Yet Susy thought she detected relief behind the bluster. It was possible to speculate that the late-night poring over guide books, the posters of shimmering Californian beaches, were merely an elaborate piece of camouflage.

While Mom vacillated, stuck metaphorical toes in water and pulled them out, Susy found her sense of purpose continually resuscitated. Just walking down the main street did that. Tara City had only one function as a population centre. It was a place you moved out of. Doctors fresh out of medical school who thought they fancied a year or two seeing the sights of the mid-west stayed a month and then applied for hospital jobs back east. Ranchers whose social pretensions advised the purchase of a town house took one look at Tara and thanked God they were hoosyar boys from the flatlands. Curiously, this revulsion rubbed off even on casual visitors. The bikers who sneaked in off the freeway and cruised the streets looking for dope and tail saw within a few minutes that they wouldn't find it in Tara. Licence, even of the home-grown variety, was scarcely encouraged by the row of gloomy bars, the run-down amusement arcade and the single enervated cathouse that made shift as civic amenities. The local weirdos and bomber boys went east if they wanted diversion, to Denver and Castle Rock. There was too much respectability, and too much decay. Reagan-voting, gun-toting, its cinema screens cleared of anything that might cause offence to tender sensibilities, its library shelves relieved of the weight of tomes immoral or unAmerican, its streets populated by Godfearing rednecks just itching to pump lead into the asses of Jews, queers and liberals, Tara City nevertheless harboured more subtle depravities. The niggers were moving in; longhairs, Ricans – 'yaller trash' Mom, trained in Southern schools of prejudice, would murmur whenever an Hispanic loped silently towards them down the street. At night the apartment block resounded to the thud of hectic jungle jive. Mom cried a little every time she walked past Trapido's and saw the Ricans clustering round the green baize tables, monitored the nigger kids drinking 7 Up on car bonnets. Pa had taken his beer in Trapido's every day for twenty years, back in the days when the buck occasionally stopped and (as Pa used to say) you could still buy something with it. Distant days, of which Susy preserved only a few recollections: swimming in Tara Creek with Artie Tripp, watching the hippy convoys heading west, coming back across the railway line, Artie Tripp saying as they blundered through the dusky scrub that in ten years they could get married and what did Susy think of that?

Artie Tripp, Susy had decided – a reflection prompted by a decade's marginal straying inside her consciousness – was a paradigm of what Tara did to you. Artie Tripp, Susy thought as they sat in McKechnie's Coffee Piazza, *had been talking that shit for eight years*. Susy remembered a sixteen-year-old Artie Tripp who had stolen rubbers off his father and driven the latter's

Ford Pontiac with negligent abandon, an eighteen-year-old Artie Tripp who featured as the shit-hot quarterback angling for a football scholarship, a twenty-year-old Artie Tripp who had talked about evading the draft and heading off east, looked across the table at a twenty-five-year-old Artie Tripp who had spent the last nine years working the forecourt of his father's gas station. 'Yeah,' Artie Tripp was saying, as he shovelled ice-cream through mild, uncombative jaws, 'I told him how it was, you know, politely, that you know I oughta think of changing things. I really gave it to him,' Artie Tripp went on, giving a swift, nervous little grin, spoon halfway from his plate. Susy gazed out of the window at the clotted high-summer streets, wanting to say *like fuck you did Artie Tripp*, wishing that Artie Tripp had turned out different. As he approached maturity a strain of nervousness, hitherto unobserved, had proved to be the principal feature of his character. 'Hell,' he said, as a blob of ice-cream flicked airily on to the sleeve of the blue sports jacket he wore on afternoons off from the gas station. Susy watched dispassionately. 'So I guess,' Artie Tripp went on, still dabbing gingerly at the vermilion stain, 'I'll be heading east soon. Pa's promised to give me a start, like with money and stuff.' Yeah, like with twenty dollars and you can kiss my ass, Susy thought. She said: 'That'll be nice Artie. Guess I can come and see you sometimes.' 'Reckon you can,' said Artie Tripp, showing his teeth as they walked into the molten sunshine. Five years ago, or even three years ago, the remark would have been enough. As it was, when Artie Tripp half an hour later drove her back to the apartment block she said: 'You can keep y'fuckin' hands off. OK?' Crestfallen yet resigned, Artie Tripp had backed away. Curiously, Susy found that this craven acceptance of her decision only increased her contempt. What else, she wondered, could you expect from a man who had spent nine years tending his father's gas station, or for that matter from Tara City?

But then it did not do, Susy thought, to condemn. By condemning others, implicitly you condemned yourself. Arid, airless mornings in the flat, Mom making interminable phone calls to Larry Vosper, Susy leafing through expensive designer magazines, lodged this fact irrevocably in her consciousness. Larry Vosper was a fat, elderly cowboy run to seed who owned a ranch twenty miles west of Tara. This, however, was not the only thing that Susy had against Larry Vosper. There was the fact that he was five foot six and wore built-up high-heeled boots, the fact that his first action when Mom opened the door was to hand her a bunch of carnations and holler 'how's my best girl?', the fact that after supper he went to sleep in front of baseball games on the TV. Larry Vosper, in short, did not have a great deal going for him. One thing Larry Vosper did have going for him was that Mom rather liked him. 'When ya get to my age,' she had once remarked, 'ya'd settle for a lot worse than Larry Vosper.' Susy, eyeing the quarter-inch of foundation, the miracles of corsetry stemming a tide of adipose tissue could believe it.

And if Mom had Larry Vosper – who had twice proposed to her, once on the sofa after dinner, once during the course of a day trip to Salt Lake (Mom was not averse to coaxed confidences) – Susy supposed that she had her job. That was, if you could call the three days a week she put in at Rosati's delicatessen a job. Rosati's delicatessen lay in a grimy sidewalk that ajoined the main street and sold pizza to truck-drivers too shell-shocked to travel the extra quarter-mile that took you to McDonald's. Trade, inevitably, was bad (there was hardly any trade in Tara that could positively be described as good), the schoolkids and garage hands who slouched in at lunchtime indifferent to the delicate strands of tagliatelle, the pert blobs of tortellini that Mr Rosati arranged with some artistry in his window. 'Animals,' he would say, as another trucker sniffed suspiciously at a tray of bubbling lasagna before moving on to finger the discus-shaped pizzas, 'fuckin' animals. For Chrissakes. Give those bastards a truffle and they'd probably think it was a fuckin' meatball.' Susy, stationed behind the counter in a pinstripe waitress's mini-skirt, blue cap askew athwart her right temple, found these performances acutely embarrassing.

Generally they were of short duration and he would disappear upstairs to apply himself with deep loathing to the accounts. Leaving Susy to wiggle her backside at exopthalmic bikers and juggle with the change. On one occasion, however, a *pasta con funghi* of generous dimensions and enviable texture having failed to attract sufficient custom, Mr Rosati had gone outside and thrown it against the side of a passing truck. 'That,' he had been heard to remark subsequently, 'was a fuckin' *art statement*.' In a small way the gesture established him as an ally.

Summer wore on. Larry Vosper took Mom on a trip to Yellowstone which culminated – Larry Vosper's shiny estate car having negotiated the winding mountain highway – in a tour of the Vosper ranch. Mom had been impressed. 'Thirteen hundred head of cattle,' she reported, 'a nigger houseboy and ya can walk for three hours and the land ain't nobody's but Larry's.' 'Great,' Susy retorted, 'Larry Vosper has a nigger houseboy. Is that any reason to haul your ass over there?' This had been sufficient to silence Mom, but it was not enough to silence the feeling of disquiet. From afar came other signs of the essential instability of the middle-aged. Postcards came from Aunt Berkmann in Amsterdam, Helsinki and Freiburg. Though Susy rather disliked Aunt Berkmann (whom she had once described to Mom as a fat klutz), this itinerary awakened her envy. There was a world out there, outside of Tara City and the hills, in which things happened; a world in which Susy felt, obscurely, she was being denied a role. Susy tried explaining this to Lulu Sinde over afternoon tea in Lulu Sinde's smart little chocolate box of a house, a house whose portals you were not allowed to cross without wiping your feet. 'For Chrissakes,' Susy had said, 'you never used to be like this.' 'Paul says I have to smarten up a little,' said Lulu Sinde. 'Like he says it's a personal and a social responsibility.' 'Cock,' said Susy. 'No, I agree with him,' said Lulu Sinde defiantly. It was hard to evoke sympathy from Lulu Sinde, dumbly awaiting the arrival of the dentist's progeny. 'And Christ the *names* of places,' Susy instructed. 'You ever realized how weird they are? How'd they get there. I mean, Kentucky, Missouri, Michigan . . . You ever been there?' 'I been to Missouri,' said Lulu Sinde, curving the palm of her hand over the slight bump of her stomach, 'yeah with Paul, two years back, I remember, I was awful sick . . .' Susy gave it up as a bad job, went home to dream long, comfortable dreams of US road maps in which squat, green-coloured states went on for ever like the squares in a patchwork quilt.

Halfway through August Larry Vosper bought Mom a plunging black cocktail dress which he wanted her to wear for a party at the Vosper ranch. 'It's kinda nice ain't it?' Mom asked doubtfully as together they manhandled the stretched fabric into place. 'You look about a hundred,' Susy told her and then, relenting slightly, 'shit, you look OK. Enjoy yourself.' That night Susy allowed Artie Tripp to take her to a movie, Christ, just like it was eight years ago and Artie Tripp still the same octopus-handed youth who had tried to get fresh with her in the back of his father's car. Though she had allowed Artie Tripp to put his hand inside her blouse the expedition was not a success and went unrepeated. Most evenings Susy spent in her room, the view from whose window presented a vista of leprous concrete and cunning piccaninny kids playing baseball, reading Kerouac and thumbing through her record collection. 'What you doing in there?' Mom would enquire through the door about once an hour and Susy would reply: 'Just shiftin' the stale air around Mom,' and slide over to the record deck to whip another disc out of its sleeve. Sixties music. 'Hippy junk' Artie Tripp used to say in the days when he ventured opinions. The sixties and Susy went back a long way: The Dead; the Airplane; Steppenwolf singing 'Born To Be Wild'. Thus:

> Catch your motor running
> Head out on the highway
> Looking for adventure
> Whatever comes our way

Susy discovered that the loud electric music cutting through the empty air had a strangely galvanic effect. As the song reached its crescendo ('And the night's gonna make it happen/for the world is a loving place/fire over the guns and watch them/ explode into space' da dum thud) she drifted round the room, propelling her limbs with jerky, ataxic movements. At times like these it was possible to imagine that you were seventeen again, smoking dope at weekend parties, screwing Artie Tripp on his parents' wide double bed with the flock mattress, thinking that any day now Peter Fonda would be sailing over the horizon on a Harley Davidson 950, just waiting to light out with you, engines gunning, into the sunset. The illusion seldom persisted. Christ, Susy thought, sometimes when you were twenty-four and a half years old and your experience ran only as far as Tara City and Artie Tripp then imagining yourself as a biker's moll was pretty goddamned funny. In fact it was about the funniest thing Susy could think of.

Saturday was a bad day in Tara City, though it possessed its consolations. Prominent among these was the fact that Mr Rosati let her have the afternoon off from the delicatessen. Things were at a low ebb in Rosati's. The fans, suspended so uncompromisingly from the ceiling that customers ducked instinctively as they approached the checkout counter, rasped lackadaisically. A monstrous *lasagna alla buoni* lay unregarded in the window. Two apprentice street hoodlums – baseball caps and wrapround sunglasses – sat drinking 7 Up by the door. Mr Rosati perched by the till, a thin, saturnine Italian with greying hair and a resentful expression. Occasionally he would raise his head and snap his eyes at the *lasagna alla buoni*, a glance that mingled the pride of the creator with the contempt of the entrepreneur . . . 'Peasants,' said Mr Rosati, not looking up as Susy, changed out of the waitress get-up into slacks and a ZZ Top T-shirt, lingered in front of the counter. 'Better put it back in the cooler,' Susy advised, 'sure as hell won't last in this heat. Hey, you got a match?' She leaned over the bar, whipped a box out of the bulging shirtfront and lit a drooping Marlborough.

'For Chrissakes,' said Mr Rosati, a shade more amiably. 'Buy your own goddam matches.'

Taking a rise out of Mr Rosati was an activity from which Susy derived inexhaustible pleasure. 'Hey,' she said. 'You wanna see me dance?' Mr Rosati shook his head. 'Guess I'll show you anyway.' Beneath his indifferent gaze she described an inelegant pirouette, hands raised above her head. 'Waddya think?' 'Shit–awful,' said Mr Rosati. 'Anyway,' Susy went on, 'you owe me twenty dollars,' 'Monday,' said Mr Rosati defensively, eye flickering for a moment over the two baseball caps and then returning to rest on the *lasagna alla buoni*, 'pay you Monday.' 'Well *fuck you*,' said Susy.

Outside in the street it was appallingly hot, the interior of Rosati's seen through the green plate-glass strangely aquarium-like. Susy stared back sullenly at the neon sign, experiencing a sudden stab of hate at whichever fate had ordained this monotonous thraldom. Much was made in Tara City of Mr Rosati's idiosyncrasies which were thought possibly to compensate for more obvious disadvantages. As Susy saw it, she had been taking shit from Mr Rosati for too long. About three years too long. Leaving Rosati's behind, a blur of green glass and reflected sunlight, she set off in the direction of the main street, past the accumulation of loping mongrels, fat woman in out-of-date frocks and gook kids that were just part of the scenery at this time of the day in this part of Tara fucking City.

In the foyer of Baxter's she flashed her membership card at the blonde receptionist. 'Swimming or solarium?' enquired the blonde receptionist. 'Swimming huh? Honey it's seventy-five degrees in there, the water I mean, so it won't make much difference.' Susy nodded, stood a while on the faded red carpet reading the noticeboard, her nose wrinkling slightly at the faint smell of chlorine. Baxter's gymnasium and solarium represented all that was lustrous and go-ahead in Tara City. When a local politician talked about civic amenities the chances were that he meant Baxter's. Prompted by a half-hearted public wrangle about facilities, nearly stifled by a committee that had sat for eight years, its funding frozen or misappropriated by a succession of suspicious mayors, Baxter's had – rather to its own surprise – emerged into the glare of public scrutiny. Nominally it was a sporting club. Which was to say that you paid your fifteen dollars a month and could swim, work out, flap ping-pong balls across green baize to your heart's content. But the crop-headed youths and the gap-toothed girls who clustered round the bar drinking coke out of plastic cups didn't come to Baxter's to play table tennis. No. Baxter's was a social catwalk. If you were anyone in Tara City – that's to say if you weren't a nigger or a pauper or congenitally insane – you came to Baxter's to see and be seen. Susy had met Artie Tripp there, light years ago when the world was green and Artie Tripp's Pontiac the nearest thing Tara City possessed to Dennis Hopper's dirt-bike.

In the women's changing room Susy traded gossip with Lulu Sinde who was glumly cramming her breasts into a somewhat otiose bikini top. 'Jesus,' said Lulu Sinde, 'my tits are swelling up, I can feel it. Hey, waddya think?' Susy prodded the proferred torso without interest. 'I guess you have to accept that sort of thing.' 'I guess you do,' said Lulu Sinde, squatting her rump on a nearby radiator while Susy changed into her one-piece bathing costume. 'Christ. The *heat*. I nearly passed out out there on the sidewalk. But Paul said I ought to take some exercise: I guess he was right.' 'I guess so,' said Susy, wanting to say: for God's sake *shut up* about your fucking husband. Together they walked through the chlorinated foot-bath towards the swimming pool.

The pool was deserted, apart from a couple of kids torpedo diving off the springboard at the far end: twenty yards of calm, sticky water. Susy swam a couple of lengths on her back, dived downwards to touch the palms of her hands on the bottom, rose to the surface. Lulu Sinde was wading resentfully through the shallows, hands clasped over her stomach. 'Hey,' she called, 'd'ya think it's showing?' Susy dived, swam three or four strokes under water to end up within clutching distance of one of Lulu Sinde's bolster thighs. 'Hey,' said Lulu Sinde nervously, several hundred cubic feet of water away, 'be careful.' Susy relin-

quished the fistful of flesh, wondered about upending Lulu
Sinde, thought better of it, contented herself with directing
cascades of water in her direction. 'You be careful d'ya hear?'
squeaked Lulu Sinde. Susy floated on her back, gazing
skywards at the scalloped overhang of the ceiling, remembered
long-ago excursions to Baxter's, a fourteen-year-old Lulu Sinde
shrieking in terror because Artie Tripp had threatened to
snatch off her bikini top, drinking coke with Lulu Sinde,
short-skirted and expectant in the bar, Lulu Sinde saying she
thought she was pregnant and was her father going to get mad
or wasn't he? As the water swirled and receded above her head,
the lineaments of the pool veering jaggedly in and out of focus,
Susy contemplated a Lulu Sinde whose pregnancy was indubit-
able, legal and approved and felt a swift, sharp pang of regret.
'Paul said I ought to take care,' Lulu Sinde confided from the
pool's edge and Susy twisted and dived like a versatile eel down
into the murky water, wanting to get away from Lulu Sinde,
from Lulu Sinde's foetus, but most of all from this disturbing,
unheralded vision of the past which the two of them had
managed to engender.

It was this image that remained afterwards in the changing
room as Lulu Sinde conjectured that she might be about to
throw up, persisted as she declined Lulu Sinde's offer of a drink
('just a coke you know') and strode out into the sunlight.
Outside Baxter's the street was empty, apart from a Rican on a
skateboard and, on the far side, a fat cadillac with white-wall
tyres. For some reason, probably the mental activities of the
past half-hour, this prompted Susy to think contemptuously of
Artie Tripp. As she watched, the car's engine revved and in an
elegant semi-circle it came to rest beside her. Rather to Susy's
surprise Artie Tripp leaned out of the window.

'Hiya Suse,' he said. There was an odd jauntiness in his
manner that Susy could not remember having seen before.
'Like the car?' 'Sure,' said Susy, 'sure I like it.' 'Well get in,'
said Artie Tripp easily. He was wearing his blue shirt and a
white BMX biker hat. There was a suitcase, Susy noticed, lying
on the back seat. 'So where are we going?' asked Susy warily as

they bowled down the High Street (Please God, am I dreaming? Artie Tripp in a cadillac?), one eye on Artie Tripp, the other on the clouds of dust that swarmed out on to the sidewalk. 'Out East,' said Artie Tripp. 'Out East?' 'Like I said,' he went on, 'I couldn't take that shit from the old man any more.' They flashed past Trapido's so that the nigger kids scrabbling in the dirt scuttled for safety, watched wide-eyed as they passed. 'You want to get out?' Artie Tripp asked. Susy shook her head. Afterwards she was only able to remember it as one would a scene from a film: the empty street, the girl turning to meet the car, and beyond (fire over the guns and *explode* . . .) the open road and Artie Tripp, his enormous forearms resting on the steering wheel, beside her.

Subsequently, if you had asked Susy to recall the details of what passed in the ensuing weeks (and Mom at least made the effort), they would have existed merely as single, isolated images: sharply focused snaps pulled at random from an interminable roll of film: standing on the hills above Baton Rouge watching the Mississippi stream away towards the Gulf; an open-air concert at Jefferson where they walked airily through the fringes of the crowd as the evening sky turned the colour of blue velvet; driving through Alabama at night with Artie Tripp continually falling asleep at the wheel and having to be nudged awake, until in the haggard light of dawn they hit Montgomery and crashed out in the back seat of the car in the middle of a municipal car-park.

Crackling, moving pictures: with soundtrack. Susy saying *freedom is the road*, Springsteen singing 'Born To Run' out of the car radio above the din of the freeway, Artie Tripp getting mad with a bullet-headed Arkansas straw-chewer who had given Susy the eye in Little Rock, Susy in a diner call-box outside of Nashville saying to Mom that honestly it was OK honestly it was and Mom not saying anything at all and finally hanging up and going out to be comforted by Artie Tripp who put his arms round her and hugged her while families in Hawaiian shirts and sunglasses looked on with prurient interest.

And always the road – the wide, eight-lane Missouri highways, winding mountain motorways that took them out of Colorado and into the wheatfields beyond, tiny Godforsaken dirt tracks that snaked along parallel to the freeway and you could travel for hours without sighting another vehicle – going on for ever, south and east to the Ocean.

So where did they go in these weeks of late summer and early fall? Eastwards of course. 'So what's so fuckin' great about California?' Artie Tripp had demanded. Through Cheyenne and across the South Platte towards Kansas. Late August found them in Oklahoma, cruising on towards the Ozark mountains, the view from the cadillac window a bewildering mixture of flat fields and undulating hills, of movement and inanition, of things going on and things not happening at all. At Clarkesville they fell in with a hippy convoy heading north towards the Lakes where there was supposed to be a free festival in the spring. Susy had wanted to go with them, finding in the buckskin-clad babies, the karma-chewing docility, something that transcended simple curiosity, but Artie Tripp dissuaded her. They left the hippy camp one morning in September, waved on by a regretful crowd of long-haired children. A week later they were in New Orleans, holed up in a cheap motel while they went on day-trips to Breton Bay and Grand Lake. The day they went to Grand Lake it rained – the first time it had rained since Tara City – and Susy stood looking at the sky in disbelief.

Throughout these days of ceaseless travelling, this frenetic dash from the northwestern corner to the southeastern extremity of this great nation of theirs, the question of motive remained curiously unresolved. Two weeks, three weeks into the journey Susy could not have told you for what purpose the grey cadillac sped eastwards through field and town and mountain, could not have told you at dawn where they would fetch up at dusk. Artie Tripp remained strangely taciturn. 'Reckon on making Tulsa this evening,' he would remark as they unfurled stiff limbs from about each other in the grey, early-morning light, the prelude to long, abstracted silences and the consultation of road maps. It did not occur to him as necessary to explain the provenance of the cadillac, just as it did not occur to him to reveal its ultimate destination. Sometimes he talked about getting a job in the East, 'New York, Chicago, someplace – I got references.' At night Susy, watching the intense, white body purposefully gyrating above her, occasionally wondered if he were a little mad, wondered whether nine years on the gas station forecourt had done something weird and irrevocable to Artie Tripp's (admittedly negligible) mind. But then the sixteen-year-old Artie Tripp had begun to recede from vision, so much so that Susy often found it safer to pretend that he had never really existed.

From the outset Susy had always incubated a sneaking suspicion that it wouldn't last. They started off staying in halfway decent hotels, whose receptionists eyed the 'Mr and Mrs Arthur Tripp' that Artie signed with a flourish in the visitors' book with tolerant disdain, progressed to roadside motels full of teenagers balling their girlfriends and glassy-eyed English tourists (the pound was having a bad time against the dollar that summer). Late September found them holed up in grubby rooms above freeway diners where the hum of car engines could be heard outside the window until dawn. Artie Tripp said nothing about this decline in the quality of their accommodation. It could not be that he was running out of cash. The twenty dollar bills, Susy noted, still flicked across the station forecourt when they stopped for gas. Oddly, or perhaps predictably, it was only at gas stations that Artie Tripp became talkative. 'Look at the dumb bastard,' he would grin, as the garage hand lurched towards the car, 'well he can kiss *my* ass goodbye.'

October, as they turned northwards and New York became not just a speculative talking-point but a possibility, a real-live name up there on the distance boards, the weather broke. Baltimore remained in Susy's mind as a confused impression of wet concrete and endless avenues of dripping trees. In Baltimore they had an argument, a grinding night-long argument at the conclusion of which Artie Tripp told her how he had come by the money and the cadillac. 'All of it?' questioned

Susy incredulously. 'You mean to say?' 'Uh huh' said Artie
Tripp proudly. 'A week's takings outta the till. What the fuck?
He owed it me.' 'Christ,' said Susy, thinking of Peter Fonda and
Dennis Hopper, 'some fuckin' wild man you turned out to be.'
'I got a hundred dollars left,' said Artie Tripp nervously. 'It'll
last till the end of the month.' His hair, which was wet and had
not been barbered since leaving Tara City, hung limply down
either side of his face. 'You can give me twenty dollars to see
me home,' said Susy, 'to see me home, because this is where I
quit.' Though it was the last thing she expected Artie Tripp
handed it over without a murmur. Susy checked out of the hotel
at first light, trudged in tears through the moist streets to find a
Greyhound bus depot. Although it had been possible to predict
that it wouldn't last and that Artie Tripp wouldn't last, nothing
else in her whole twenty-four and a half years had ever made
her feel this sad.

Tara City, glimpsed through the rain-streaked window of a
Greyhound bus early one leaden Sunday morning, did not seem
outwardly to have changed. Inwardly Susy, checking off the
features of the main street against the mental kaleidoscope of
the last two months, found it had shrunk: that Trapido's,
display-case for so much local *éclat*, was no more than a
glorified dime store, that Baxter's – outside whose porch it now
seemed impossible that Artie Tripp had ever lingered – was no
more than a second-rate sports club. Walking into the apartment Susy found Mom and Larry Vosper sitting together on the
sofa, a spectacle so unusual as to defer more obvious questions
and explanations. 'So what's he doing here?' Susy enquired,
examining Larry Vosper's brilliantined hair and stacked boots.
'We're getting married next month,' said Mom. 'Anyhow,' he's
got a *right* to be here.' 'Susy baby,' said Larry Vosper, Adam's
Apple working up and down his throat like a tomahawk. 'Eat
shit,' said Susy. For the rest of the day she refused to speak
either to Mom or to Larry Vosper. It was not, when you
thought about it, a particularly auspicious homecoming.

In Rosati's delicatessen the warm reek of overcooked spaghetti rose impenitently to the ceiling. 'Shit,' said Mr Rosati quietly as Susy slammed a plate down on an adjacent table, 'that ain't no way to serve an order.' 'You wanna see me dance?' said Susy, twitching her ass at him. Mr Rosati shook his head. It was curious, Susy reflected, considering the past week, the way in which things changed, how, bolstered by external camouflage, inner mechanisms simply ground to a halt. Mr Rosati was an altered man, his window bereft of exotic pasta, himself resigned to dispensing pizza to undiscriminating gooks. There had, it transpired, in Susy's absence been a regrettable incident in which Mr Rosati, disgusted by public indifference to ·a stupendous *canneloni all Campagnola* had pushed a customer's face into a plate of lasagna and been bound over to keep the peace. Susy thrust her head close up to the till. 'Hey,' she told him, testing this newfound good nature, 'you owe me twenty dollars, remember?' 'For Chrissakes I remember,' said Mr Rosati. Just as there had been other changes, small yet significant, to the complexion of Rosati's delicatessen, so other aspects of the known world had not escaped alteration. Lulu Sinde, unable to contemplate the rigours of parturition, had had an abortion. Aunt Berkmann, jilted by her lover in favour of a Swedish hotel receptionist had returned from Europe ('and serve her dam' right' in Mom's opinion). Susy felt that in some way her return was a small example of the past fighting back in the face of present assaults, that while accepted matter-of-factly it possessed deeper implications. 'About fuckin' time,' Mr Rosati had said, but there had been a painful gleam of recognition in his eye. 'Shift you ass over there,' he shouted as Susy, stirred from rapt contemplation, heaved a plate crosstable into the midriff of a waiting diner. Obscurely the thought comforted her. Outside the rain rattled on the windows. 'OK, OK,' Mr Rosati was saying. Susy thought for the last time of Artie Tripp, framed in the doorway of Baxter's, the gleaming Iowa cornfields, before turning to consider the more pressing details of Mom's wedding suit, the expression on her face half fretful resignation, half dreamy content.

135

SUZI ROBINSON

Half-day Closing

It's extraordinary really, because I've so often walked along that street and I've never before noticed the shop. By often, I mean about twice a week. It is not what you would call a favourite walk. There are many more attractive streets but I often find myself in this particular street. Well, at least twice a week! But you would think I would have noticed the shop, wouldn't you? I used to notice shops. I used to love to go shopping.

Perhaps you know the street I mean? I can tell you exactly how to get there. You walk down the High Road, going towards the big supermarket, then you turn left at the first set of traffic lights and then left again, just before the 87 bus stop. That's the beginning of it. It's a long, straight road with many side turnings. I've been down two of the turnings but they were crescents and led back to the main street.

There are a few shops at the beginning of the street. There's a tobacconist and then a grocery store that stays open until midnight, every night. You should make a note of that, you might need to buy something late at night. You never know. Opposite the grocery store, there's a second-hand dress shop and, next to that, a place where they cut keys while you wait. Then, there's a small café with the menu written up on the window in white paint. I've never been in there. Rather a lot of chips.

After the café, the street becomes residential. There's a series of terraced houses on both sides. Small, red brick houses, all exactly alike. Further on, the houses get bigger; double-fronted and set back from the road. I don't know what happens after that. I've never walked all the way down. Not yet, anyway. I always turn back after the second of the double-fronted houses. I usually walk up on one side of the street and down the other side. That is why I'm surprised I didn't notice the shop. Not until last Wednesday afternoon.

Wednesday is a very hollow sort of day for me. A day in parenthesis. Monday is a colon. Tuesday is an exclamation mark, but Wednesday is round bracketed and empty. I felt very low on Wednesday. I sat in my room all morning and I waited. But nothing happened and so, after lunch, I put on my coat and my boots – it was very cold on Wednesday – and I went for a walk. I went to the street. It was my intention just to go as far as the tobacconist. I thought I might buy some cigarettes and a magazine. And, perhaps a bar of chocolate. It was a very hollow day.

I walked up on the side of the second-hand dress shop. It was closed. It's half-day closing on Wednesday afternoons. The key-cutter was also closed. The café was open, but empty. I walked on until the second of the double-fronted houses came into view and it was as I turned to cross the street, that I saw the shop.

I can't understand why I haven't noticed it before. It is set back from the road but it must always have been there. It doesn't look new. Perhaps I have seen it before and I thought it was just another house. There is nothing to say it is a shop. There's no sign over the door. Nothing in the windows. I just knew it was a shop in that strange, sudden way, one does just know things. I knew it was a shop and I knew what it offered for sale.

I had to push the door hard to make it open. Inside, it was warm and bright and welcoming. The floor was covered with wood shavings and they crunched as I walked. But, they weren't ordinary wood shavings. They were all shaped like letters, letters of the alphabet! I picked up a capital 'T' and a small 'g' with a beautifully curled tail. I put them in my pocket.

There was a long wooden counter running along three sides

of the shop and all the walls were covered with boxes. Long white cardboard boxes, each with a letter of the alphabet handwritten on it in black ink. There were twenty-six boxes just for the A's. I was starting to count the B boxes, when a man's voice said: 'Good afternoon.' And a man appeared, bald and smiling, from behind the counter. He was small and plump and neat and he had a little moustache. It was brown, like his overall.

'Good afternoon,' I said. 'I should like to buy some words.'

'And what sort of words would you like, miss?' The shopkeeper seemed very pleased to see me. He smiled broadly and he had such kind eyes, brown and soft, like melted chocolate.

'English,' I said. 'I want lots of English words.'

'You'll find no foreign words here,' said the shopkeeper. 'We don't import. Although we export all over the world. Everyone wants our English words.'

'They are the best,' I said.

'The very best. The very best in the world. Look about you, miss. All these boxes are full of words. Nouns and pronouns. Conjuctions and prepositions. Verbs and adverbs. And every description of adjective.' The man turned towards the shelves of boxes and gestured from floor to ceiling. 'The very best in the world,' he said and he sighed.

In one corner of the shop, I discovered a carousel. There were many phrases hanging from it, each one mounted on white card and shrink-wrapped in clear plastic.

'What are these?' I asked.

'That's our range of ready-mades,' said the shopkeeper. 'Metaphors, similies, one or two proverbs and some clichés.'

I spun the carousel and read through the selection. I recognized many well-known phrases and quotes from plays and poems. 'Once Upon A Time' was there and 'Happy Ever After'. But they didn't appeal to me and I turned away.

'You'd be surprised how many of those we sell,' said the shopkeeper. 'It's very popular line.'

Just then the telephone rang. There was an old-fashioned

black telephone on the counter and the man went to answer it.

'Good afternoon, sir,' he said, 'how can I help you? Yes. This morning's was it? Seventeen down. Eight letters. First letter "p". Second letter "a". Last letter "e". I see, sir. Was there a clue? Yes. "An obvious lie". Very good sir. Hold the line please.' He scanned the shelves and took down a box marked 'PA'. He peered inside and took out something that looked like a piece of black lace. He went back to the telephone. 'Got it, sir. It's "palpable". P-A-L-P-A-B-L-E. Eight letters. No trouble at all, sir. Glad to be of assistance. I'll put it on your account, sir. Good afternoon.'

I was so excited. I couldn't help myself. I had to see inside that box. Before he could close the lid, I took the box and looked inside.

There were dozens of them and they were so beautiful. Ornate chains of letters in a swirling copper-plate. They looked like pieces of black filigree against the white of the box. And, I know you won't believe this. And you can write it down, if you damn well like. I don't care. I swear, I saw 'palpitate' twitch. Ever so slightly. It quivered, ever so slightly, as it lay in the box.

The shopkeeper took the box and very carefully put 'palpitate' back. He closed the lid. He didn't seem to mind that I had looked inside. He smiled and he whispered, 'They're very fine, aren't they?'

'Very fine,' I said, 'and I would like to buy some.'

'We sell them by the hundred,' he said as he replaced the 'PA' box. 'Minimum order: two hundred words. But you can mix them up. Nouns, verbs, anything you fancy. They're all the same price. You can make your own selection.'

'That seems very reasonable,' I said.

'These words you want to buy, miss. Are they for poetry or prose?'

'Prose,' I said. 'I'm writing a story. At least, I'm trying to.'

'A love story, is it?'

'No. I don't think you could call it a love story. Although love does come into it. It's difficult to explain.'

'Try,' he said and he smiled his kind-eyed smile. He leaned

towards me across the counter and he listened.

'Well,' I said, 'the story concerns a woman. This woman has had a great shock. A very bad thing has happened to her and she is very ill. Very ill, for a long time. She is in hospital for a long time and then, they send her home. She stays at home and she takes her pills and she eats and she sleeps and she goes to the doctor and, all the time, she waits to get better. The doctor and, all the people who know her, they all tell her she will get better. So she sits at home, and she goes for walks, and she waits.

Many months go by. Six, seven, eight months and still she waits and then she begins to realize that she has lost her life. Of course, she's not dead. It's not a ghost story! She is still living, but she knows she has lost the life she used to have. And she knows she will never be better, because she is as well now as she ever can be. That is her secret and her strength. She is wiser than the doctors and those others who say: Wait. Be Patient. They don't know what it's like. How can they? The don't know that all she is waiting for now, is death. And when you've lost your life, well then, death doesn't matter, does it? That's her secret. And that's the story I want to write. But I can't find the words.'

'But you've got some words,' said the shopkeeper.

'Oh yes,' I told him, 'I have some. I found some in an old shoe box under my bed. But they won't be enough. I shall need more.'

The shopkeeper stroked his little moustache and frowned. Then he took a box from the shelf and put it on the counter. 'Have a look in here, miss,' he said. 'From what you've told me, I think these might suit you very well.'

I took two words from the box. I took 'loss' and love'. I was disappointed at first. They weren't pretty, not like 'palpable' and the words in the 'PA' box. These weren't handwritten. The letters had been cut away from a piece of white card. They were like stencils. I poked my finger through the 'o' of loss.

'Hold it up to the light, miss,' said the shopkeeper, 'hold it up and look into it.'

I did and it was fantastic! Just like watching television. I saw a man sitting at a table in a restaurant. Before him was a plate with the bill on it. He was searching through the pockets of his suit. I think he had lost his wallet.

'How clever,' I said.

'My idea,' said the shopkeeper. 'Saves a lot of trouble. People could never find the right sort, you see. They kept saying: "Haven't you got something with more bereavement in it?" Well, I can't go running up and down that ladder all day . . .'

'Of course not,' I said.

'I'm all on my own here and I'm not as young as I was. It was too much.'

'Too much,' I said but I wasn't really listening. I was looking again into 'loss' but this time the picture was different.

I saw a nursery. A blue and white nursery with lots of stuffed toys, teddy bears and rabbits sitting on a shelf and on the floor were some alphabet bricks. I saw a little white bed with all the sheets and blankets neatly folded and piled up. And then the picture faded.

The shopkeeper was busy taking boxes from the shelves and piling then on the counter. 'You're going to need some verbs as well,' he said. 'I've got a good selection for you here, but I must ask you, miss. You will be careful. They're all infinitives, you won't split . . .'

'Never in my life!' I said. I picked up the 'love' stencil. I held it up to the light and looked into it. I saw a boy and a dog playing in a field. A little fair-haired boy in a duffle coat and red wellington boots. He was running along beside a frisky black labrador. The dog was nearly as tall as the boy. The boy was laughing and trying to hold on to the dog's collar. But the dog was strong and lively and she broke away. And she bounded forward into the road. And the boy ran after her. And I stood at the kitchen window and I wanted to shout. I tried to shout. I wanted to shout. But the words wouldn't come.

I felt so cold then. My teeth were chattering. It was very cold on Wednesday afternoon. The night was closing in and it was dark outside. I wrapped my coat around me but I couldn't stop the shivereing. The shopkeeper was very concerned for me. He fetched a chair and made me sit down. He held my hand and he wanted to make me some tea. He was so good to me. and he had such kind eyes.

You know, I'm really very tired now. I would like to go home. I think it must be time for me to go home. But, before I go, I want to show you the letters. The letters I picked up from the floor of the shop. I thought you would like to see them. I thought you would be interested. They're still in my coat pocket. Here they are. They're a bit squashed from being in my pocket. Look. There's a capital 'T' and a small 'b' and a 'y' with a beautifully curled tail. They are very fine, aren't they? You do like them, don't you? Next time I come, I will show you the bag I brought my words home in. The shopkeeper put my words in a bag for me to take home. It's a plain brown bag, but I've washed and ironed it, so it looks very nice. I'll bring it with me. I'll show it to you next week. But now, I'm very tired and I want to go home.

WILLIAM NEW

Six Heated Tales

VANELLUS VENELLUS

And searing pains in the eyes and ears doctor.

How well I remember the day it first struck, I had taken my secretary into the country areas for a bit of peace. We left the car and went looking for a secluded spot. where passing traffic would be out of sight. But even along a footpath made nigh impassable with overgrowth, thorns, and flies, we were not able to find such a place, because if it was not motors it was trippers, and if it was not trippers it was solitary hikers, and if it was not solitary hikers it was the hi-de-ho of a scout camp outing.

I was greatly agitated by this time, in the pit of the stomach, then my companion suggested turning back along the path the way we came, oh dear me no! If you think I am going to go back, through that bliddy morris! We will have to come out on the road again soon. And indeed it was not five minutes before I pushed through a hedge and could see my Triumph's side shaking in the hot light, half a mile up the hill.

This was April.

Give me yr hand Miss Sspt I said, for she had fallen behind me, to sulk perhaps, and was in trouble over a ditch. We are home and dry.

And as our hands touched, that was our first of skin barring the occasional letter passed in the way of business, a bird got up in the field behind us and *span* in the air, uttering long whoops. Whoo-oop. Whoo-oo-op. I am unable to imitate. Like little fast sirens wheeling. No, I cannot do it.

It surprised me by its unexpected NATURE. And its actions, that I can only describe it *span* above the field like it was not right, on a band.

Miss Sspt laughed at its motions but it was then that my stomach unbuckled, and a pain came into my eyes as I watched, into my ears as I listened. That has rarely left me since.

Some black and white creature.

Not a natural thing, I fear.

> H hs cm p qck gnst th fr f lf.
> T brnd.

BEAN WOM

I am one who suffers from unnatural beings.

The front street was crowded with running dogs (in heat) so I made my way home through the scrubground at the back, and came to the fence of my garden (householder).

For the first time I noticed an iron tap fastened to one of my fenceposts, a council job I thought, and idly, out of sheer curiosity, to see if it worked, I turned it on, yes, and kept it on though some spring in its mechanics would have shut it off again, so I had to hold it, while flies and bees bit at my steady hand, till the splashing set me to daydreams.

Then cramps brought me round and I let the tap go, and saw, propping herself against the fence so that water ran down her belly and between her legs, it, rubbing her marbled armpits and tangling for fun.

Her hair.

Was a bean woman.

Nodded.

Her pale blue.

Head.

Soos ghost.

When I was a boy of fifteen, a wee sprk, I had met a girl the night before who, shyly fingering her hem, said to me come to my house tomorrow afternoon when my mamandad are out and we will act like mad.

Do you know what I'm talking about?

I know what I'm talking abt.

Next day I easily played the truant and took half an hour to walk to her address, and how I walked! I walked shaking! That's right.

But when I came to her window (it was only soos ghost) a white face plus red holes in it, six in pairs plus one alone, plus tassels for hair sticking round about.

No good to me.

No good *for* me.

That's that.

Only, I might have flamed for a bit, for a little bit on the pavement outside afterwards, as far as I can remember.

That's all.

THE FOUNTAIN

Was I right to have done this?

Should I not have taken him to one side and pointed out the error of his ways?

Pah I thought, who am I to point out the error of his ways?

It was a demon sent to muddle me, probably.

Then I went down to The Fountain.

In the bar I found all my friends lined up at drinks Pete and Mich.

And they were all well pissed peet.

Pete.

Said to Mich.

I had known they would be there, for I had seen their bikes outside, but they were not real bikers, Pete and Mich, what were they they were imitations of it.

Their bikes outside where children, halting from their URGENT PLAY, had gathered in curious knots to view.

Hello my men (he shouts) my bonny men room for a little one I said why aye they said sit your self down chiff.

I said I see yr bike mich and he said if those kids are buggering with it yall pull their fir-king legs off.

Pause.

Mich said Pete says he's going to dip the new barmaid aren't you pete oh, he said, I'll dip her alrit.

Don't you worry.

There's been a bit of the old, eyecontact.

Already?'

I'll say.

This time next week, I will have been through her.

But this time next week he was in hospital, for all his talk, and happening quickly too when we left the bar and in no fit state he *gunned* his bike, as they say, and went for a quick demonstration around the block in the excitement of his feelings, and went over a traffic island very badly into the path of a passing car, breaking both legs.

I said, now he knows it doesn't always pay to be too confident.

I mean, when memmie-endeddie were away on the pier!

And one glance was enough to show me that he *too* shared my excitement, especially after I am not used to having a lot to drink!

And, in rapid succession, four or five times, till I felt the adjacent amusements arcade, until I felt the amusements arcade roll my eyes in its lights (in a spin), that is to say not that I'd done it that way before, and especially not for money!

> Shut up.
> More exciting.
> Shut up.

Feeling them drops lik new rain on the backs of my hands flexing on the pierstone, oh, his mouth went in and out, I blushed, I mean what to say . . .?

Then a seagull flew in pecking his mirror frames until it broke one lens and pulled out, it, that, there was glass all over my new sandals and him feeling his features all over as if to say: oh I hev had an ACCIDENT. Oh I am disabled!

I mean has bloodeye, has wetwet, has spitlip.

Split.

MISERABLE OLD LORD

Do you know what I'd do withim?
Thed a would hev every one of the bass-tids castrated!
Ad castrate thim.

Do it, I would do it, I wld do it.

To them, that kind, it is a frigg-in side better than they deserve!

(Breathe).

Animals?
Animals?
Don't talk to me abt frigg-in animals.
Ther wuss an animals, ten times, an hundred times.
Fuck in hell!
Worse than *the* frigging beasts of the FIELD!
Yat ness!

Ssi oot doog rif ad stnc, eh nirg.

Lord, a moral man to speak: I hev bin translated!

Angel

She realized the moment she set down the receiver that she was going to have a struggle on her hands. Millie could get George to agree to anything, on a moment's notice, providing she could find a babysitter, but Ed hated having things sprung on him. Ed preferred things planned out in advance, chewed over, circled on the calendar.

She marshalled her arguments as she showered. George would drive. They wouldn't be late. They hadn't been into town in ages. The couldn't just let themselves stagnate.

—Look, Ed, she would simply have to say, trust me on this one, I'm thirty-four years old and *compos mentis* . . .

She waited for him in the bedroom, listening to him come in and make himself a drink, picking her time.

—There you are, he said.

His eyes fell on the slacks and the turtleneck she had laid out for him. She could delay it no longer. She was brief, forceful.

—This was Millie's idea, Ed complained, sitting down on a corner of the bed in his shorts, not yours.

It had been both of their ideas, she countered. She had been wanting to get out, she thought, Millie's call had merely served to crystallize that desire. George would drive, she said. So what, she thought, if it had been Millie's idea?

—Zip me up? she asked.

He unzipped her first, slipping his hand first under the elastic of her pants, but she refused to be diverted.

—No bra? he said.

No bra. She could still get away with it. She checked her hair in the mirror and stepped into a pair of pumps. The best way to get him moving, she decided now, was to go downstairs and leave him sitting there alone.

George, as promised, drove. Millie, in front beside him, sat sideways, as sideways as she could sit in her condition. This was absolutely and positively the last, Millie swore, the *pièce de résistance*, but she had heard Millie sing that tune before.

—The Colts and five points is a sucker's bet, Ed was saying.

—The Colts and eight points then, George offered.

It was football they were negotiating, not horseflesh. She asked Millie if there had been any complications – she knew the terminology at least. Yes and no, said Millie, giving her a look which meant change the subject, no complications so far as the mother was concerned.

They got off the freeway somewhere near the university. Students, talking, with books under their arms, jaywalked, regarding the traffic disdainfully. It was Millie who finally spotted the small sign.

—The Green Pea, said Ed, sounds French.

—If anyone doesn't like it, said Millie, they can wait in the car.

They found a place to park. George locked the doors and put down the antenna.

—You coming in, Ed, said Millie, or should we send you something out?

The place was down a flight of stairs, in a basement beneath a beauty parlour. 'Looks Can Kill' the beauty parlour was called. Clever, she thought. Looks *Can* Kill.

Ed held the door for everyone, not just out of politeness she knew him well enough to know by now but so that he would be the last one in, so that the rest of them would already have borne the brunt of the strangeness. Stomach first, it was Millie who led the way.

The place was more or less what she would have expected, studiedly shabby, with bare brick walls and unmatched furniture, columns decorated with posters, candles flickering on the tables beneath overhead lighting.

A table was free near the small stage. George took her coat and Ed took Millie's. Out, they always sat as if they were married the other way around. George lit her a cigarette and Ed offered one to Millie but Millie refused, patting her stomach.

—Millie the mother, George laughed.

The waiter was a skinny man, no longer young, but with his hair, what was left of it, in a pigtail down the back of his Green Pea T-shirt. Ed asked if they could see the menu. The waiter indicated a blackboard on the wall.

Ed took off his glasses and began to clean them. Ed would have expected himself to know that the blackboard was the wall. George asked if the soybeanburgers came with steak-sauce.

—If you're not ready to order, said the waiter, I'll come back.

Millie grabbed his wrist to prevent him from doing any such thing. Could he just bring them a platter with a little bit of everything on it? Millie smiled. He agreed, unenthusiastically, to ask. It was no longer revolution or napalm that these places were about, she was thinking, but food.

It was on Saturday mornings, in his oldest clothes, with a hammer or a screwdriver in his back pocket, with his mouth full of screws or carpet tacks and the Four Seasons going full blast on the stereo that Ed was most in his element. She didn't mind, she had known that when she married him, but you couldn't let yourself stagnate.

She stubbed out her cigarette. She smoked now only when they were out. Somehow, she felt, you had to resist the temptation to wall yourself in.

The platter when it came had labels stuck on toothpicks on everything, flying like little flags, to tell them what it was. See the tourists, she winced. George and Ed started reading them aloud. There had been a mistake, she saw herself explaining to the waiter, they lived there, if they enjoyed themselves they would be back. She saw him hastily pocketing the offending flags.

—Bread? George was saying. It looks like the cardboard off the bottom of a frozen pizza.

So she had been giving him frozen pizzas.

—Eat it, said Millie, you can use the roughage.

—Put some steaksauce on it, George, said Ed.

Tourist. Housewife. Over-thirty. Suburban. Childless. It wasn't the words *per se* that she objected to, it was their excess baggage, their connotations. Words could pick up such a cargo. Bra or no bra for her had nothing to do with liberation, nothing to do with politics, but with putting one layer more or less between herself and the world outside.

—You're sure the silent one tonight, Millie prompted.

She was just enjoying herself, she said. People found it hard to believe that they were sisters.

—Still waters, George defended her. Do not disturb.

Millie turned on Ed, who had hardly eaten anything. Ed said that beside not liking the taste he didn't see the mechanism through which their eating beans and nuts instead of meat would help to feed the starving.

—Tell Uncle George, said George, leaning toward her to indicate conspiracy, whisper in Uncle George's ear what you know that no one else does.

—Mechanism? said Millie. Can't you just eat to be polite?

Some day, she put him off, maybe some day all would be revealed.

The overhead lights began to dim. A spotlight came on. A ragdoll was her first impression as a tall, scruffy, stoopshouldered man slowly shambled through the tables and towards the stage.

—Ivan Something-or-other, Millie informed. The poet.

Was he a Russian then? she wondered. A dissident? Wouldn't a defector have been better looked after?

She accepted another of George's cigarettes and turned sideways in her chair. A stool and a microphone had been placed on the stage. She could hear a blender going in the kitchen.

—Any guesses what he's on? George asked.

She let Millie shush him. The man, the poet, Ivan, draped himself over the stool, remained like that for a moment as if resting, and then folded himself forward, resting his elbows on his knees, his head bowed now in thought or silent prayer.

—Is there a cover charge for this? Ed hissed.

She crossed her legs. She reached back to tap ash off her cigarette. Of all the people there, she thought, she was probably the one least embarrassed by silence.

The man wasn't, as it turned out, Russian, nor was his name Ivan, it was Ivor. As for his poetry, it seemed to be composed mainly of sound effects, the few words which managed to find their way in being for the most part expletives. There were grunts, groans, he crowed, he cackled, he did carhorns, foghorns, explosions.

Was it to do with entrophy? she wondered. The running down of information? Death by noise?

There was no rhythm, no beat, there was not even that to hold on to, there were no recognizable repetitions. Was it a comment on art itself, she wondered, a comment on modern music, a comment on painters who painted with sticky tape, on sculptors who sculpted in car bodies?

'He who was living is now dead,' she recalled admiring. 'We who were living are now dying.'

Since then, however, she had seen *Casablanca* twelve times, *Love Story* twice, and God knows how much television. No one had forced her to, she just had. The next time *Casablanca* was on, if she knew herself at all, she would probably watch it again.

Even before the lights were fully up, Ed and George were lighting cigarettes. The better time he was having the less Ed smoked.

—Well, said Millie.

—I wonder if he's made any records, said Ed.

—We had a clanging radiator like that where we first lived, said George.

She accepted the cigarette George placed between her lips, took, a drag, and returned it. Certain primitive peoples, she had read somewhere, more alert to symbolism, refused to allow their wives to be offered cigarettes by other men.

The waiter returned to ask if they wanted a little bit of everything for dessert as well. Millie ordered carrot cake and then started in on the school system.

—Tell you what, Ed said now, as if an hour and a half hadn't passed, I'll give you the Colts and ten points.

The cake came and four tiny cups of espresso. Sunday afternoons during the football season, she thought, would be the time for the Communists to invade. She agreed with Millie about the school system. She stirred a cube of sugar into her coffee. She imagined herself being called upon to stand up and present an exegesis of the poem. Somewhere in town there was a club where women from the audience were offered fifty dollars it they would go up on stage and strip.

The lights went dim again. A girl walked past them with a guitar, a short, a heavyset girl, but with luxurious hiplength hair, jet black. It shimmered beneath the spotlight as the girl stepped up on to the stage, perched on the stool, balanced the instrument on her knee, and began to tune.

A string snapped. The girl cursed.

—Cocksucker! said the girl.

A few people applauded.

—Does she eat with that mouth? said Ed.

How many hours a day, she thought, to have hair like that? How many hours a day for how many years when there were a million other things which you could have been doing?

The girl's face, when she lifted her head, was plain. Her breasts were large but shapeless beneath a man's flannel shirt. Her voice, when she finally got around to singing, was pleasant but not special. Her fingers appeared barely to be able to manage the chords.

But that hair, she thought, someone, sometime, somewhere, was sure to fall in love with her for her hair, and then what would the girl decide?

As soon as the girl was off, Millie gave her the signal and they got up and headed for the Ladies. It was minuscule but clean. Sunflowers had been painted on the walls. Millie locked the door behind them and sat down on the toilet seat.

—I've got a favour to ask, Millie began.

She caught a glimpse of them in the tiny mirror. Anything, she said. Millie looked so pale. Millie, in most people's opinions, had been the pretty one.

—It's about George, said Millie wearily.

She turned and squatted down and took Millie's hands. Millie's hands were puffy. She could recognize Millie's smell through her perfume. It was the smell, she had come to accept, of fecundity.

—What about George? she said, knowing full well.

It was probably nothing. They had been down this road before. It was probably, Millie admitted, only her imagination acting up again. The other times it had either been Millie's imagination or the thing had burned itself out of its own accord.

She rubbed Millie's hands. Millie had frostbite, she imagined, and she was restoring circulation. She agreed to ask Ed if George had mentioned anything. She promised to do a little snooping. Then someone started knocking.

It wasn't just what it cost to go out, George was saying, it was paying for a babysitter, it was driving into town at night and trying to find a place to park and all the time not knowing what might be waiting for you in an alley.

Ed agreed.

She and Millie sat back down.

Ed took out his wallet and removed a newspaper clipping and unfolded it. It was about a couple who had bought a place in town and started to renovate it only to be discovered by the police one morning hacked to pieces in their sleeping bags. Ed hadn't even known the couple. It was some sort of talisman, she supposed.

She refused another cigarette and instead got out a mint.

—It's the courts, Millie said.

—It's parents, Ed contradicted.

She couldn't have said with any authority what it was. She tried to overhear what people at the next table were talking about. It was something to do with Wittgenstein. If she had had to say what it was that she herself most feared, she would have had to have said being buried, metaphorically speaking, alive. She was claustrophobic, she supposed, if that was any explanation. She heard the tinkling of a bell.

Once more she turned toward the stage but this time she made no attempt at interpretation, preferring just to let it all wash over her. He had brought props with him this time, a bell and a harmonica. The purpose of the harmonica, it seemed, was to drown out the bell. Probably he had made a record, she thought. Probably it had sold well. Eventually her thoughts got back to Millie.

Once at a party, dancing with her, a little drunk, George had said that he couldn't help wondering what it would be like making love with someone who didn't keep up a running commentary.

—Ask Ed, she had laughed.

Shout, scream, recite a poem, talk dirty, Ed was always after her, anything to let him know that she was still there. Covered by blasts from the harmonica, she crunched what remained of her mint. Ed was right, at times she wasn't there, not properly there, at times she found herself, not usually when they were making love but sometimes even then, drifting out of a situation which she was supposedly involved in, rising above it, as it were, in order to survey if from commanding heights.

—When did you first notice, she heard the doctor questioning her, that you were schizophrenic?

It wasn't schizophrenia, she was convinced, it wasn't escapism or lack of commitment, it wasn't disinterest or disloyalty, which brought her back to Millie.

—Look, George, she would simply have to say, having cornered him somewhere, if it's still waters that you're after . . .

She would, of course, in all likelihood, say no such thing. His overture at the party she had turned into a joke, laughed off, not unappreciative of the irony. Only once in all the time that she had been married, one New Year's Eve, had she ever so much as kissed another man in passion, shortly after which she had thrown up.

One final blast on the harmonica and the set was over. She turned back to the table. Ed was yawning. George started looking around for the waiter. Millie was wrapping up the remains of the carot cake in a paper napkin. They were leaving, she realized.

Ed didn't think that the waiter deserved a tip but Millie left one anyway. He was probably an ex-con, Millie reasoned. There was more, she realized as George helped her on with her coat, people were still coming in, it wasn't even midnight yet, a small charge of envy ran through her.

Outside they stopped for a moment to get their bearings.

—Everybody here? said Millie.

George started counting heads. Uncle George her foot, she thought. She saw his face, still boyish, to all appearances innocent, grinning from the cover of a supermarket magazine: How To Tell When He Starts Cheating.

The car was where they had left it. A few flakes of snow were coming down as George unlocked the doors and put up the antenna. She slid into the back, leaving just enough room for Ed. George knew how to get back on to the freeway, she thought, why did Millie have to tell him?

She closed her eyes and saw the freeway stretched out, white as a sheet, before them.

—Hon? said Ed softly.

A hand probed inside her coat. She squirmed to make it easier for him, to keep him from stretching the neck of her dress. Her boobs, she thought, her tits, once upon a midnight dreary.

—It's not a blizzard, George laughed, it's only flurries.

She smelled stale smoke and aftershave, heard Millie fooling with the radio to try to get a forecast, felt the heat from the heater start creeping up her legs. And then she thought, and then she asked herself again, and then what would the blackhaired girl decide?

SANDRA McADAM CLARK

The Foreigner

The morning was grey with a gleam of pale sun sparkling over
the river, then swallowed by the dark rain, green water, brown
foam on the shore. Only the seagulls moved on the beach. It
was too early for the Miss Flowers to be out on their morning
walk along the sea-front, their coats floating in the wind,
holding on to each other as they faced the east wind. On the
marshes, curlews and lapwings cried out, sharp, yodelling little
cries that were whisked away by the wind. A few yachts were
moored on the river. November was the month most of the
yachts were put on shore for winter. It was only mid-October, a
wet, windy and disturbing time.

It was in the morning that she arrived – a dark, young/old
woman and a foreigner. She moved into a rented house on the
sea-front, removing the flood gate from her front door, closing
the curtains when it got dark, like everyone else, and going for
walks on the marshes, by herself. She was spotted in the first
week by the yacht club members, those that remained after the
season had ended and who drank whisky or gin and tonic,
staring at their boats and at the weather. One member,
Commander French, remarked that she seemed a little strange,
what with those long walks, an artist maybe or someone from
London. The locals also noticed her, said hello when they
passed her on the narrow path by the river or on the public path
by the gorse-bush fields. She would smile, nod, walk past. She
spoke English with a strong accent and in the shops they would
often ask her to repeat herself. She did, but then asked for
things they didn't have. 'Not here,' they would say, 'in London,

or even Ipswich, but we don't stock that here.' It was mainly fruit she asked for, strange cuts of meat or out-of-season vegetables. The wine merchant said she bought quite a lot of red wine, a packet of cigarettes a day. She got the paper regularly and rented a television. She didn't have a car and had apparently arrived by train at the nearest station and taken a taxi. The houses next door to her were empty, only rented to families during the holiday season or to artists during the Arts Festival in September. She didn't use the bookshop or library much either. Perhaps she wasn't an artist or writer after all. There was no phone in her house; she went to the post office to post letters abroad, not to use the phone boxes.

Charity collectors came round, the usual ones like the British Legion, RSPCA, RSPB, but never managed to get any contributions. Mrs Johnson was said to be especially annoyed. Collecting for the British Legion was usually quite profitable as people were so generous.

'*She* never gave anything; just stood at the door, with a bright red frock on, I ask you my dear in October! . . . she seemed slightly tipsy to me, I must say – '

'But what did she say?' one of her friends asked, a veteran himself and deputy mayor.

'She just said "what is it for?" and I told her about the Legion and our local branch. I'm not sure she understood what I was saying, that's why I thought she was probably drunk – she looked so blank – anyway she said "there are other wars now" and tried to close the door in my face!'

'What did you do old girl? her friend asked.

Mrs Johnson sipped her tea, then put her cup down, wiping her mouth with a tiny napkin. 'I can't exactly remember; but I wasn't going to let her get away with it. I told her that people living in England ought to be grateful.'

'Quite right; after all we've sacrificed and done for others,' her friend broke in.

Mrs Johnson looked at him briefly, looked away. 'Yes. Naturally we can't expect a foreigner to understand. She did say something else but I couldn't understand her accent.'

Afterwards, she felt, she would probably say she enjoyed her exile in this little town. The cold greyness of the sky, the empty seashore, walks along the marshes where salt encrusted her hair, rain washed her face. The cold was bearable, sometimes it was colder in her country, she didn't miss the heat, the food, her house, all the things she'd imagined she couldn't do without. Her lover, her friends, her family, her comrades were all sealed inside her, were her, the despair only surfaced at night and only infrequently. Then she would get up, have a glass of wine, smoke cigarettes, watch the foam breaking on the shore. She found it easier to let their faces wash over her all at once, for there to be two, four, seven people in the damp room with her, than to take each one separately, to be split into two. Perhaps she was closer to madness that way, perhaps it was unbearable, but she found she could bear it. She avoided the mirror in the bathroom on those nights, her eyes seemed blank, like the brownish glass she sometimes found on the beach during her walks, her hair had white dots, her face was no longer hers.

Otherwise, during the day and early evening, she was almost happy. She wrote to the others in London, Paris, Amsterdam, saying she was all right, she would surface soon, join them. In the meantime, she sent them money, she was lucky to have been able to take some out. It would be gone soon. *Then* she would leave, find a job, speak out, campaign, but whose voice would she use? Rosa's? Jaime's? Her mother's? Her father's? She felt it was no longer possible to speak in her own voice, to repeat what had happened to her. She had got out, was here, they were with her, but still remained in her country.

One morning, a woman had called to collect charity. Others had come before, about animals, but this was different. It was for the Second World War ex-soldiers who were poor now and needed money. She would have given something until she saw the lady's eyes looking past her to the room, papers on the floor, her few books lying around, then back to her dress. She swayed slightly, the long night by the window had drained her, she saw herself tiny, reflected in the eyes of the woman. 'There are other wars now,' she had said, trying to cut out the woman's reflection by closing the door. But the woman stayed, talking about being grateful to the State, then she grew taller, brown hair cut sharply, dark brown eyes, wearing a familiar black shirt. 'Rosa?' Then it was gone. Sealed back inside her. The woman left. She was alone and there was only one war. She went back to the room and started to write a letter.

November came and it was dark at 3 o'clock. People sat in pubs, at home, drinking, watching television, eating. One evening at the yacht club Commander French mentioned that the foreigner had left. The flood gate was back on, she had paid rent to the estate agents, taken the train to London, earlyl He had seen her when giving a lift to his son.

When his son next came down for the weekend, both he and his father were invited to a meal by Mrs Johnson, his father's old friend. He had brought a paper with him and after coffee, asked casually, 'Isn't that the woman I saw on the platform when I was down here last?'

Mrs Johnson took a look. 'Yes, that's her, look, Ben.'

Commander French took the paper and read the small paragraph. 'I don't know how you can buy this paper, Peter. Biased, left-wing journalism!' he said after reading it.

'Good God, Dad, read what she's been through; her friends and family are still there, she's speaking for them, not even herself.'

'What rubbish you talk, when will you grow up?' his father sighed.

'I think she was going to give me something, at first anyway, for the Legion,' Mrs Johnson murmured, tidying the coffee cups.

'What did you say, dear?' said Commander French.

WENDY BRANDMARK

Irony

Phil had almost refused her. His writing workshop was overbooked, but by the end of the day he felt too weary to resist. Jane Wood was not even attractive: a small tight face on the end of a bony body. He should have known what to expect; she did not plead or flatter to get into the class.

'Mr Rosen?' not even 'Professor' or the mistaken 'Doctor'. When he nodded, she shoved the registration card in his direction as if he were a machine.

Phil Rosen, the creative writing department of a tiny city college, the sole writer-in-residence respected by the other members of the English faculty and by students because he could be counted on to produce a novel every two years.

He wrote about married professional men having affairs with young women in New York, in Los Angeles, in Denver, where he now lived. Phil's heroes sounded much like him, although he was careful to change hair and eye colouring. His wife Carol and the wives in his novels wore identical housedresses and hung with the same unappetizing flesh. He dedicated all his novels to Carol.

The local library carried one of his books, and occasionally the back pages of the *New York Times Book Review* mentioned his newest novel. 'Life hasn't given me all its cookies,' Phil liked to say with a sneer.

But he was lucky, he told himself, to have a secure academic job in these times, lucky too to be handsome and youthful in middle age. A big man with broad shoulders, thick wavy hair, a 'Jewish Rock Hudson' one of his lovers said.

With each freshman class, he found a new mistress, usually in his writing class, for whom he was mentor, father and seducer. Although he would say they seduced him, coming to his office for criticism and the like.

Phil hardly noticed Jane Wood in the first week of class. Never very good with names, he referred to her once as 'the girl in black'. At this she said her name loudly as if he were both deaf and senile. 'Wooden faced' he thought but forgot her for a time. In the beginning Jane did not say much.

Phil was intent on another, Julie, a golden-skinned blonde. He criticized her story mercilessly but at the end of the hour when he could see the beginnings of tears in Julie's blue discs, he began to point out certain possibilities, room for improvement. Phil was hoping this would send her to his office before the weekend.

'What do you think of the grandmother?' he asked the class, a calculated question.

'I don't really know her. I mean her character is not really developed,' offered the ex-marine, an innocuous lad whose crew cut was growing into a hedge.

Phil nodded with satisfaction, the second week and already they were picking up his words. 'Yes I agree with that and the character traits which are given don't fit together.'

Julie's eyes remained fixed on his face the whole time.

'I wonder if this character is based on a real person?'

Julie shook her head with a frankness Phil found idiotic. He wondered if her mind would turn him off physically.

Then she said it, Jane Wooden or whatever her name was. 'Why does that matter?' She had not even raised her hand.

Phil broke in immediately. 'I have never known a character to work which was not based on a real person, in all my experience,' he added humbly.

'How do you know that all of Tolstoy's characters or Joyce's were not made up?'

Phil's smile emerged a sneer. He was going to give a rational explanation with historic examples but something about her tone upset him. 'It won't work, I can tell you.'

Jane did not argue the point further. The class ended in silence. As his students stood up to leave, Phil's foot was tapping involuntarily as it did on the accelerator pedal when a driver cut out in front of him.

Afterwards he sat alone in the empty classroom, too apathetic to gather his papers and leave. When students for the next class began to file in with puzzled expressions, he was jolted to his feet.

Julie came that afternoon with her story, asking for advice. Phil felt assuaged. She had changed into a sleeveless dress; her hair was pulled back by two tiny clips but a few golden strands fell on her smooth forehead. She was charming. And had talent, if only she would stop writing about wrinkled old women.

'Write about what you know.'

Julie perked her head up as if he had coined this advice. 'It's only the second story I've written,' she said in her defence.

Yes, the course was open to anyone practically; soon he'd be getting geriatric lady writers, the ones he taught at night in his hungry days.

After their initial disagreement, Jane Wood became more vocal in class. When she wasn't arguing with his judgements on a student's story, she brought up odd questions, ones he could neither answer nor laugh off although he tried. Why didn't she smile at him, even at his poor jokes? Her small hard face incongruously framed by brown curls never relaxed.

Phil praised a story by the ex-marine, predictably about boot camp. Two soldiers shared the local prostitue one night and found each other better company. There was just a tinge of homosexuality in the story, enough to make Phil feel broad-minded about praising it.

'But I don't care about either of them. I don't like the main characters,' Jane interjected.

'That's not the point,' muttered the author.

Phil waited for once, hoping the rest of the class would finish her off, but they looked to him.

'Do you sympathize with these men, I think we're supposed

to?' Jane turned to him.

No he didn't but was not going to make it easy for her. 'I can and do admire a piece of fiction objectively for its merits.'

'But shouldn't our hearts and minds be involved?' Jane spoke with absurd sincerity.

Yes, this had been his intention as a young writer, but more and more, Phil grew disdainful of his creations.

'It's a matter of opinion.' He drew the class's attention to the next story.

At the end of that week Jane handed him three stories. At last he could pick apart her words in front of the class, regain his hold. For he was losing them gradually. There were signs. The ex-marine no longer accosted him after class with plaintive questions: 'Why do you write? How do you know when you're professional?'

Even Julie, that relationship was not progressing as rapidly as he wished. They were still at the discussing writing stage, still had not left the confines of his office. Phil grew tired of her questions which artlessly flattered him. The freshness which attracted him at the beginning, he saw as gullibility.

One quick reading revealed flaws in Jane's stories: stilted dialogue, unbelievable actions. Phil felt relieved but rereading was struck by the main character in each story: a young woman who spoke to herself in a stream of brilliant images, sentence fragments. It was as if an exotic bird flew out of her mouth, that set, critical mouth, singing wild, high-pitched songs.

Phil always tried to separate the student from the story in order to judge impartially, but he could not stop thinking of Jane's desires. Was she not embarrassed to reveal herself, or would she hide behind the writer's ploy: 'That is not me, not really'. A ploy with truth.

In workmanlike fashion Phil dismembered each of Jane's stories. The class was good that day, echoing his criticisms like a chorus. Phil wondered how Jane could sit there so cool and silent while the crescendo built. He waited for her protest but when it came at the next meeting, he was surprised.

Phil began by praising the interior monologue in one story

166

about a murder. Jane stared at him with just a hint of a smile as if she scorned his conciliatory words.

'But the actions of this girl don't make sense in view of what she tells us about herself.' Phil wished she would stop trying to out-stare him. 'Someone who professes to be so passionate would not let herself be victimized so easily,' Phil concluded.

'You missed the irony,' Jane said.

'What irony?' Phil looked around the table for smiles, but found none. She does not even know the meaning of the word.

Jane began to point out sentences, whole passages with so-called double meanings, twists; passion turned to passivity under her scrutiny.

'You see?' she demanded. One by one the students around the table began to nod their heads in agreement.

'Like dogs,' Phil thought.

'A story is not a puzzle. For the irony to work, it must not be obscure,' he said.

'It's not, is it?' Jane looked around.

'I don't think we need to discuss this further.' Phil felt ashamed of himself. He noticed Jane exchanging sympathetic smiles with the other students. He couldn't believe he had lost so much.

At the end of the hour, when Julie came up to ask if he had time in the afternoon for a conference, Phil turned away with a brusque 'no'. What was he doing making love to a girl of eighteen who believed everything he said, while another had challenged his right to sit in judgement?

Phil left the classroom before everyone else. His body felt cumbersome as he strode through the campus to his office. There he sat through the afternoon, trying to read student papers, picking up, putting down a new journal and finally staring out the window at the distant bluish hills.

In the next office, two of his colleagues were planning the annual spring departmental outing. Phil picked up the journal again. Someone in Texas had written on the 'Ineluctable Modality of the Visible in Virginia Woolf'. He could never read this stuff. No academic he, you couldn't call yourself one

167

without a doctorate.

Phil sat up in his chair. A craftsman he, a wordsmith carefully creating little boxes for little people to pop their heads out of at predictable moments. Phil focused his attention out the window again.

Jane startled him appearing so suddenly on the other side of his desk. Had she watched him stare at nothing through the window, as though with sightless eyes.

'Sit down,' he responded to her 'Are you busy?'

'I don't agree with any of your criticisms of my stories.'

'Well, that was obvious today,' he smiled in what he hoped was a fatherly way.

'I was reading your comments; they don't really tell me anything but your opinions.'

'I can't tell you how to write your stories if that's what you mean.'

'I'm not asking that. It's just that you don't really read the stories, you have preconceived ideas. You're very opinionated in a certain way.'

'Yes I do have opinions. Students have always found my judgements very helpful.' He laughed to keep above her, to make her a child throwing tantrums.

'You dominate the whole class. Everyone's afraid to say anything.'

Phil watched her mouth as she said this, a wide mouth, 'generous' he would have described it in his earlier novels before he was sensitive to being called trite. Phil wanted to strike that mouth; it offered none of the solace for which it was intended.

And then, he felt excited, why when she was flatchested, had no ass, a stick figure he used to draw for a woman? If only the desk wasn't in the way.

Jane was talking, but Phil could not listen for he must calm himself down, look out of the window. The moment passed. He was able to deliver a mildly patronizing statement: 'Young lady, you have a chip on your shoulder. None of my students have ever complained.'

He saw her flinch at this as if the charge had been made before. In her vulnerability she became desirable again.

Jane stood up awkwardly; for once she had trouble meeting his eyes. Phil moved from behind the desk as she walked toward the door. He caught her by the arm, jerking her towards him. Before he could reach her face with his lips, Jane gave him a quick push and he had to step backwards to regain his balance. She was out of the door.

Jane Wood disappeared for a week, during which Phil regained respect in the class. The small group of writers sitting around the oblong table needed him or at least they thought they did.

'The writing in here is improving,' he announced at the end of the week. They were just past mid-term when students itched to see results.

Then he asked, although he could have just as well remained silent, 'Has anyone seen Jane Wood? Is she sick, do you know?'

No reaction. If they were all compatriots, if she had talked, he should know.

The ex-marine asked, 'Is she the one with the murder story, the real skinny girl?' He shrugged his shoulders. 'I don't know her outside of class.'

No one knew her number. The advantages of a commuter school: students could not compare notes, could not organize in the dorm. And Jane seemed like a loner, probably sat home angrily nursing her wounds.

'Well, no matter. She's probably sick.' Phil dismissed her from the class communal mind. No one looked at him accusingly or much worse with amusement.

Julie approached him after class with a special favour, that he look over her revision before she sent it to the college literary rag. He took advantage of the occasion to put a fatherly arm around her. They made an appointment for next week, late in the day, a time when Phil knew no one else would be around the office. It might work out after all.

The air felt fresh as he emerged from the building. The college was up on a hill above the yellow haze of the city. On the walk between the classroom and his office, Phil began to formulate his next novel: a successful novelist suffering a prolonged writer's block meets a flighty young poetess at a writers' conference. He felt better than he had in weeks, free to stretch without breaking delicate objects.

Phil greeted the department secretary, a grim, plump woman of fifty, with an unaccustomed smile. He was not one of her boys, did not not bring flowers on Secretary Day or compliment her on the arrangement of velvet bows in her hair.

She did not return his smile. 'Bob was looking for you.'

Just then the chairman popped his head out of his office. 'Do you have some free time now Phil?'

Something about the official air of the request disturbed Phil. He rarely talked to Bob Williams, a white haired Harvard man, a real scholar, so everyone said, who looked New England wasp but talked Kansas. A pleasant enough fellow, but someone you could only exchange greetings with.

Phil stared across the desk at the stern portrait of Jonathan Swift, not one of his favourites.

'A rather serious situation has developed. You have a student in your writing class, Jane Wood?'

Phil nodded, shifted his body around in the narrow chair. The chairman's voice sounded as if from the stage of a hushed theatre.

'She lodged a complaint against you.' Here Bob Williams paused, searching for some way to express the next statement. He grimaced, not really the right word to express the gravity of his thin dry mouth.

'She told me you had harassed her sexually.' The chairman looked at him, probably with the hope that he would deny the charge.

'Are you the only one she's talked to?'

'Yes I believe so, but I'm afraid she wants to bring the matter before the dean.'

'That's ridiculous. I've taught here for fifteen years.' If only he could really explain the situation but not to Bob Williams; someone else could see the nuances of the situation, someone else might laugh the girl away.

Williams unfolded his hands, his expression that of the sick room. 'We'll back you as much as we can. You've always been popular with students.'

'Thank you,' Phil said contritely, like a gigantic schoolboy.

'But if she raises the issue before the whole college, I don't know.'

Phil wanted to say he hadn't touched her, not really. It was blackmail, some anger she had, the bitch. 'I didn't harass her.'

'Yes, of course.' The chairman produced a bleak smile. 'But it's her word against yours and your reputation. If she goes to the dean, the president, we'll have to have a hearing. Who knows how far it could go?' He paused. 'You could lose your position.'

'Christ! So what can I do?'

'Nothing at the moment till we know what she's going to do. But I wanted you to be aware of the situation.'

Bob asked after Phil's wife and they both mentioned vague invitations for dinner.

Phil left the office, his face moist, his clothes clinging to his body. He did not look at the secretary although he felt her glance, but walked silently by her shiny topknot of hair.

No one to talk to. Phil closed his office door. He pushed a pile of student papers from the centre of his desk, rested his hands, then his elbows on the cool metal. He rubbed his eyes, then peered out the window at the city, not his town. He could leave without sadness.

A knock at the door. A small man in a wrinkled striped shirt entered before Phil could speak. Dave Javits calling round for their usual Friday afternoon drink. Poor Dave, a widower with fantasies about young women. For a moment Phil thought of pouring it all out; Dave might make a good joke of it.

'Not today. My wife's having some friends over, you know, she wants me home early,' Phil invented. Even Dave with his obvious sexual jokes would think Phil mad for grabbing a student. They had had long discussions on the art of manipulation, but it was not clear that Dave Javits had ever seduced anyone but his dead wife.

Dave mumbled something about a paper he was working on. An eighteenth-century man who hadn't published anything in twenty years. One of the small department's many mediocrities.

After he left, Phil felt paralysed. Finally he began to gather up his papers and books. When he reached his car he knew he could not go home, not without his wife seeing his distress. Instead he walked down the hill to the city, a walk Phil hadn't taken in years.

Third Street. Even the name had no identity. Cars rolled down the wide avenue toward the small bluish foothills of the Rockies. How disappointed Phil had been when he arrived fifteen years ago to find the great mountains did not embrace the city, that Denver existed quite apart from the Rockies, a sham of a city with no heart, no brain.

Phil wanted to burrow in some alleyway, away from the march of white towers, J.C.Penney's and Woolworths. Young girls rushed by, running to catch buses, feet aching from a day behind the counter, fingers numb from the typewriter. Everyone leaving for the weekend, a soon-to-be-desert city. Phil realized he was walking against the tide and moved to the inner part of the sidewalk.

A thin girl with curly hair approached him. If it were Jane, what would he say, would he plead or shout at her? But it was not. He must not faint, for a middle-aged man who fainted was either ridiculous or very ill.

Phil pushed open the door of the Satire Lounge. Soothing darkness. He stumbled down the steps to the bar, blinking to rid himself of the bright dots.

Two old men watched him approach. One nodded to Phil, who, seeing the grizzled face of a derelict, turned away and sat at the other end of the bar.

'A Martini,' he called out to the bartender.

A woman in a grey raincoat jiggled the pinball machine in the far corner of the large room and cursed.

He could leave, maybe survive by writing, just writing. Phil smiled at his fantasy, but it was possible even this late. His life, the quotidian, had become dull especially when looked at from the outside.

The woman at the pinball machine turned, but seemed afraid to leave off jiggling and slamming the machine. She had a desperate look about her pale, horsey face.

Phil ordered another Martini. Jane was pitiful and he a fool. No need to be angry, to make a scene. He would talk to her.

'Hey, are you ready?' The derelict's question resounded throughout the room.

He walked over to Phil and pulled at his shoulder. 'Are you ready for today?' A shattering laugh. Phil pulled away and walked out of the bar.

Garbage swirled through the empty streets like tumbleweed. A plastic bag flew towards him; latched on to his leg.

Phil laughed at the red lights as he drove home. When he turned into his driveway, he let the car travel almost to the door of the garage before he stepped on the brakes.

He walked in humming. But after his wife greeted him with a look of irritation because he was late, Phil felt despair again.

He sat unmoving at his accustomed place at the table while Carol called down the two boys and then set the dishes down. His voice as he greeted his sons sounded like it came from someone else, a loud, peremptory voice sternly enquiring after school.

His wife had a manly look, her grey hair tied back in a short ponytail, her broad shoulders held straight as she dished out the potatoes and beef stew. She might ask for a divorce. All these years Carol knew about his affairs, must know, but none were serious, not really, none threatened her position. Carol had kept her silence, so had he. If it all came out in the open?

Now she was clearing off the plates. The boys brought in the pie and his coffee. They finished quickly and raced off to the television room.

'You look tired,' Carol said. 'Have you talked to a lot of students today?' The irritation hadn't lasted long, it never did.

'Just the usual.' He felt no passion for this heavy woman, nothing like that for years, typical he supposed. They were friendly companions. He felt tears rising. She was the mother of his children.

What was she saying? What was she saying?

'Do you want to have Harriet and Joel over next Friday? I was thinking it was about time.'

Phil brooded the whole weekend. His wife kept tactfully away, thinking probably it was one his moods between books. But he would have welcomed any conversation, if only to take his mind off his predicament.

Phil did not banter with his sons in the usual half-sarcastic, half-patronizing way, but they scarcely noticed. The older one was dating, the younger preferred to chase a frisbee around the yard. What difference did he make to anyone! Phil sat on the patio, his face sour.

When he arrived at his office on Monday, Phil expected to see a note from the chairman, but his mailbox was empty. He waited all Monday and subsequent days for some sign, some event which would signal the beginning of his 'undoing' as he half-jokingly referred to it in his mind.

Then he fantasized about relief. Jane Wood left the school; she became very ill over the weekend, a horrible accident, a death in the family, for he expected no mercy from her. The crazy bitch, she would never relent.

Phil stopped himself from knocking on the chairman's door to ask if anything had happened. He did not want to appear desperate; then it would all be over for him.

Phil told Julie he could not see her that week; he did not want to risk himself further. And Julie seemed so young, her soft face lacking not intelligence but the awareness which comes with age and sexual experience. He would be seducing a child.

On Friday afternoon after his class, Phil was sorting through some student stories when Jane Wood slipped into his office. Phil had to swallow before he could talk, managing only a wry 'Hello, where have you been?' She was still his student, a student who had disappeared from class for two weeks now. He had a right to ask.

She pushed a pink slip of paper across the desk. 'You don't

have to worry, I'm dropping your course. You have to sign because it's so late into the term.' She explained her presence in his office.

Without a word Phil signed the wrinkled paper. Probably she had clutched it all the way from the registrar to his office. Her pass to freedom, his reprieve. His signature was a scrawl.

Jane pushed the slip into her pocket, stood up and adjusted her knapsack on her back. Dressed like a boy in straight jeans and a plaid shirt, she was rather appealing. Phil surveyed her body with an amused expression.

Jane followed his glance. 'I read one of your novels this weekend.'

'Could you find a copy? I'm surprised.' The old joke about literary failure. Phil grinned at her. Perhaps the thing need not end on a bad note.

She kept a straight face, the humourless bitch.

'I thought I'd find out more about you, but it wasn't you.'

Phil didn't know what to say to this.

'I mean you couldn't have had those affairs and left your wife. It's all fantasy isn't it and you're a coward.' It was the first time he had seen her smile, not a smile really. Though his hand shook with rage, he wanted to touch her mouth.

'Get out of here!'

Jane fumbled with her knapsack, pulled out a black and shiny object. It was a gun she was pointing at him almost nonchalantly.

'How ridiculous.' Phil made an effort to keep his voice low and calm. It could not be real.

'How does it feel?'

He wanted to say 'you're mad' but the words didn't emerge thought he felt his lips move.

'Do you know anything, do you feel anything? Tell me, tell me.'

She came towards him silently now, holding the gun like a live animal, the smile gone from her face.

'You give that to me.' His chin and lower lip were twitching. His flesh, his body always so solid, so firm around him, grew soft. He could not have moved. She wanted to give him something, he understood now, the gun was her present; she wanted him to have its eruption.

'Please give me . . .' His voice had gone high.

'Here,' she whispered, lifting the gun higher, pointing it at his face. She squeezed the trigger.

A spray of icy water struck his forehead. Phil struggled to see through a stream of water, sweat and tears. They were tears he had not experienced since childhood, tears of rage as if some precious toy had been torn from him, mocked and destroyed. Yet till that moment he had not known it was precious.

Phil began wiping his face first with his hand and then with a handkerchief which he remembered was in his pocket. There was a knock at the open door. Jane turned and darted out past Dave Javits.

'What was that all about? She looked pretty upset.'

'Oh nothing.' Phil was trembling, was hoping he wouldn't be sick.

'Not one of your heartbreaks?' Dave winked.

'Yeah.' Phil marvelled at the cool sound of his voice. 'That's it, if you really want to know.'

PENELOPE SHUTTLE

The Prisoner of Zenda

Liv found Lewis sprawled out full-length on the floor. He'd
gone to sleep watching *The Prisoner of Zenda* on television. His
head and shoulders were cushioned against the base of the
grubby second-hand sofa and his pulled-off sneakers made a
neat blue vee on the carpet near her feet.

She picked up his dirty supper dishes and the two crumpled
cans of Harp lager, stacked everything on a battered tin tray
and carried it out into the kitchen. Round the border of the tray
ran the legend, 'We have seen the Lions of Longleat'. Then she
came back into the room. It smelled of curry, tobacco, sleep,
lager and hyacinths.

She watched Lewis with an amused self-important look in
which pleasure and irritation were equally present. Such is the
vulnerability of a sleeping peron. Maybe he dreamt about her.

The black and white images on the little screen folded and
unfolded, smiled, mimed, parried and bobbed this way and
that. She ignored the swordsmen. The volume was turned
down. Smiling, she kicked the man quite roughly with the toe of
her furry pink-slippered foot.

'Get up,' she said, 'get up, you.'

He flinched, shook his head, saw the men with rapiers darting
at him, blinked, felt confused by everything, but innocent.
Then yawned, raised his arms above his head, stretched, came
full awake.

'What?'

'Come on,' she said, taking his hand, pulling him up.

An hour later, their bodies were still coiled together. Their breath was sour and delicate with sex. She watched him, the sweat shiny on his forehead, eyes closed in peaceful astonishment, and she smiled, binding and encircling him. She slept.

In the morning she woke up alone. Lewis had gone for his swim. In her dream last night Liv met a man who was important to her. He was not mad or drunk or in debt. If he was not pure then he was good-tempered. He was her half-brother and he came skiing down the steep white slope to meet her, laughing in the glitter and sparkle of the snow, delighting in the icy air, greeting his sister with pleasure, his skin a jet-black shock even to her in this cold bright white world. It was Paul, with his familiar comforting expression of questioning serenity; she smiled back at him lovingly.

In Paul's features the independent humour and thick assurance of his black father and the supple Puritan gravity of their mother mingled and became glamorous. It was the mother she shared with him, the woman whose sky-blue eyes she saw through, whose talkative gifts she lacked, whose blonde hair snaked down her own back, the ache of the tight plait.

In the dream Paul showed her books about magic and gardening. Their dream conversation began seriously, there was a cruel streak in it, but laughter happened as well. We laughed loudly, childishly. What did Paul say that was so funny and lovely? thought Liv, puzzled and disappointed. She sat up in bed, yawning.

The mirror is waiting for her to get up. Shivering, she confronts it. Her slippers scratch softly on the wooden floor. She leans forward eagerly, as if her life is going to be explained here, written out in the enchanted grammar of the glass. Nothing but her own face. She puffs out a breath of exasperation, raising her eyebrows sullenly at her reflection, that stiff unhelpful girl.

In her dream she asked Paul, 'what shall I do?' She meant, as he understood at once, what shall I do, I am not happy. He looked offended, impatient. He brushed her puzzled face gently with his large warm hand. Then he told her, 'Liv, you make a boat or you make a bridge. Sail the water, or cross it.'

She repeats his words. Paul's advice, if it was advice, does not help. So why did I wake happy? It was a happy dream. Don't drown, he said. Yesterday's tropical fish in their shopwindow tank do not drown. She has admired them every afternoon this week, their bright-as-kite colours, their fearless glad ever-open eyes.

'Are you up yet?'

She frowns at her husband's voice. The classroom children call out longingly, tautingly to her; she remembers that she loves them. Soon in their rows they will wait for her to reward them for their finished sums, their neat writing.

To stay by the mirror is dangerous. She moves hurriedly away.

'Look,' she said to her husband, 'a postcard from Paul.' The picture was of the bronze head of Hypnos, the winged head of the bringer of sleep.

Lewis smiled and gave the card back without comment.

'Why do you smile like that?'

'Like what?' He got up, glanced at his watch, flicked off the radio.

'You smiled in an unpleasant cunning way . . . like a liar.'

'Who, me?' He laughed and wrinkled his nose in a way he had of stifling his anger. He was too lazy to be deliberately destructive, but he let his own particular lack of conviviality towards Paul stand between them, so that no matter how much she wanted to stop speaking she could not.

'What's your game, Lewis?'

She heard without pleasure her voice rising too high, as it always did when she got angry or nervous.

Lewis leaned in the doorway, not looking at her, indolently resentful.

'He sends you that card, Liv, so emblematic, so packed with his personality, his aura, and you expect me to . . . what; admire it, congratulate him?'

'You're talking nonsense.' She forced herself to speak in a low calm voice.

'Am I?' Lewis could crack her with his smiling, she'd crack

like an eggshell. It was one of his lawyer's tricks.

His dislike of Paul had been automatic and absolute, from the beginning. He disliked Paul in the same way that he would have disliked a Chinaman. That her half-brother, with his brown skin and African features, should be an eminent surgeon annoyed Lewis even more. If Paul were a nightwatchman or a labourer in a car factory or an unemployed musician, Lewis would be happier. By nature thoughtful towards others, Lewis could not accept the piquancy of having a relative, even by marriage, who was half-white, half-black. He felt it soiled him. Sometimes he would examine Liv closely, afraid of finding that his wife had turned black or at least too suntanned overnight; as if her own Welsh father might have been posthumously supplanted by Paul's father and her own blood altered.

Earlier in their life together Liv had insisted on a more amenable and friendly response towards Paul. But Lewis had jettisoned this now and she did not have the knack these days of bluffing her way back to that earlier strength. So her brother was a humiliation she bore. Paul's own life required nothing from them; it had its own power. If he felt angry about Lewis then he had not announced it. Paul doesn't care, Liv thought, and felt unhappy.

'Yes,' she said, 'you're talking nonsense.' Paul's postcard lay on the table, the god's calm wings of stone unmoving. She screwed it up and threw it in the bin.

'No!' said Lewis, flinching.

'Why not?' she asked brutally.

He hesitated. 'It seems unlucky, somehow,' he said lamely.

'OK.' She picked it up, smoothed it out and put the card back on the table with exaggerated caution, before bowing to Lewis in a theatrical manner, one arm folded and tucked behind her waist, the other resting lightly and comically on her breast.

A bank of grey cloud rose from behind the pale green hill fields and moved coldly across the sky. The afternoon had another hour of changeable light up its sleeve.

'Paul,' she said quietly. She was alone. She addressed her

words to her absent brother. 'The Japanese have a beautiful deceitful phrase, "sleeping upon the water". It means, to sleep with a prostitute. In Japan some prostitutes ply their trade on river boats. If I were a man I'd go out tonight and sleep upon the water, to get rid of this hunger. I need to go beyond what has been set as my limit, Paul, to break some taboo, to risk something sexually. I want to use my body in a new way, make my mouth strong around some man's sex, feel his tongue against my own sex, until like two arrows we shoot into sleep. Then an hour later I'd wake, pay the man, and leave him to his next client.

'Perhaps one day you will be able to explain why I'm disgusted by you and your women, Paul, yet still want to purchase someone I can fuck in my own way. From your experience of women you've bought on boats, in gardens, in bars, in locked and unlocked rooms, can you tell me if my desire is real or a fantasy and why it excites and scares me?'

Liv stood up and walked about the room, her heart pounding inside her, her body hot and then cold and then blazing again, as if men were coming in an hour to arrest her.

Will Lewis leave me? she thought suddenly. Perhaps tonight he'll say, that's it, I've had enough of you, I'm a bastard I know, but there you are, I'm bored, I'm off. Or suppose he came into the room and another man's head was between my legs and I was a willing partner? Can he read my thoughts? She was frightened. Energy that she kept for an emergency welled up in her and she rushed about the house, tidying, polishing, vacuuming, perparing a meal, performing the domestic tasks with a heightened blend of her usual accuracy and sloppiness. As she worked, she tried to forget what she really wanted.

Later, when she came out to hang some washing to dry, the secret happy life of trees, bushes, grass and hills hurt her. The autumn was almost over. She went back into the house and lay on her bed.

The dog wallows and barks at the water's edge but the swan glides on and round, neither hurrying nor loitering. Its feathers are mild. The swan neither loosens nor tightens his circles, simply creates and considers them. He is neither mischievous nor sad. From time to time he dips his head and lithe neck beneath the surface, seeking the sweet and tender frogs.

Lewis and Liv walked uphill from the pond until they came to the old mine shaft. Nearby the reddish earth was ripped up in long casual gouges from motorbike scramblers. The long disused mine shaft was fenced off but most of the fenceposts had rotted and the barrier had been pushed down by curious, destructive or amorous visitors.

Liv followed Lewis reluctantly to the mouth of the shaft and peered down the narrow dark rocky vent of the mine. Stagnant air tasted foul in her mouth. She closed her eyes, then blinked them open very wide and pulled a disgusted face. Out of the shaft rose a smell of urine, chalk, gorse, dust and death. It scared her, threatened her. She stepped back. Despite the cool day, she was sweating. Lewis peered down the shaft eagerly.

'Before the man-engines were built, back in the very early days,' she said, 'the men went down the shaft on timber ladders. We did a project on the mines with the kids last term. Imagine, going down there.'

'Yeah,' he said, not listening.

But Liv knew that the lower levels went down so deep that the men took several hours to descend and come to surface again, clinging to the rough rungs of the ladder. She knew that the miners were the élite of workers in this region, because of their closeness to the richness and danger of the earth. Down there rivers flowed; underground bridges had to be constructed. Often the men waded through icy water; they stood and worked in it, by candlelight. Later the miners rode up and down on the man-engine, balancing on wooden platforms attached to the massive engine rod that worked in unison with the pumping mechanism to keep the mine from flooding. Liv knew that the levels went far down into the dark, gallery after hacked-out gallery, deep into the earth to farm its tin and copper, arsenic and silver. She knew also that when the men surfaced again, faces blackened, they would walk home still clad in wet and fifthy clothes.

'Miles down it goes,' said Lewis. He crouched enthusiastically by the lip of the mine, animated by the deep dark shaft. He was excited. His eyes glinted.

Down there, she thought, men would have used few words. They worked as fast as they dared, being paid only for what they got out of the earth. Sometimes a shout of pain broke the silence, a fit of cursing, or a hallooed direction when one was lost. Maybe there'd be some teasing when a youth was new to the work. More usual would be the silence of caution and endurance. Liv moved further away from the shaft. She concealed her thoughts from Lewis as competently as he hid his from her.

'Be careful,' she warned automatically as he tossed a stone down the shaft. They listened tensely for the stone's clatter. They waited but no sound came.

'Is it bottomless?'

She shook her head. 'No, but deep as hell nearly. Last winter when the wind howled, I thought I heard the oldtime miners groaning. As if limb by limb their hard lives still racked them.'

'I think of them differently,' he said. 'I hear them singing, a thoughtful choir, strong and happy.' He took three paces back from the edge of the shaft, straightened his shoulders, lifted his head and sang in his light clear baritone,

> 'Plunged in a gulf of deep despair
>   We wretched sinners lay,
> Without one cheerful beam of hope,
>   Or spark of glimmering day.
>
> With pitying eyes the Prince of Peace
>   Beheld our helpless grief;
> He saw, and – O amazing Love!
>   He flew to our relief.'

III

The energy of the frog! How it leapt, its long muscular legs throbbing with life. In the dream it came to her, the green of it, the leaping, the pliance of it, its huge affectionate eyes. Liv woke up, a helpless young woman laughing at the clear bright rain.

'Who in the house is hungry?' she sang out at breakfast.

'I am!' sang back Lewis.

All that day they were fortunate. It was one of the mysterious days of marriage, when wants and exhaustions vanish; when nothing is left in the lurch; when no one goes in different directions; when the evil spirits molest others but not you or me. It was like that for Liv and Lewis. They went through it with joy, like swimming under water all day, safely.

Months later she bought several enlarged reproductions of old photographs at a local auction, intending to use them as exhibition items in another school project on regional history. Most were village or farm scenes, the others of mines and miners. One showed the trammers at work on the three hundred and ten fathom level. In another men were dumping wagon-loads of ore into a crushing machine. A group of bal-maidens (girls and women who broke up the ore into small workable pieces and shovelled it into carts, outdoor work), stared from the rainy yard of the photograph, unsmiling in their ochre and mud-stained hessian aprons, their heads stiffly shawled. A fourth photograph showed the massed bearded shareholders of the biggest mining company in the area on proud parade in the forecourt of the mine office. The senior men with foaming chest-deep biblical white beards sat upon a row of chairs, while less senior and smaller-bearded men stood in two rows behind. The merely-moustached junior men sat cross-legged on the ground in front, with one of their group reclining full-length, supporting his tweed-suited body on a braced elbow, his bowler hat held decoratively over his stomach. He grins. But the other shareholders look solemnly into the camera, without irony.

All these photographs were for school. Only one interested Liv personally. She showed it to Lewis as soon as he came in. It was, at first glance, an unremarkable picture of two children taken in a nearby village over one hundred years ago.

'It fascinates me,' she said.

The two children were a boy and girl. The stood back to back, heads turned to the camera, with the boy smiling and the girl serious. They wore the usual clothes of the period, heavy coarse boots on their feet. They stood in front of an old cottage, grey door closed and grey windows shuttered, a house that no one lived in any more. The sky was full of a dusky light. The season was hard to tell. Beside the house was a collapsing shed, and indifferent garden, but with one richly-blooming bush, vivid even through the sepia tints. By the side of the smiling boy a thin dog is sniffing the ground. The boy's face is alight with love of the world despite all the evidence to the contrary around him. The girl's watchfulness is a wiser response to their surroundings. But she is therefore not beautiful; her guarded gaze is without desire and so looks like disgrace.

Lewis turned the photograph over and read the description, 'miners' children, 1887'. The picture did not interest him. He coughed. He was hungry. He yawned. He felt Liv's peculiar deliberate docility filling the room, like a smell almost.

'What fascinates you?' he asked.

'Here are two lives no phoenix renewed,' she said almost angrily. 'These children died, maybe even before they grew up. Probably no one knows their names now. This photograph is about impossibilities. What happened to them? Did their father die down that shaft we visited? Did the boy grow up to work in similar darkness? Did the girl marry a miner? Maybe she got away and had a different life, sordid perhaps, but with some happiness in it.'

'Does it matter?' he asked. She rested her hand on his shoulder, looking at him nervously, then blurted out,

'I feel as if they were my children, who died. But at the same time I feel as if Paul and I are those children.'

Her mention of Paul angered him. She accompanied her words with a long cool direct shameless look, asking him to what? wound her, comfort her?

He laughed out loud.

'You and Paul! What a crazy idea, Liv.'

He felt her whole body shudder and she drew back from him. He thought with satisfaction and remorse, I have extracted that shudder from her dishonourably. He laughed again and she took a long deep painful breath. The photograph of the children shook slightly in her hand. Lewis looked again at the smiling boy.

'But the boy is very beautiful,' he added.

RALPH GOLDSWAIN

The Examination

It is a hot summer but my garden is unpleasant this year. The shrubs are dead because of the harsh winter when the snow lay heavily on them for five weeks, and broke their stems. Everything was frozen for weeks. There are not even insects; the low temperature ensured that. I come out every day though, because I've always sat here in the summer.

I retired in July but I am still an examiner. Every day I sit in my garden and read scripts. I don't enjoy it any more. I don't enjoy anything any more. I am just fifty-five but I feel like an old man. Perhaps I shall be a examiner for ever.

Last year the garden was beautiful. My wife was still with me then. She has green fingers and used to spend all her spare time gardening. The daffodils wrung memories of our courting days. The tulips were beautiful – a banquet of colour. In June the peonies announced themselves as dramatically as ever, and died just as soon as ever. By the middle of July everything was out. It was a moderate summer with warm days and plenty of rain. Now it is just hot. No rain.

I have always marked history A level examinations. This year they wrote to me. They regret that they are unable to fit me into their examining programme, they said. After all those years. I don't believe them. I know they were determined to get rid of me. It is part of the deliberate lowering of standards. Anyway, I had my say. I spoke out against the new syllabus at the examiners' meeting. That silenced quite a few people.

I wrote off to some other boards and the only thing I was offered was an adult education social studies paper. Personal

187

development. Yes, that's a subject, they tell me.

The standard is very low. I am appalled.

They had to attempt three questions and although there was plenty of choice most candidates answered the same ones. Number one was popular: 'What was your greatest achievement during the year?'

Here is an extract.

I gave up smoking. After thirty years of addiction and several unsuccessful attempts I finally did it. I just woke up one morning, clenched my teeth and said, 'no more'. It worked. I had tried everything from peppermints to hypnotism. None of it worked. But one morning I did it all by myself. It has changed my life; indicated new avenues. Every morning when I open my eyes I rejoice.

That's not much of an achievement. Any intelligent person should be able to do that. I had to mark him down for the severe lack of stature in his choice of material. Moreover, his style is questionable. He cannot get away with that repetition – I just woke up one morning, one morning, every morning and so on. And he mixes his tenses. No, very poor.

There are others like that. One had stopped biting her nails. She claimed it had given her a new confidence and allowed her more freedom. I'm not impressed. I'm nervous of young people having too much freedom.

My department, for example. There was always a bigger turnover than in any other department and I found myself with more than my share of inexperienced young teachers. I found their enthusiasm misguided. Ater all, I was the one who had to take the responsibility if anything went wrong.

There was once a Miss Fisher who wanted to do a *son et lumière* to help pupils to understand better the issues involved in the Magna Carta. I was warned by the excited, almost fanatical gleam in her eyes. And I was right. She wanted to abandon lessons for two weeks, build sets, arrange lighting and then do a performance. She even wanted to invite parents. If I had ever been inclined to waver the last item brought me to my senses.

'Parents, Miss Fisher?' I said from behind my desk. 'Parents? Here? During school time?'

'Why not, Mr Bilder?'

'Because, young lady, I have always found that it doesn't pay to let parents in. They only come here to criticize.'

She sat right on the edge of the huge armchair and looked up at me with puzzled eyes.

'But that's their right surely? Their duty even.'

I'd never been challenged like that so I put a stop to it, before she had a chance to expound on her extraordinary pedagogical theory, which she looked as though she was about to do. Part of a new breed, she would actually invite parental criticism. Definitely one of the headmaster's own. He had probably put her up to it.

I reached slowly for a cigarette from the box on my desk and lit it. Then I looked straight at her.

'No, Miss Fisher,' I said. 'The answer is no.'

The fanatical gleam subsided and she sank back into the chair. Then she stood up and sighed.

'Thank you, Mr Bilder,' she said.

She became more subdued after that. She didn't bother me with trivialities either; in fact she hardly spoke to me. Within a few terms she had gone.

Without the discipline of going in to school I've fallen out of the habit of taking exercise. I sit in the garden all day and when I get up in the late afternoon I can hardly walk. I am in pain most of the time – a terrible burning sensation all over my body. I should see a doctor.

Another popular question is number three: 'What qualities do you value in your friends?' You would think that with such a choice candidates would take care to give a considered answer. 'People must accept me for what I am. If anybody does that he is my friend. I also value the ability to take. Anybody can give but how many know how to take?'

Now that's pure nonsense. It seems to me that everyone

knows how to take. I've always been surrounded by grasping people. No, friendship is a rare thing. I am proud to say that I have never made one friend among my colleagues. People use the term 'friend' loosely. I have never had a colleague in my house and I have never been to a colleague's home.

The deputy head, John Wilde, came to me a few years ago.

'Mr Bilder,' he said, 'I've been looking for you.'

He had his usual suave lopsided smile, broad beneath hornrimmed spectacles.

'Oh yes?' I replied.

'Yes,' he said. 'You haven't put you name on the list.'

'Which list?' I asked. 'As you know, Mr Wilde, there are always several lists up on the board at any given time.'

He shook his head. 'You know which list I mean, Mr Bilder.'

I did know which list he meant. He'd put a notice up inviting the whole staff to his silver wedding and he'd asked them to indicate if they would like to come. He was a popular man in an uncouth way and it had seemed to me that the whole lot had put their names down, including the headmaster. Well the last thing I wanted then was to join them in merrymaking. I thought quickly. There were a few other teachers nearby, taking a close interest in the conversation.

'Ah yes, Mr Wilde,' I said. 'Thank you for the invitation but I think not.'

'May I ask why?' he said.

'Because I have better things to do.'

I saw the eavesdroppers exchange glances. I know some of the younger ones laugh at me. I once overheard one trying to do an imitation of me. It wasn't very good but the others laughed as though it was.

Wilde was more cautious in his approach to me after that. I understood the party was vulgar. For weeks afterwards I couldn't get away from it. Wherever I went in the school people were talking about it, rehearsing its pathetic episodes to each other. I was glad I didn't go. They didn't want me anyway and would only have been interested in my wife. She likes parties. And she actually enjoyed some of the tedious functions I had to attend. But I don't go to parties for other people's benefit.

There is an old man two doors up from me and he burns things in his garden every afternoon. His name is Mr Gillaume and he's almost a hundred. One afternoon I strolled up along the service alley and asked him not to burn things on Sundays. I spoke politely to him – not in any way offensively. He was all dressed up in a suit with a white shirt and tie. He stopped his stoking and looked at me with his sharp little eyes.

'Piss off,' he said.

He's just lit a fire and I'm afraid he must have put some old tyres on it because the smoke is thick and black and there is a strong smell of burning rubber. I wish he wouldn't do that. I have always believed in communication and I find Mr Gillaume a challenge to that belief.

I haven't seen much of the neighbours all summer. Their gardens are scorched like mine. I sometimes wonder where they all are. I've not talked to anyone since my wife left.

She said they all felt sorry for her but I didn't believe that. They knew she had everything she wanted – more than many of them would ever have. And she seemed happy. She often used to hum tunes as she worked in the garden. I frequently had to point that out to her because she didn't realize she was doing it. Then she would stop. She knew how it got on my nerves.

At least we never had any children. There was one family a few doors down with six – always screaming. I often used to say to my wife; 'Now aren't you glad we never had any?'

They must have gone on holiday. I haven't heard them at all this year.

There is a child somewhere around here though – at first I thought it was one of theirs but they couldn't have left just one behind. She comes and stands behind the fence looking in through the gaps. She sometimes throws acorns at me. She's very ugly. When I stand up she runs away.

The question 'What can you offer?' was badly answered. I could answer that one right from the heart. In a nutshell, I gave myself unstintingly for so many years but I was never appreciated.

The headmaster invited me in one day. He stood up, smiling, as I entered his study. Little wrinkles formed at the sides of his eyes as his smile broadened.

'Ah, Mr Bilder,' he said and indicated a lounge chair with an expansive sweep of his arm.

He came round the desk as I sat down and settled gracefully into the chair's twin on the other side of a coffee table. There's something wrong with a man with so many ties. I've never seen him wear the same one twice. And always a silk pocket handkerchief to match.

'Well Mr Bilder,' he said. 'We've known each other for quite a long time.' He smiled at me. 'May I call you Eric?' He crossed one leg over the other and leant toward me quite intimately.

Although I didn't usually encourage that sort of thing – first name terms – among colleagues, I thought it a reasonable request, coming from the headmaster. So I nodded, although he was wrong. He hadn't known me for a long time; only five years.

'Certainly, Headmaster,' I said, 'if you wish it.'

He smiled. 'Thank you Eric,' he said. He leant forward and tugged at one of his thin black silk socks with the forefinger and thumb of both hands. His shoes shone, catching the light from the windows in bright little squares.

Then he looked hard at me. 'You've been here a long time.'

I nodded.

'And this is where you started your teaching career, isn't it?'

'Indeed, Headmaster,' I said. I wondered where this was leading. But I could guess. I don't trust anybody who smiles so much.

He sat back and smiled again. 'You've given you life to generations of boys. That's something to be really proud of.'

I smiled then. He was right.

'A splendid effort,' he said. 'Tell me, Eric, does it ever get you down?'

I thought carefully about my reply. One doesn't complain to the headmaster if one has any sense.

'Not in a general way, Headmaster,' I said. 'Only the

ingratitude one sometimes encounters along the way.'

He beamed. 'Ah, the monster ingratitude, eh Eric? The serpent's tooth.'

I bowed my head in acknowledgement of the apt quotation.

'Have you ever thought you've had enough?'

I was puzzled. What did he mean? He was making me nervous. I hoped he hadn't noticed.

'I couldn't change at this stage . . .' I began but he waved his fingers gently.

'No, no, I meant retirement.'

'I'm only fifty-four,' I said. I don't usually divulge my age to anybody but I didn't want him to labour under any mis-apprehensions.

'That's just it,' he said. 'There are splendid opportunities for early retirement these days. Let's face it Eric, you've done well. Thirty-five years in the classroom; rising to head of the history department; doing a good job there . . . Don't you think you deserve an easier time?'

'But retirement at fifty-five!' I said, trying to keep the dismay out of my voice. I knew that arrangement was only for those who couldn't cope. 'They wouldn't give it to me.'

He lifted both hands in a Mediterranean-type gesture. 'But my dear Eric, if you want it we can arrange it,' he said. 'It's all in your hands.'

We sat in silence for a few moments. Then he spoke again.

'Education's changing fast. We all have to develop new attitudes. You know – more appropriate ways of dealing with the problems of our times.'

He had touched on one of my hobby horses and I responded. 'There's no need for a liberal education to be any different from what it was in Classical times,' I said. 'We can learn from them. They worked out the perfect curriculum for an all-round education.'

'Well,' he said, smiling affably, 'it's a perfectly valid point of view. Not everyone would agree with you but you're certainly entitled to hold it.'

I knew he had made up his mind so I ended the meeting by

getting up. He stood up too and put his arm round my shoulders.

'Think about it, Eric,' he said, giving my shoulders a little squeeze. 'Just think about it.'

During the weeks which followed I decided not to retire but it was useless. He got his way.

And my wife left me on her fiftieth birthday. I tiptoed into her bedroom at seven o'clock with her tea as usual and she wasn't there. There was an envelope on the bed. The note simply said, 'I've left you. I'll come and see you in a few days.' As I set out for school that morning I could already feel the drought coming. I had only six weeks to go; I didn't have time to think about my domestic affairs; there was too much to do.

I had to get my own meals. Then one evening she came.

'How are you, Eric?' she said. She looked younger. It was strange seeing her sitting on the sofa like a visitor rather than an inhabitant. She was also dressed like a visitor – handbag and make-up. She wore her blue dress.

I wanted to ask her to come back. I missed seeing her bent over a flower bed in her straw hat and thick gloves.

'I'm hurt, of course, as you can imagine,' I said, determined not to let her see the pain as I remembered the young woman who had so infatuated me. And, yet, even then, I wanted to tell her but I couldn't.

'Do you know, we've never once had a good row?' she said. 'Like other people.'

Domestic rows are vulgar. I wanted to ask her to come back.

'You realize, of course, that you have put youself completely in the wrong?' I said instead.

'Oh Eric,' she said, 'that's exactly the kind of thing that's made me leave. I just can't live with you any more.'

I shrugged.

'All those years,' she said. 'I'm exhausted.'

I think she had tears in her eyes. I still didn't say anything. She stood up. I stayed where I was. I haven't seen her since.

I'm thinking of taking up gardening but I would have to give up examining if I did and I don't think I could do that.

KARA LIND

The Caper 11: Clifton

They went with intentions of bringing him to a peaceful end, chattering with increasing excitement as the train cut closer, closer, filling the darkness breifly with sound and light.

Their first surprise came at Parkway where the Old Padré stood chuggily on the platform. 'I didn't wear my dog collar,' he whispered mischievously, taking Cynthia's bags. She'd wanted to powder and lipstick, arrange her head for a warm welcome brilliantly concealing the future plot. 'Thought I'd head you off. – Weren't expecting me till Temple Meads, chaps,' he smacked Vince's shoulder with innocent affection; then added accusingly: 'You're taller.'

They exchanged glances in the back seat of his yellow car, a cheap disappointment, driven ruthlessly by the old man to the Gothic gates of the old school.

He gibbered happily about hot food arrangements on the way in; they said very little. Clutching suspiciously, pushing each other half-humouredly into middle position, they followed the fly of the old fool's cloak through the Quadrangle, past the vast open swirl of stairway, then held hands in the cloisters, wondering if perhaps he had something in mind for them too. 'It's a full moon.' 'Maybe he's a psycho,' they whispered before he found the right key, swinging the oak door open on a lighted dining-hall, laid for three. 'Count Dracula's, I assume.' Cynthia threw off her os, warming to the irony.

*

Her room overlooking the cobbled Quadrangle had a fire in the

195

brass grate and four large pink thoughtful towels warming on the bathroom radiator.

She lay awake thinking of a poem she'd once written about a big brass bed in Moscow, enjoying the wind until even the expectancy of tomorrow couldn't keep her two blue eyes open.

Buying Poison

The slim girl's heels clipped along the stone to the waiting car. The reflection surveyed with casual care by the driver was one of cleverly co-ordinated anonymous elegance. – A pale green raincoat of the style worn by any youngish woman of her sort – the very cut of the cloth, meticulous stitch of its threads revealing a certain non-individuality. Her accessories were of soft leather in a quiet mink, the scarf giving just the right amount of comfort from the chill sun; her pink suede gloves delicately betraying an inner frivolousness the mastermind behind the outfit had taken pains, today, to conceal.

Dismissing her black glasses as hyperbole, Cynthia removed them, clipping down the lane towards Halem's shop. There was no one else inside.

'It's a bright day but there's no warmth in the sun,' she said at the arranged time, to the short, stooped man who expected her.

'You'll be from the college then?'

'Just visiting. I'm off to Paris at the week's end.'

Unasked, he picked a tiny package from below the counter, putting it into the dainty pink hand. Cynthia paid and left.

Meanwhile . . .

Balancing his breakfast tray on his knees like the professional he is, Vince slipped on his silk dresser on time for the Padré's unannounced entrance. 'Where's the dear girl this morning?' Reverend Brile allowed himself a visible touch of emphasis on this last word. Vincent winced, hoping the old fool wasn't going to be a bore about what time they breakfasted; and a little put out at the decadent assumption Cyn would be in his rooms.

'Gone out. Surprise,' Vince replied in his clipped but nonetheless charming voice.

The afternoon being taken up with a swift succession of
appointments organized by the Reverend for their entertain-
ment, it wasn't until evening Vincent managed to whisper:

'Did you get the stuff?'

She nodded.

'And you?'

'Yes.'

before the old man glided them in to dinner with that
unsubtlety scolded in children, tolerated in the aged.

Plan A

The Masters pretended complete interest on their plates until it
was their turn to feign surprise and look up smilingly at Cynthia
and Vincent in answer to the Reverend's tap on each respective
shoulder. After the briefest introduction they carried on with
dinner, obviously careful not to overstare at Cynthia's slitted
black gown – in the most unusual places.

Headmaster took Old Brile aside later, telling him with a
radical smirk that he – as one of the rather Modern School –
wouldn't dream of consciously subduing decadence; instead
preferring to let it dissolve naturally and outlive its welcome.
Reverend Brile was in no doubt as to what he was referring to,
and permitted himself a reciprocal smirk. He even went so far
as to broach the topic with those assembled in the Recital Hall
later, saying: 'Your gown is certainly exceptional, dear girl.
Very attractive – but so unfortunately black. A chap longs for
variety, you see. And in my business, I see such a lot of that
shade,' with all the audacity of one who knows his financial
position to be secure until death.

(They wouldn't dare cut him off – thereby slandering both
their reputation as a fairly democratic Public School and taking
yet another swipe at the poor old Church – not to mention a
poor old man. Brile's personal fortune had been consumed in
his glittering middle age, his policy re: finance having been
'Save till you're forty then Spend, Spend, Spend, who cares-

about-the-vulgarity.' His financial dependency on the school was no great secret; Headmaster was painfully aware of those reasons, aforementioned, that meant he'd never be rid of the old fool.)

*

Recital over and applauded, a party of five consisting of Cynthia, Vincent, the old man, and the two most openly-inquisitive of the masters ascended the stone stairway to a small upstairs sitting-room.

At the right moment – her timing always so perfect – Cynthia distracted the trio, giggling as her dress, apparently unbidden, looped forward at one of the discreet slits above the cleavage exposing a little more white flesh than the designer's original tasteful intention, but still less than the vulgar. Leaving Vince the opportunity to give Old Brile an almost imperceptible dunt that would send him crashing to destruction.

'Isn't that a bit passé?' Cyn had worried when he first suggested this plan.

'Simplest most effective,' Vince replied convincingly, as ever.

'And what could be more simply unimaginative than shoving him downstairs!'

'According to the architectural plans, the gradient should be steep enough to finish him.'

Naturally suspicion would fall on the young visitors – once the police discovered his daughter, Verity, was to inherit the lot. Then Phase 2 of Plan A went into operation. Vince would show Ver the photographs – clever trickery implying the Reverend a practising transvestite with no colour co-ordination. 'He probably is anyway,' Cyn assured her priest before leaving town. She always discusses everything with him. 'These old masters always are,' he readily agreed, 'either that or fruits.'

You may well be wondering why they don't just blackmail him. Brile. Cynthia was against this, arousing Vince's suspicions that her interest in the old boy wasn't purely material. Didn't want to lose his esteem. She countered this with the real reason (she claimed) for her reluctance to touch him rather than the renownedly snobbishly bourgeois Verity. Old Brile, she observed, would enjoy such a photograph, pounce on it immediately, rejoice in its technical cleverness demanding a copy for the Family Album. Ver would be shamed beyond all redemption. Besides, an old man's death is never too suspicious anyway.

Alack! The old sport regained his footing with a satisfied smile that seemed, to Cynthia, to guess at their plot.

Seated in the plush room, a red and gilt cliché more suited to a French tart's boudoir than supposedly sober schoolmaster's smoker, her suspicions increased. 'Perhaps we underestimated him, I'm sure he's shrewder than we thought,' she said to Vince later as he warmed his toes at her fire. His new room, the one he'd been moved to that morning after breakfast, was dank and freezing, stuck at the top of a spiral complete with predictable cobwebs. 'For one thing, he kept harping on death – as if trying to jinx our plot.'

'What sort of music do you favour?' she asked Collins, the younger of the 2–inquisitives, who also happened to be the one with the largest nose and a walk that made one want to enquire how badly his tummy hurt? Before the idiot could answer Old Brile cut in with: 'I prefer the Death March myself. Used to it, you see.' Then rampaged into a detailed account regarding the scattering of his ashes – as if expecting them to become available in the very near future.

Vince deftly manoeuvred the conversation to tomorrow's agenda. – A rigid arena beginning at the Lord Mayor's 9.30; The Country Club, 11.00; The Seaside; The Zoo; The Suspension Bridge; The Downs; The School Libraries and grounds at times he couldn't remember, but feigned an interest in anyway. 'I'm so looking forward to the Panto,' he smiled directly at Brile.

'Oh – are you going? Jolly good!' the old man said slyly.

'I've seen it,' the younger master enthused, adding, as if it were expected of him, 'There's no smut.'

'Whatsoever.'

Old Brile turned intimately on Cynthia, excluding the others with one of his hunched shoulders, saying in a low voice, coquettish as a radical minister can be: 'I'd love to take you to a funeral.' To which she laughed outright, liking him, almost abandoning in her mind the idea of the plot.

'Ho, Joce,' he called to the large-nosed master, showing off. 'How much did it set you back? Your cat's funeral?'

At that, the winning-over process was almost complete; enough for Cyn to risk annoying her partner by suggesting a change of plan later.

'Why don't we give him another year?' she said casually, as if his reply wasn't that important to her, or to a man's mortality.

'We're a bit short,' Vince reminded with a master stroke of common sense, withdrawing his toes, them being quite warm enough now. 'Besides,' he added, in his calm, secure, logical voice, 'he may not invite me back again.'

'When did you need an invitation,' Cyn enquired lightly; but he noted the tense undercurrent which suggested the necessity of climbing the spiral and being tucked chilly alone.

Jealous of even a hint of affection from her for somebody else, even one ruined and decrepit as Brile, with nothing left to amuse himself but his affected rude joviality, Vince said decisively: 'It must be completed tonight. Besides, Beryl's waiting in Paris ready for that lethal compound to be slipped in her tea.' Cyn giggled a little at that. If anyone deserved the unusual callous tone in his voice it was Beryl. And it was rather clever, even for Vince, to discover two substances innocent alone, deadly mixed, and virtually untraceable – especially in an old hag who gobbles tranquillizers all day anyway and is simply longing to die as a last act of spite.

'Plan B?' he raised his eyebrows confidently.

Cyn nodded.

How To Do It And Not Get Caught
By prior arrangement, it was Vince who softly trod the dark narrow halls of the upper floor wearing the anonymous black master's cape and a protective false nose, excellent in silhouette. 'It's my idea so you can carry it out,' she said with that

irrationality that always seems sensible when she's sitting on the floor with a pen and notebook taking jots for their next caper (naturally to be destroyed after memorizing).

Of course, he had no trouble finding the correct room. Vince always does his homework. Turn left at the end of the hall, second on the right, first door on the right. Conveniently unlocked (these old men always trust each other), making his master-key unnecessary.

Once inside, Vince gave up the strangled walk of a man with diarrhoetic cramps – briefly wondering how Joce Collins keeps it up all day – and, after the safe few minutes of close listening, proceeded to the bed without conscience. Picking up a tassled cushion from the armchair which lurched forward at the top to accommodate Brile's hump, Vincent listened again for the contented regular breaths of sleep. Still hearing nothing, he stuck his ear daringly close, almost expecting the old thing to struggle just when he got his finger on the lethal gland. Brile's unprepared features, as terrifying at close range as anyone's of that age group, would have convinced Vince – had he needed such persuassion – that murder in this case was more a favour than an outrage.

He touched the old neck with his left hand, seeking the gland with his right index finger, his mind ready to defeat any last minute will to survive. The chill flesh first disturbed him, the feel of it, then the pallor – more like death than the chap with the slit throat he'd identified in the morgue at Amsterdam, when his name was Jack, his assistant Cérise.

Oi Oi, something queer here, he thought to himself. The old man's dead already.

*

Le Petit Déjeuner
You can imagine their surprise next morning to find him sitting upright without any aid from a suspended string, eating a china plate of crisp bacon and lemon scrambled eggs with a cheerfully vital appetite. Or the surprise they would have felt, had they not been the sort of people that absolutely nothing fazes.

'Reincarnation,' Cyn whispered, between a pretty smile and a Good Morning that resounded of nothing but ease and affection.

Vince winced. 'He was definitely dead last night.'

A pact with the devil, he idled, as Old Brile helped Cyn into her chair and prepared for one of his cosy chats, made private again with use of shoulder.

'Dear girl, I do believe I'd marry you,' he said, loud enough for everyone at table to hear, 'if I had enough time left . . .'

Cynthia gave a charming laugh, grateful for the weak sun straining in the big windows, the absence of which would have made his suggestion obscene.

'Of course you do,' she said pleasantly. 'But what would Vincent think?'

Vince was fast proceeding to the stage of envying even the people she made fun of; and he was in no mood to make an exception for this flirtatious old corpse. He bit into a bit of marmaladed toast, unconsciously reflecting Cynthia's wide expression in his own.

She always had people imitating her. Even later, when it all seemed over, and she was quite insane instead of just partly, the other crazies on her wing liked to look as she did, reposed before the looking-glass with carelessly elegant expressions; pretending to worry about nothing at all. But the reciprocal element is there too. Cynthia, often quite against her will, soaks up the best and worst characteristics of those around her, attaching these weights to an already intricate personality. Like the time she copied the laugh of a cheap but commercially successful Fortune Teller in the Grande Place until he thought she was making fun of him and stalked off without his crystal. Cynthia researches herself well. With Vincent in Clifton she expected the explosion that was bound to come, believing herself unable to prevent it.

'I'm sure what I'm about to say must sound very insulting,' the old man chuckled, giving the signal for another cup of coffee to be poured, 'so I'll apologize in advance – but say it anyway!'

Vince grimaces.

'I'd love to conduct you funeral, old fellow,' The Reverend finished in the manner of a punchline. 'You mustn't think I dislike you,' Vincent almost shrank back visibly from the touch of the dead flesh clapping his shoulder, 'I simply think of you as a black – oops mustn't say that, must we? – as a dark person, and I've always wanted to conduct the service over such a one.' He laughed merrily, making the others join in.

'I would've thought you'd have experienced most things by now,' Vince said. – Rather shortly, Cyn thought.

*

'I rather like him, after all,' she said as they stood admiring the steep drop from the modern bridge to the ageless water, cracked at the edges with rock and the roots of trees. Brile was still puffing away back at the Samaritan sign on a seat provided by the charitable Toll Keeper.

'I'm glad you've finally decided to admit it,' but there was a touch of humour in his clipped tone now, somehow reassured by the glinting flick of her hair that he wasn't yet about to lose her.

'He's invited us to Patrons' Day in September,' she smiled with the edge of her lips. 'It gets darker early then,' looking down longingly at the water. Then she looked at him and he understood. She loves me now. At this moment. And that's the only guarantee anyone can ever have.

*

Next morning they weren't sorry to leave. The food had certainly been good – but it would be better in Paris. And one can only take so much of an old man's banter, particularly when he's temporarily outsmarted one. And so they left the fortune that doesn't really exist to accumulate interest until Patrons' Day, waving from the train that would take them to the coast, concealed hands clutched below the window line, content, for now, perhaps a little smug that their love was still safe and hadn't become just another commonplace threat in the business of living.

ELAINE FEINSTEIN

A Late Spring

Jenny knew it was a mistake to go back to Cambridge as soon as she got into the old green diesel at Liverpool Street Station. What could she have hoped for? Travelling back across that hedgeless, treeless fen, past all the April landscape of puddled fields, piles of old cars and yellow cranes, back into the past. Her own past, ten years lost.

But then she was running away, really, as much as running back. And when you're running away, you make mistakes.

Easter weekend was always Maurice's favourite time of year; and, until that weekend, he had always thought of himself as contented. He had peace, lucidity and a chance to work. He had no wish to travel. All this trotting here and there, he couldn't see the pleasure in it. Nasty, modern habit. People pretending to care about the world. Looking in guide books. Shallow, silly business. What he enjoyed was getting his knees under a desk. Getting his head down.

He put weekend invitations off with bewildered politeness. Why did people feel they had to have parties? He'd never met anyone actually enjoying them. Well, he couldn't prove that, of course; some people did look quite animated from a distance, but he never found anything much going on when he listened in.

What he liked about Easter was the pause. The clean, uncluttered silence of it.

Since that particular Easter, though, he had to acknowledge it had never tasted quite the same again.

Jenny had been given a room in what had once been a totally male college. And, at first sight, little had changed. There were the very same two porters; grey always, in skin as well as in hair. They went about their business as they always had, sparing no attention for the young woman from across the Atlantic who stood waiting for their attention.

—Thank gawd for the vacation, said the elder.

—Just Maurice Williams will it be? the other enquired.

—Just him, more or less. Over Easter, anyway.

And she stood there as two Fellows of the College entered, and one of them asked:

—Any letters for me?

The other greeted him sardonically.

—Hello, James. Where are you off to?

—The Auvergne.

—Lucky sod.

Then one of the porters coughed.

—There's just a note, sir.

—Thanks.

—Is it from Maurice Williams again?

—Yes.

—I had one of those. About silk stockings hanging from the girls' windows. Getting in the wisteria or something.

—I don't think they *wear* stockings much these days.

—Not silk, anyway. Worse luck.

They both giggled, and Jenny wondered if some magic had rendered her invisible.

—Well.

—Are you taking Sybil? To France, I mean.

—Have to. It's her uncle's farmhouse.

As they drifted out of the College together, she heard their voices receding, plaintively.

—I think they specially *selected* the girls.

—To be no trouble?

—Not to disturb.

—Well, *twelve*, after all. Do you teach any?

—Next term . . . Maybe.

205

At length, Jenny found herself irritably knocking on the wooden porters' desk.

—Excuse me.

—Yes?

—Professor Michaelson, she said firmly.

—Professor Michaelson? replied the porter. Right. I'll just look for you. Mmm. Sorry, he's not arrived from the States yet.

—No, no. *I'm* Professor Michaelson, Jenny laughed.

—The visiting Fellow? asked the porter, appalled.

—Don't you have my name on a list?

—It's the vacation, he said apologetically. People going. The list now. Where's the list?

—I'll carry your bag, offered his fellow.

As the door closed, she heard his wizened superior mutter:

—She's opposite Maurice Williams' room. Whose idea of a joke was that?

As they walked, Jenny observed that what had once been Lavatory Court was now some kind of coffee bar. But then, she hadn't been back since 1968. A different country. When her bags were set down, she offered the astonished porter a pound note.

Always a bad sign, overtipping, she knew. It meant the place was starting to get to her. She opened a window, and it was cold and wet. Victorian Gothic. And yellow everywhere. Jasmine. Forsythia. Barberry. She knew she should have stayed in London at Easter. And she looked out at the familiar lane and against her will remembered Tom in New York. What a failure, when the whole point was not to think of Tom.

That evening, Maurice was entirely content. No students. Reports filed. The last few notes to dilatory supervisors. Just a quiet sherry in his own room, with the light going. Waiting for Hall. He could just see the gold hands of the College clock, slowly turning. Except a most irritating letter from his mother that morning had roused her voice in his head.

—I'm always surprised at what you find to spend your money *on*, Maurice.

—Things, Mother.

—You don't even have a decent car.

—I don't really need a car at all.

—You are becoming quite selfish as you grow older. Bachelors do, I suppose. It's very disappointing.

Maurice's mother had a strong preference for objects that moved. Or did complicated tasks. Preferably, *new* objects. Maurice liked to take his time over all purchases. When he wanted a bookcase, he went to Saffron Walden, or Swaffham to an auction at some big house. And made a day of it. That's where he'd picked up the decanter that so much angered her.

—I think you're very extravagant.

—It's Georgian.

—And a snob too. Much you care about what happens to ordinary people. This government is tryng to starve the older generation to death. No heart. No compassion. I can't even afford a packet of fags. My son collects glass.

Maurice and Jenny collided for the first time as they hurried along the stone corridor towards Hall.

—Hello. Is this the way to the Combination Room? Jenny asked.

—Too late for sherry, I'd have thought. Are you a wife? he replied.

—What?

—Somebody's guest?

—I'm Professor Michaelson from Columbia. How do you do?

—Gracious me.

They entered the Hall just in time to hear the Master saying:

—Benedictus Benedicat.

—Hardly seems worth saying grace, with so few of us, Jenny murmured to him as the chairs scraped back, and the High Table sat down.

—Our customs are still a little behind your fashions I'm glad to say. I expect you have abandoned grace altogether, said Maurice gruffly.

—You can't have travelled in the Middle West.

—I've never wanted to visit any part of the United States, said Maurice complacently.

Jenny was stung.

—And what is your discipline, may I ask?

—Medieval History.

—The Church side, naturally?

—Early Church. Latin tradition of monastic transmission. That kind of thing. Won't be of any interest to you. What about you? One of these new-fangled structuralists, I suppose?

—Our fields relate, actually, said Jenny demurely. Only I think we probably take a rather different view of that monastic tradition of yours. I'm an Arabist.

—Never much been interested in that bit of the world.

—Come on, you can't ignore the Arab contribution to the Renaissance, can you? I mean, your Christians didn't even have the books until later, did they? Think of the luck of a Moslem like Avicenna. There he was with a whole library of Aristotle, Greek medicine and mathematics round him in Bukhara, and what did the Christian West have? A few poets, Latin schoolmasters and the Church fathers.

—That's rather . . .

—What's more, they didn't always let in the poets. Think of St Odo on Virgil.

—You're a very opinionated young woman. I am, of course, aware of all these arguments.

A young waiter, probably a student Jenny thought, was trying to remove Maurice's bowl unsuccessfully.

—The survival of the Church was at stake, young woman. There were pagans on every side.

—I know all that.

Her voice was cool and amused. Maurice's own voice rose to a yelp as he replied:

—I don't want to hear all over again about the beginnings of scientific thought. I've often thought that without Christian faith it's impossible to understand medieval history.

—Ooh.

In his irritation his gowned shoulder caught the silver platter of courgettes now poised at his ear by the same uncertain adolescent hand.

—Clumsy idiot.

—Sorry, sir.

—If the College *will* employ unskilled staff.

—You jogged my arm, sir, the boy protested.

—Do stop patting me.

—I was only trying to help.

—Don't, said Maurice curtly.

—How appallingly rude! Jenny tried to intervene.

But Maurice misunderstood.

—Yes.

—I meant *you*. Jenny clarified the situation. There was a terrifying pause, and then a young man from across the table made an effort to restore calm.

—Seen *The Times* today, Maurice? Old Age Pensioners have found a good racket. Selling barbiturates at so much a pill. To teenagers. How about that for a way of recycling inflation?

—Don't read the papers, said Maurice, huffily.

—No time?

—No patience, young lady. For all that liberal cant. It takes some time, I suppose. To understand what's happening in England now.

—The economic crisis, do you mean? Or bombs? Ireland?

—I'm talking about moral collapse, said Maurice. Then he stood and left without a smile.

—What a *monster*, Jenny stared after him.

—Oh no. You can't hate old Maurice, protested her neighbour.

—Why not? she asked sharply.

—World changing around him, you see. A lost soul. And this is where he lives, you know, College.

—Well, that's his choice, I expect.

Back in his own familiar room, Maurice was by no means at ease with the task he had set himself that evening.

He was trying to reply to his mother's letter, but even as he read over what he had written, he could feel his blood prickle with anger as he recalled his dinner encounter.

Dear Mother, Of course I understand your delicate situation in these troubled times though I shall never share your political attitudes as you know . . .

He groaned aloud as he read the letter over. What can I really say to the old slut? he wondered. Perhaps two hundred and fifty pounds would do it?

I wish you would not concern yourself over my matrimonial situation. Few of my friends enjoy simple homely pleasures as I do, or have anything like so orderly and structured a life.

His mind wandered uncomfortably again. That American bitch. I must have been in Norfolk when they put her Fellowship through. Insolent eyes she has. He crumpled the first draft of his letter.

Dear Mother, Perhaps we should try and put your financial affairs in some kind of order. I don't want to sound like Father, but perhaps you should put an end to your habit of using charge accounts. It would take a financial genius, which you are not, to calculate how you are doing . . .

The next day found Jenny, uncertainly, at the porter's lodge. She, too, had troubles.

—Good morning Miss.

—Yes, isn't it? She said, rather flatly. I'm just going to take a walk round town. Will there be any shops open?

—Good Friday? *Well*. The food shops are open, if you need to stock in. But the others make their own minds up. Some do, some don't.

—I don't suppose there's been a message for me, has there? she asked, just a shade too casually. The porter looked doubtful.

—Well, I'll see.

He saw.

—No. Thought not.

—Perhaps there's another post today? Well, if anyone *phones* or anything, would you say I'll be back for lunch? There *is* a College lunch, isn't there?

—I wouldn't have thought so; but I'll check for you, if you like.

—Never mind. Thanks.

She turned away, reflecting upon the multiplicity of her mistakes. She could see her return to Cambridge was not going to be an idyll. They'd sandblasted Rose Crescent. Looked like a smart bit of Florence with leather shops stuck in the wall. Memories teased her. Who used to live over that restaurant? She remembered. There was a party, and she was the only one who knew how to heat up cannabis resin on a pin. She supposed everyone had to come through all that, by now. Lost in thought, she was astonished to find a male hand on her arm.

—Well, you've arrived. Wonderful. You remember my wife don't you?

Jenny looked at two strangers. The other woman spoke first.

—Good heavens, Jenny Michaelson, isn't it?

—Sybil? Jenny enquired uncertainly.

—Of course. Well, I just wish you'd told me you and Tom were coming before Easter, we could have had some kind of supper party for you both; now we're just off to France.

Jenny said dourly:

—I'm not here with Tom. How are you, anyway.

—Frightful, said Sybil: we're moving house. You can't imagine how exhausting it is, showing people up and downstairs all day long. I just wonder if it's all worth it for the extra space. Do you still live in the same apartment?

—Tom does, said Jenny: I've moved out somewhere less fashionable.

—Forgive me, I didn't know. Oh, dear, said Sybil, and you seemed so happy together.

—*I* was happy together. Tom wasn't, said Jenny, so, don't let me hold you up if you're shopping for last minute things.

Sybil sounded relieved.

—Well, I'm afraid the shops *will* close on us, if you wouldn't think me terribly rude.

And now, against her will, the reasons for her presence in this desolate city, this desert of absence, presented themselves to Jenny's unwilling mind. Tom's voice. Her own rejoinders.

—Why couldn't you share the things I like to do? You don't want to do anything active. I can't see why that is. Plenty of academic women like to ski or learn to sail. You don't seem to want any fun.

—But I'm no good on skis. You know that. And not everyone likes the Adirondacs in winter. It's still winter in April, Tom.

—The snow is part of the adventure.

—I remember. And the trees up there. They look as if they've been cursed. Every year. Grey and withered. I can never believe they'll go green.

—We'll be having a sabbatical. A good log fire at night, a bit of shooting during the day . . .

—I hate guns.

—Listen, you are just goddamn *dull*. I know a lot of people ready and willing *tomorrow* to fly off and share a jar of Jack Daniels in my cabin. Excited to. Eager.

—I'd rather have a week in the sun, Jenny had roused herself to mild mutiny.

—Toad. Well, I'm not going alone. Why should I go alone? I could have married someone who shared my world. If that's what you want, I'll leave you in peace. I just hope you enjoy *that*. Let you get on with whatever you do. I hope you like it.

Jenny felt tears sting her eyes. She had walked down Garret Hostel Lane and now was looking over the new bridge into the silver water of the Cam and trying to like it. But it was hopeless. She knew what she'd have to do was go back and read a book. And even then she'd probably have Tom's voice in her head all week.

At the porter's lodge, she was signalled to, eagerly.

—Professor Michaelson.

—Yes?

—There's a cable for you. International.

Thanks, Jenny said shakily.

Here you are, he said importantly.

But it wasn't important. Only the Adirondacs address and some phone number nearby.

—I see, she smiled, dully.

—Not bad news, I hope? said the porter, who had begun to respond almost like a human being: I found out the College schedule for meals if you want to see it.

—Oh it doesn't matter. Doesn't matter. Thank you, I won't bother now.

Maurice made a habit of attending Evensong in chapel, and that evening he had an enormous need for everything to be just as it always had been, even though he found his concentration drifting away from the hymnal towards his mother, who had always said she couldn't quite believe in God. In his view, she was just being lazy. He could never remember going to church much until he was up at College. Since then it had been a great solace. He knew some people had religion confused with Third World poverty, and politics, but that was the fault of the clergy. Infiltrated, he often thought. Certainly not doing their pastoral duty.

Afterwards, he thought he would have a word with the Chaplain.

—Nice to see you here again. Music's good this year, isn't it?

—I'm more or less tone deaf, Maurice confessed, in what was intended as jocular exaggeration.

—What a dreadful affliction.

—But you're doing a fine job. Godless age this, your devotion is a great comfort.

The praise seemed to embarrass the Chaplain.

—Well, I think the last coda could have been . . .

—Christian devotion, I mean. Will you take a brandy with me in the Combination Room?

—I'm afraid I promised my wife . . .

Maurice sighed.

—I can remember when there was a real community of bachelor Fellows. These days . . .

—Quite. Well, I'll be running along. The Chaplain tapped a young boy on the shoulder: Hey, have you got a lift with that cello?

Maurice was appalled. The Chaplain was a perfectly amiable man, but somehow his style made Maurice more than usually restless. So that evening, because he didn't want to go straight back to his room, he took a short walk through Clare. He stood a long while. Just stood on a bridge. Not watching anything. Just listening to the water. Before he decided he might as well go back to the Common Room.

There, to his astonishment and horror, he found he was not alone.

—Oh, I do beg your pardon. I didn't know you were here.

Jenny had evidently had a brandy or two before him.

—I thought I'd look at the papers. Found I was all alone. Strangely silent in here. Perhaps you will join me in a brandy?

—Thank you, no, said Maurice, drawing away: I'm just looking for the *Church Times* myself.

—Well here it is. Funny, I've just been reading about Ulster in it. Aren't they in a knot?

Maurice looked at the confused pages.

—You've messed it up, he said: Horribly. *Look* what you've done. *All* the papers. Why on earth do women have to do that? Good heavens. I hope you aren't going to cry.

Jenny sniffed, with the same hope:—I was down anyway. Do you have to look so fierce? The perfectly ordered male.

—I try not to fritter my time away.

—You'd never admit it, even it you did, would you? It's not part of the ethic is it? You can't imagine being a failure. It's not allowed. Not in Cambridge. To lose out. Can you imagine asking anyone for help?

—Can't say I ever felt the need.

—I wonder what you were like as a young boy, Jenny

214

shouted: a pimply little beast probably. No wonder you've turned out such a pig.

There was an awkward pause. Then, to her surprise, Maurice replied mildly enough:

—I believe you're married to Tom Dawson. He's been very successful, I hear. Surprising, I thought.

—I don't want to talk about Tom. We've split up and that's why I'm here.

—Dear me.

—To work instead of brooding. Oh, go away. You've no idea what I'm talking about, you – you old monk!

—I see you've been drinking a great deal, said Maurice.

—Oh yes. I have. Drinking, and taking a good many Mogadon. *Not* trying to do myself an *injury*. Don't worry. Simply *trying*. To get through the night. I don't supposed a nice self-contained gentleman like you has that kind of trouble.

In the silence, the College clock sounded the quarter hour.

—I know all about insomnia, as a matter of fact, said Maurice with unexpected kindness. I'd say you'd overplayed the brandy. Here. What you need is a walk. I've got a coat hanging over here. Slip it on. That's a good girl.

—It's too big for me.

—Cold out. Belt it up. That's right. Now. We'll take a walk. She followed meekly.

—Mind the Library door. This way.

—Starlight.

—Yes.

—No moon.

There were water noises in the night outside, as their two pairs of feet scrunched into the gravel. For a while they walked in silence, which Jenny broke:

—I'd have thought you'd get into your righteous little bed easily enough. What do you get insomnia about?

—Well. I always wanted to be left alone, you know. All my life. First by my father. Then by my mother. I *thought* I loved my mother until I had to put up with her. And then at last I got away from everyone and I *was* on my own.

—And?

—That's how I am.

—Do you like it? Jenny risked the question, even as she felt his arm stiffen.

—Order. That's what I wanted. After my mother's house, anyone would crave it, he replied quietly.

—I've never been very interested in being tidy, exclaimed Jenny.

—Tidiness isn't the point. It's having some kind of organized world. Well. In answer to your question. I've never minded living on my own.

—How extraordinary! I'm terrified of it. I suppose that's why I took my sabbatical here. Not to be alone in New York. Oh, I can see what you are thinking; but it isn't violence I was afraid of. It was *just* being alone that scared me. Listening to the silence, and looking into the room. Perhaps that's why people keep dogs. Just to confirm they exist.

Maurice laughed.

—Tell me about your father. Was he an academic?

—Not he. Ex-army; then failed grocer.

—Did you hate him? she asked, sympathetically.

—Well. I hated his bitter ways, and the ways he talked to Mother. Until he died. Then I had to run things, and I learnt to sympathize. Are you feeling better?

—Well, yes. Now you ask. You're being very kind.

—I often walk round the grounds at night. Stand here a moment. Do you like that smell?

—I'm so puffed up with all this crying my membranes can't distinguish *anything*. Wait. It's very heavy and sweet.

—Lilac, he said.

—White lilac. Lovely.

And as they walked on, there was something new in the way Maurice supported her.

—Tell me more about yourself, Jenny encouraged him.

—Well. You know that Henry James story about the man who was afraid of the Beast in the jungle? Who thought all his life something terrible was going to happen to him? And

216

nothing did? Well, I'm like that, really. Nothing much happened to me at all.

Jenny smiled.

—Weren't you ever in love? Well, you're wrong to grieve over that. Doesn't do you any good, believe me. All you need are friends, good friends. And sex, OK. Not love. And certainly not marriage.

—I'd no idea marriage was so passionte, Maurice returned.

—That's it. It shouldn't be. It's some modern rubbishy idea, that it should be anything more than a bit of comfort and loyalty. But sometimes someone asks you to turn to them, and you do; and then if they move away, even a little, it hurts.

He blinked like a night animal.

—You don't know what I'm talking about, do you? she concluded.

—I don't suppose anyone ever turned to me like that.

—Would you want them to?

—Yes. I don't know. It's not likely, is it?

—Let me look at you. Well. You've got a good, generous mouth. Surprising, that, I never looked before. Let me feel the shape of your cheek. I can't see in this light. There.

She kissed him.

Maurice was shaken.

—Why did you do that?

—You looked as if you wanted me to. Shall we go on walking? said Jenny demurely.

—No. That is. No. Let's just stand here a moment.

The next morning, Jenny woke up with birdsong in her ears. Must have been very early. And the weather had changed. There was one bird very loud and clear; might have been a blackbird. A very sharp, pure note. Piercing. She felt very calm. There was an odd silence in her head. Even Tom's voice had disappeared.

For the life of him, Maurice could never remember what he did that morning. Did he go to the University Library? Lie in bed? Unlikely. He was always up at six. But then, it wasn't an

217

ordinary day. For all he knew he might have slept until ten-thirty. Anyway, absolutely the first thing he could remember was arranging an evening meal for the two of them. That and the sunshine. The sun came in the window all the while he was talking. Hot sunshine. On his bare skin. He must have been standing at the window in his pyjamas.

On the telephone he spoke with a brusque authority:

—And make sure the Stilton is ripe. Ah, while I think of it. Have you a bottle of Barsac? Yes, the one we had at the last Feast.

He could hardly wait for the evening.

—Welcome, he said at last, Mozart on the turntable, and his heart racing.

—My goodness, Maurice. Do you always live like this? You said a simple cold snack.

—And so it is, said Maurice, delighted.

—Beeswax candles.

—And College candlesticks. It's easy really. Can I take your coat? Have a glass of wine.

—Well. All this splendour.

—Try this first. Smoked roe. Do you know, I've been reading your book all morning? Sensitive, but I wanted to argue with you furiously all the way through.

—Your neighbour at table explained it was almost a College rule. Not to talk seriously over food.

—Now don't tease me. What shall we drink to?

—The glories of the Past?

He was pleased with the suggestion.

—Yes, this rubbishy age. Do you realize how this age is going to look to people living after us? Meretricious. They aren't going to envy us living in this age, I can tell you.

—So when was it good?

—People scrabbling after fame. Where are the fine minds of this age? The decent human endeavour?

—Some people still believe in the possibility.

—Like that Tom of yours no doubt. I always thought him a

218

lout, you know. It's only fair to say.

—No, well, he doesn't admire what *you* call civilization. It's another discipline.

—I meant humanly civilized, said Maurice gruffly.

—I don't want to talk about that. You know, *this* is a wonderful room, said Jenny, rising briskly.

—Is it? said Maurice, with a certain wistfulness. Don't you think it's rather heavy. The panelling?

—I learnt to like dark wood in California where they have too much sun.

—You didn't say you were from the West Coast. Were you happy there?

—I can't really remember, it's so long ago. I think I was a happy child.

—You mean your parents didn't quarrel?

—Never. I don't know why. It wasn't a very good preparation for contemporary life, was it?

—I can't see how someone like you ever came to marry . . .

—Please.

—He *was* my contemporary, you know. He cared about nothing but success. Getting his name on as many papers as possible.

—Oh, don't grudge him his energy, Jenny said gently. He loved to make everyone a present of it. That's how he gave me New York.

—How do you mean?

—Well, he walked me south of Houston Street one day, over rubble and waste land, and there were the seagulls overhead and salt in the air and he wouldn't let me turn round. Until he said NOW. And then. Rising up above like a huge glass boat were all the buildings of the city. Their windows blind to protect their occupants against the sun. And it was like a fairytale, shining boat. I could never have beaten my way into it, but he had no problem.

—But you had no need. Jenny . . .

—And now, I must go. You've been terribly kind. I'm glad you forgive me my maverick views . . .

219

—It's early yet, he risked.

—I'm tired, though.

—Of course. I'm sorry, said Maurice, almost visibly drawing away.

—It's been a lovely evening.

—And I'm not a monster?

—Of course not. Who told you that?

Maurice laughed.

—Will you come for a walk in the morning? We could look at the crocuses. They're late this year.

—All right. I love the way they come out of the earth whatever kind of weather it is.

—Later on it's all Japanese tourists. Waddling about and peering in at us.

He opened the door, and then could not resist pursuing her.

—Wait. I was thinking. You know I've got a little cottage. Nothing very grand, of course, but comfortable. In Norfolk. About two hours' drive. If you wanted to . . .

—Maurice. There's no need to be so kind just because you're sorry for me. I'm tougher than I look.

And off she stepped into the night. She left Maurice in a turmoil. All night he tried to make a real list with the pros and cons on each side. Of course, he was afraid. He knew the sensible thing was to say nothing at all, pretend nothing had happened. And yet, even the word *matrimony* no longer sounded quite so forbiddingly domestic as it once had. There was no question of sleep. He couldn't even bring himself to lie down. A glimpse of himself in the mirror looked gaunt and haggard. Like a stranger.

Afterwards, Jenny blamed herself. How badly she had behaved, since she knew exactly what was going on. And yet, she had skipped off down that stone passage like a young girl, knowing exactly what he meant, and not giving him a chance to say it.

And with a funny kind of prescience she *knew*. The first evening she had managed to escape from needing Tom had returned an advantage to her. And her new confidence seemed to have reached across and reminded him of her existence, at a remote unthinkable distance. Reminded him she existed, was still young, could act for herself and not just wait for him.

As she remembered it, she was certain even *before* she opened the door of her room, even before she put on the light, that there would be a yellow envelope on the floor. A cable. And she knew what it said even before she opened it, and the words she had been waiting for didn't touch her at all.

The next morning the College served breakfast. Not quite as grand as an Oxford college, but she enjoyed it, ate heartily, and felt happier than she had in months for no reason at all. But there was Maurice, beaming and nervous.

Suddenly, with anxiety, she remembered their promised walk. She could hardly refuse.

He studied her face as soon as they were outside.

—I walked around all night waiting for a chance to say this. But your face has changed.

—Yes.

—I suppose you've heard from Tom.

—He's coming over. We may go away for a while.

—I see.

—Oh don't keep saying that. You don't know anything about me, she said crossly.

—Perhaps. But I must say, it's surprisingly painful.

—What do you mean?

—For a late developer like me. To wake up.

Maurice bowed stiffly, and made an effort at dignity that took all his courage.

Much later, he tried to feel he had been lucky. After all, there was some hidden guiding hand in the affairs of men. Who knows what a terrifying suburban life he might have been leading? Out in Cherry Hinton, worrying about the mortgage. No cellar. No company. Little sticky-fingered children pulling at his clothes. And Jenny weeping. Women always weep at you, he told himself.

And yet.

It wasn't easy.

It wasn't easy to forget.

Jenny, too, remembered. She could have been radiantly happy when Tom came back to her, but she wasn't. Oh, she didn't foul it up or anything, and she had enough sense not to tell him what was bothering her.

The strangest thing of all was that, apart from the time she kissed him in the garden, Maurice had never even touched her.

JONATHAN STEFFEN

Meeting the Majors

If you have ever had qualms about making use of an introduction, read on.

Some years ago I visited Berlin. I had a rucksack, and a typewriter, and a burning ambition to become the Christopher Isherwood of the eighties. I also had one address, that of a British army officer stationed in Berlin whom I shall call Major Savory. I had been given his address by a third party, likewise unknown to me, whose existence was subsequently to prove a complete mystery to the major and an acute embarrassment to myself. This mysterious third party – of whose existence I still have my doubts to this day – was a colonel in the Greenjackets by the name of Broughton. Colonel Broughton was, in theory at least, a friend of Major Savory's. He was also a vague acquaintance of my uncle's. On hearing from my uncle that I was going to Berlin, the colonel had exclaimed, 'Oh, but he must look up St John and Camilla Savory!' – and promptly scribbled down their address and phone number on a piece of paper. He handed my uncle the piece of paper, promising to drop the Savorys a line to let them known that I was coming to Berlin; my uncle passed it on to me; and I took it all the way to Berlin Zoo Station, guarding it as jealously as my passport with its yellow-and-green East German stamp. On arriving in Berlin, therefore, one of my first acts was to telephone the Savorys. The result was one of the most excruciatingly interesting evenings I have ever had, an experience which really put the grist in the well-worn phrase about the writer's mill.

The telephone conversation did not go well. It was Mrs

Savory who answered the phone; and Mrs Savory had never heard of me. This might not have mattered had I been able to remember the name of the colonel in the Greenjackets who had given me the Savorys' address; but right at that moment I couldn't. All I could tell her with any degree of certainty was that there *was* a colonel in the Greenjackets whose name probably, but not definitely, began with a B; that this colonel had given me the Savorys' address and *urged* me to get in contact with them (I perhaps overstressed this point); and that the colonel had *definitely* promised to write to the Savorys to warn them of my impending visit. Mrs Savory handled these anecdotal intricacies with aplomb. Although audibly taken aback, she nevertheless reacted with impeccable politeness, propping up her falling intonation with a plethora of 'supers', 'wonderfuls' and 'lovelys', and inviting me to dinner in a couple of days' time. I was to 'come scruffy', and St John and she would be 'absolutely delighted' to see me.

I put down the receiver feeling like a cross between a beggar and a bully. I had been prepared for the possibility of the Savorys' being away from Berlin; prepared for the possibility of their being too busy to see me; but nothing had prepared me for this. I had, in effect, just invited myself to dinner with a set of complete strangers. I had foisted myself upon them. I had conned my way into their good graces. I had, not to put too fine a point on it, shoved my great big foot in their door, and there it was now, stuck fast, and looking every bit the size thirteen it was.

Standing in the telephone booth, I made a silent and solemn vow never again to act upon any sort of introduction whatsoever.

However, the damage was done now, and I had no option but to turn up to dinner. To back out at this stage would be unbearably embarrassing, and the Savorys for their part couldn't cancel the arrangement because I had forgotten to give Mrs Savory the telephone number of the hotel at which I was staying. I was committed, they were committed, and there was no way out on either side. If I am to be completely honest, though, I must confess that my resignation was not entirely unmixed with *Realpolitik*. Cheap as my hotel was, it was a deal too expensive for me, and I knew that I wouldn'tbe able to stay there for very long. I wanted to stay in Berlin as long as possible; and that meant, of course, renting a room. The Savorys might just conceivably know of someone with a room to let; and even if they didn't, they might at least be able to advise me as to how best to go about finding one. Besides which – and here the 'I am a camera' fantasy comes into play, as it did so often during those weeks in Berlin – the Savorys lived in a world to which I would normally have no access whatsoever; and an encounter with this world, however fleeting, should be all grist for my (as yet, totally empty) mill. I decided to put a brave face on it, persuade the Savorys that I was in fact possessed of some manners, and do my best not to spill wine on their undoubtedly white tablecloth.

I had been invited for seven-thirty, which I took to mean a quarter to eight. Seven-thirty saw me getting off the bus at the Scholzplatz: seven-thirty-five saw me in front of the Savorys' house. Seven-forty saw me back at the Scholzplatz, studying timetables and contemplating a last-minute retreat; and a quarter to eight saw me back at the Savorys' front door with my finger on the bell.

'Camilla Savory,' said my hostess, inclining her head slightly and extending a hand like a dry leaf. 'Come in, do, you're just on time.'

I took Mrs Savory's hand, shook it much too hard, and had the impression that I was as it were pushing her back across her own threshold.

'It's Nicholas, isn't it?' she asked, disengaging her hand.

'Jonathan,' I corrected her.

'Of course, how silly of me,'said Mrs Savory. 'Shall I take your coat?'

She was referring to my leather jacket. It was brand new, very expensive, and it gave me an obscure feeling of strength.

'I think I'd rather keep it on for the moment, if you don't mind,' I said.

Mrs Savory smiled a smile of all suavity.

'As you wish,' she said. 'Go on through and St John will get you a drink.'

I thanked her and stepped through a cool cloud of powder into the sitting-room.

It was a typical army house: foursquare, white, and sturdily plush. One felt the whole thing could be dismantled in a day, shipped off in boxes, and reassembled somewhere else. I noticed thick red velvet curtains, a few regimental mementoes, a general absence of clutter. Three men and two women stood in the sitting-room, the men drinking heavily watered whiskies and the women holding full glasses of sherry. The men shouted at each other while the women smiled and watched their sherry glasses, turning the bracelets on their wrists from time to time. I stood in the doorway for a few seconds until the oldest of the three men, noticing me, turned and broke away from the group.

'Come in, come in,' he called, approaching to within two feet of me. 'St John Savory.' He held out a hand which I missed the first time and caught the second. 'You're . . . ?'

'Jonathan.'

'Jonathan what?' asked one of the other men.

'Jonathan Steffen.'

'Great,' said Major Savory. He brushed a thick flat lock of hair off his forehead and put his hands in his pockets. 'I'm St John, call me St John, we're all majors here. This is Patrick, Donald, Fenella and Felicity. Confusing, isn't it? What can I get you to drink?'

I said that a whisky would go down very well.

'With Perrier?'

I was about to say 'without', but the major was already on his way to the door. I smiled at the wallpaper and readjusted my tie.

'So,' said the major who had asked after my surname, 'how d'you come to know St John and Camilla? I'm Patrick Donald, by the way, this is Donald Jackson, it's awfully confusing.'

'Well, I don't know them, actually,' I said. 'I was given their address by a friend of my uncle's who's a colonel in the

226

Greenjackets.'

'Your uncle's in the Greenjackets?'

'No, my uncle's friend is in the Greenjackets.'

'Aha,' said Major Donald. 'Terrific. And what brings you to Berlin, then?'

'Curiosity,' I said. I had been meditating this answer all day.

'It's a fascinating city, absolutely fascinating city,' said Major Donald. 'Great for a young chap to come to Berlin, isn't it, Donald?'

Everyone turned to look at Major Jackson, who was the shortest of the majors, and the slightest.

'Marvellous,' he said, and took another sip of whisky.

'What do you do?' asked one of the women, blinking as she spoke and placing great emphasis on the second 'do'.

'I write,' I said, with an involuntary blink.

'This chap's a writer, St John,' said Major Donald.

'Splendid,' said Major Savory, who had just returned with my whisky-and-Perrier. 'What does he write about?'

'What do you write about?' asked Major Donald. 'Really, St John, you could ask him the question yourself.'

'At the moment,' I said, with a slight clearing of the throat, 'I'm working on a retelling of the story of Troilus and Cressida.'

There was a silence. Not a pause, but actually a silence.

'Troilus and Cressida . . . ' Major Donald scratched his Adam's apple. 'Out of my province, I'm afraid. I stick at John le Carré.'

'Would anyone care for a smoked oyster?' asked Mrs Savory, sliding to the rescue with a plate.

I took a smoked oyster and retreated to the armchair Mrs Savory indicated. The conversation switched to polo ponies and officers' salaries. The two seemed intimately related. Major Savory told a long and involved story about the polo-players and parachutists of a certain regiment stationed in Germany, both of which groups had wished to use the same grounds for their practice-sessions on a particular Saturday afternoon. The story seemed to go on forever, not least because of constant interruptions on the part of Major Donald, but at least it wound up with a parachutist landing in the middle of a polo match and one of the team captains threatening to knock his head off with a polo mallet if he ever did it again. This was also intimately related to the cost of polo ponies. Major Savory seemed to hold sway most of the time, but it was Major Donald who shouted the loudest, throwing smoked oysters into his mouth like peanuts and then spitting a good part of them out on to the carpet. 'Sorry, Camilla, sorry,' he would say as he bent down and scrubbed the carpet with his hand. Mrs Savory smiled and nodded. It was only after some while that I noticed that all the majors seemed to be wearing exactly the same make of pullover.

Mrs Savory called everyone to dinner. The men threw down the last of their whiskies and the women placed their half-drunk sherries on the sideboard. I found myself seated between Major and Mrs Savory, and faced with a plateful of gambas. I spent a long time tucking in my napkin and studying techniques before nonchalantly picking up my first one.

'So,' said Major Savory, twisting the head off a gamba and making little circles with it in the air, 'how is it exactly we know you?'

'Colonel Broughton in the Greenjackets is a friend of my uncle's,' I said (I had remembered his name only that morning); 'and when he heard that I was coming to Berlin he gave me your address and suggested that I look you up. He promised to write ahead and let you know that I was coming.'

'We've been through this, St John,' said Mrs Savory.

'Broughton, Broughton . . . ?' mused the major, crunching audibly. 'Do you know a Broughton in the Greenjackets, Don?'

'There's a Reggie Brampton,' said Major Jackson.

'He doesn't mean Colin Houghton in the Guards, does he?' offered Major Donald.

'You don't mean Colin Houghton in the Guards, do you?' Major Savory asked.

I shook my head.

'Beats me,' the major said. 'Anyway, you're here now. So what are your plans?'

'Are you going to write about Berlin?' spat Major Donald.

'I might do,' I said. 'It would depend.'

'On what?' asked Major Donald, helping himself to more wine.

'On what happened.'

'Of course, you've got to know your cities,' said Major Savory. 'Take that chap who wrote *The Alexandria Quartet*, what's his name now, Gerald Durrell, he really knew the place like the back of his hand. He'd really done his homework, hadn't he?'

'How do you find it, being stationed in Berlin?' I asked, with a wave of a gamba.

'Well, of course, it's terrific,' said Major Savory, 'it's a terrific life. Most exciting city in Europe, if you ask me. Wouldn't you say so, Patrick?'

'I wouldn't be anywhere else,' Major Donald replied. 'The rest of Germany's boring, frankly, but you've got everything in Berlin. And you've got this marvellous standard of living, of course.'

'And what about when the tanks come rolling in?' I asked, handing my plate to Mrs Savory, who was clearing away the first course. Three immaculate gambas lolled among the debris.

'Well, they won't,' said Major Savory. His face was blank and he propped his chin on the back of his folded palms.

'Oh, come on, St John, they must,' said Major Donald.

'Well, of course, they will,' said Major Savory, 'but not for a good while yet. Not while we're stationed here, anyway. We've only got two more years, of course.'

'Then back to bloody Blighty,' said Major Donald.

'St John's in tanks,' said Mrs Savory, as she brought in the plates for the next course. 'He's always knocking trees down.'

'Christ, yes,' said Major Savory. 'Only the other day, you know Patrick, we knocked out another during the rehearsal. The Germans went bananas, absolutely bloody bananas.'

'Well, they always do, don't they?' said Major Donald. 'I have hell to pay with my chaps, they can't see the road for the trees.'

Everybody laughed, and the conversation petered out as Major Savory carved. When it picked up again it switched to retrievers for a while, then back to polo once more.

Over dessert Mrs Savory asked me: 'Have you published anything?'

'One or two pieces,' I replied. 'In literary magazines.' My 'one or two' in fact meant 'one'. The printing error on page sixteen still caused me pain.

'I don't suppose I would have heard of them?'

'Probably not.'

'Of course it's the women's magazines that pay a lot of money, isn't it?'

'Hit 'em with a romance every time,' said Major Donald. 'Zonk – between the eyes. You can't go wrong.'

'I'd write pornography if I was you,' said Major Savory. 'That's where the money is.'

'*I'd* write pornography, but I haven't got the bloody imagination,' put in Major Donald. 'Eh, Fenella?' He kicked his wife under the table and snorted.

'Returning to Berlin, though,' I said, beginning to warm to my role as Observer of the Contemporary Scene, 'what do the Germans think of the army here?'

'Oh, come on, Fenella,' said Major Donald, stretching across the table and trying to catch his wife's hand. 'Come on, Frumps.'

'Shut up, Patrick, he's trying to be serious,' said Major Jackson. 'It's a serious question.'

'Sorry.'

'Well, it depends which Germans you're talking about,' said Major Savory. 'The old ones like us and the young ones don't.'

'Why's that?'

'Well, the older generation are shit-scared of the Russians and the younger generation haven't got the sense to be shit-scared of them.' Major Savory sat forward in his chair. 'You see,' he went on, 'the Germans aren't allowed to have a standing army in Berlin – that's why the Four Powers are here. The East Germans break that agreement, of course, because

230

they have soldiers manning the Wall, but there's no military service in West Berlin, it's the only place in West Germany where you don't have to do it. So all the lefties and bolshies and general drop-outs come here.'

'I seem to remember hearing that there were a lot of squatters here.'

'That's right, there are. They have demonstrations and they shout a lot of bloody nonsense, of course, but they're not really dangerous. I mean, a few bricks get thrown at the riot police from time to time, but they're not really violent. If they were violent' – the major scratched his chin in search of a conclusion – 'If they were violent, well, they'd be in the army.'

'They want us out, of course,' said Major Donald, 'but if we left they'd be knee-deep in Russians, and they know it.'

'How long can it last, then?' I asked.

'Not long,' said Major Donald, tipping back his chair and rocking in it.

'Of course it'll last,' said Major Jackson, a touch of scorn in his voice.

'It won't, Don.'

'It will.'

'It won't!' Major Donald brought his hand down on the table. 'The unification of Germany caused the first two world wars and it'll cause the next one.'

'Rubbish!' said Major Jackson. He turned to me. Calmly, almost urbanely, he said, 'If there were to be a flashpoint somewhere else then of course Berlin would be overrun in a second and we couldn't hold it. West Berlin, I mean. But it wouldn't start here.'

'Look, Don,' said Major Donald, 'I didn't specialize in modern German history at Oxford for nothing. The unification of . . . '

'You didn't specialize in modern German history at Oxford,' said Major Jackson, 'you played rugger.'

'And cricket!' said Major Donald, 'and cricket!' He chortled, rocking harder in his chair. 'But I still maintain that the – '

'We all know what you maintain,' said Major Savory, 'stop

being a bore.'

'Well, how much do you want to bet?' asked Major Donald.

'I don't want to bet,' said Major Jackson.

'No, come on, how much do you want to bet? A tenner?'

'All right, then, a tenner, but you're talking through your hat.'

'I think the coffee's ready,' said Mrs Savory.

We adjourned to the sitting-room. Mrs Savory went round with the coffee, Major Savory with the liqueurs. Major Donald sat at his wife's feet and played with her knees. Major Jackson twiddled his thumbs. Mrs Jackson wore the look of glazed interest she had worn all evening.

'So how long d'you think you'll be staying in Berlin?' Major Savory asked me.

'I don't know,' I said, it depends how the money goes.' In a voice which seemed to be coming out of a cassette recorder, I added: 'I'd like to find a room to rent if I could.'

'Damned expensive city,' said the major. 'You get through the shekels like a dose of salts. No, that's not right . . . '

'Where are you living at the moment?' asked Mrs Savory.

'I'm staying at a hotel in the Mommsenstrasse.'

'Oh, that's lovely,' she said. 'So central.'

'Yes, it's very central,' I said.

There was a pause. As if prompted, Mrs Savory said: 'We'd offer to put you up, of course, but unfortunately army regulations forbid it. Don't they, St John?'

''Fraid so,' said Major Savory.

'Well, it's kind of you to – '

'What you want,' said Major Savory, crossing his legs and leaning back in his armchair, 'what you *want*, is to get shacked up with a German girl. Don't you think, Patrick?'

'Sorry, St John,' Major Donald said, 'I thought you were talking about me for a second.' He punched his wife and grinned. 'Yes, yes, of course.'

'Then you'd have your rent and food and everything,' continued Major Savory. 'D'you speak German?'

'I'm afraid I don't.'

232

'Well, you could learn a bit of German as well. Although they all speak English here, there's not much point unless you're staying for a while.'

'Yes,' I agreed, 'that would be ideal.' I sniffed my cognac.

'But if we hear of anything going,' said Mrs Savory, 'we'll give you a ring. I mean, some of our German friends might have a room to let, or something.'

'That's very kind of you,' I said, in the full knowledge that Mrs Savory didn't have my telephone number.

'We'll ask, anyway,' said Mrs Savory, with one of her exquisitely meaningless smiles.

'Thank you very much,' I said, returning her smile with redoubled meaninglessness.

Another pause. I looked at my watch. It was just about late enough to leave.

'Well,' I said, 'I think I'd better be off now. I'd like to do a bit more work before going to bed.'

'Burning the midnight oil, eh?' said Major Savory.

'An occupational hazard,' I replied.

Major Savory smiled. Turning to his wife, he said: 'Camilla, how about bringing Philippa down now?'

'She'll be asleep,' said Mrs Savory.

'Oh, come on,' said the major, 'you know she always wakes up wanting a cuddle about this time.'

'St John and Camilla's baby,' Major Jackson clarified. 'She's eleven months old.'

'I'll fetch her myself,' said Major Savory, and left the room.

I stood up.

'Well . . . ' I started.

'Well,' said Mrs Savory, 'it's been lovely seeing you. So interesting. Do call any time you're bored, or needing help.'

'Thank you,' I said. 'It's been a most enjoyable evening.'

I shook hands all round and made towards the door.

'Who's Daddy's little beanbag, eh? Who's Daddy's little beanbag?'

Major Savory was coming downstairs with a small white bundle in his arms. A miniscule pink hand tugged at his

233

forelock. Major Savory's face was radiant as he stood on the threshold of the sitting-room, gently jigging the baby in his arms and crooning nonsense-talk at it.

'I'll see myself out,' I murmured, squeezing rather awkwardly past the major.

'Oh, right,' said Major Savory. 'Good to see you, anyway.'

I waved a discreet – actually, unnoticed – farewell and let myself out. As I closed the front door behind me I heard Major Savory's voice saying: 'Camilla, you know I'm sure she said 'Daddy' when I picked her up, I'm sure she did . . . '

That was not the last I saw of the Savorys, though it was the last they saw of me. Two weeks later, at the annual parade of the Allied troops down the Strasse des 17 Juni, I saw Major Savory in one of his tanks. Immaculately turned out, as straight as a die, and absolutely expressionless, he looked not so much the commander of his battalion as an adornment to it, the perfect finishing touch. The sun was beating down out of a cloudless sky, but the major did not blink. The pavements were lined with demonstrators shouting 'Go home! Go home! Go home!', but the major did not look to right or left. I was reminded for an instant of George II, the last British sovereign to lead his troops into battle. I only saw him for an instant, however; for just as his tank rumbled into view, a riot policeman called to me to get down out of the linden tree I had climbed and to stop taking photographs. The climbing of linden trees was *verboten*. As for the taking of photographs, that was not *verboten*, but simply impolitic. You think you're taking a snapshot, the policeman explained to me as I scrambled down out of the tree, but the demonstrators think you're doing something different. 'For your own safety,' said the policeman, running his finger underneath the chinstrap of his riot helmet and casting a bored glance at the shoal of waving fists.

EDITH COPE

The Veils

The wooden chair in Mrs Morrison's shop had a dark blue enamel advertisement for Recketts Blue slotted in its back. I was told not to sit on it while ladies were standing and, as I slid off its high seat, I felt a hot dislike for Mrs Morrison because she had shamed me in public. I told my mother that I wasn't going in there again but next time we needed biscuits I went back to choose them from the glass-topped tins, where a half-pound of assorted could be made up as you pointed. Granny Gibson's shop didn't have tins like that and was further away. What's more, she gave tick and on one occasion I had seen a cockroach in the window. My mother accepted Mrs Morrison's manner as the price to be paid for financial respectability and cleanliness. 'You can see she wasn't brought up to serve behind a counter.'

Mrs Morrison signified her breeding by wearing a black velvet choker. With her piled-up hair and impressively projecting but undifferentiated bosom, she resembled her idol, Queen Mary. I believe that my mother felt that our terraced street gained some status from the Morrisons' shop. It was on the corner where Barton Street intersected at right-angles with our own. On the first floor was a projecting corner bay window and up there Mrs Morrison had her parlour and surveyed the neighbourhood in three directions from behind her lace curtains. All the other shopkeepers lived in rooms behind their shops but Mrs Morrison's parlour reminded us of how privileged we were when she came down to serve us.

Mr Morrison was hardly ever seen because he did the baking in the great bread ovens which were across the yard at the rear.

White-coated, cadaverous, with a persistent cough, he produced irresistible bread, bread that made the saliva spurt in your mouth at the smell and tempted you to twist off a crust before you got home. He baked overnight so was only seen by early workers at dawn when, exhausted, he slipped in the back entrance.

Yet it was the quality of his bread that brought the customers, and at some point he must have had energy enough to convert Miss Grace Pomphrey into Mrs Morrison and install her behind the counter.

Given the age of Mrs Morrison when she condescended to marriage and given her husband's overnight work obligations, it was not surprising that they had only one child, Florence. She was the same age as my sister, which made her some seven years older than I. Although the corner shop was virtually opposite us, Florence's life was quite remote from ours. She did not attend the local school but was paid for at a private establishment on the outskirts of Liverpool. She never played in the street but spent her evenings having piano lessons, going to dancing class, or sitting in the parlour with her mother while her father toiled at his ovens. Mrs Morrison would give bulletins on Florence's progress to such customers as were of sufficient standing to enquire. But the girl as she grew up was never involved in the local outings, never went to the pictures or to parties. It was understood, without resentment, that Florence was being saved for better things.

Not long after the episode of the chair, Mrs Morrison suggested that since I was almost ten I might like to take over the delivery of some of the bread. Most customers picked up their own loaves from the shop but a few trusted children were given the task of carrying a couple of 'tins' or 'oven bottoms' to such householders as could not manage to call. There was no payment but at the end of the week each of us received a bag of sweets for our trouble. Since all the houses were near, it did not take up much time and all it required was the self-restraint not to gnaw the bread *en route*. I felt I could manage it and my mother agreed.

236

At the end of the third week I had reached a decision and was anxious to see Mrs Morrison alone. I had thought about the matter carefully and wanted to enter into negotiations with no one else present. I waited until the shop emptied, then slipped in. 'Please, Mrs Morrison,' I said, thrusting the proferred bag of sweets firmly back across the counter, 'please could I have a few good ones rather than a bagful of cheap ones.'

Mrs Morrison stood, speechless. She finally took hold of the sweets, in silence, and looked into the bag as if to check the contents. 'There's nothing wrong with them,' I hurriedly explained. 'They're quite all right. But they're two pence a quarter. Please, I'd rather have a few good ones from the four pence bottles. Or, just four or five Milk Tray.'

The effect was more profound than I had anticipated. Mrs Morrison put aside the rejected bag, tore off a fresh one from the bundle suspended by their corners and carefully placed in it five chocolates. She handed them over and then said ominously, 'I must have a word with your mother.'

I thought that this would mean the end of my bread round. So since Mrs Morrison was going to have a word with my mother, I decided I had better tell her myself. Her only comment was, 'You did right. I bet her Florence is only given the best.' I could tell that in an odd way she was pleased with me for keeping our end up. She never did tell me what Mrs Morrison said to her but I went on delivering the loaves.

It was from then on that Mrs Morrison unbent enough to converse with me. I was tall for nearly ten but even so she had to incline towards me over the high counter.

'Florence enjoys the fig rolls, but not the rich tea,' she would murmur as my finger hovered indecisively over the boxes. Or, 'I notice that you are wearing a new dress. Be careful that the flour from the loaves doesn't dust off on to it.'

To which I replied, 'It doesn't matter. My sister cut it down for me from one of hers,' because I didn't always remember about keeping our end up. I told her about the toy theatre that had been brought for me from the Christmas club and asked for cardboard pieces from the packing boxes so that I could paint new scenery. There was an advertisement for Crawfords biscuits which I particularly coveted. It showed a mother, with hair in a soft roll at the nape of her neck, seated in an armchair by a tea table. There was a silver teapot and a china plate of biscuits on a tray. Standing before her was a girl of my age with brown bobbed hair and frilled blue dress, holding a biscuit out in an affectionate teasing gesture, as if to a puppy, to a golden haired little boy who was sitting at the mother's feet. The rich carpet, the elegant tray, the mother's smile, the absence of any father to disrupt the calm of the charming scene, powerfully attracted me. I badly wanted the picture and one week I asked for it. Mrs Morrison said, 'I can tell you appreciate nice things,' and came round the counter and unpinned it from the wall. My sister objected to it in our shared bedroom and my father said it wasn't a real painting, but I pinned it on the wall all the same.

Florence remained at school until she was seventeen but was not clever enough for School Certificate. She came home to the parlour, never descending to the shop. It was at this time that Mrs Morrison, who had up till then restricted her powerful influence to the narrow territory of the corner shop, began to go further afield. She hired Mrs Foster as a counter assistant for the afternoons. Impressively toqued, she would take Florence in a hired car to the tea dances at the Adelphi. Florence in Macclesfield silk would glance apologetically up and down the street before following her into the vehicle.

Although my sister took a sour view of Florence's social life, I wished her well. I'd heard my mother say it wasn't right for poor Florence always to be with her mother. 'The lass can't have a mind of her own, brought up the way she's been. As for a father, he's been glad to hide in the bakehouse.' So I hoped Florence was doing well at the Adelphi, so that someone could carry her away from the parlour.

It was a party at the Adelphi after the Grand National that led to Mrs Morrison's triumph. When the party ended, Florence was virtually engaged. The man was called Ralph Higham, pronounced Rafe, as Mrs Morrison explained to my mother. He had excellent prospects because he worked in his father's firm and his father had a network of office furniture shops and showrooms throughout the North West. The street was amazed at the achievement.

Florence was a well-built girl, with a hint of her mother's stately bulk but lacking her handsome authority. Instead, she had a passive timidity which would have been charming in a fragile girl but which in her appeared as awkwardness. Mrs Morrison had had no easy task. My mother had her doubts.

'What's in it for him? He doesn't need the shop. I'm sorry for that poor girl. Why she can't marry a decent local lad as will really fancy her I don't know.' The rest of us were behind Mrs Morrison. We were pleased that Rafe had been captured. We wanted Florence to rise to the cocktail set, the afternoons at Haydock Park, the villa at Southport. Our notions of the sophisticated life were hazy but, when Rafe was considered safe enough to be permitted to see our street and call at the shop, we felt that his red MG came up to our expectations. The smartly Brylcreamed hair, the navy blazer and the car made amends for the hornrimmed glasses.

After the sightings of the red MG, we waited for the wedding and the honeymoon cruise. Mrs Morrison took to fending off questions, saying she did not wish to lose her girl just yet. I heard my mother and sister talking and knew how much credit to give to that. 'She'd have the wedding tomorrow if she could just get him up the aisle.' It was noticed that the red MG was appearing less frequently and the street took to morbid speculation, which was only halted when Florence made a blushing appearance in the shop to show her sapphire engagement ring.

'Hasn't she done well,' was the marvelling comment, the 'she' being, of course, Mrs Morrison. We had no doubt who deserved the credit. Only my mother remained grimly silent, taking no part in the excited speculations. Rafe and his family now featured in across-the-counter bulletins, graciously conveyed with the quarters of tea or ounces of pepper.

'Rafe is thinking of getting a new car. An MG is hardly suitable for a married man, though excellent for a bachelor.'

'Rafe's mother had such a charming chat with Florence, and is planning to give her a teapot which belonged to his father's side.'

The wedding date, however, remained curiously elusive.

The Grand National Party came round a second time, and Mrs Morrison announced that she and Florence would this year be taking rooms overnight at the Adelphi to avoid a tedious late taxi drive home. Of course, Rafe's parents would be only too delighted to offer hospitality but Southport was just as far away. I had a feeling from the reactions of my mother and sister that the Adelphi weekend was some sort of desperate strategy.

Even with all these warning signs, it came as a profound shock when six weeks later we heard that the engagement had been broken off. Mrs Morrison showed her true metal in coping with the announcement. The Queen Empress jowls sagged, the eyes were pouched and sunken, but the neck above the choker was as firmly held as ever.

'I could not risk a girl of as sensitive a nature as Florence sharing the rest of her life with a young man who was not, in *every* way, thoroughly dependable. Rafe is a delightful person, but he has been a little indulged. It is natural that with a wealthy background like his, he should take life's pleasures for granted. Mr Morrison and I have given it very careful thought but we have both decided that Florence might be happier with a more mature partner.'

When a keen-eyed reader of the *Liverpool Echo* saw the announcement of Rafe's engagement to Dorothy, daughter of Colonel and Mrs Grant, The Towers, Formby, the news spread like wild-fire through the street, but by general consent no one mentioned it within the shop.

It was some weeks after the announcement had been spotted that Florence left to stay with an aunt who lived at Kendall. Apparently the aunt had been in failing health for some time and would welcome the companionship of an attentive niece, while the change would be good for Florence. My mother said darkly that she would be surprised if Florence was back much under nine months. I wondered why she had to stay away so long with an aunt none of us had heard of before, but my mother said she had been talking to my sister, not to me, and would I get from under their feet.

It was some time after Florence's departure, Mrs Foster has been dismissed and Mrs Morrison had resumed her daily position behind the counter. She seemed to me much as before but my mother claimed to detect signs of ageing and loss of command. This particular day I had finished my bread delivery and had come back into the shop for my weekly sweets. Instead of handing over the customary bag, Mrs Morrison said, 'Come upstairs. I've got something special for you.' She led me round the side of the counter into a corridor at the rear from which the staircase rose. She went ahead and I followed her into the parlour. It was just as I had imagined it. The carpet was as richly flowered as in the Crawfords advertisement, long blue velvet curtains hung at the bay windows behind the white lace, the settee and easy chairs were in blue moquette with quilted satin cushions. Mrs Morrison walked over to a mahogany chest of drawers. She draw out a flat brown paper package.

'I've been tidying up and clearing things out. I don't need these any more, and I've put them on one side for you. I know you like nice things and you like to dress up. Do you think you could play with these?'

She opened the package, and lifted an object from the tissue paper. It was a veil, pale lilac, diaphanous, with tiny mauve spots, of the kind that swathed the face and surmounted a purple toque. There were others beneath. I was silenced by the unexpectedness of the package and stunned to be in the parlour, where no one else in our street had ever penetrated. I nodded and mumbled, 'Thank you very much, Mrs Morrison.' I picked up the package and went downstairs and across the street to home.

My mother cleared the table in the kitchen and I spread out the tissue paper. I lifted out the lilac veil, which was delicate enough almost to float. There was a fine black one, like cob-webs, and a heavier one with tiny black velvet bows scattered over it. There was a purple one, richly regal and edged with sequins. And finally a pale grey one so magical that it made me think of

> Slowly, silently, now the moon,
> Walks the night in her silver shoon.

I sat spellbound, with the table covered with these gauzy wonders. A faint and faded smell from Mrs Morrison's powdered cheeks clung to them when I raised them to my face and sniffed. My mother picked up a veil. 'She must have saved these for years. No one wears them now, except the Queen. I wonder what's made her get rid of them now? Why did she give them to you?'

I was puzzled by my mother's surprise. Although I couldn't put it into words I thought I knew why Mrs Morrison had chosen me for the veils. 'She said she didn't need them any more. She wanted me to dress up in them.' That was as much as I could manage.

I did dress up in them and in the next few weeks I was an Eastern princess, a Spanish dancer, a goddess. The veils became crumpled, battered and ultimately torn.

All except the grey one. That I kept in its package. It was stored away in its tissue paper, diaphanous, moth-like, too precious for play. I have it still, as fragile and as clinging as these memories.

JOHN BAINBRIDGE

The Clay Horses

It had been the coldest night of the winter. Jennifer had watched Keith scrape the ice from his car before leaving for work. Twigs bent under the weight of the frost. The tap outside was frozen. There was no sun to thaw the white ice crystals that covered every leaf and every blade of grass in the garden; only a pale glimmer of light showed feebly through the mist.

Samantha had rung just after breakfast. 'Why don't you bring Penny down to the mill today? We haven't seen you for ages.'

It was true. Jennifer had been meaning to go for weeks but things kept cropping up. She had spent the last fortnight of term teaching at the local school, covering for a teacher who was ill. The holiday had begun, the days had gone by and still she had not taken Penny to the mill. But now it was getting very close to Christmas and today they would go.

Penny helped her wrap the bright red and gold paper around Theresa's present. Penny was a mature, intelligent ten-year-old. She would never have her mother's good looks. She had too many of Keith's features for that: straight brown hair, a dark complexion, a thin, pointed face and a nose that was rather too long. But she had his good nature too. She was a patient, understanding girl who had never given them a moment's anxiety. At times like this Jennifer was glad to have her around.

'I hope Theresa likes her present,' Penny sighed as she stuck down the last piece of tape.

'I'm sure she will. But we mustn't let her see it today.'

Jennifer called Theresa 'the miracle child'. After eight years

Derek and Samantha had almost given up hope of having children. Jennifer knew how fond Samantha was of Penny and how much she longed for a child of their own. And then Samantha had unexpectedly become pregnant. Theresa had been born a little prematurely but she had grown stronger and now she was over three years old.

Penny tidied away the wrapping paper while Jennifer cooked lunch. Yesterday they had decorated the room. Together they had hung the baubles and the lights on the tree and then Jennifer had hung up the trimmings, leaving Penny to arrange the cards. Perhaps today they would find some holly.

'You like going to the mill, don't you?' said Jennifer as they washed up.

'Most of all I like seeing Theresa and Samantha.' Jennifer noticed the glow on her daughter's face at the thought of their impending visit. You don't need my blonde hair and blue eyes to look beautiful, she thought.

Jennifer was glad that her friendship with Samantha meant so much to Penny. Samantha was the one college friend that she had kept. They had both settled down in the area and had married local men. Derek was now a lecturer at the college. Five years ago he and Samantha had bought the old water mill outside the village. It had been practically a ruin and it had taken nearly all of their savings to put it right.

Jennifer thought of the many hours she and Keith had spent there, Keith helping Derek with the woodwork while she and Samantha painted and wallpapered. It had been hard work but they had enjoyed it. They had laughed when things had gone wrong and sat on the half-built stairs in their paint-stained jeans and drunk beer from cans and thought only of the work they had completed and not of the mountain that was still to be done.

When it was all finished, when the carpets were laid and Samantha's abstract paintings were hung on the walls, when it really looked like a home that Jennifer might have envied if there had been a trace of envy in her nature, then they had drunk their beer from glasses and relaxed on the antique furniture and felt satisfied. There had been parties too. Jennifer remembered it as one of the happiest times of her life. Then Keith had been promoted and his job took up more of his time. And of course Samantha had been busy with the baby. Gradually their visits because less frequent. Now Jennifer felt guilty that Samantha had had to remind her to call.

The mist was clearing when Jennifer and Penny set out on their walk. It was still bitterly cold and too late in the day to expect the ice to thaw. The air was sharp against their faces but they wore thick coats and scarves and the walk soon warmed them. They passed the neat, detached bungalows on the edge of the village and soon there were only fields ahead of them; white fields and a few patches of gaunt, grey woodland that broke the skyline. The frost lay thick on the thorn hedges and had fossilized dead cow parsley by the edge of the road, Rooks combed the still, lifeless fields.

They passed the farm where a sheepdog barked at them and the smell of ripe manure drifted into the road. And then they saw the mill, partly hidden by the copse of willows that grew along the banks of the mill stream. Before they reached it they stopped to watch the horses at the riding school. There were four of them out today, big, powerful-looking animals, three chestnuts and a grey. They had been pulling hay from a rack but when they saw Jennifer and Penny watching them they stopped and stared back at them but they did not approach. Clouds of white steam rose from their nostrils. They pawed the ground as if resentful at the intrusion. Then two of them began nudging each other in mock battle and together they galloped off across the field. Their hooves rang on the frozen earth.

'They're showing off,' said Jennifer. Penny laughed.

The mill stream was frozen solid. The ice looked like steel. White strands of willow hung down over the stream, the tips of the branches frozen into the ice. Outside the mill, a blue tit pecked at a string of peanuts but they startled it and it flew off.

They found Samantha in her studio, her hands covered in wet clay. Theresa sat on a tall stool watching her.

'Penny! Jennifer!' The little girl ran first to Penny and then to

Jennifer and they both knelt down to hug her.

'Sorry about my hands,' Samantha said, getting up from the wheel to kiss her friend. She had tied a brightly patterned scarf around her head to keep her long, black hair out of her eyes and she wore a nylon overall to protect her clothes.

'What are you making?' asked Penny.

'Just a vase. It can wait.'

'Oh no,' said Jennifer. 'Don't stop. Penny would love to watch you.' Samantha looked at the girl and saw it in her face.

'All right,' she said, returning to the wheel.

'And then I'm going to show you my rabbits!' Theresa announced.

They watched Samantha mould the shapeless slab of clay until it rose from the wheel, delicately shaped by her skilful fingers.

'It's beautiful,' Penny gasped. Samantha smiled at her.

'Come on,' she said, wiping her hands. 'I've a present for you.

She led them through into the shop. Here Samantha sold the various vases and other ornaments that she made. Now that she was well known in the neighbourhood she had quite a successful business. Among all the beautiful objects on display there was one collection that immediately caught Penny's eye. It was a group of horses, several inches tall, each one meticulously modelled out of clay, perfect in every detail.

'They're lovely!' Penny exclaimed.

'I used the horses down the road as models.' And they were so life-like that Penny could see the resemblance. Each horse was different. One stood with its head turned to one side and she remembered one had stood just like that when it had watched them on the road. Another was galloping, its head tossed back, its mane streaming out from its neck.

'Would you like one for your Christmas present?' Samantha asked.

'Oh, yes please!'

'Then pick the one you'd like.'

It wasn't hard for her to choose. She had already spotted her

246

favourite. It stood with one leg slightly raised and its neck arched. Its nostrils flared and every muscle was taut. It looked as if it was about to burst into life. Samantha wrapped the horse and put it into a box.

'Now will you come and see my rabbits?' demanded Theresa. Samantha dressed her daughter in a warm coat and woollen scarf and gloves.

'Don't stay out too long. And do as Penny tells you,' Penny smiled at the little girl and squeezed her hand.

'Can we give them some carrots?'

'All right. There's some in the bag.'

The two women watched them tramp off, hand in hand, crushing the frozen blades of grass with their boots. They disappeared into the shed where the rabbits were kept, leaving two lines of footprints in the frost.

'They get on so well together,' remarked Samantha.

'Like us,' said Jennifer.

'Oh Jenny, it *is* good to see you again!' Samantha threw her arms around her and they clung to each other.

'I've been meaning to come . . . '

'It's all right. I know you've been busy. But you're here now and I'm glad you've come.' She released her grasp. 'Would you like some coffee?'

They sat by the warm glow of the open coal fire drinking fresh coffee from mugs that Samantha had made herself. She had also made the ceramic table lamp. The large picture of the mill on the wall above the fireplace was her work as well.

'It's good for Theresa to have Penny here,' said Samantha. 'We're too far from the village for her to have many friends.'

'Penny loves coming. She was so excited after you rang.'

'She's very mature for her age.'

'She's like Keith. Very practical. Not like us artistic types who panic every time there's a problem.'

Samantha sipped her coffee thoughtfully. A coal fell in the fire and sent a shower of sparks up the chimney. A dog barked in the distance. Jennifer looked at the painting. The style was unquestionably Samantha's. The mill was in black and white, as

247

were the reeds and the willows except for where a single shaft of yellow sunlight caught them and it sent a glow that seemed to shine right out of the picture into the room. Samantha had always been a 'real' artist. Her talent had shone out when they were at college together. Jennifer could draw and paint well enough but Samantha had the eye to perceive the unusual, to give her own individual interpretation of things. Jennifer had always admired her work. It was no surprise that while Jennifer had gone in for teaching Samantha had made a career out of her art.

'I threw away a lot of paper before I got it right,' she said when her friend remarked at the quality of the mill scene.

'It's lovely.'

'Very symbolic actually but we won't go into that now.'

'You've used so little colour and yet there is still so much warmth in it.'

'"Not too much colour, Samantha. Don't spoil the effectiveness of your line work." Do you remember Neil saying that to me?'

Jennifer didn't actually remember the words but she remembered Neil Strawson well enough. He was the lecturer the girls had all fallen for: a single man in his thirties with a thick black beard and the long hair that had been fashionable among artistic men at the time. She remembered his bright open-necked shirts and the gold chain around his sunburnt neck. Some of the other girls, jealous of Samantha's successful results, had spread rumours that she was having an affair with him. But Jennifer had defended her. Samantha had such obvious talent. How could they think her achievements were due to anything other than her undoubted ability?

'I remember Neil,' said Jennifer. 'He's not at the college now?'

'Oh no. He left soon after we did. He went down to London I think.'

'He was nice.' Jennifer looked up. Her friend's face looked red in the glow of the fire.

'I know what they said about us,' she said.

'They were only jealous,' said Jennifer. 'We all fancied him like mad. Remember?'

'Yes but I've always been grateful for the way you stood up for me. You were the only real friend I had.'

'I was only telling the truth. I knew you too well to believe what they said.'

Samantha put her coffee mug down on the table. Although it was only the middle of the afternoon the daylight was beginning to fail and the room was becoming appreciably darker.

'Jennifer, there was rather more between us than you thought.' Jennifer looked across at her. She had removed the scarf from around her head and her dark hair fell forward over her eyes.

'You don't have to tell me.'

'There's not really a lot to tell. We had a couple of dates. We got quite friendly. And . . ' she paused, 'I posed for him in the nude.'

You did what?' Jennifer couldn't help laughing.

'You heard,' said Samantha. She was laughing herself now. She raised her hand to brush back the hair from her eyes. 'It was terrible really. He was so sincere when he asked me. We were sitting in a pub. He had a glass of beer and I was being terribly daring drinking vodka and lime.

'"Samantha," he said. You remember his voice was so strong and masculine? "Samantha, I'd love to paint you." I just laughed.

'"What for?" I said. "I'm sure you can find someone more beautiful to paint."

He said "I want to paint *you*." I was so mad about him I think I'd have agreed to anything. I went to his flat on the Saturday afternoon. You thought I'd gone shopping. When I got there the room was full of nude paintings and sketches. He asked if I'd mind him painting me like that.' Samantha paused. The coal shifted in the grate. Another cascade of sparks disappeared up the chimney. 'All the time I was sitting there covered in goose pimples, I was thinking "what am I going to do if he tries anything?" In the end I was rather disappointed when he didn't.'

249

'Didn't he?'

'No he just finished off while I got dressed.'

'How did he paint you? I mean how did you pose?'

'Oh, reclining. Legs apart. The whole thing.'

'And what was it like? The painting, I mean. When he'd finished.'

'Just another nude.'

They were silent for a while. Jennifer wondered what had happened to the painting. Was the nude Samantha hanging on the wall of Neil's flat while he painted some other girl? Had she graced galleries in London? Did some wealthy businessman eye her lustfully as he sipped his whisky?

'You crafty thing,' she said at last. 'Keeping secrets from me.'

Samantha smiled. 'We've all got secrets.'

'It was a long time ago,' Jennifer reflected. She noticed that Samantha was no longer smiling. The room became colder. The fire needed more coal.

'The girls have been a long time,' Samantha said suddenly. 'Let's go and find them.'

It had been so dark in the room that it was surprising how much light there was left in the sky. It was already freezing hard.

The shed door was closed. The rabbits scuffled about in their hutches but the girls were not there.

'Where can they be?' said Samantha. 'Oh, Jennifer' you don't think Penny would have taken her on the ice?'

'I don't think so.' Penny had always been such a sensible girl. It was not the sort of thing she would do. But Jennifer's voice was unsteady. She too was becoming alarmed.

'Theresa!' Samantha's shout was almost a scream. 'Theresa darling, where are you?'

They ran across the garden into the shroud of frozen willows. There were cracks in the dead grey ice of the mill stream but no signs of a break. But upstream the bank curled round. The stream was hidden from view.

'Oh my God!' Samantha gasped, running on blindly. Frozen twigs cracked under their feet; dead thistles clawed at their legs.

Samantha's eyes were wild and wet.

'At least they're not here,' Jennifer tried to reassure her. 'You can see. The ice isn't broken.'

'But what has she done with her? Where can she have taken her?' For a moment Samantha's words stung her. How could she blame Penny? How could she think that Penny would do anything to hurt Theresa? But her own concern for the girls' safety soon pushed these thoughts from her mind. She too was becoming more than anxious. It was true that the ice seemed to be unbroken but it was freezing hard. Was it possible that it could have frozen over again? She shuddered.

Distant rooks were calling as they gathered to roost. The garden remained still and silent. They went back. The girls were waiting for them outside the house. The relief was almost as unbearable as the fear. Samantha hugged Theresa and let the tears stream down her face.

'Penny, where have you been?' Jennifer asked. She did not speak unkindly to her.

'We were looking for holly. Remember, you said we might find some. And there's a bush over that hedge with lots of red berries.'

'But why didn't you come when we called you?'

'We did. We came straight back but you weren't here.' Jennifer and Samantha looked at each other. In their panic they had rushed straight off towards the ice.

'I'm sorry', said Samantha. Jennifer smiled but her heart was still racing.

It was becoming darker. The first stars were beginning to penetrate the greyness of the sky. Samantha wanted them to wait for Derek to take them home but Jennifer thought that they had better walk.

'Don't leave it so long next time,' said Samantha as she kissed her goodbye.

'I won't. Perhaps you and Theresa will get along to see *us* soon.' The two women looked at Theresa.

'Would you like that Theresa?' Samantha asked.

'Yes please!'

'After Father Christmas has been.' Everyone laughed. Theresa was not sure why but she joined in.

There was still sufficient light for them to see their way clearly. There was almost no traffic. The moon had risen and the frost sparkled on the road. Jennifer carried Penny's horse in her bag. Penny held the bunch of holly that Samantha had cut for them before they left. Penny asked her mother questions: about Theresa and Samantha; about the mill; about her mother's college days; about their plans for Christmas. Jennifer answered her briefly. Her thoughts were elsewhere. Eventually Penny grew tired of asking and she too fell silent. A blackbird flew out of the hedge, chattering noisily. Ahead of them the streetlights of the village glittered in the evening air.

Still Jennifer walked in silence, keeping her thoughts to herself. Today, for the first time, she had noticed how much Theresa looked like Penny.

THOMAS McCARTHY

A Visit From Al

He bounced through the hall after he had cleared Customs, a tall, balding man in a crumpled off-white mackintosh that was a shapeless as a smock. His trousers were above his ankles and showed thick socks and shoes. In that he was like all the Americans: lightweight suits, thick socks, thick shoes, and button-down shirts, of course. And very crumpled looking – as if they had slept in their clothes – which Al probably had, for he had left Chicago the day before and flown straight to Shannon.

'Hi Charlie, how ya been?' He shook hands almost violently with Charlie, who stood Buddha-like.

'Hi Al,' he replied laconically, as if he were half-asleep. Charlie liked to give the impression that he was so laid-back nothing ever worried him. But things did. I knew they did. I knew about the bottles of vodka that he kept in his desk and in his briefcase and God knows where else.

'And you must be Jim Quirk, right?' Al turned to me, a big, false, smile on his face. But I saw only the cold grey eyes that showed no sign of fatigue as they appraised me.

'That's right, I'm pleased to meet you,' I said.

'And Jim, it's a great honour for me, Al Jackson, to be back in Ireland.' Al smiled again as he repeated my name: he was straight out of Dale Carnegie. Moving past me he shook hands with Seamus Healey, who was my number two.

'You want some breakfast?' Charlie asked him, as we went towards the exit. 'I guess the hotel could lay some on, that right Jim, it's not too goddamn early for them, is it?' And he laughed.

'No, it's eight-fifteen, they'll be serving now.' I laughed a little uneasily, for Charlie had been astonished that the hotel refused to serve him breakfast before eight: he seemed to need a lot of food each morning.

'Hell, don't worry about me. I guess if I can stop by some place to clean my teeth, I'll be fine and dandy,' Al said, as he walked briskly from the terminal to the car park.

Sunday morning it was, and the sun was high and warm for early March. I should have been sitting at home eating breakfast and looking at the papers before going to the golf course for the day instead of chauffeuring this lunatic around the country. Yet I blamed Charlie as much as anybody for dropping me into all of this.

The hotel was quiet and Charlie resolutely made his way to the dining-room, leaving me to show Al to my bedroom, where he took a toothbrush and a tube of toothpaste from his briefcase.

'How's business?' he asked me, as I heard the tap run and then Al start to scrub his teeth.

'Not good.' I knew that was wrong. It was considered defeatist even to admit it.

'How come?'

'The company is in a shitty condition, Al. It's been left to fester for too long. It's going to take three to four years to pull it round.'

'Oh no it isn't, buster. It's gonna take you and me about three months, otherwise your ass is on the line.'

'Al, miracles I can do today, the impossible takes a little longer.'

'Hey, I kinda like that! That's my boy! That's positive! Great! You wait until you see the convention we're gonna lay on for your boys. Boy oh boy will they be go-getters then! You'll see.' He shouted above the noise of the flushing toilet.

I smiled back at the door, but I thought, you're as full of shit as the rest of them.

'OK, let's get this goddamn show on the road.' He came out of the bathroom looking as fresh as if he had slept all night.

'Charlie is having breakfast,' I said.

This didn't please him, but Charlie and he were about equal in the complex hierarchy of the company, so he said with another false smile: 'Let's go get him then, buddy-boy.'

Charlie was munching his way through rashers and eggs and sausages and black pudding and white pudding and tomato, all of which he had cut into small pieces, so that it looked like the remains of an operation, for he had poured his favourite catsup, as he called it, over the lot, and he shovelled it in, the fork in his right hand, the knife at right angles on the plate. Seamus Healey looked pale and ill for he and Charlie had both been as drunk as skunks the previous evening when we had spent the time discussing strategy over dinner and then in the bar over drinks until I had left Charlie and Seamus at midnight.

'Coffee, Al?' Charlie said casually.

'Nope. I'm ready to go soon as you're ready.'

Charlie put some marmalade on to his toast then ate it with a forkful of the *mélange* in front of him.

'Well, Al, where I come from a man needs a damn good breakfast to do a *proper* day's work, know what I mean.'

Al didn't answer him. Instead he turned to me and said: 'Say is Bunratty Castle near here?'

'Just down the road.'

'Hey, you know I keep meaning to go visit one of these places, but somehow I never get the time. You know all the time we were in Australia I never got to the Opera House in Sydney. I guess my wife gets to be the cultural visitor in our house.'

'You moved back to Chicago, yet?' Charlie asked him between mouthfuls.

'Sure, they moved back last week. I've left Mavis with her list of jobs to do. She gets to hang the drapes this weekend and to plant out the bulbs.'

Seeing that Charlie was still eating, Al sat at the table, but still refused to have anything to eat or drink. I never eat breakfast, but my mouth was dry, due to last night's booze and my heightened adrenaline caused by Al's visit. I ordered a pot of tea.

'OK, so what's the plan for today?' Al seemed determined to be business-like. He looked at Charlie, who looked at me.

'You tell him, Jim.'

'First step is Limerick. We'll look at the depot, the manager is coming in especially to open up to show you around.'

'Good, next?'

'Then we head for Tralee, same thing. From there we go to Killarney, then Mallow, then Fermoy and into Cork this evening.'

'Say, can't we do more than that?' Al was a little petulant. 'That's, let me see, that's only six depots.'

'I doubt that we'll get to Cork before seven this evening,' I said. 'The roads are not very fast, and Sunday is a busy day in this country with sports and people visiting.'

Al looked suspicious for a moment. Charlie, now that he had finished, grinned at him.

'There ain't no turnpikes in this country, Al, just little ole roads that wind up and down and you sure as hell need patience.'

'Just like Brazil in the early days, right?' Al laughed.

'Just like any ass-hole of a country in the Third World,' Charlie said amicably. 'Only thing is the natives speak English. Well kinda.'

Now normally I didn't mind when Charlie made disparaging remarks about Ireland, for he was as likely to be equally disparaging about England, or indeed America, but that stung me.

'Well if you don't mind I'll go out and harness the donkey and cart for your lordships.'

'Hold on, buddy-boy, I'm a' coming with you,' Al said.

We were like the meat in a sandwich, I thought, as I picked my suitcase up at the porter's desk and made for my car. Charlie was the European director of sales, Al was the Western Hemisphere director of retail sales. Part of us belonged to Charlie, part to Al. Both of them were using the failure of the

256

Irish company (which had been nothing to do with me, I had been sent to try and put it right six months earlier) to score enough points to get off the international division of the company and get back to the American division, for it was well known that it was only from there that you got to make (in Charlie's words) a Vee Pee, and thus to safety.

'Say, this is a *nice* motor car,' Al said, as I unlocked my Granada.

'It's standard executive stuff,' I replied cooly. I was thinking of how all work in the company had ground to a halt over a week ago as soon as we had heard about Al's visit. And then of course Charlie had flown in on the Wednesday to double check everything we were going to show Al, which meant even longer working days as reports were typed and presentation charts painted up. All the Americans like a presentation – or *preezentation* as Charlie called it – with lots of charts of different colours. I had done many of them myself in my meteoric rise to the top of the Irish company, but I had always been dubious of their worth.

'Say Jim, what's the average age of your sales force?' Al said as we got into the car.

'Twenty-five point four years,' I replied. That was the first figure that came into my head: I had no idea what the average age was, but I knew that Al liked the answer.

'Say that's good, very good. Young and hungry, huh.'

'Very,' I said, thinking of Kevin Molloy and his perpetual hangover, or old Mickey Quinn up in Dundalk who was only interested in horses. They were both well into their fifties and in their own way did a good job. But not in Al's mind, so I had sent them away on a course to our training school in London. I sighed. More wasted money. There was nothing any training school could teach them: you can only teach those who want to learn. As we waited I began to add up the cost of Al's visit in terms of time alone. The money spent was equally vast, but I stopped myself as it merely added to my bad temper.

'OK, let's get this goddamn show on the road,' Charlie said, as he settled his bulk in the back seat behind Al. Seamus

Healey, still looking pale and sickly, squeezed in beside him.

As we drove into Limerick I saw Charlie take a quick slug from his flask before he offered it to Seamus, who looked as if he was about to throw up at the prospect. Charlie smiled, took another, longer swig and returned the flask to his briefcase which was open on his knees.

'OK,' said Al, 'what's the percentage margin at this place?'

'Nineteen per cent' I said.

'And the net?'

'It made a loss last year, it might break even this quarter.'

'This the worst one?'

'It's all in the report, Al,' I said sharply.

Al was silent, he seemed annoyed and I was amazed at my own audacity, for I had never spoken so sharply to somebody so senior in the company. But I was beginning not to care. Who could take Charlie and Al seriously? And Charlie and Al represented the company: how, therefore, could I be serious about the company?

We drove down O'Connell Street, I turned off and parked outside the depot. The office was open, and I went in followed by the others. Nobody had spoken since I had in the car.

'Hello Sean, it's good of you to turn out on a Sunday,' I said.

'Yerra 'tis nothing. I'll be home again in half an hour, not like yeerselves.' Sean hadn't shaved, he cupped a cigarette in his hand as he grinned at me. He didn't care, I thought wearily. Why should he? He had seen this happen before. The Yanks would come, then go. I would depart in time, he knew that; all he had to do was to smile and agree with everything he was told, and then, when we had gone, do as he liked.

'Hi, I'm Al Jackson, you're Sean Hackett, right. It's great to meet you Sean, real great,' Al said with his searchlight smile.

'And it's good to see yourself again too, Mr Jackson.'

'Call me Al, Sean, please call me Al. Say have we met before some place?'

'We have. Didn't you come and give us a talk one time when I was on a course in London. Do you remember that at all?'

'Oh, sure, I remember Sean, well it's good meeting you again

258

Sean. How about showing me around your depot.'

'Well 'tisn't much of a place Mr Jackson, 'tis an ould building with a hole in the fitting bay floor. The roof leaks, too.'

'And your margin is only nineteen per cent, right,' Al interrupted sharply.

'Ah sure, Mr Jackson, nobody would drive their car into a place like this, and if we get a lorry, we have to jack it up outside in the road. We have nothing to offer,' Sean said evenly.

Al looked at me in fury, but I refused to answer him. Everything that Sean Hackett had said was true; the company had not invested any money for years, and old properties like this one were too costly to replace. But Al didn't want to hear that; he had come to make his reputation, it didn't matter about the future; all he was concerned with was now and the report he would make to his boss in New York, the infamous Patrick J. Powers, the head of the company's overseas operations.

We stayed for about ten minutes before we headed south to Kerry and Tralee. Al sat reading my report; Charlie dozed in the back, numbed, no doubt, by the further swigs he had taken from his flask. How the hell, I wondered, did he not only get away with it, but manage never to be seen to be even slightly inebriated let alone as plastered as he should be on that intake of alcohol? Americans were funny, odd-balls – at least in Europe they were. Charlie's boss, Klaus Kroner, or Fritz the Kraut, as he was known behind his back, was locked in combat with Patrick J. Powers for the right to succeed the chairman of the company when he retired in eighteen months' time. And whoever won, either Al or Charlie would go with him to the seat on the main board, the much-sought-after title of Vee Pee, the power and the glory, the money, the use of the company plane, the stock options.

'This place in Tralee doesn't look too bad,' Al broke through my thoughts. 'Seems he's kinda got a good margin and sales. How come?'

'It's a new location,' I said. 'We bought it last year, it is everything that Limerick isn't, that's why it does well.'

Al, like a cat at a mouse hole, pounced.

'You call a margin of twenty-five per cent a success?' he sneered. 'I'd say that was a goddamn near disaster.'

'This is not America, Al,' I began patiently. 'We are trying to turn what has been a wholesale operation into a retail one. We don't have the staff, we don't have the premises, we don't have the know-how in sufficient quantity to achieve results over-night. Tralee is a first step, that's all.'

Come on, Charlie, I thought angrily, you drunken bum, come and help me. But Charlie slept, his head resting on the uneasy shoulder of Seamus Healey.

'Seems all I hear from you guys is why I can't do this, why I can't do that. It's too negative, you gotta kick some asses, Jim. Why don't you go drink some tiger piss, then kick 'em.'

I was about to retort but held my temper. All this was good ammunition for Al and I was doing Charlie's job for him. But of course the system worked downwards too. If Charlie went up, well so would I.

'Like I said this morning, Al, this company was ignored for too long. When you bought it in the sixties it was profitable, but nobody took any notice until it made some losses, now don't you go saying *that's* my fault.'

Al was at once conciliatory. 'Hell, you know how it is, Jim. You got a sick child, you look after him, you don't bother over-much with the healthy ones. You were healthy, now you're sick.'

Mollified somewhat, I drove on. Charlie woke up, took a further swig from his flask, then he and Al swopped gossip about people they knew. Old so-and-so was in India, someone else in the Congo, another in Greece. The new imperialists, I thought, and I am one of the lesser breeds that make up their army. They started to discuss tax, or rather its avoidance, so I concentrated on driving as fast as I could. I knew Charlie was a nervous passenger. It was a form of revenge.

In Tralee we followed the same pattern. A lightening visit, a ten-minute tour of the premises, Al's questions answered more politely – and positively – because the manager was younger and newer than Sean Hackett, and had almost certainly been phoned by Sean on the questions Al was likely to ask.

We were delayed going through Killarney, but Al saw a jaunting car and was suddenly the tourist.

'Say, they do exist, these things,' he was wide-eyed, 'well, how about that.'

We were sitting in a traffic jam and two jaunting cars went past both with Americans on board.

'We might even find you a leprechaun,' I muttered.

'What they do, get some midgets to dress up for the tourists?' Al asked. He was serious, too.

'No, Al, they don't. If you see a leprechaun, he'll be the real thing.'

'Mavis is gonna love this place when she comes over in June. Did I tell you she was coming to tour Europe? Why I promised her she could come.'

'If I'm still in London, I'd be happy to show her around the sights,' Charlie said.

'That's good of you, Charlie, but London isn't on her itinerary. She's gonna do Scotland and Ireland this time as well as France, Italy and Spain.' Al took a folded sheet of paper from his inside pocket and opened it. I saw a typewritten list of places and hotels and beside it dates.

'OK,' he resumed thoughtfully. 'June 9 she lands at Shannon and departs Dublin to Glasgow on June 16. I guess it would be kinda nice to have somebody meet her at Shannon and show her around.'

'Is she travelling alone?' I said.

'No, she's travelling with her good friend, Lucy Clayton.'

'I'd offer but I'm afraid I'm on holiday then myself,' I lied.

'Perhaps some of your people could help out,' Charlie suggested.

I didn't answer either of them, using the excuse of being able to drive again as we moved slowly to the depot. But I was seething. So this was part of the reason for Al's trip, to lay on some free chauffeurs for his bloody wife and her friend. I had been caught like that before; not only were you chauffeur but you were expected to put your hand in your pocket also and buy them dinner – or at least the company was.

After our cursory visit to Killarney depot, we headed out on the road to Mallow, and stopped for lunch – at Charlie's request – at a hotel on the outskirts of the town. Charlie headed straight for the bar.

'Say, do you know how to make a dry Martini?' he asked the boy behind the bar.

'I certainly do, sir.'

'OK, make me one with vodka.'

Al refused a drink at first, but after a little persuasion from the head waiter who took our order, condescended to have a half-pint of Guinness. Which was a good thing, for he and Charlie both fell asleep when we set out after lunch and did not wakn until we had reached Mallow.

I wondered when the matter about Al's wife would be raised again, and sure enough, over dinner in the hotel in Cork, Al said: 'I think this hotel is the one Mavis and Lucy are due to stay at.' Once more he took the itinerary from his pocket. 'Yep, Silver Springs Hotel, Cork city. This is it, all right.'

I waited but said nothing.

'Do you think some of your people would show her some of that famous old Irish hospitality?' Charlie suggested.

'I'm sure they will meet with nothing else,' I said formally. I felt Charlie's feet nudge mine. 'But as I said, unfortunately June is when I'm on holiday myself.'

'I'll show them around,' Seamus Healey said, uncomfortably

'You'll be too busy while I'm away,' I said curtly.

'I'm sure you can work something out,' Charlie said firmly.

'Oh I don't know,' I said. I was too annoyed to worry any more. 'We'll have a lot of people on holiday, but of course if you're telling me to do it, it'll get done.'

'Say, that's very good of you,' Al said, with his false smile. 'I'll write Mavis tonight to tell her that Seamus here is gonna be at Shannon to meet her and Lucy.'

'Make a note in your diary, Seamus,' I said coldly. '9 June to meet Mrs Jackson and companion and act as their chauffeur.'

Charlie looked at me in amazement, then anger clouded his fat face, while Al seemed to be oblivious of anything, and poor Seamus blushed and looked as if he wished he were far away.

'Is there anything else you want for tonight?' I asked Al as our plates were cleared.

'No, I guess not. We'll have a breakfast meeting in my room at, say, 6 a.m.' He looked to Charlie for confirmation and Charlie grinned and nodded.

'How long do you anticipate the meeting will be?' I said.

''Bout an hour, hour and a half. Get to the office about seven-thirty.'

'What about breakfast?' Charlie chuckled. I realized he was stoned out of his mind again, but I only knew because he laughed a lot when he was really drunk – it was his only slip.

'Say, why don't we have it as we meet. Lay on some coffee and Danish pastries, that would be good, huh.' Al was full of it now.

'I'll see you at six in your room, then,' I said and left them there. Seamus was also staying in the hotel but I drove home.

I was back at the hotel at five-forty-five the next morning. As I parked my car a boat slid along the Lee and a train hurtled by on its way to Glanmire Station. I felt terrible. I had hardly slept, yet I had been very tired.

Sharp at six, I knocked on Al's door.

'Come on in, it's open.'

He was dressed and had all his papers spread out on the bed. 'I read all of your report last night,' he began. I thought, you ignorant bastard, you don't even start the day with a greeting.

'*GOOD* morning,' Charlie said cheerfully, as he walked in.

'And I guess what we're gonna have to do,' Al continued, looking for some paper from the mounds on his bed, 'is to take three or four of the depots, pour everything into them, make them the object of very regular and critical scrutiny, then when they're right, build up another four, then another four.'

'Al, we're already doing that,' I said wearily. 'That's what Tralee is all about.'

'And I guess,' Al went on as if I had not spoken, 'the people you put in these places have got to be made to perform.'

'What time you order breakfast for?' Charlie demanded. I realized now why he ate so much: never drink on an empty stomach he had confided to me once – and I guessed that he was approaching the time when his first drink would be vital to him.

'I said six, but I don't know if the receptionist understood me too well,' Al conceded.

'Say, why don't you find out what's happened?' Charlie ordered me.

'I'll see where Seamus is at the same time.'

Down in the foyer I found the night porter. I asked him about Al's order.

'I can make you some tea and toast,' he said slowly, as he put his glasses on to read the orders in his book.

'Fine, but could you do it as quickly as possible, please.'

'One moment, now, sir. I have the switchboard to mind and I'm on my own until the receptionist comes on at eight.' There was an indignant tone in his voice.

'Sure, I understand,' I said, smiling. 'But as soon as you can, I'd be very grateful.' I slipped him a pound and made a mental note to claim it back on my expenses.

'So I say we make Tralee, Cork, Dublin and Galway our four pilot depots,' Al was saying when I got back.

'We already have done,' I told him tartly, but he again ignored me.

Charlie looked at me angrily. 'Where's this goddamn breakfast?'

'It's on its way, but he'll be about ten minutes.'

'*Jesus Christ*,' Charlie said exasperatedly. 'Does anything come on time in this bloody country? I gotta use the bathroom, Al.' And he went back to his own room.

Al had set a tape recorder on his bedside table and began to dictate his report. Seamus Healey knocked and came in, his eyes bloodshot and heavy with sleep, a look of intense worry on his face.

'Sorry I'm late,' he began, but I shushed him.

When Charlie came back he looked angry, and I wondered if he had had a drink and it hadn't worked, or whether it had and its effect on an empty stomach was not to his liking. The meeting continued in its shambolic way. Charlie said nothing, he just sat in a chair by the window looking at his watch or through the trees to the river. Al kept talking about improving profitability, using methods I had already put into a twenty-page report I had written three months earlier, a copy of which had gone to Al's desk-man in Chicago – along with the monthly report I submitted – but which I had long suspected nobody read.

'So, to conclude and finally wrap up this whole ball of wax,' Al said, as there was a knock on the door and the porter came in with a tray of tea and toast.

'No Danish pastry, huh!' Al was not pleased.

'Ah, no sir, you'd have to wait until the shops open for that. Will that be all, sir?'

'More toast and jam,' Charlie said brusquely.

We had finished everything by seven-fifteen so I drove them to the company office across the river by City Hall. The streets were quiet, only an occasional bus or the odd lorry or car were on the move, and we were in the office – which I unlocked – about five minutes after we left the hotel.

'All-righty,' Al said briskly, 'let's have the first *preezentation*.'

Before I replied I looked pointedly at the clock on the wall of my office. It was seven-twenty-five.

'Al, we don't start work until nine o'clock.'

'What kind of goddamn way is that to run a business, I'm not surprised you guys are in trouble.'

'Let me explain,' I began.

'Hell NO!' Al shouted his face contorted in fury. 'You will get your people here on *time*, and I mean *on time!*'

'Al, nine o'clock is on time.' My voice was loud. 'As I was about to tell you before you interrupted me, nine o'clock is when *everybody* in this country starts work. We have an hour's break for lunch from one until two and we finish at six in the evening. There are exceptions, of course. I'm usually here by eight and I don't very often leave before seven in the evening.

Al started to study some figures. I had noticed that whenever he lost an argument he ignored it.

'Of course' I continued, as Charlie gave me another dirty look (I knew I was in trouble with him as well, now), 'had I known that you wanted me to get people to be here for seven-thirty, well of course I would have arranged that. It's no problem.

'I guess we could look at some figures I've brought over from some of our stores in the States,' Al said, taking another of his files from his briefcase. 'Now see here how these guys sell up and sell five tyres and just look at their level of lower-half servicing. And you know the most interesting thing? Over sixty per cent of their business comes on their own credit card. Do you have your own credit card?'

'No, we've looked at it, but it's got more problems for us than benefits.'

'I think you should get into that market. I mean the spin-offs are incredible. Like, OK, a guy comes in for two tyres. We sell up, persuade him to have five better ones. OK, so he doesn't have enough cash on him or his checking account. No sweat. We check his credit ratings, if they're OK, we give him our house credit card. So he spends two hundred dollars, right, and our opening credit limit is five hundred. The next morning in the mail he gets our mailing shot with our special offers on our refrigerators, freezers, food processors, cookers, washing machines, and,' Al grinned, he was immersed in his subject like a born-again preacher, 'here's the perfect hit. We say you have three hundred dollars credit in your account, our special offers are always pitched right there between the cost of the average first sale and our average credit limit. So his wife says, "Come on, honey, we need a new washing machine, you've got the money." Maybe she gets him a little horny first, but in ninety per cent of our first sales we get an order for electrical goods. Then, when he's locked into us for five hundred bucks, boy he's locked into us for good!'

'Very impressive,' I said – which it was. 'But this market is not that sophisticated. Credit cards are here but in a small way. And as for the wife telling him what to buy.' I shook my head.

Al didn't like that. Nor did Charlie.

'Maybe we could try it out in one place,' Seamus Healey said timidly.

Al nodded. 'Right, good thinking, I like that. What about Dublin, Galway?'

'Anywhere will do,' I said, 'it won't matter.'

Charlie went out to Seamus's office, ostensibly to make a phonecall, but he was seen (by old Miss Farrell, the cashier, who started work at eight-thirty) to take swigs from his flask. (She told me this after they'd gone, in shocked tones.)

We started our presentations sharp at nine. The chief accountant, Oliver Desmond, was first, and he looked as if he were half-asleep – which he probably was, for he was a heavy drinker and a womanizer – and he stumbled through, pointing out the wrong figures on the chart, and fumbling over his words when I corrected him.

Through all this Al sat writing copiously, he asked a question now and then, but they were asked, I thought, merely to demonstrate that he was awake. Charlie asked the odd question, too, as if to keep his end up, but unlike Al, he made no notes, he had this incredible memory and could reel off figures from ten years ago.

As the presentations progressed, we were freqently interrupted by telephone calls for Al and Charlie. Al took three calls from London, two from Belgium, then, later on in the morning at about twelve-thirty, one from the States.

'You sure 'bout that?' His tone had risen. 'When? What! Shit! OK, be seeing you.' He slammed the phone into the cradle and stood, looking white-faced and grim.

'Something up?' Charlie enquired.

'I just heard that Patrick J. is flying into London tomorrow. He's gonna tour Europe.'

'Comin' to see what *you've* been doing, huh,' Charlie chuckled.

'He'll want to see everybody, but *everybody*,' Al muttered worriedly. All the bounce and zip had gone from him; he looked as if somebody had kneed him in the groin.

'Say Jim, get your people to book me on the next flight to London, OK.'

'Certainly,' I said with pleasure. I walked out to my secretary's office, passing the worried-looking Seamus Healey who was waiting with his charts to give his presentation of the Irish market.

'Relax Seamus, it's almost over, I don't think you'll be needed.'

When I got back Al was saying to Charlie: 'I guess you don't have to come back.'

'No siree, my brief is to send a report back to ole Fritz, that's it. I guess that's gonna take a few days longer.'

The phone rang on my desk. 'Yes,' I said softly.

'A call from America for Mr Peterson.'

'It's for you,' I said to Charlie, and just as he held the receiver to his ear, I added: 'It's from the States,' and I noticed the sudden look of fear on his face.

'Yes SIR!' he said, having listened for a few moments. 'No sir, first I knew about it was ten minutes ago when the call came through.'

I could hear the roar even though Charlie had the receiver pressed tight to his ear. He looked as if he were about to have a heart attack.

'No, sure, I understand, yes sir, I'll be there, you can count on me, sure thing.' And the phone went slowly back into the cradle.

'Get your people to book me the next flight to London,' he said slowly as he sank back into his chair.

'Got a problem?' Al asked nonchalantly.

'Nope, just got to be there when the man arrives, that's all.'

'Same old story, I guess,' Al said, with a short laugh. 'You bird-dog my guy and I'll bird-dog yours.'

Charlie didn't answer him. His face was grey, beads of perspiration flecked his forehead and upper lip, his breathing was heavy, and not for the first time I wondered what drove Charlie and Al to put up with such treatment. Then I thought of the stock option, the company plane, the money, the power and the glory – and I realized – the prospect of one day being able to treat people the way they had been treated and get away with it. The prize is so great, I thought, they will literally eat shit to get it if they have to.

There were seats on the afternoon plane. As I drove up the hill to Cork airport, I wondered what their reports would say. Al would favour keeping the company open; Charlie would want to close it down. Of that I was sure. And I realized that there was nothing I could do about it. As long as we were losing money we would be forever a pawn in the power game of Al and Charlie's ambitions, just as they were servants to their respective masters, and would, at even the merest hint, drop whatever they were doing and run to do the man's bidding.

I didn't offer to go and wait with them, using the presence of the heavy deployment of Gardia around the terminal building as my reason. It was raining, the wind gusted in from the sea and it was a long walk from the car park.

Al and Charlie hurried into the building without a word, so I drove slowly back to the office. The charts were being stored away by Seamus.

'What about the sales conference?' he asked me.

'We'll go ahead without them. Life returns to normal now – until the next visit.'

'Or they close us down,' Seamus said gloomily.

'Yes, or that.' I saw no reason any more to pretend.

MANSEL STIMPSON

A Mouthful of Sushi

Waiting for the train to arrive, Andrew found himself watching a man on the platform. The man was so absorbed in his own actions, so intent on emulating the swing of a master golfer, that he was quite oblivious of how comic he might appear to others, standing there and practising the motion, while the book grasped between his hands did duty for the club. This was Tokyo in the autumn of 1981 and Andrew, further from home than ever before on a business trip, had entered the underground station on his way to a gay bar in the Shinjuku area.

Although the greater part of his time had been organized for him by his hosts – interviews and receptions set up for journalists specializing in economics – he had known that there would be some free periods too. So from the start he had planned to go primed, his strategy to be built upon the information in the Spartacus gay guide which listed two recommended bars close together and not far from the Isetan Department Store, Then, by chance, a friend had mentioned an acquaintance who taught English in Tokyo and who might be glad to greet a visitor from England. Accordingly, Andrew wrote to Eric, explaining how he had heard of him, giving the dates of his stay and suggesting a meeting. Their encounter, however brief, should offer Andrew an opportunity to learn something of gay life in Japan, something beyond the surface impressions which are all that most visitors experience. What happened in fact justified this view, for, however atypical Eric's situation, Andrew was to recognize in retrospect how much more he had learnt from their meeting than from his own excursion to the two bars, the Mako and the Regent, which he had undertaken alone. Even so his impressions while there had served to illustrate clearly several aspects of Tokyo's gay scene.

Andrew had found his way to the bars without too much difficulty – although the maze-like exits from the Shinjuku-Sanchome station had momentarily caused him to lose his sense of direction. Having selected an exit (he did not have enough information to make a meaningful choice), he had come out into the street and paused. He discovered an atmosphere in keeping with the night-life of the area. Despite the cleanliness – the absence of litter was a feature of Tokyo – the district, marked by the presence here and there of a strip joint, gave a neon-lit welcome reassuring those who were looking for an evening which would be slightly sleazy. But the young man who approached Andrew as he stood map in hand had no ulterior motive in offering to direct him. It was Fodor not Spartacus which had informed the traveller that the young Japanese are most anxious to try out their English on tourists who need assistance.

Andrew wondered if there would have been any reaction had he asked for one of the bars instead of the Isetan Department Store, from which he could find his way unaided. Standing a little way back from a substantial road, the two bars were almost next to one another facing a side street. Their names, visible in English lettering, were made all the more conspicuous by the open space opposite. Making assurance doubly sure, the Mako offered 'dancing for men'. Andrew went in and up, to be faced by premises which immediately upturned any preconceptions about the nature of a well-known gay bar in a capital city. It could equally well have been a temporary meeting place in Barking or Finsbury Park: two small adjoining rooms for drinking and dancing and a lack of elegance so complete that the bare plaster of the walls provided the surround. Those present during Andrew's visit, largely innocent of the macho look and with a tendency towards the camp or the effeminate, were mainly young and spoke only Japanese. The host, the man behind the bar, was the exception: he spoke a few words of

English and apologized because the only sake he could offer was cold. Despite the povery of the setting, the atmosphere was a friendly one. Before long the record player for the disco blared out the LP version of 'Stars On 45' but that familiar sound was overshadowed by the next attraction. This was a recording new to Andrew and clearly favoured by the young men present. It was called 'We're All American Girls'.

Nearby at the Regent, which Andrew also sampled, the space was just as cramped; but an attempt had been made to create style, albeit of two kinds simultaneously. The plush tone suggested that the owner would feel only contempt for the lack of decor at the Regent; but eighties chic, evidenced by the pictures on the ceiling and on a large calendar on the wall, provided its own contrast, what was on display in each case being a full-frontal male western nude. There were very few seats in the Regent and little communication. The message for the visitor was that this was not a place for strangers: those Japanese who spoke English took no notice of them, while the Englishmen present also kept their distance, as though protecting their territorial rights. By providing a view of gay life in Tokyo it possessed interest, but Andrew was surprised to find it all so modest, so lacking in excitement. If it had a flavour, it suggested not the Big Apple but pecan pie.

Yet it was this same world which provided for Eric a source of fantasy at once fearful and enticing. Or such was the opinion which Andrew formed after meeting him. This encounter with the friend of a friend had taken place the day preceding Andrew's night-time venture to Shinjuku and, intriguing as it was to discover for oneself the character of the bars, he had to admit that, when it came to insight, it was the day with Eric which had been significant.

Having planned to spend half of the day together, they had met early on the Sunday afternoon at the hotel in the centre of Tokyo where Andrew was staying. Eric had brought with him a friend, Alan, who, being in his late twenties, was at least ten years younger than Eric. Alan appeared the smarter and had made more concessions than his friend to dressing for a warm day. But neither was possessed of special characteristics and they stood out here only by virtue of their nationality. Although Alan was also gay, their friendship appeared to be platonic; it was as two Englishmen living in Tokyo that they kept in touch despite differences in their backgrounds. 'I'm a photographer,' explained Alan, when Andrew enquired about the nature of his work, but it was perhaps more significant that this enabled him to keep up a higher standard of living than Eric, occupying a western-style flat in a central area.

Within minutes of meeting, the three men set out for the Meiji Shrine and then made a point of visiting the garden located nearby. This was a place which Eric and Alan enjoyed visiting at weekends whether alone or together. The green leafiness which was a feature of some of the trees may have explained this, for it carried echoes of England; yet the pond within the garden was the abode of turtles and at least one huge carp and a tea house stood beside it. From there it took but a few minutes to reach Omote-Sando, a road closed to traffic on Sunday afternoons, an encouragement to the crowds of pedestrians who would roam from shop to shop or visit a café.

During these wanderings Andrew found himself becoming increasingly responsive to the character of Tokyo; he was also tuning in to his companions. It quickly became apparent that Alan was the more straightforward and also the less interesting. In contrast, Eric was to emerge before the day was out as a character who could exist in a novel by Graham Greene, that master of façades and insecurity. In a film version he would be played by Denholm Elliott. First impressions, however, were conflicting. On the one hand, Andrew was aware that Eric had put himself out for his benefit: nothing could have been more friendly than his readiness to be useful. As against that, there was something in his character to which Andrew was unable to warm. It was revealed obliquely, just hinted at really, by the manner which Eric adopted on entering some of the shops on the Omote-Sando. Once among the art objects and the antiques, he would make a point of disdaining the gaudily popular only to rhapsodize over other objects which to

Andrew's eye had little merit. Observing this behaviour with detachment, Andrew quickly became aware of the reiterated refrain which expressed enthusiasm and yet, allowing Eric to cast half a glance over his shoulder, provided also the safeguard of a qualification: 'this is interesting; not great but interesting'.

It was late in the afternoon when Alan went his own way and Eric fulfilled a promise to show Andrew his home. Eric lived in one of the many suburbs of Tokyo accessible by train and, by offering the hospitality of his home, he was enabling his guest to see an aspect of life in Tokyo unfamiliar to most tourists. The way from the station to his abode, a simple one in true Japanese style, led along a shopping street characteristic of suburbia with its rows of small establishments catering for a variety of needs. Goods and produce on display ranged from food to furniture to hi-fi and among these establishments was a sushi shop frequented by Eric. He pointed it out to Andrew as the place where they could eat, adding, however, that if the raw fish proved to be unpalatable to him they could readily adjourn to Eric's home where food of a different kind was available.

Before venturing into the sushi shop, Andrew was taken down a side turning nearby and introduced to Eric's home. He had already registered the small, squat exteriors of Japanese homes in many parts of Tokyo and therefore was not surprised by what he saw on entering. A mere space by the door, where outdoor shoes could be discarded in favour of slippers, gave on to a kitchen area with toilet to one side and two modest rooms beyond. The far room was the only one to have a window and the vista thus provided revealed a narrow strip of land available for plants; it was little bigger than a long London window-box, while above it washing could be seen hanging out. A lane, comparable to the one at the front, made a demarcation line, flat but imperative, marking off the limits of Eric's territory.

Acting as host, Eric supplied green tea which Andrew accepted and Bull's Blood which, not being fond of alcohol, he declined. In private now, their talk became more concentrated, more personal. Eric, admitting his sensitivity, referred to the conflict he had experienced between his gayness and the

274

religious beliefs implanted in his childhood. He revealed for the first time to Andrew that it was as a priest that he had been sent out to Japan. Subsequently, however, having rejected his calling, he had chosen to stay on in the country where he had settled, discovering there a demand for teachers of English.

More followed in this flow of speech, not all of it coherent. He mentioned that recent events had given him a measure of notoriety in the district where he lived. He spoke in anger of an Anglican church in Tokyo which, having agreed to homophile meetings on premises which it owned, had suddenly rejected the plan to hold these on a Sunday which happened to be the day most suitable. Andrew wondered if it was the stand taken by his host on this matter which had resulted in the story which had put Eric into the local headlines. 'Ninety-five per cent of what was printed was quite untrue,' he was asserting, 'but the result is that I am now regarded as the district's gay man.' Andrew wanted to known more about this, and realized that he was feeling more sympathetic towards Eric as a result of these disclosures. But before he could pursue the matter it was time to leave for the sushi shop where, as it happened, events were to take a new course.

On entering the shop, Andrew was once again aware of Japanese cleanliness. These were simple premises in an unfashionable area and yet, whether one looked at the counter extending down one side or at the tables at the back, spotless surfaces met the eye. Eric was greeted as a familiar figure by the man behind the counter; they spoke together in Japanese, with Eric offering not so much a translation as a précis to Andrew. Although he had insisted that the meal should be at his expense, Andrew left it to Eric to order; even so, he was able to study the large board handed to them on which the range of fish, local or universal, from shrimps to eels, was illustrated. Eric made a selection for both of them, explaining that the portions of raw fish, some wrapped in seaweed, could be dipped in a sauce which was also supplied. To accompany this, sake was available which the customer would then pour a little at a time into a small glass.

275

They had not been long in the sushi shop when Andrew suddenly became aware of a weariness which was spreading through his body; he recognized this as the penalty of too little sleep on the flight out which had ended only twenty-four hours previously. Originally he had intended to go to the bars in Shinjuku with Eric as his companion later that evening, Alan having drawn a map since he knew them well and Eric did not. But now he was too tired to keep to the plan. With his mind partly on this and partly taken up with investigation of the sushi (he found some fish more palatable than others but was nevertheless dubious about trying sushi again), he was not aware at first of the drama which had built up around him with Eric as its central figure. He had been half aware of figures, Japanese figures, entering and taking one of the tables but now their presence took on a new focus for him. 'I'm sorry,' one of them was saying, addressing himself to Eric in English; 'I'm sorry.' The repetition of the phrase suggested that the speaker was in earnest, but at the same time he became fully aware of the degree of tension which existed. Apart from the apology, everything spoken was said in Japanese, leaving Andrew becalmed but decidedly uneasy in the eye of the storm. Possibly it was the Japanese who had created this atmosphere and yet as young men they appeared reserved rather than rowdy, rude at most, not menacing. Taking this in, Andrew recognized the present source of the tension as being in Eric; the sense of raw hostility capable of erupting into violence came from him and only the apology offered in English suggested that it would not come to that.

The situation was defused a few minutes later when the Japanese party withdrew, leaving the two Englishmen as the lone customers once more. Only then did Eric force himself to explain. One of the men at the table had, it appeared, reacted to Eric's presence by describing him as a man who seeks young men. Seeking to justify his own fiery response to this, Eric added the remark: 'You can't sit back and take it all the time.' He said this in a tone far from apologetic, as though he had chosen to take the line he did because he regarded such strong retaliation as a moral duty.

Andrew knew men who would have acted entirely from such motivation. But Eric was not one of them, and his actions gave him away. What he said suggested a man in control who had deliberately unleashed righteous anger but his behaviour revealed a perturbation he was determined to deny. He stopped eating before he had consumed half of what he had ordered. Stressing to Andrew its limited alcoholic content, he turned instead to the drinking of sake and then, as soon as Andrew tried to express his concern over the incident, he persisted in declaring that he was not upset at all. He could not admit to being hurt, to having played any role than the one which he had described; and he felt this the more strongly because the man behind the counter, sensing his lack of control, implied that he was over-reacting. Eric had to believe in his own bravado.

Andrew became rather silent but knew that his companion might attribute this to his tiredness after the flight, for he had now revealed this and it had been agreed to cut short the evening instead of going to Shinjuku. It remained only for Eric to accompany his guest to the station. Getting down from his bar stool, he gave a sudden lurch; it was the first indication that his drinking was having an effect on him. The second sign was the way he stumbled on one of the steps at the station, muttering an excuse as though it were a chance accident. His mood may also have indicated his response to the cancellation of their shared trip to the gay bars. Denying their appeal, he declared: 'I never go there.' But, in case this could be attributed to cowardice, he added at once: 'Of course, I could go there if I wanted to. I could go there every night if I wanted to.' And the last comment was the lie which may have been nearer to the truth than he thought: 'You see I don't believe anything ever happens there.'

Eric, intending to guide Andrew to the right track for trains bound for the centre of Tokyo, led him down to a platform. 'Tell them in London,' he said, 'that if ever I get back I would like to help over gay rights. They could count on me.' At this point a train arrived and Andrew was about to board it when for the first time Eric expressed doubt as to whether the train they had been awaiting was the right one. 'Just a minute,' he said, stepping inside the train to check its destination with one of the passengers. A second later the doors clanged shut and the bemused Eric, thus imprisoned, was carried out of Andrew's sight for ever.

Having no words of Japanese, Andrew was not sure if he could make himself understood but he attempted an enquiry of the station staff and a few minutes later boarded the train which he believed to be the one he wanted. For a little while he was uneasy. As station followed station in these vast engulfing suburbs, he could see names but they were useless to him; his railway map showed only the central area of Tokyo and at least ten minutes passed before the names at last began to match up, thereby confirming his whereabouts. If he had felt a slight anxiety, now assuaged, there was good cause. For Eric had not only entered the wrong train but had taken one which, moving in the opposite direction, was travelling away from Tokyo.

DAN CORRY

In A Way – It Hurts

Ah, the big fella. He's been around as long as I can remember, dressed in his ill-fitting trousers and his too-short coat. It was a parka a long time ago but now it's one of those blue scruffy things with a fluffy bit of synthetic fur inside. His arms are too long for the coat; he just looks crammed into his clothes. And all through the years, as brogues gave way to stacked heels and clogs and on to the new realism of the eighties, he has worn vast plain black shoes – never particularly dirty or tatty but never, ever, shiny.

Lots of people seem to know the big fella, acknowledging him by a look or a wave and giving him some respect. Not the new young professionals who are just moving into the area and not the rising middle classes who arrive to form Community Organizations, action groups, Council lobbys and dog-free bits of the common. But those who for one reason or another, have grown up and learned about life in this place. You couldn't grow up, you couldn't watch the signets turn to swans and not known the big fella.

In plain language I suppose he is something like autistic. Who cares. The only word for him is simple; a gentle giant who finds our crazy world hard to comprehend. Oh yes, I'm being reasonable now but I have shouted 'Crazy' at him in the past. Most times that was down at the recreation ground where we might go after school. You would rush over to the swings and see how high you dared go (and it wasn't very far for me), then race on to the slide and run down it (unless you were a chicken).

And then everyone would pile on to the scaffolding-like, pyramid-shaped roundabout called the 'Witch's Hat' (that has now been banned – probably rightly). And we'd sit on it and some would climb dangerously high. The tougher kids would push it to and fro so that the circular ring that we sat on crashed violently into the central metal pole from which the whole thing was suspended. It took a bit of nerve to stay on when they started doing it. That juddering of the bones as the impact happened and the horrible jarring sound of metal crashing into metal. For the brave it was a great game but for the meek it was a terrifying ordeal that you had to go through – oh so regularly – to be able to save face.

The big fella (who wasn't so big then) would watch all these goings on. He'd stand a little way off on the grass, sometimes with his hands in his pockets, often with them behind his back, and just watch. His face was always dirty and often disgustingly snotty-nosed, but it didn't seem to worry him much.

But nobody really treated him too badly, not Simon the terror of the Witch's Hat, or Arthur who once went right over the top on the swing and lost all his front teeth, or Sheila who stunk to high heaven but was willing to show off her anatomy for an outrageously small sum. It was only those like me who were down near the bottom of the pecking order who would occasionally shout out, 'Come on, come and have a go', and answer his lack of movement with an exclamation of 'chicken'. Mind you, I was only near the bottom on things like the Witch's Hat. Give me a football and it was all a bit different. That was when the other kids always wanted the big fella to play so that there was someone they could beat. But he wouldn't play really, though he would kick the ball back if it went near him. He had a yo-yo which he couldn't really work and he seemed quite happy with that. It would go up and down a few times and you'd think that he'd worked it out after all, but then he'd begin swinging it from side to side, watching it as though hypnotized by its movement. He didn't seem very worried about having to wind it all up again after that and having to start all over again. It used to annoy me like crazy though; I once shouted at him:

'Can't you work it then? Do you want me to show you?' But he didn't seem very interested.

And so in general we didn't really worry too much about him. He didn't annoy us and wasn't much fun to tease. But though he never joined in with our games and stuff, he was definitely one of *our* group; there was no doubt about that. Once a gang of kids from Westfields School turned up at *our* 'Rec'. We ignored them for a time (which was quite a relief to me as I didn't really fancy any trouble). Inevitably they soon got bored with their games and decided to take on the one member of our group who was not with us, who was different and vulnerable. It was obvious they were teasing him, making fun, but we kind of ignored them. And then a rare thing from the big fella; he let out a loud, piercing scream and went red in the face. 'Give it back', he shouted. 'Give it back!' They had stolen his bloody yo-yo and he was mad. He went towards the kid who had taken his precious toy but as he got near him the yo-yo was thrown over his head to another kid. And then as he made his way determinedly, but in his awkward manner, to that child, then he threw it to someone else. Round and round they threw it and round and round he walked. Then they began to speed it up so that he had to run to keep up. It went on and on with the taunters laughing more and more cruelly. A gruesome version of piggy in the middle.

Somewhere along the line, the assailants broke the bounds of decorum. And you could sense that they knew it. They had overstepped some unwritten code and something would have to happen, but they couldn't stop.

And so in some kind of slow motion caricature of a Western, we slowly but deliberately began to make our way over to the part of the park where all this was going on. We did not need to say anything at all. They waited until we were up to them and then threw the yo-yo down in front of the big fella.

'Come on let's get out of here,' they chorused as they left. 'Let him have his stupid yo-yo.' And as if in partial explanation, 'He's a spastic anyway.'

It's funny to think back like that. To think about those days. When do I see the big fella now? Usually it's just at the bus-stop on my way home from work. I'm in my suit with my briefcase and umbrella, returning from the City to my small but comfortable flat. My mind is usually focused on the evening ahead, when I might go out with my girlfriend for a meal or to one of the local pubs to meet up with my friends – most of whom I know through university or work. Or maybe I'll just stay in and listen to a few of my records. It's with my mind on these kind of things (and cursing the lack of a bus) that I see the plod, plod of those big black shoes as he arrives at the bus stop. He smiles and acknowledges a few old ladies, but he doesn't recognize me; no reason he should really. I wonder where he's been? My mind tends to place him on the way back from some sort of day-school for the mentally subnormal. But maybe I'm wrong. I see him quite often but we never talk. What would we talk about? We've gone our own ways and that's not my fault.

Do you know he was even in our cub-pack, even in my six at one stage. But he wasn't much good at most of the games, like treasure hunt and guess-the-object. He was all right at tug-of-war but surprisingly useless at British bulldog. He'd just stand watching everyone. The game he was best at was submarines; he always won that. You had to creep across the whole length of the hall, all along the floor, until you were pointed at by blindfolded listeners. He would slither along on his stomach, sometimes not moving for minutes at a time. He had so much patience.

It used to annoy me that he lost us points at inspection with his garters often missing and his green sweater stained with leftovers of meals. His shoes were never shiny like they were supposed to be.

But he drifted out of cubs. I don't know why. Our Akela said that he had something else to do after school but she wouldn't say what. My mum said she thought he probably found it all a bit much, with so many people and so many rules.

I asked my mum, 'Is he stupid? Is he a spastic or something?'

'I don't think so,' she answered, 'but he isn't very quick and he gets confused easily.' I often pondered on those words – and I still do sometimes,

'Will they put him in a home or something?'

'No I don't think so. He just needs people to be understanding.'

'That's good, because he is my friend.'

'That's good,' answered my mum.

It *was* good mum, but it all got lost along the way. I just don't know where.

When I was a little older I used to go and help my mum in the launderette every Sunday. It was pretty boring in a way, but I used to be rewarded for my pains with bribes of chocolate. The big fella always used to arrive at the launderette when we were there to do some washing. It seemed to be a regular errand for him and he'd do it all like clockwork. He'd lift up the lid of the machine, check there was nothing in it and then pile in the washing. He carefully checked that the knobs of the machine were on the right settings and then get out his washing powder. He'd meticulously measure out the soap in a plastic cup and then pour half of it down the middle of the machine and half of it all round the washing. And then he'd get out the money for the machine from a little plastic money bag.

I know all this because I used to watch him – every Sunday. My mum would sit down with the paper and I would have a couple of comics to read. She never looked up when he came in, but I did. I watched all that ritual and I watched everything he did; except when he might catch my gaze – and then I looked away. Occasionally one of the other Sunday regulars would say, 'How are you?' to the big fella. 'Fine thank you,' he'd smile back. Then he'd sit down and stare at his washing, or sometimes he'd go to the glass front of the launderette and look out at the cars passing by.

Watching him was all part of my ritual too and I quite enjoyed it. But by the time I was about twelve it had begun to frighten me. The guy was simply odd. The bus that took me back from my secondary school dropped my off just near the launderette and I always glanced in when I walked by. And the big fella was so often in there – doing washing. It wasn't just Sundays. I don't know why he was there, or why he wasn't at school. I know that he is still to be found there fairly regularly and I reckon that he must spend his life doing the washing for the old folk who find the effort too much. That's why they all know him. God help him if a time ever comes when everyone has a washing machine. I knew though that he scared me in those days. On one occasion, when I was watching him in the launderette, I noticed a one pound note about to drop out of his pocket, and I almost said something. But I just couldn't tell him that it was going to happen. I got quite frantic about it. I never spoke to him in the launderette.

Eventually I reached an age where one no longer goes to the launderette with mum and so I tended to see the big fella only rarely. Things went pretty well for me. My secondary school was a direct-grant school, so I wasn't with most of my friends from the recreation ground. In fact I soon stopped seeing them. I haven't seen any of them since I was about eleven. But I made new friends after a time, and with them I began to explore the outside world. I was in school plays, in the football team on Saturday mornings and went on trips to Wales to look at the rocks and to Hampton Court to get lost in the maze. Soon O levels came along and I worked very hard for them, passing eight with pretty good grades. Then I had to choose what A levels to do and even what subject I might want to do at university. It was all a long way from the Witch's Hat.

I also started going to parties and arguing with my parents over whether or not I should. And all that meant girls. Not that I liked a lot of the girls that I came across. The crowd we saw at parties were all a little pretentious – far advanced on the boys and somewhat frightening. For a long time I was pretty rotten at parties, and with girls. The cattle market aspects of these events both attracted me and repelled me. But eventually – and in retrospect it seems like it was inevitable – I began to go out, on-and-off, with Clare. She was not the prettiest girl in town, with her short brown fair hair and her roundish face, but she was very friendly and concerned and she wasn't showing off all the time. And she did have lovely eyes. On one of our first dates we went to a pub near where I lived – the Kings Arms, I think it was. I desperately wanted an evening face to face, talking, with the talking being encouraged to flow by a few drinks. Going to the cinema or whatever didn't give us time to talk or to look at each other. But now the prospect of an evening more or less alone with Clare made me nervous, worrying about how the evening would go, fretting that I would run out of words. I shouldn't have worried really though. The words didn't dry up appreciably. I learned a lot about what went on in Clare's mind and let her know enough about myself so that some kind of closeness was established. A few looks into her eyes told me that she wasn't just coming out for a drink with me out of politeness. A few looks into her eyes made my whole body quiver and let my imagination plot endless happy days. An evening in a lovely pub with my girl. Life seemed to be turning yet another of its corners.

I was lost somewhere in these enjoyable thoughts, when the big fella walked into the pub. A person I hadn't seen for three or four years. He really was a 'big fella' now; a very large man in stature. But his shuffling gait, the gentleness of his hands, his neck-less head and childlike face were still there even if they were now attached to a powerful-looking frame. But as I looked at him I was aware of a big change in his appearance, now that he was an adult. It was now rather obvious that he wasn't normal.

He went towards a corner bit of the bar, where the old-timers hung out, and by the way they greeted him it was clear that he was a bit of a regular. His drink – which looked like a half of shandy – appeared far more promptly then anything I'd ever ordered in that pub. He stood with his drink as though part of the bunch in the corner but with his role as that of a concerned listener, rather than an active participant.

When I realized how comfortable he was in this setting I felt relaxed again, because when the big fella first came in, it jogged me. He and what he stood for in my life seemed suddenly to take over from, and make trivial, me and Clare. Only for a minute though. I said to Clare: 'I knew that big guy over there when I was much younger, the one with the big head and the black shoes.'

'Oh,' she said, interested a little, I suppose because of the connection with me and my younger days, and because she was far too bloody polite not to be. 'Who is he?'

'He's a person who just drifts along,' I said not really trying to answer her question. 'I once knew him, but haven't spoken to him in years.'

'Why not?' she asked.

'I don't really know,' I paused. 'It was a long time ago.' Clare looked at the wall behind me, with a somewhat blank expression. But her eyes came back to focus on me as a sudden enthusiasm and keenness came into my eyes, 'I don't know if this means anything to you, but he is a *real* person. You see I've known him from when I was a kid.' I don't think it did mean much to Clare, but she appeared to appreciate the fact that I was trying to let her into my thoughts. I didn't try and explain any further; indeed I didn't really know what I was trying to say.

And so our evening drifted back into its previous mood. It wasn't that easy at first, my mind was not there. I didn't like catching sight of the big fella and made sure that I avoided looking towards him. But after a short while I didn't find that very difficult since all I wanted to stare at was Clare. Very soon I had completely lost interest in the big fella and was back to enjoying my growing feeling of love for Clare.

It was much later – when the drink had brought a pleasant buzz into the evening, when I was beginning to wonder how I could possibly work it so that I ended up with Clare tonight – that there was a sudden sound of a pint crashing to the ground. Everyone turned round to look. A youngish guy up at the bar, who had had one too many, appeared to have knocked over his drink; that was all. It was not of much interest and people quickly returned to their conversations.

But in looking up, my eye had again caught sight of the big fella and my attention had once again been drawn. He was leaning, his back to the bar, with just one person between him and the young glass-smasher. Although nothing seemed to be happening, I felt instantly scared and anxious for the big fella; as though he were my sister. He was too close to this drunken lout. And so although I carried on talking to Clare, half of my attention was on the scene behind her shoulder. She didn't realize for a bit.

The young guy had got himself another pint but was now taking up the issue of his fallen pint with the man standing between him and the big fella; a rather posh man with a trendy peaked cap. He was being accused of having knocked over the previous pint. It wasn't nice, I could see that. But nobody else seemed aware. Nobody else seemed to realize that this could turn nasty and that the big fella was perilously close to the action.

I did not say anything to Clare – nothing had really happened. She chatted merrily about one of her friends who was rumoured to be about to leave school to go into acting, and I did not need to pay much attention. No, I watched them up at the bar, and wondered.

From the little I could hear I knew that the young drunk had begun to ask the posh man why he had knocked over the drink. It was all fairly good natured yet in watching I felt myself frightened but almost exhilarated. It could so easily go wrong and I felt protective.

'What are you watching?' Clare had become aware of my divided attention.

'Oh not much,' I replied, 'just that bloke who knocked his glass over. He's trying to blame the man with the cap.'

She turned round but couldn't really understand what the interest was. She carried on with her story and I pretended to pay attention.

The drunk swung round to get his pint but knocked his pint over again spilling it all along the bar. And at this that harmless big fella just threw back his head and laughed and laughed and laughed. In the drunk's opinion it was not the right thing to do. He moved over to the big fella and my stomach knotted.

'Oh God,' I said, involuntarily.

'What's wrong?' Clare said.

'That big fella, he is going to get in trouble.' She looked round but all she could see was a big man having a good laugh. I felt Clare's leg push against mine beneath the table. It did not have a sexual feel because it was so clearly just for comfort and protection. I held her hand over the table.

The big fella had stopped laughing and was being interrogated by the drunk. What was so funny, eh? It wasn't nice, the whole thing had me knotted up. The big fella was pushed, just a small push, but a push. Why didn't anybody do anything, why didn't they notice? And why was I sitting like this all knotted up when such a whole chunk of me wanted to do something. I guess it was not a big enough chunk.

He was pushed again and then once more. I squeezed Clare's hand tight and said, 'Look what's happening. Oh my God, I should do something.'

At that moment one of the girls behind the bar came up to the drunk. 'Leave him alone,' she said, 'or I'll have you thrown out. He's not done any harm, he isn't that bright and he just likes a good laugh. All right?'

And the young drunk slunk back to his place quietly, and my knots began to loosen. And that big fella just carried on enjoying his evening and Clare and I held hands.

He does that to me that 'big fella', he does that to me. Even though he doesn't know who the hell I am. I think he will always do that to me.

When I see the big fella at the bus stop I just can't help feeling odd because I knew him when I was a kid. Because that big, gentle man will always be a part of me, gnawing away.

CONNIE BENSLEY

The Bad Day

The day that was to come back to Emily repeatedly in
nightmares started well enough. As she watered the geraniums
on the patio, the sun was warm on her shoulders, and already
she felt she could do without her cardigan. A half-forgotten
feeling stirred in her, and seemed to shape itself into a wish to
do something new or different. She thought that she would go
for a walk on the Common. It would give her something to
describe when Marion rang that evening, which she did each
Friday: it would be a little surprise, a little interruption to
Marion's relentless account of her own activities. Of course she
liked to hear about Marion and the boys, and Marion's good
works but . . . she straightened up and went to fetch her old
shoes. She had not been up to the Common since she moved
out of The Laurels down to the flat, and that would be two
years ago. Of course it would take her a good fifteen minutes to
get there – it was a bit of a pull up Sheen Lane, even with her
stick, but there were seats on the way. The doctor had told her
to keep active when she'd seen him for the check-up on her
eightieth birthday. 'I miss The Laurels,' she had told him. 'Of
course you do Mrs Grenville,' he said. He forebore to ask if she
also missed her husband, whose death had led, in due course, to
her move from the big house to the bijou flat. He knew better
than to ask such open-ended questions on a Friday afternoon
with six people drumming their fingers in the waiting room.
Perhaps she missed them both, but in the inhibited way of some
ladies, found it easier to speak of the house than the husband.
  Emily laced on her old brown leather brogues, raising each

foot on the petit point footstool. She took the bag with the shoulder strap that Marion had given her ('it will leave both your hands free mother, much more sensible') and put the strap over her head, and settled it across her thin body. Then she took her garden straw, for the sun was already hot, and settled it firmly over her straight silver hair.

Her route, of course, took her past The Laurels. For forty years or more she had trodden the few yards from the front gate of The Laurels to the Common: in the early days with Marion in a pram; later, on her own; later still with Marion's two children – playing the same games, hearing her voice making the same admonitions: 'Mind the stinging nettles', 'Don't put your face down to strange dogs', 'Don't go any higher dear, the branches are so slippery'.

As she passed the house, she examined it furtively, pulling her hat well forward. It looked much as before – the garden perhaps rather over-bright with so many petunias, and the virginia creeper needing discipline. No prams or toys – it seemed that the nice couple who bought it hadn't any children yet. It was difficult to see much more without lurking and staring. She walked on, her heart thumping slightly – not seriously, but just as when there was an unexpected knock at the front door, or when she had to cross a main road.

Soon she was on the Common, picking her way along the bumpy paths past the football pitches, watching her step and pushing aside stones and the odd coke tin with her stick. There were one or two women about in sundresses and sensible shoes, with assorted dogs. She stood still as each dog bounded along, to brace herself against being bumped or jumped at. A man and a girl ran slowly past her in sports gear, glistening with sweat, their rubber shoes thumping in unison on the sandy path. 'How far are you going this morning?' the girl was asking, but Emily could not catch the man's answer. How nice, these easy friendships between men and girls; but how could they run in this heat? It quite took her breath away to see them. They were on their way to the park, but she turned off towards the cemetery. She was glad to get into the shade of the trees, but the brambles had grown forward since she had last walked here, and they caught at her skirt, so that she had to pick herself free. It seemed that as she freed herself from one, another coiled forward.

At last she turned off to the wild patch near the churchyard, where all was deserted. The sun shone fully down on a tangled mass of grasses, clover and vetch. On the left of the path ahead of her, something brown moved, more solid than a leaf. She pushed the spectacles up her nose. It was a young rabbit, munching, the sun shining pinkly through its ears. She stood very still. This made the expedition worthwhile. It was years since she had seen a rabbit, or any wild animal, in its own surroundings. They held each other's gaze for one minute, two minutes; at last she moved to ease her painful ankle, and the rabbit bolted into the earth.

As she turned away, Emily realized that she was very hot indeed and that there was nowhere to sit down. Also, she wanted to go to the bathroom or, as Marion insisted that the children call it, the loo. As a matter of fact the children called it 'the toilet', a habit formed at school and not easily altered. Emily turned for home. The first part of the return journey was through the shade and past the tiring brambles. A small fear was forming in her mind about the distance she had to cover to get back home. For once, she wished herself inside her cool flat, behind the lace curtains, with her feet up on the stool. She wiped her face and her spectacles with a neatly pressed handkerchief. As she left the trees, the heat hit her like a smothering curtain. There was nobody about and the open sports ground shimmered in the vertical light. The grass was drained of colour and nothing moved. The length of two football pitches had to be crossed to get back to the road. She put out a hand to a tree trunk to steady herself. She did not think she could walk so far, yet she must. In the distance, near the road, the sun glinted on something metallic and she set out towards it, her mouth dry, the blood singing in her ears. If she could only reach the road she would be on home territory, though of course it was all familiar, it was only she who had changed, become weak and faint. She seemed to see two tree trunks in place of each single one, and now there were twin metallic glintings. She stared, willing them to return to one. One litter bin; it must be the litter bin near the entrance to the Common. She kept her eyes on it, forcing herself to walk carefully over the interminable, hot, open ground.

Slowly it came into focus, became clearer, and at last loomed up at her out of a mist. She put out a shaking hand to touch it. Now she was almost home, and why she had come out on such a hot day she could not recall. She would soon be back at The Laurels and up the path past the petunias. Now she saw, with alarm, that the front door was open. What on earth had possessed her to leave the front door open; Philip was always telling her to make sure to lock up. Perhaps she need not tell him. The great thing was to get to the bathroom. Limping into the dim coolness of the hall, she gave a half sob of relief. As she climbed the stairs, the carpet looked weirdly different – where were the threadbare patches? No matter now – the thing to do was to reach the bathroom. From somewhere below, in a kind of pulsating loudness and softness, scraps of talk between a man and a woman floated up: 'The bloody hose has come off and there's water all over the kitchen floor' . . . 'Well shove it back on, I can't be everywhere.' She reached the bathroom, dragged herself inside, and locked the door.

Some minutes passed, which she could not afterwards recall, but then, running cold water over her wrists, she stiffened at the sound of footsteps coming up the stairs. Her breath came short. Who could be on her stairs with such a confident tread, at this time of day? The footsteps came closer, and to her horror, the handle of the door turned. There was a thump, as if someone was trying to budge a door that had stuck. Then the handle again, turning and rattling horribly. A man's voice called out doubtfully – 'Jean? I thought you were downstairs.'

There was a silence, and after a moment the steps receded. Emily strained her ears and heard scraps of conversation – a woman's voice laughing, then becoming serious. Emily heard the word 'police'. She shrank into a corner, twisting a towel between her fingers. Her stick was hanging from the towel rail, and she took it down and held it in front of her. After a few moments there was a scraping and banging, near the window. This was the sort of noise a window cleaner made, and she realized, fearfully, that someone was coming up a ladder to the window. Should she made a dash to get out of the door? Her legs felt so weak. As she hesitated, a man's face appeared at the glass. Emily, half whimpering with fear, saw a young man with brown, dishevelled hair and a thin face, streaked with mud. It was a face she half-recognized. After a moment, he made a flapping gesture with his hands, and, mouthing something that she could not understand, he disappeared again.

What could it mean? Why were people trying to get into her home, into her bathroom? In that second, turning to the mirror and seeing the unfamiliar wallpaper behind her reflection, she was struck by the terrible revelation that this was not her bathroom. She looked around her and, as if waking up, saw gleaming chromium where there had been dull metal, and flowered tiles where she remembered scuffed cream paint. Dear God, let her be dreaming. Surely she must wake up and find herself safely in bed, not trespassing in someone else's house. The word 'police' came sickeningly back to her. Now, footsteps had started on the stairs again, and someone was outside the door. A woman's voice called soothingly: 'Mrs Grenville, would you like to come down now and have a cup of tea?' Emily remembered the voice. Jameson, Mrs Jameson. The young couple. After a pause she said: 'I am coming,' and she fumbled at the unfamiliar lock.

As she came out she was crying, could not help herself, and the young woman put an arm round her shoulders. Emily said: 'Please do not tell my daughter. I should be so grateful if you would not tell her. I'm so sorry, I . . .,' she stopped, unable to explain the matter, and allowed herself to be shepherded downstairs.

The Jamesons made her rest on the sofa and drink tea, and said that anyone could get confused in the heat, and in due course they drove her slowly home and saw her settled in the armchair, with her feet on the stool. Was she sure that her daughter shouldn't pop over? Or the doctor look in, just to give her something for a good night's rest? Emily shook her head, and they left, closing the door gently. After a while she crept out to the patio, where the geraniums were casting long, spidery shadows across the paving stones. She remembered the morning with nostalgia, and longed to go back to it, for nothing now would be the same. She would not leave the flat on her own again except to go to the shops. But supposing she left the flat without realizing it? She had sometimes braced herself against the prospect of death, but this fear was something altogether worse.

The telephone rang. 'Hello dear,' she said. 'Oh no, nothing special. And what have you been doing with yourself?'

PETER WHITEBROOK

Gauguin's Leg

Her two marital engagements, one at twenty-two and the other ten years ago at twenty-eight, having proved both protracted and inconclusive, Jane Honeyman now lived alone in the nineteenth-century quiet of Queen Victoria Street, one of Edinburgh's most highly rated and widely admired backwaters of solid grey private houses.

The large and staid buildings, set just out of line so that you didn't actually see them as terraces, rose two floors high from basements sunk deep into their surrounding gardens of smooth lawns and prodigious flowerbeds shielded from each other and the street by chest-high iron railings. Every May blossom from cherry trees flew across the cobbled road and lay thick on the roof of a newish Volkswagen Golf or other preferably foreign car parked outside each gate. One by one the Queen Victoria Street residents had refurbished their basements ('garden flats', the estate agents who found suitable tenants called them), either renting to young lawyers whose partnerships would take another couple of years or to university lecturers, tenants whose social and professional standing were an embryo of their landlords', or else, with a private grimace, storing their parents or other elderly relatives in them.

Jane Honeyman had let her own basement flat in November to an appropriate but fat woman in her early thirties called Rosalind McEwan, a cataloguing assistant in the antique furniture department of an international auction house. Rosalind was recently divorced from a QC who, Jane Honeyman discovered, cropped up with surprising regularity in the

Scotsman newspaper in connection with the more lucrative civil cases. According to Rosalind, who spoke of him little but with some spite when she did, he had prosecuted his own divorce with no less relish or thoroughness.

Since Rosalind came to live below, Jane increasingly saw herself as her custodian for Rosalind clearly needed a cushion to protect her from the world. Although, Jane Honeyman thought to herself, in private moments such as in her bath when she considered her own lean body beneath the water, Rosalind's fat would be a cushion against most things.

Her assumption of Rosalind's embittered retreat into seclusion was jolted at precisely ten-thirty at night on the second of June, just after she had switched off the television news. She heard, unmistakably, Prokofiev's fourth symphony from the flat below penetrating her floorboards and carpet. Standing in the blue shadows by her sash windows and peering downwards, she saw the reflection of light from the basement window on the grey stone wall directly opposite it and on the steps leading up from the tiny courtyard to the garden path.

After a few moments she dismissed the sound as uncharacteristic of her tenant. Possible Rosalind often played music on the stereo; possibly she had inadvertently set the volume too high or was in the loo and momentarily unable to rectify a sudden crescendo.

Yet as she stood there long enough for anyone to come out of the loo the noise became if anything more insistent, more passionate. On the top of the stone courtyard wall a few clumps of bluebells leaned towards the street as if in a high wind. Probably shuddering, she thought.

Next morning, as she closed her front door on her way to work as an editor at Miles Publishing, she was greeted by a young man emerging from Rosalind McEwan's. Jogging up the steps he offered her a lift into town in a green snub-nosed Citroën she had not noticed parked at the gate.

Closely watched by Geraldine Couchman who just happened to be supervising the street's school transport rota from her house directly opposite, she got into the passenger seat.

Stewart, the end of his thin red leather tie over his left shoulder, was an architect and told her as they nosed their way through the Georgian new town that he was professionally interested in her street.

During the following nights Stewart's car was often parked outside, his professional interest, Jane Honeyman thought acidly, becoming obsessive. The developments were commented on by her neighbours.

Jane knew that her neighbours, the Couchmans, McCabes and Robertsons, saw her as the subject of mild but distant concern, rather in the way they viewed famine in Africa.

Roger Couchman made television travel documentaries, Bobby McCabe was a partner in a law firm and Edgar Robertson the director of an advertising agency. In each case their wives, Geraldine, Sue and Ginny had no job and thought Jane wonderful for managing. Their children, with names like Marcus and Annalouise, attended the best private schools.

Only the Grants were different. The Couchmans, McCabes and Robertsons looked on Colin, a socialist playwright, and Clare, who was attached to the local Council in some vague capacity as a community anthropologist, with bemused tolerance. Geraldine Couchman called them their social consciences and said they were fun. Edger Robertson said they read the *Guardian*. None of them had ever seen any of Colin's plays which were either performed in Council housing estates in Glasgow or transmitted on Channel 4, but their St Andrews education and hardwood patio doors were admired and Martyn with a 'y' attended the same school as Marcus.

Dinner parties were the Queen Victoria Street social focus and regulator. The Couchmans excelled at giving them and a few weeks ago had held one so that Roger, the first of them to acquire a gold American Express card, could show it off.

'How I ever managed abroad without it, I'll never know,' he said, shaking his head as he cut another wedge of Stilton. 'Especially in New York last month.'

'Darling,' said Geraldine, and put her arm around his.

Each of the guests held the card in turn, Bobby McCabe and

Edgar Robertson rather resentfully, thought Jane, except Colin Grant who poured himself more wine, dug his fingers into his hair and loudly asked God to save them all.

The card was returned to its place in front of its owner's cheeseplate.

'Only in this house,' said Colin, 'could the centre-piece of a dinner table be a gold credit card. And that's only because Bobby and Edgar don't have one yet. Now it won't be any fun for them when they do.'

Poor Clare, thought Jane, as she saw the irritation in their eyes and the alarmed expression of the escort Geraldine had provided for her 'just to make up the numbers, darling', some press-ganged colleague of Roger's, poor Clare will do her little round of apologies tomorrow morning.

'I can draw ten grand,' said Roger, snapping his fingers, 'just like that. Anywhere in the world. Then juggle the old expenses and claim it all back, of course.'

Jane's escort laughed heartily. Roger must be your boss rather than a colleague, Jane thought. Colin said it. Poor Clare would get his telephone number from Geraldine at some opportune moment and make a fourth call in the morning.

Colin made the Grants' dinner parties unpredictable affairs. Once, when he was midway through writing what he called an alternative *Scarlet Pimpernel*, a socialist musical which he said would show the true French Revolution, he had suddenly delivered a lecture over the dessert.

'The trouble with all of you,' he had said, 'is that you believe your lives are about accomplishment, but they're nothing of the sort. They're not even about ambition which of course makes successive accomplishments valueless. Your lives are all about acquisition. Power. Or, putting it another way, doing each other down. Your emotions are all wrong as well. You think that actually to be associated with an emotion is an achievement in itself. You try to be sincere and clever and witty without knowing why or what to be sincere, clever and witty about. Which is why you're dependent on each other. You're a damned race, the lot of you. All except you, Jane.'

All except me, thought Jane, pleased that Clare Grant was her only neighbour who did not worry about numbers at dinner. However, Clare had once broken the assumed code of not inviting basement-dwellers to these above-ground evenings. Polishing her spectacles one day while taking a break from hoeing under her rhododendrons, Clare had suggested to Jane that Stewart and Rosalind be invited to a moussaka evening her own basement tenants, a Greek businessman and his wife, were giving as a token of farewell. So they're already a couple, thought Jane as she changed the subject. Stewart and Rosalind. Something fixed.

One Saturday evening as Jane returned from shopping, she met them on the garden path on their way to a party near the river. Rosalind was dressed in the current fashion in imitation of a man, a suit of some sort of silvery fabric, trousers, double-breasted jacket, a white shirt and striped tie. Jane Honeyman watched Rosalind's curious rolling walk as she and Stewart moved towards the gate, the suit clinging and digging obscenely into all Rosalind's many fatty lumps and folds.

This was a month before Jane went on holiday during the Edinburgh Festival. It was not that Jane shared the indifference of the Couchmans, McCabes and Robertsons towards the arts, quite the reverse, she attended concerts at the Usher Hall, buying a subscription ticket each season for the Scottish National Orchestra. She took her holiday during the Edinburgh Festival because, in common with the Couchmans, McCabes and Robertsons, she let her house during the three August weeks to foreign visitors. While the others did it for the gifts they had come to expect along with the rent Jane did it out of necessity, needing both money and a rest.

And so Jane Honeyman ate alone in the little restaurant near her hotel in Concarneau, fish, Camembert and a glass of red wine, always with a book at her side. The awkwardness of eating alone in a public place meant that during her first week she had finished *Farewell My Lovely* and was halfway through *Killer in the Rain*. No rain here, thank goodness: she strolled along the waterfront in the humid dusk and had a nightcap each evening sitting outside different cafés watching the friends and lovers at other tables.

One morning during her second week she took an early morning walk before breakfast to the shop where she had arranged to have a daily newspaper kept aside for her and found herself standing behind a man whose methodical and questioning recital of the names of English papers made her laugh out loud.

'Look,' she said, 'it's all right, you can read mine. For some reason the only one they get is the *Express*, anyway.'

David was alone, an art historian on a working holiday from the Tate Gallery, researching for a book he was writing on Gauguin.

'It's extraordinary,' he said, 'because my French is more or less restricted to *la plume de ma tante*. And the names of paintings and museums, of course. In restaurants I point at something on the menu and take pot luck with whatever comes. In towns I pick someone out of the crowd, look helpless and say "Musée?"'

She laughed again.

They became friends.

'I'll translate for you,' she said.

She ordered crab for them in restaurants and drinks in cafés. His French was better than he had made out and he said the same about her knowledge of Gauguin's paintings. Together they visited Pont Aven and had lunch by the river, took day trips to museums and looked at paintings and one day drove to Arles and to the Place Lamartine.

'Gauguin would have walked across here,' said David, 'on Christmas Eve in 1888, when he heard footsteps behind him. He turned around and saw Van Gogh holding an open razor, obviously meant for him. That night Vincent hacked his ear off at the skull.'

Back in Concarneau they walked arm in arm and she leant her head against his shoulder as he told her about his work. She told him about her house and Miles Publishing. That night, sitting outside the café, he stroked her forearm as she cupped her chin in her palm and watched the shine on his teeth as he laughed when she spoke to him in French. Later, as the warm breeze swung the paper lanterns hanging from the café awning, he held her shoulders and their lips brushed gently across each other's while from a nearby table somebody applauded them good-naturedly.

'Bon appetit,' someone said as they turned and walked away.

They parted on the Wednesday of her third week, after their café breakfast, David to drive to Rouen in his orange Beetle, she to take a train to Paris and the airport. Before their meal they had gone to the harbour where David took many photographs. It was there, he said, that Gauguin began the journey that eventually took him to Tahiti where he would consolidate his colour theories and paint his greatest pictures. In France he was depressed and despised. Also, he said, his appetite for women had earned him the wrath of not a few husbands. And before he left Concarneau a group of local men, cuckolds probably, caught up with him at the harbour here and savagely assaulted him, beating him and breaking his leg.

They looked around at the few old fisherman on the quayside.

'Perhaps one of their grandfathers did it,' he said. 'We could find out,' she said, 'I could ask them.'

'No,' he said. 'I like the story the way it is.' He looked at her. 'There's always retribution. Everyone gets their come-uppance sometime. Some people it destroys, while others . . . ' He spread his arms and grinned. 'Like Gauguin. He went on to paint wonderful pictures.'

Jane repeated the last week in her mind as the train sped through France, the sunlight bouncing off the window beside her making the landscape and tall cypress trees rushing past seem at times like a bright flickering film.

When she returned to Queen Victoria Street she found that Rosalind McEwan was away on holiday with Stewart. She smiled at the thought of Rosalind on a beach somewhere, a bloated pink form, the two parts of a bikini stretched around her like string around an uncooked joint of meat, and took her film to be developed at the photographic shop next door to Miles Publishing.

At the first party after her return (the McCabes: drinks on Sunday twelve noon, in the garden if it's warm enough, inside if not, and guess which it'll be, dear, we're back in Britain now), she took pleasure in showing her pictures. She described each in turn to the Couchmans, McCabes, Robertsons, Grants and the compiler of a gazetteer of historic Scottish burial grounds Sue McCabe had invited 'just to balance things out', making David sound rather important.

'He's in almost all of them, darling,' said Geraldine Couchman, 'you must have spent a lot of time together.'

Roger turned the hint into an innuendo.

Clare nodded studiously at Jane and said she was 'really pleased for her. Well, they both were, actually.'

Ginny Robertson took her to one side and said her skin looked stunning. 'It's good for your complexion,' she said.

While the gifts her neighbours had been left by their summer tenants were substantial, and in the Couchmans case (an antique silver cigarette box), saleable, their holidays had been less successful.

Roger had pulled strings to swing a free holiday for the Couchmans in Florence. Photographs showed Marcus in sta-prest tennis shorts gazing smugly at old buildings and Geraldine outside some boutiques with some darling things she just couldn't say no to. Roger, however, had paid with his new credit card on the assumption that he would be making a travel film and be able to claim the extravagance back. But the television company had scrapped the Florence idea and proposed autumn residential craft weekends in Lancashire instead.

Edgar and Ginny Robertson had been to Miami where Edgar had his travellers' cheques stolen and Ginny her handbag.

The McCabes had returned from Corsica. Their photographs showed Bobby by some rocks on a small moped and later standing by more rocks with a bandaged knee. Sue had burned her breasts trying topless sunbathing which explained her stooped and fully clothed posture while standing on even more rocks.

Colin's alternative *Scarlet Pimpernel* had been staged in a disused warehouse in Leith and won a Fringe First award from the *Scotsman*, but Martyn's cat had been run over.

The next day Jane enrolled for a course of evening classes in art history at the university and bought Thames and Hudson books on the Impressionists and Post-Impressionists. This she told David in a letter to London, writing another after the introductory lecture.

Yet there was no letter or telephone call in return. At first she was curious and then, as another week went past, disappointed. Twice she telephoned him and twice left a rather plaintive message on an answerphone machine. 'Don't you think Cézanne is fascinating?' she said on the second occasion. 'I can see his shapes and forms in the garden, even.'

She attended the second class but missed the third. A group excursion to London and the galleries, the National and the Tate, was planned but she said she was busy on the dates arranged.

She gave up writing David letters.

Rosalind McEwan returned from her holiday and most nights the green snub-nosed Citroën stood outside the gate. Some nights she met Rosalind walking along Queen Victoria Street on her way back from work. In the gloom Jane hardly recognized her at first, attractive and smiling in a fashionable long coat, a copy of *Cosmopolitan* magazine under her arm. Rosalind chatted while Jane fiddled with her key.

Rosalind and Stewart began to be invited to the dinner parties, the Grants breaking the basement-dweller code first, followed by the Robertsons. Jane went along to the Grants almost as a guest of Rosalind and Stewart rather than those giving the dinner. She missed the Robertsons. It was better somehow, tidier around the table.

At weekends, disappointment replaced by anger, she took her pruning shears to the dead heads on the rose bushes, letting them fall in a flurry of browning pink and white petals through thorny branches to the hardening earth.

She gave up the art history classes.

Anger lolled into futility. One grey Saturday, as a malign treat, she bought a frozen cream sponge cake, let it thaw in the kitchen and ate it while watching television.

Waking on bleak Sunday mornings Jane Honeyman moved slowly from her bed to the bathroom where the scales were. As she stepped on to them the calibrated dial at her toes whizzed round and shook to a standstill. Each week she saw, without feeling, that there was more weight. Fat. Podge. Flab. Blubber. Rosalind had got shot of it. She was piling it on.

VAL WARNER

His Shining Knight

It was the picture of himself that had haunted him during the
frenzied few minutes of the taxi ride between Battersea and
Victoria, with every set of traffic lights like a Berlin Wall
between two states; Trevor stood outside the grey locked door
of May's room, wondering what to do. The taxi meter outside
and conceivably May's life inside the locked door ticked away,
while he wondered what to do. After the drama of bursting into
the house by kicking in the front door under the apathetic eyes
of the taxi-driver – not really so dramatic as he'd remembered
May moaning how the lock was so loose that most of the other
tenants in the house didn't bother with a front-door key – and
bounding up the stairs to the top floor like any silver-screen
hero, it seemed especially inadequate to be doing nothing now.

But probably May was out living it up at a friend's. Or at least
living. She'd never struck him as cut out for living it up, any
more than he was himself. He tried to think lucidly and quickly
– not very practicable for him at the best of times. He
remembered she often worked in the British Museum Reading
Room from late afternoon on the midweek days when it stayed
open late, but today was a Friday so she couldn't be there, even
if she was still able to carry on working as before after what had
happened. Perhaps she was away for the weekend. He could
remember her occasionally mentioning she'd been away for the
weekend, generally in connection with her work – very May.
And there was the shadowy figure of a man in the background,
though recently he'd had the impression that the shadows had
finally got him. Perhaps if he'd been around now, he could have

done something to lift her spirits? All Trevor himself could grasp was that her life was her work, so that it was difficult to see how she could ever recover from what had happened.

He'd like to think of May spending the weekend with a sympathetic friend and being soothed, but when he envisaged her ravaged face as he'd seen her the evening before, that seemed a rose-tinted image. Somehow, it was the calmness of her resignation that he'd found so chilling. That had haunted his mind over the past twenty-four hours, as he'd ended up telling Tim. Tim had seemed so possessed of the emergency of the moment, and had momentarily so possessed Trevor of this, that he was now outside the fateful door taking the long, cool look at the situation which had eluded him sitting in his elegant sitting-room with Tim.

'Shouldn't you *do* something?' For the first time that afternoon, Tim had turned his cool, grey eyes full on him. So he had phoned May. No answer, of course. Tim's eyebrows (not plucked?) had seemed even more quizzical as he watched him replace the receiver. 'Speed is of the essence,' he said, reclining on the *chaise longue*. Trevor had a nasty suspicion that if Tim was familiar with any kind of speed, it was not the kind he was urging on him. He'd muttered, 'Perhaps I should go round there. I'm sorry to break up things.' He hoped Tim would offer to come with him, but he'd said, 'Not at all. I'd have to be making tracks soon.' Trevor rang for a taxi and Tim slipped away as he filled in the minutes dashing round closing windows and switching off the electric fire and generally fussing.

He'd met Tim at one of the huge parties given by his ex-sister-in-law and on an impulse which he didn't quite understand had invited him round for tea – tea! a meal he never ate and which had to take place at an hour which broke into his sacrosanct working day at home as a publisher's reader. And then in the stately silence of his sitting-room, whose peace Trevor generally appreciated in London, Tim had proved harder to talk with than against the party's background noise. In fact, he could hardly get two words out of him about his life as an English teacher in Saudi Arabia, from where he was on leave, due to return in a fortnight's time. Playing mum over the teacups, Trevor had wondered how soon he could decently offer a stronger drink. In desperation, he had been telling Tim how May's publisher had rewritten the biographical part of her book to make it measure up to the correct feminist formula to which Vyvian, in life, had regrettably failed to conform. Then somehow, under Tim's flitting eyes and his memory of May's stony gaze the night before, there didn't seem to be *any* humorous dimension to that story and, in what by now had become a monologue, he had found himself revealing how worried he really was about her. So thanks to Tim he was now staring miserably at the door of her room, wondering if he would expect him to knock it down.

He looked around for help, but of course there was none. No note from May, conveniently left for some expected visitor, saying 'Back at 7 p.m. Please wait', complete with today's date. But even if there had been, it could have been a red herring, a false trail laid by the all-planning May before she ceased to plan. He'd occasionally come here to supper with her and now those casual goodbyes at the top of the stairs mocked him – not that at the time they didn't each seem to have more than a fair share of the northern hemisphere's problems.

He looked more carefully at the matter in hand. The door with its maddening inch-wide gap at the top was on the landing at right angles to another door into May's other room, normally entered by a communicating door through the big room; he'd never seen that door to the landing opened and suspected it might be bolted from inside. Opposite, a dresser and a gas cooker were crammed on the tiny landing. Trevor had worried that the cooker was a fire risk, and that her rich absentee Rachmanesque landlord was heartlessly breaking some fire regulation? Nor, personally, would he have cared for all the tenants below to sniff precisely what and at what hour he was cooking, though he'd always got the impression that May cooked only for visitors and didn't care too much what anyone thought about the cooking or anything else. Under a quiet manner, she'd struck him as curiously self-possessed though at the same time bereft of confidence.

He remembered noticing the long, uncurtained sash-window above the deep stairwell, over the little half-landing where the staircase bent round. Standing at the top of the stairs with your back to the bloody door, you almost had the impression of being on stage, especially after dark, playing to some invisible audience out there among the orange lozenges of the house lights, across the yard. Or perhaps on a scaffold. Perhaps, sometime, he'd heard Big Ben chiming through the lowered window – May always left that window open all through the winter (as like so much else in the house, it didn't work properly?) – and vaguely remembered Charles I stepping on to the scaffold through a window in Whitehall. This window overlooked a builder's yard that had once been a mews, he remembered May telling him. Especially at night, he'd always felt it would be very easy to take a step into the dark, framed in the light.

There was a minor explosion downstairs, followed by a rush of smoky air. After a moment, Trevor realized that this was what it felt like on the inside when the front door was kicked open. The tenants were coming home from work: he imagined May sighing that the house's relative peace was over for another day. Doors were unlocked and slammed, apparently jack-booted feet ran down to the basement and up, a lavatory cistern flushed – he remembered making his way down through the house to the communal bathroom in the basement. The electric bulb had always gone on one or other landing so that the house had seemed a death-trap. Now, a fragrance of cooking wafted up the stairwell.

He wondered if by any chance the ground-floor tenants would have a spare key to May's flat, though more likely if anyone had a key it would be the occupant of the first-floor flat, from which he'd noticed no sign of life. From what he remembered of the constant changes and general unreliability of tenants in these multi-occupied houses from the years before he and Elaine had bought their first flat, he doubted May would leave a key with her neighbours. In any case, he'd have to explain why he wanted the key. They might think that he was a burglar, though May was certainly too poor to have anything worth stealing. Not, of course, that a burglar would know that before breaking into the anteclimax of her untidy, paper-littered room. And a methodical burglar, intending to clean out the premises, might well start on the top floor of a building and work down. Then he remembered reading in the newspaper that the early afternoon was the prime time for burglaries, at least premeditated ones, and in any case he imagined these multi-occupied houses would offer poor pickings, so he stopped worrying about being mistaken for a burglar, should he decide to sally down to appeal to the ground-floor tenants.

In any case, it wasn't really the prospect of being mistaken for a burglar that chilled him. Rather, extrapolating from May's life to his own, it was the devastating prospect of the other residents in his own building being asked for a spare key on the grounds that he might be getting up to no good in his flat, might in fact be busy doing away with himself. The Hargreaves! John Day! Mrs Campton! He blenched. He knew this was only another transmogrification of the what-would-the-neighbours-think? syndrome, the nightmare of any bourgeois, which he supposed he had now perforce become. Yet, he found it the most appalling scenario – the kind of thing that would make him contemplate suicide. He saw himself large as life trying to persuade his neighbours in turn that his compassionate, enquiring, imaginary friend had been just a little the worse for drink, which had sharpened his concern, though, as far as the Hargreaves at least went, he wasn't sure he wouldn't be out of the frying-pan into the fire. May's cooker glowered at him, grimy with generations of grease, he felt sure, though mercifully the light was fading. But no, Trevor felt decisive about this one; while there was any possibility May was alive he couldn't go running round her neighbours with suicide stories, ruining any reputation she might have as a well-balanced, sober, respectable body. And if he said he'd left some piece of property in her room – something which he simply couldn't live without – if they had any sense they'd take him for a con man.

Then he worried that one of the tenants might wander up to the top of the house where he was skulking, though he could think of no good reason for his or her doing so and the little half-landing under the window put him out of sight of the comings and goings of the first-floor tenant, also invisible at the moment. All that was drifting up was the fragrance of cooking, as if the stairwell were a huge cauldron. Where *was* their cooker for God's sake? He hadn't remembered seeing a cooker in the hall. He decided that the fragrance was rosemary, and he rued it. It gave him a bad moment. Rosemary for remembrance.

Somehow, away from Tim's steely eyes, May's suicide had seemed rather less likely. It was almost as if Tevor's expenditure of vigour and indeed cash – the taxi throbbed on below – so far had provided enough displacement of energy to check his worrying. As he looked round at May's makeshift kitchen and saw superimposed Tim sprawled on his *chaise longue*, he tried to go on feeling it had all been a storm in a teacup.

For not least among May's problems was her landlord, who would be unlikely to believe that the door of her flat had been battered down in a potentially life-saving emergency, and even if that truth could be drummed into his thick skull (Trevor had never met this latter-day Rachman, but he'd heard plenty), he might not think a potential suicide a suitable tenant. If not properly hushed up, a successful attempt might get the house a bad name, though rented accommodation being as difficult as it was to come by in central London, Trevor couldn't seriously foresee any difficulty in reletting a flat. Still, if May had to add immediate threat of eviction to her other problems, she would be even less grateful to him for accidentally battering down her front door, that is to say her room door, on a wild goose chase to save her life, quite unnecessary in the event. And given that the front door of the house yielded to the slightest pressure, she might feel even more strongly about the security of her own door. It wasn't even as if she'd *threatened* suicide, What had alarmed him had been her very resignation, her calmness, but perhaps that betrayed his own irrationality rather than hers – not of course that he would agree that suicide was an intrinsically irrational act. After all, he had to keep his own lines of retreat open. 'Be prepared' had been his motto since boyhood.

And even if her life was there to be saved, although he now considered that unlikely, Trevor wondered if he'd really be doing her a favour, dragging her bodily back to the land of the living. May was certainly not the kind of person, he reckoned, likely to indulge in a silly hysterical cry for help, a not-quite-final *cri de coeur*. If May had done this act, it was for real. For good. Shouldn't he let things be, however, she'd arranged them, for good or ill?

And what if she moaned 'Let me go', as he'd read in one suicide account that a reviving doctor had been besought. He didn't quite see himself standing up in the coroner's court, clearing his throat and announcing complacently, 'So I let her go.' Wouldn't that make him accessory to manslaughter? Prison? Life sentence? He braked his imagination, which was careering off to crash the helpless passenger of his reason, and pulled himself together; all the same, if he were intending to respect May's hypothetical wishes, he'd best start by respecting her locked door and ride home in his increasingly expensive taxi. Also, there could be the insurmountable problem of explaining to the coroner the motive for her suicide. He only hoped she would have had the presence of mind to leave a note spelling out precisely how her publishers had driven her to take this drastic step. Perhaps he would be doing May more of a favour if he were to phone the press rather than the ambulance if – *if* he broke down the door and found . . . her. Not that that would be the case, and in any case her name was not sufficiently well known to excite much interest dead or alive, so that he would have to sell the story on the name of her publisher – who would sue, if her lawyers could get stuck into any technical loophole.

He tried to review May's life – what he knew of it – like the mythic drowning man, except of course it was she who might be drowning, actually or metaphorically, though as he reflected again, that was pretty unlikely. Still, she would certainly find it difficult if not impossible to recover from what the publishers had done to her. He'd worked in publishing all his life before going into semi-retirement as a reader for his old firm and he could tell bad publishing stories with the best of them, but he'd never known anything as scandalous as the fundamental changes made to May's book on the pretext of shortening it. The pretext was unbelievably specious given that she had written it to the length originally specified by the publisher. If only he'd known about the affair during that crucial week between May's being informed of the 'shortening' and the manuscript being whipped off to the printer, perhaps he could have advised her how to fight – Society of Authors? – Writers' Guild? – though with only *one week* . . . As it was, any reputation May might have had as a critic would scarcely survive the facile praise the publisher had heaped on Vyvian's very indifferent prose and juvenilia. And as for May's scholarship, that could now never be anything but suspect given the way the publisher had suppressed key facts to present a more sensational Vyvian. To make matters worse, he feared that the biographical issue was a time-bomb that would explode on May in the future, when she might have been beginning to pick herself up again, as it was unlikely any of the reviewers would have the knowledge to challenge the 'facts' given about this hitherto obscure poet who had published only a handful of poems in the interwar years under the name 'Vyvian'. Beside the critical perversity and the biographical fraudulence of May's publisher, that lady's imposition of a ridiculous feminist straitjacket on to Vyvian was just a pathetic joke.

Although he was by no means a close friend of May's, he had the impression that she had very little else in her life beside her work and a number of friends. Things had clearly been hard enough for her. He doubted how many more successful authors would have been prepared to exist mainly on a diet of oats and potatoes in order to buy the time to write, though May always parried any comments on anything she let slip about her standard of living with, 'Oh well in the Third World I'd most likely be dead by thirty-five anyway.' But it was difficult to see how she could fight back after the way her publisher had destroyed her. Sooner or later, a corrective book on Vyvian would be published to set the record straight, and May could expect only to be pilloried for her publisher's anonymous lies.

He would be pilloried by Tim if he thought to ask after the upshot of his frantic visit to May, if he said he'd arrived there and done nothing . . . if he saw him again. He could see very clearly the cold contempt in Tim's eyes. But he hadn't done anything. He hadn't offered to come with him. But then, for all his off-the-cuff advice, Tim hadn't known May. He hadn't known her very well himself, but they'd had things in common. Literature. It had been through him that she'd first got the free-lance proof-reading that had become her main source of income, though later he'd wondered if he'd done her much of a favour; he'd always felt she'd given up too easily as a novelist after her previous publisher turned down her third novel, though come to think of it, for all he knew she might have gone on to produce other manuscripts that were in turn rejected. She was always working very hard. It had been a casual friendship, but shared interests were what mattered. Yet, for all the non-communication with Tim that afternoon, they'd had things in common.

At the party, he'd been drawn to Tim because someone had mentioned a new novel by one of his favourite authors and the youth's eyes had filled with tears. Later, Tim had declared how much he adored the work of A or B, but that was not the memory that Trevor had carried out into the night back to his book-lined, empty flat, like a rosebud from a buttonhole.

Cowering outside May's door in the falling dusk, Trevor reflected that if he really succeeded in baulking May's hunger for oblivion, she could always have another shot . . . later. It was not as if he were proposing to hang round her like some kind of human life-support machine to keep her body functioning after her spirit had died, snuffed out by her publisher. When he'd seen May yesterday, it had struck him as odd the way he'd felt more anger than she. Of course, May had lived for some time with the knowledge of what they'd done to her book, whereas that was the first he'd heard of it, but he'd been appalled by her utter resignation. It had been he, the equable, world-weary Trevor, who had spluttered, 'This is unspeakable. Publishers can't *set out* to disseminate lies. Oh damnit, I know there's the gutter press. But serious book publishers! Who needs censorship with publishers like that woman? And May had smiled sarcastically and said, 'But don't you see? If the book sells better because the biographical part is a lie, it means more people will read Vyvian's poems, which are the important part of the book, so it's all to the good.' And as he had stared incredulously at her, she'd gone on, 'It's all to the good from Vyvian's point of view. Who'd object to their life story being posthumously tarted up if that brought their work to more people?' Trevor gave May's door a tentative thump, too hard for another polite knock for admission but not really calculated to rock it back on its Victorian hinges. He felt he was hitting out at May's dishonest but highly successful publisher, woman or no, as much as doing what he'd have done if Tim was there. He would, of course, pay for any damage. And, once broken into, the flat couldn't be left, for all that May owned nothing except the stock for a modest second-hand bookshop. If the flat was empty, as seemed likely, he would have to wait in it until she came back, to explain. And if she was away overnight, perhaps turning out to have a more interesting private life than he'd suspected, he'd have to wait in the flat till tomorrow morning and then phone to get someone to come and fix it. And he must remember to go down and pay off the taxi once he'd checked the room was empty.

As he advanced on the door more seriously, the line went through his mind 'I am putting my poor shoulder to the task.' It was probably an adulterated quote – he could never quote two words without misquoting one. His flippancy was fleeting. He soon realized demolishing the door was no light matter, if indeed it ever had been, under the circumstances. In fact, he wasn't quite sure he *could* demolish the door with his bare hands, with his sore shoulder as battering-ram.

Now that he'd decided on his course of action and, regardless of noise, damage and general fuss, had crossed his Rubicon, he was in a blind panic. As if he were drowning down the stairwell, he became conscious of clock-time and taxi-time pulsing in his skull, most surrealistically. Never mind that he'd wasted whole minutes with his cogitations, kicking around so many King Charles's heads. Now every second was a matter of life or death. It went through his mind that the tenants downstairs might well have tools that could batter down the door in the batting of an eyelid, or at least stalwart cooking utensils. A wooden rolling-pin could be pressed into service as a battering-ram. But he'd give one more frenzied shove before wasting precious time running downstairs.

Then he thought he felt something give – a small crack. He reminded himself that the wood in the panels of the door, which did not look a very strongly built door, was possibly quite flimsy and if he got the top left-hand panel out, he could probably put his hand through the hole to unlock the door from the inside, like a burglar with a glass-paned door.

When he got in and saw her lying on the floor and found she was breathing and was wondering why her phone was not on her desk, he tripped on what he thought was her coat lying on the floor. The coat revealed itself to be wrapped round the phone, on whose flex he'd tripped. If she'd tried to muffle the phone, not wishing to be disturbed while dying, he wondered irrelevantly why she hadn't used her little back room for that purpose. After the 999 call and the ambulance and helping to collect up the surprisingly large number of pill bottles from each of which she'd apparently swallowed something and the later telephoned assurance that he was 'in time' – only wasn't he too early, that was the question? – after all that, sitting in his elegant sitting-room, he heard himself saying in future in his so-English diffident way, 'It was nothing. I just happened to be there.' And he would know Tim had saved May. Later still, he reflected that perhaps Tim had been so keen for him to sally forth on that probable wild goose chase to May's aid as a heaven-sent opportunity to terminate what he was finding a very boring tea-party?

Bonfire Night

I, for one, shall not be sorry if the bonfire party is quietly dropped this year. Now that Andrew has decided to move and will probably be gone by November there is no reason why it should not be held but, if it is, I think I shall make some excuse and stay away.

Andrew and Gillian Bradshaw lived opposite us in a house similar to ours – not the sort of house you would expect a part-time actor like Andrew to be living in, but then Gillian was the chief bread-winner in the Bradshaw household.

Andrew is the archetypal he-man: dark, thick-set, athletic and sexy down to the tips of his rather square fingers. In addition he is, once you get to know him, extremely funny, kind and sensitive. Paul, my husband, says that he does not think Andrew has much 'on top', as he puts it, but this is probably jealousy on his part. Gillian, on the other hand, for all her sweetness and amiability (not unlike that expressed by the winsome children and cuddly animals in her highly popular drawings), never struck me as anything other than a rather dull, overweight, suburban housewife, in spite of her talent and efficiency. She was completely indifferent to her appearance. She cut her hair herself and went in for shapeless Laura Ashley type pinafores and fussy floral smocks with prim high collars: they did nothing for her.

We knew Andrew better than Gillian. Gillian always seemed to be busy working, leaving Andrew to do many of the everyday chores like taking the children to and from school and going shopping. But whenever Andrew was away on location, Gillian would be regularly in attendance before and after school and we sometimes chatted together about the children, the school and how Andrew was enjoying his work – never intimately. I felt diffident about asking how her own work was going, she never referred to it herself. Her books, by this time, were selling in America and various details like their new car (they now had two), Andrew's growing collection of trendy jackets and the children's clothes, made it clear that the cash was flowing in.

One morning when Andrew was away shooting an episode in some ITV cops and robbers type serial, Gillian telephoned at breakfast time to ask if I would collect her children after school and keep them until she got home. She said she would try to be back by seven but she might be delayed and would I give them supper. She had done this a couple of times before and as usual I said that I would be delighted to have Matthew and Sarah for as long as she liked. I am fond of the children; my boys – Luke and Sam – are both older but the four of them play well together, as do most of the children in the road, which is probably why the bonfire party has become such a well-established tradition among us.

By seven-thirty Gillian had not come for the children. By eight I was worried. At nine Paul rang the ITV studios and got a telephone number where Andrew could be reached. At ten a policeman called at the house and told us that Gillian had been killed in a car crash earlier that evening.

We did not see Andrew for several weeks after the accident. Gillian's mother came to collect the children the next day. There was only one week of school left before the summer holidays and she thought that they should have a change of scene as quickly as possible. She said that Andrew would be staying with her too. I promised to keep an eye on the house and offered to do anything else I could to help. My offer was waved aside; she appeared to be every bit as well organized as her daughter had been.

When Andrew returned from staying with his parents-in-law, he looked worn out and scruffy. He avoided talking about Gillian and the accident. His chief topics were the children and money. He spoke of selling the house. I could see that on his own he would not be able to support himself and the children in such a large house, and it would have been tactless just then to mention Gillian's royalties, which presumably would be good for several years to come, or to enquire whether there had been a clause in their mortgage agreement whereby the house would be paid off if either partner died, so I confined myself to belittling his problems and making practical suggestions such as taking in lodgers or even dividing the house into two flats.

For the next few days Andrew went to ground. No one saw him. I would look across into the house from our upstairs windows but there was never any sign of him. When I told Paul that I was worried he said that Andrew probably wanted to be left alone, his tone implying that I should mind my own business: Paul is not very imaginative. One morning while the boys were out playing with friends, I knocked on Andrew's door. He took a long time to open it. I had woken him, he was in his dressing-gown and still half-asleep. I insisted on making him a cup of coffee. As I washed the few dirty plates in the kitchen sink and waited for the kettle to boil, I could not help reflecting that it would probably not be long before he started to look around for new female companionship. It would be a great pity if at this point he were suddenly to leave the neighbourhood.

Over coffee I explained to Andrew that I had come to offer my services should he need any help with Gillian's clothes. He looked up gratefully at me, his large dark eyes tragically mournful as they fixed on mine: I could never understand why he was not more of a success as an actor.

Andrew arranged to be out on the day I was to sort through Gillian's clothes. I got a friend to help me and together we cleared out every article of female clothing we could find. We bundled them into plastic bags, took them across the road to my house and spilt them out on to the floor where we went through them item by item, stacking them in various bundles destined for Oxfam, needy friends and forthcoming jumble sales. Andrew had told me to take anything I wanted but Gillian's curduroy smocks and jejune flowery summer wear appealed to neither of us, they all went to charity.

The next day Andrew appeared at my door holding a bunch of roses which he must have picked from his garden. He said he wanted to thank me. I was touched by the roses and asked him in for a coffee. In response he lowered his head and pushed past me into the hall. He was still a long way from being the cheery Andrew I wanted to see but that, I told myself, was only to be expected. He sat on a stool in the kitchen, contemplating the cup of coffee I had placed in front of him, breathing heavily and paying no attention to Luke or Sam when they put their heads round the door to see who had come in. I tried to make casual conversation. I asked after the children and his mother-in-law; then I asked about himself, how he was sleeping and whether there were any jobs in the offing. Monosyllables and shrugs were his only response. I was in the middle of issuing an invitation to have a meal with us later in the week when he interrupted me, completely changing the subject. He said: 'But what was she doing in Brighton?'

At first I had no idea what he was referring to, then I remembered the newspaper report of Gillian's death. Paul had spotted it and thrust it at me, somewhat thoughtlessly, while I was trying to relax in front of the television and rid my mind of such horror stories for a couple of hours. The report made gruesome reading. She had collided with a lorry at a round-about a few miles outside Brighton. The car had been incinerated with Gillian inside it.

'Do *you* know what she was doing?' He glared at me; it was the first time I had ever seen Andrew angry: it suited him. As to the question, it was now my turn to shrug. I had no idea what Gillian had been doing in Brighton and it was only Andrew's apparent concern that made me wonder about it for the first time. Various possibilities immediately suggested themselves. Perhaps Gillian had not been quite so straightforward as she appeared on the surface. But even if she had been up to something, such as a few afternoons of dalliance in Brighton, I could not believe that it would have meant all that much to

Andrew. I was prepared to bet that few of his nights on location were spent in lonely single beds. So I tried to ignore his query and when he repeated it, said, with perfect honesty, that I did not know. To change the subject I again asked him to eat with us and this time he acknowledged the invitation and accepted. He thanked me for the coffee, clapped his hands on his thighs, said 'Well!' in a purposeful way and got up to go, shouting out a greeting to the boys from the hall. I waited until he had let himself into his house before closing the door – in case he should turn to look back.

When the autumn term started, I volunteered to cope with getting Matthew and Sarah to and from school. Andrew had done some radio work over the summer and was optimistic that more would follow. He had such a good voice that I thought it likely that radio might prove his ideal medium. He told me he was also writing a play to keep himself busy during slack periods. He no longer mentioned money worries and had made no effort to look round for lodgers.

November came. I have already mentioned the bonfire party. It is an unpretentious affair with plenty of cheap wine and coke for the children. Afterwards there are baked potatoes, saus-ages, quiche and french bread. Because it mostly takes place out of doors, in the dark, to the noisy accompaniment of fireworks and excited children, with the bonfire providing a spectacular focal point – all the usual barriers that would arise at any normal social function that included everyone living in the road, are submerged in the general mêlée. And the children love it. They all play together, regardless of sex and age, as one dreams of them playing in a Utopian playground. This is why we all tacitly agreed that the bonfire party was a good thing for the neighbourhood and should happen every year.

Last year, the year that Gillian died, the party was being given by the Lloyds, a couple we do not know well. They live further down the road where the houses are slightly newer and smaller than ours, the gardens a few feet shorter and the children younger. Andrew did not know them at all but this made no difference. Jane Lloyd knew Sarah and Matthew from school and invitations automatically included children and parents. Up until then Andrew had been avoiding parties and he suggested that Paul and I take the children along with our two, leaving him out of it. I became jokingly bossy and said that I would not hear of it; he must come. I could understand that the evening would be something of an ordeal for him but much less of one than an ordinary drinks party. I saw myself as being particularly well placed to help him through such an evening since Matthew and Sarah would provide an extra link with him and any attention shown to them by me would include their father should he be feeling in need of moral support.

As usual people brought what they could afford in the way of fireworks and sparklers for the younger children. Graham Lloyd was supervising the bonfire and the fireworks display. We were all safety-conscious and privately confident that none of our children would ever add to the statistics that are read out by the media every year, warning the public against the hazards of trifling with fireworks.

'Keep well back there!' Paul shouted at Luke and Sam, as Graham threw some paraffin on the bonfire and started the blaze. Sarah held one of my hands and one of Andrew's. I remembered her being terrified two years earlier and clinging to Andrew's neck until Gillian eventually had to take her inside. This time Andrew could let her go and slip back into the house to refill his glass without her even noticing; she was perfectly happy to stay with me and watch the bonfire.

Jane Lloyd had made a particularly good guy with a hat, a pipe, a pocket handkerchief and gardening gloves for hands, not that his splendour made him burn any slower: he went up in a whoosh of flames. There were squeals from the children as his hat fell flaming to the ground and his top half followed, leaving a pair of much patched jeans rammed on to an old broom handle still on the pyre.

As the 'oohs' and 'ahs' subsided, we were distracted by shouts coming from the side entrance to the garden as another family arrived pushing a wheelbarrow and shouting, 'Make way for Mrs Guy.' I and some other mothers cheered loudly and joked about this novel blow for sexual equality. Paul and Graham hoisted Mrs Guy on to the burning lap of Mr Guy. The grown-ups whooped, the children cheered. Mrs Guy was a splendid creation and I was just thinking how much more dramatic a female guy was when, out of the corner of my eye, I saw Andrew, drink in hand, stepping back into the garden. I had been waiting for him and hoping that he would again take Sarah's hand and re-establish the chain between the three of us. He headed towards us, ducking to avoid an overhanging branch from an apple tree and I quickly switched my gaze back to the bonfire in time to see Mrs Guy's skirt billowing up in front of her face. For an instant the flames projected the light material, as if it were a filmed transparency, throwing the delicate pattern of daisies and cornflowers into relief and bleaching out the paler background. I recognized that dress: it was Gillian's. Coming up behind me, Andrew recognized it too. He let out a roar. His glass shattered against the tree trunk as he lunged towards the bonfire, knocking me over on top of Sarah, and leapt on to the burning effigy of his wife, howling her name incoherently. The wigwam structure of the bonfire caved in; smouldering timbers keeled over to left and right. Parents grabbed at the children to pull them out of danger. Matthew had caught hold of his father's sheepskin jacket and was screaming as he tried to pull him back, like a man hopelessly overpowered by a lunging animal on the end of a rope; beneath Matthew's screams Andrew's roaring continued as he floundered in the chaos of the demolished bonfire. The rest of us just stood there, too stunned by this vision of a human gone berserk to do anything but watch his performance. Then someone shouted, snapping us out of our trance. Paul swung Matthew clear of the fire. Graham tumbled on top of Andrew and rolled him on to the grass. I saw a foot kicking the remains of Mrs Guy out of his grasp and on to a flower bed. Darkness fell over the garden, broken only by the occasional shower of coloured lights disgorged overhead by rockets from other bonfire parties.

The children were quickly herded into the house and distracted with food. The doors to the garden were closed to muffle Andrew's spasmodic groans. An ambulance was summoned. Matthew, although not burned, was taken away to be treated for shock. Sarah had been distracted by my falling on her and bruising her ankle and was still only half aware of what had happened. Paul gave her a sedative and she fell asleep in my arms as I was carrying her home with us. It was impossible to say how badly Andrew had been burnt.

The Lloyds' garden looked a wreck the next day: sodden firework wrappers hung from rose bushes, the lawn was a mudflat strewn with the ashes of the bonfire. I looked out from Jane's kitchen window and stared at the spot in front of the apple tree where I had stood the night before flattering myself that I was working my way towards filling a gap in Andrew's life as Gillian could never have done – until that moment when the fire had flared up exposing the ferocity of his love for her as clearly as it had illuminated the daisies and cornflowers on the skirt of her old summer dress.

Biographical Details

G.E. ARMITAGE is the author of two novels, *A Season of Peace* (1985) and *Across the Autumn Grass* (1986). He lives in Hornsea, East Yorkshire.

JOHN BAINBRIDGE was born in Northumberland in 1951. He has taught in a middle school in Grimsby for twelve years. He had a short story published in *New Stories 4* in 1979. He has since written a number of stories for young children and some magazine articles.

CAROL BARKER BA was born in Amersham in 1960, but now lives in Otley, near Leeds. Her interest in writing began at school and developed during the three years she spent at Leeds University, where she took a degree in English Literature. Other interests include opera and medieval history.

CONNIE BENSLEY lives in London, has had two collections of poetry published (Peterloo), and has had short plays on radio and television.

WENDY BRANDMARK is a freelance writer and editor. She is American and lives in London. Her short stories have appeared in *Writing Women* and Sheba Press's anthology

Everyday Matters, and in literary magazines in the United States. She has reviewed books for a number of British and American periodicals including *City Limits* and the *Listener*.

MARGARET BROWNE was born in Birkenhead. Her poetry has been published in South East Arts anthologies, *Wascana Review* and other poetry magazines. Her fiction has appeared in *Twenty Stories*, a South East Arts collection, and in magazines. She has won the Radio Kent Play Award and Kent Creative Writing Award.

SANDRA McADAM CLARK'S short stories have been published in, among others, *Spare Rib*, *Everywoman* and *Girls next Door*, an anthology of lesbian feminist writing. An ex-social anthropologist, she now works in medical administration. She is active in her trade union. She is half French and half Scots.

EDITH COPE has been a Senior Research Officer at Bristol and Edinburgh Universities and was Deputy Director of a large college. She has written many research articles and a few works of non-fiction. She is at present living in Cheshire and is now developing her writing of fiction and poetry.

ELSA CORBLUTH has published poetry in many poetry magazines and anthologies (including several numbers of Arts Council of Great Britain's *New Poetry*), has won a number of poetry prizes, including Cheltenham, 1981, and has lived in London, Wiltshire, Nottingham, Cumbria, Staffordshire, Lancashire and Dorset. She has a forthcoming collection in the Peterloo Poets series.

DAN CORRY was born in 1959. His recent activities include a year as deputy president of a student union and a year living in Ontario. He now earns his living as a professional economist. To keep himself sane he watches Chelsea, supports the Labour Party, listens to Archie Shepp and writes the occasional short story.

ELAINE FEINSTEIN is a poet and novelist living in London. Her most recent book of poems is *Badlands* (Hutchinson, 1986); her latest novel, *The Border*, is available in paperback from Methuen. Her biography of Marina Tsvetayeva, *A Captive Lion*, appears in January 1987. She is at present working on a new novel.

FRANCES FYFIELD was born in 1948, of delightful medical parents, in Derbyshire. Her roots are northern, overriden by many years in London.She is single, lives off the proceeds of crime as a solicitor, and has been writing short stories for four years while searching for a novel.

RALPH GOLDSWAIN was born and educated in South Africa. In 1971 he came to England and has taught English in comprehensive schools ever since. One day three years ago, at the age of forty-one, he turned his long dream of writing into reality when he sat down and began.

GILES GORDON has published six novels and three collections of short stories. He has edited *Shakespeare Stories*, *Modern Scottish Short Stories* (with Fred Urquhart), Everyman's *Modern Short Stories 1940–1980*, and – with David Hughes – *Best Short Stories 1986*. He has been theatre critic of the *Spectator* and is currently theatre critic of the *London Daily News*. He also writes on theatre for *Punch*, *Observer* and

Tatler. He is a literary agent with Anthony Sheil Associates. He lives in Kentish Town with his wife, the children's illustrator and author, Margaret Gordon, and their three children, two cats, two hamsters and a white boxer, Sniffy.

MARY HADINGHAM is of Scotch-Irish parentage. She was educated in America (Northwestern University) and worked as a journalist there. She has been settled permanently in Britain for the past twenty years. Her stories have appeared in *Blackwoods*, *Short Story International*, *South West Arts Review* and the *Literary Review*.

KARA LIND was educated in the United States and Scotland and has lived in London since 1985. Previous publications include *2 Plus 2* (Time Free Press), *Bridport Prizewinners' Anthology*, *Scottish Review*.

THOMAS McCARTHY was born in Mallow, Co. Cork, in 1941, and spent his childhood in Ireland. He now lives near Peterborough, in Cambridgeshire. He has had stories published by the Northampton Community Press and in *P.E.N. New Fiction I*.

DUNCAN McLAREN was born in Perthshire in 1957. He was educated at various institutions in Scotland and England. He spends half the year working and in 'time off' writes. He has recently completed a novel. This is his first published story.

ROBERT MULLEN is an American-born naturalized Canadian presently residing in Edinburgh. He holds degrees in computer science and educational psychology and has taught high school mathematics, data processing at McGill University and the English language in Spain.

WILLIAM NEW was born in South Shields in 1952. Pieces from his two unpublished collections of stories, *Studies* and *Gesta Daemonorum*, have appeared in *P.E.N. New Fiction I*, *Firebird 3* and *Ambit*.

PETER PARKER's stories have appeared in *Fiction Magazine*, *London Magazine, Honey* and two previous P.E.N. anthologies. He is the author of *The Old Lie: The Great War and the Public-School Ethos* (Constable 1987), and is writing a biography of J.R. Ackerley. He is a regular contributor to *London Magazine* and *Books and Bookmen*.

IAN RANKIN was born in Fife in 1960. His short stories have appeared in various newspapers, anthologies and magazines, and have been broadcast widely. He was runner-up in the 1983 *Scotsman* Short Story Competition, and won the 1984 TSB Scotland Short Story Award. His first novel, *The Flood*, appeared in 1986 and his second, *Knots & Crosses* (The Bodley Head), in 1987. He lives in London.

SUZI ROBINSON read English at Sussex University and now writes advertising copy for a living. Her fiction has appeared in *Just Seventeen* and in 1986 she won first prize in the *Over 21* magazine short story competition. She lives in her native North London with two very literary cats.

KATHRINE TALBOT. Born in Germany, came to England before the war. Published novels in the fifties and sixties, since then short stories and poetry. Has translated much fiction and non-fiction. Lives in Sussex, married to painter Kit Barker, son Thomas one year out of art college.

D.J. TAYLOR was born in Norwich in 1960 and works in London as a copywriter. His stories and criticism have appeared in *Encounter*, *London Magazine* and *P.E.N. New Fiction I*. His first novel, *Great Eastern Land*, was published by Secker & Warburg early in 1986.

PENELOPE SHUTTLE was born in 1947. She lives in Cornwall with her husband Peter Redgrove and their daughter. Her most recent publication is *The Lion from Rio*, a collection of poems from Oxford University Press, 1986. 1986 also saw the reissue of *The Wise Wound* (Paladin), the pioneer study of menstruation she wrote in collaboration with Peter Redgrove, now considered a classic contribution to the subject.

DEBORAH SINGMASTER is Irish and writes short stories and radio plays. She won the *Observer*/Virago Short Story Competition in 1981. She is married, has one daughter and lives in London.

MANSEL STIMPSON was born in 1937 and now lives and works in London as a freelance critic of films and books. His reviews have appeared in *Literary Review*, *TLS*, *Film* and *Films and Filming*. His first short story, runner-up in a competition, was published by *Gay News* in 1982.

VAL WARNER is a freelance writer who translated Corbière – *The Centenary Corbière* (Carcanet), and edited *Collected Poems & Prose of Charlotte Mew* (Carcanet/Virago). She has received a Gregory Award for Poetry. Her poetry books are *Under the Penthouse* (Carcanet) and *Before Lunch* (Carcanet), nominated for The Duff Cooper Memorial Prize, 1986.

DAVID WELSH was born in 1955, educated at comprehensive school and Oxford, and has worked as an editor and journalist. Although he is well known as a non-fiction writer for schools, *A Mugging* is his first accepted story.

PETER WHITEBROOK, born in London, is an arts journalist in Edinburgh. He contributes reviews and interviews to the *Scotsman*, to BBC Radio Scotland (*Prospect*), BBC Radio 4 (*Kaleidoscope*), and writes profiles for *Scottish Opera News*. His stories have been published in *New Edinburgh Review* and broadcast on Radio 4.